Sarah

by Shirley Dummer

Before she could step off the porch, Lee grabbed her arm and asked, "Why do you always fight Ma on everything. You just got to be difficult. What the hell is the difference if she knows when your birthday is?"

Try as hard as she could, she couldn't shake Lee's grasp of her arm. Taking a deep breath, she finally spat at him, "'Cause my ma told me that I was a curse when I was born. That she wished that day have never come and she hoped that I'd die, only I never did. She told me so many times that she hated me and that the devil gave me to her.

"She hated me. You understand that? She hated me. I never had any of the love you have in this house. I don't know what that is. And, by the way, my birthday is Christmas Day and that's tomorrow and that's why we never had anything for Christmas when she was alive. Because it was my birthday and she hated my guts."

As Lee let go of her arm, she whirled and ran down the steps and up the hill toward the safety of the little house and the dog, Bud. The expression on Lee's face as he watched her go was of shock, dismay and discovery wrapped up in one.

SARAH

by Shirley Dummer

SARAH
First printing, 1997

International Standard Book Number 0-9633479-4-2
Printed in the United States of America

DEDICATION

Dedicated to Mildred Castek in appreciation for all she has done for me. Her expertise in helping me with the details, financial figures of the 1930s, the ideas and her appreciation of what I was trying to do has been an inspiration to me. She was only a telephone call away when I needed something. And always so glad to give me the assistance I wanted.

What a great day it was when my mother and I found Mildred. She had lived for so many years at Chadron, near where we had lived for a number of years and now lived about twelve miles from us here in Wisconsin. My mother and Mildred spent hours reliving the years spent at Chadron and the many people they both knew. And during this time I asked them so many questions that needed to be answered so my writing would be authentic. Whom better to ask than those who had lived during this era of time near the place where my writing is based?

In all my books, the characters and the story are strictly out of my imagination, make-believe, but the day-by-day happenings are how my parents and others lived during that era of time. It is with pleasure that I dedicate this book to Mildred Castek, as she has helped me fill in the gaps of the day-by-day happenings. Such a neat lady!

ACKNOWLEDGMENTS

My daughter-in-law Christine again designed the cover for *Sarah*. As with the others she has done, the finished product was exactly what I wanted. Many, many thanks.

And a big thank you to my granddaughter Beth, who was my photographer. Not wanting a stiff, posed picture from a photo shop, I enlisted her help and with a camera we spent time trying to get something I could live with. Funny thing how a picture tells the story of all those wrinkles you overlook in a mirror, but I pacify myself by telling myself that I earned every one of them. Thanks, Beth.

And a thank you to Mike Durpenhaus who read the first, rough draft of *Sarah* to see if I was writing something that would be acceptable.

And to Colleen Kanieski, there just aren't words good enough to say my thank you to you for all those hours you spent reading the manuscript and taking the time to write down suggestions to make the finished product something that was very feasible. I appreciate this so much. Again, thanks for helping me with your knowledge.

CHAPTER I

OCTOBER 10, 1930

"Sarah, would you like to come home with us?" Mary asked the woman. "You shouldn't stay here alone.".

"I'm not afraid," she answered.

"I still don't think you should be here alone," Mary told her.

"There's the chickens and cows to be taken care of," Sarah answered.

"The men can come back and do that. You can come back with them or tell 'em what to do. Ain't that right, Victor?" The tall, dark-headed man beside her nodded yes. "At least until after the funeral. Just pack a few clothes, also a dress for your ma's funeral".

The young woman hesitated a moment and then left the room. In a few minutes she was back with a small satchel.

"I just took clothes for one change. I'll come back when it's chore time and get my dress for the funeral and shoes."

"The undertaker'll have to have a dress for her," Victor told her.

"There's only one dress for good and I have to wear that."

"I can find you something to wear," Mary answered, her eyes going quickly to her husband. "Victor can take the things needed to the funeral parlor this afternoon. Maybe you had better get them now so he can take them with him when he goes after dinner. And you need to put on an everyday dress too. Those overalls are all right for doing chores but not for all the time, only for the barn."

"I don't have a dress or any other clothes but another pair of overalls and a flannel shirt that I took with me," Sarah answered. "Ma said I didn't need a dress on account of I never went anywhere, only the barn and there a pair of bibbies would do for that."

"Well." Mary said, shrugging. "Guess that'll have to do then. I think I've got something at home you can wear for everyday for now. We'll just have to make a dress for the funeral. Do you have a pair of shoes you can wear?" Mary asked, glancing down at the young woman's feet. She had on a pair of old worn-out black, men's shoes.

"My ma's," was the answer.

"They fit?"

"Yes."

"Well, come along then. You got a key for the door?"

Sarah went into the other room and brought back a key. Locking the door behind them, they were soon in the car going down the dirt driveway. In a few minutes they were in another yard.

"I should have told you how Ma feeds the cattle and how she wants the chickens taken care of," Sarah told Victor as they got out of the car.

"You can tell me before I go back this evening," he answered.

"You just come into the house here now," Mary told her , leading the way. " I'm going to make a little dinner and then after dinner, while Victor's in town, we'll have to see what we can find or do about a dress for the funeral tomorrow afternoon."

Mary knew she had nothing that would fit Sarah. Although as tall as Sarah, she couldn't ever remember being that slight in build, even in her childhood years. Glancing in the dresser mirror, she looked at her own blonde hair streaked with grey. Even though the hair showed her years, her round face showed very little aging lines.

Sarah, sitting on the bed behind her, had a smaller thin face. The reddish tinge in her hair seemed to come alive as it was being picked up by the rays of sunshine coming in through the window. Even with the distance between them, Mary could smell the barn odor coming from the other woman. Her clothes looked clean, so Mary thought it must have been a while since she washed her hair. As it was braided into a single braid that hung down the back, she could see it had been sometime since it had been combed, probably when it had been washed, as was common with long hair. She would have to remind her in the morning to take time for a bath and a hair washing.

Looking through her box of material she took from the corner, Mary found a dark green piece of yardage that she thought would make a nice dress suitable for the next day. Using a pattern she had used for her daughter, when she was younger and thinner, she quickly cut out the pieces while Sarah watched her in silence. As the afternoon progressed the pieces were sewed and fitted together. By supper the dress was almost completed.

"Here," Mary said, handing Sarah the dress as Victor came into the house. "You can do the hem while I fry up some potatoes and scramble some eggs for supper. You get to the undertakers?" she asked him.

"Yes," he answered. "I'll change clothes and then eat before I go out to help with the chores. I suppose Tony has a good share of them done by now. You remember Tony?" he asked Sarah, as she sat in the corner of the room hemming the dress.

She nodded her head yes, before looking up at him. Mary shrugged her shoulders, then quickly began putting the meal on the table.

After supper was over and the chores done at both places, Victor and Mary walked down to the corral. Watching the animals in the distance, they spent some time talking. Finally they came back to the house and asked Sarah to join them for a cup of coffee before going to bed.

"Sarah," Victor asked, "what you gonna do with that ranch now that your ma has died?"

She shrugged her shoulders, then finally answered, "I know that she had a will and it was going to be left to me."

"What are you going to do with it now that you inherited it?" Victor asked. "She's been sick now, what, going on a couple of years. She had time to tell you what she wanted you to do with it after she was gone."

"She figured she'd live a long time yet, I guess. At least until right before she died. And then I don't think she figured to die that soon."

"She ever have the doctor?" Victor asked.

"No!"

"I don't know if he could have done anything anyway. I been thinking that we would like to rent your ranch, for maybe five years. You know Tony is getting married?" Sarah looked blankly at him while Mary and Victor exchanged glances. "Well, anyway, he is and we could use the extra land and buildings too. I wondered if you would like to live in the little house, behind this house that my ma lived in while she was alive. Tony would live in your house and then we could keep some cattle and chickens down there and he'd take care of them. That would give you time to think about what you wanted to do with the ranch and give us time to decide what to do about a house and some more land for Tony. The little house Grandma lived in has only two rooms, a kitchen and a bedroom. That would be big enough for Tony and Johanna after they're married, but when babies come along, it would get small in a hurry. I thought that would be big enough for you for now and in five years, when the rental agreement was up, then you would know what you wanted to do more than you do now." Again exchanging glances with his wife, Victor continued, "Sarah, I'm afraid for you to stay down there alone. Earl Conway has been saying all kinds of strange things all around town for a week or so already and I'm afraid for you."

"Ma liked him. They talked several times. Ma was gonna work out something with him — only she died first. I... don't... like... him," Sarah told them, talking very slowly, then added in a rush, "He came to the house, last week, and looked around the rooms like he was looking for something."

"Your ma keep any money there?" Victor asked her.

"No, Ma kept all her money in the bank." She hesitated a long moment, then continued, "But my uncle never put any of his money in the bank. It's all buried there under the house".

"All right," Victor answered, letting the breath out of his mouth in a big sigh. " I think maybe me and Tony had better stay over there tonight. I don't know how many know of your ma's death but just to be safe, I think we had better. It didn't sound like Conway knew she had died yet, from what I heard and I didn't say anything to anybody either about her dying." Thinking a few moments, he continued," You know where that money is, your uncle's?" he asked.

Sarah nodded her head yes.

" I think it had better be put somewhere else, if you know where to find it. Earl's not to be trusted at any time. If he thinks there's money there he'll tear the place apart."

Sarah looked at him, the terror that flitted across her face was instantly replaced with a blank look. A moment or two later she told them, "I'd like you to rent the ranch. I know where Uncle John's money is, or at least close enough so I think I can find it. I know how much Ma had in the bank and how much everything is worth."

They looked at her in amazement.

"How do you know that? Victor asked.

"Ma told me that and I wrote everything down for her

and kept the records for her. I know everything about the money. Ma couldn't read or write. My uncle did all that and when he died last fall she had me do it then. And if you think it would be good, then I'll stay over here and Tony can live in Ma's house."

"I think that would be the best and also a five-year rental agreement," Victor told her.

"What would I do with my time, when I don't have any chores any more and Ma ain't there to take care of anymore?" Sarah asked.

"Oh, I can find plenty for you to do," Mary answered her. " My ma had a stroke and she's coming here for a while. We, all of us girls, are going to take turns taking care of her. She had the stroke about two weeks ago and she's been in the hospital until now so I'm going to take the first turn at keeping her. She can't walk, is in a wheelchair and can't talk either. She needs someone taking care of her most of the time. Now I don't expect you to do that but I do bake for one of the eating places in town and I wondered how I would ever be able to do all of it with Ma here. With you helping, it would work out fine."

"I know how to bake some," Sarah replied. "Ma always said what I had to do. She always told me how to do it, even when she was sick. I always did everything how she said."

"For a while I probably will too," Mary told her. "'Cause there's a set menu that they want done everyday. This restaurant is called the Labit's, you know where it is?"

"No. I never ate anywhere but at home. Ma said it was sinful for anyone to eat anywhere but at home. She called it wasting money and that was a sin. She called it eating with the devils."

"Well, once in a while I eat there," Victor assured her, " and I don't think I ate with any devil. Some of the people in town, like the doctor and even some of the ranchers eat there, when they go into town to do their business. There's nothing wrong with it."

"Ma had her own ideas," Sarah softly answered, looking down at her work-worn hands.

"Going back to Earl and your ma," Victor said. "Can you tell us more about his coming over to see her?"

"Earl came over several times this past month and asked her about running the ranch. Ma told him she'd think about it. Ma said he'd make a good husband for me," Sarah told them, never looking up. Victor puckered his brow in a frown while Mary gave a quick shudder.

"Do you think he would make a good husband?" Mary gently asked her.

Sarah did not respond at first. Finally she shook her head no.

"Ma said I should be glad anyone would look at me 'cause I'm nothing to look at, with my red, awful-looking hair and homely face and so old. Old maid, a homely witch of an old maid, she called me. She said I should be glad Earl came around 'cause I had no brains, was behind the door when they were passed out. Said I had no sense at all."

"I'll get the lawyer out here right away in the morning, when I go into town to deliver your baking, Mary, I'll go and see him. I'll go to his house so he comes out right away so we draw up the papers and they are signed. I think your ma knew she was dying and she planned for you to marry Conway. That would have been one big awful mistake. He would have made life a living hell. And with that lazy ma of his and that tribe of sisters of his, you'd have been their slave. Parry Paul is our lawyer's name. He'll have an idea of what rent is worth, I have some idea too and we'll work something out on that. We'll buy the cattle that are there and the chickens too. And Mary will pay you for helping here," Victor told Sarah.

"Sakes alive, child," Mary added, " You need to get to bed. You can hardly keep your eyes open. You look so tired."

"I've been up at night, many nights taking care of Ma,

these last days. I sat in the rocker and slept what I could. I..." she hesitated a moment, then added, " I've talked here more tonight than I talked at home for a long time put together. I hope I haven't showed you what a fool I am."

"You're no fool or a witch either. You did the money work for your ma and that shows that you're no fool. You took care of her and did all the work and chores. You are far from a fool," Victor answered her as Sarah got up and made her way upstairs.

"Earl Conway," Mary said in disgust after Sarah left the room. "I know I wouldn't want any daughter of mine to marry him."

"That ma of hers knew she wasn't going to last long and she was going to set up Sarah with him. She just died sooner than she thought she would, which was a blessing for Sarah. Her ma wasn't a very nice person from what I know about her. 'Course we never knew her very well."

"No one did cause she never went to anything or let Sarah go to anything either. I'm surprised she let her go to school for that long. I don't think she finished eighth grade though. Her ma was a funny person, so different. Never would associate with the rest of us, thought she was too good I guess," Mary said, adding, "Although I remember she used to come to the Christmas programs at school, by herself, never brought Sarah, but after Sarah started school, she never came again. What a good thing the undertaker stopped here this afternoon and told us about the old lady dying and wondering if we would take the time to go over by Sarah for a little while 'cause she seemed so lost."

"Yeah," Victor answered. "That way we got to talk to Sarah and got her to come here before Conway heard of her ma's dying." Mary poured the last of the coffee into his cup while Victor asked, "Only one dress for both of them?"

"One dress between both of the them," Mary answered. "Honestly, and one pair of good shoes and those are a man's shoes. I don't know if they fit Sarah or not but she's gonna wear them tomorrow. And I made her a dress this afternoon, just a simple shirtwaist dress with a collar. She finished the hem after supper. Only bib overalls and flannel shirts to wear. I got to find her some dress of mine to wear until we get some sewed for her. It'll have to be gathered together at the waist with a belt cause I'm bigger than she is. And she never has an expression on her face. That gets me. It is just blank looking all the time. You never know what she's thinking."

"Maybe it was just easier at home if she didn't look like she knew anything. I wonder how many times you'll have to tell her what to do and how to do it."

"That's all right 'cause then it'll be done like I want it done. When I think about it, I just don't understand it. Why would a mother want to say those kinds of things to her daughter? Sarah ain't homely or dumb or a witch either like her ma said she was. If her hair was cut some, it would look real nice. It looks like it could be curly and it's a beautiful reddish light brown color and she's got the nicest, biggest brown eyes when she looks at you, which ain't very often. She has a habit of looking down most of the time. I remember going over there after they moved in and that ma of hers saying she had only one girl and that was enough. If I remember rightly, she said something about a woman could have a lot of sons but only a daughter can take care of her ma. It was her duty to take care of her ma," Mary told Victor.

"Well, Sarah did just that. She took care of her until she died. Thankfully, she didn't marry Conway first, before the old lady died. Now, after we get those papers signed tomorrow morning, she has five years to learn to think for herself and get her life in order. I hear Tony coming in from seeing Johanna, so we'll go over there to sleep now for tonight, maybe for a couple of nights until we get the place cleaned out and then see what happens. Maybe Tony can go there at night then by himself."

"You see Mr. Paul this morning?" Mary asked Victor at breakfast the next morning.

"Yeah. After taking in your baking, I drove past his house and went in and talked to him. He thought it a good idea to take care of it right away so he'll be here about nine this morning with rental papers to draw up. He said he would have his secretary type up something and then all we would have to do is fill in the blank spaces."

"He'll have it typed on a typewriter?" Mary wondered aloud.

"I guess so. That's what he said anyway. I think his daughter works for him. She took a course somewhere to learn how to run the machine after he got it. Maybe from wherever he got the machine from, they gave lessons, I don't know," Victor answered. "Sarah up yet?"

"Yes. She went outside to the toilet."

"I got the idea that Paul was relieved when her ma had died. He hadn't heard that she died but he seemed relieved when I told him she had and that Sarah was here and that we were going to rent the farm and she was going to live in the little house."

"He didn't say any more than that?" Mary asked.

"No. Only that it would have been a real mess if she had lived for a while yet," Victor answered. "He asked how we knew and I said the undertaker had stopped and wondered if we'd go over by her for a little while. Paul said that was a blessing in disguise. I'm not sure what he meant by that."

Before nine o'clock Parry Paul drove into their yard. Looking dapper in his black suit, freshly starched and ironed white shirt and tie, he got out of his car.

"Nice car you have there," Victor told him as he walked around the 1929 Pontiac. "And just look at that rumble seat. You're really coming up in the world. Pretty fancy, there."

"I like it. Got it for a good price too. Someone died and the widow didn't want it, couldn't drive, so she told my brother who lives in Hillsdrove to sell it for her. It was taken care of. Looks like new inside. Morning, Mrs. Labella and good morning, Miss Hysell. May I call you Sarah? And you Mary?" At their nod, he continued. "Sorry to hear about your mother's passing but seems we must all go sometime. Now you wanted to rent your mother's ranch to the Labellas."

Sarah told him she did, adding " I don't know what else to do."

"Your ma had a will, did you know that?"

"Yes. And the ranch was left to me in the will. At least that's what she told me."

"That is correct. It is. I have a rental agreement drawn up here with the spaces left open to be filled in this morning."

"I didn't tell Sarah any figure for the rent cause we hadn't gotten that far. I thought maybe we could rent it on thirds for the cattle and the winter wheat we thresh, also a third of the straw. One third for Sarah and two thirds for us. I thought that should be a fair price for the ranch. There's three sections of land, nineteen hundred and twenty acres there, and the buildings and the house," Victor told all of them.

"That sounds fair enough. Is that agreeable with you, Sarah?"

" Yes," she answered. "Ma used that agreement when she rented to Don Kelly when Uncle Pete was too sick to work the land."

" I'm surprised you know this," Paul told her.

Since she did not seem inclined to answer the lawyer, Victor told him Sarah had been taking care of the book work for her ma.

"What about the personal property ?" Paul asked.

" We're going to buy what there is. There's three cows, two milking Thirty head of beef cattle and some young stock, including a heifer that's ready to freshen that would be a milk cow."

"Do you have any idea what they are worth?" Paul asked Sarah.

" My ma said cows were worth about two cents a pound. Calves about fifty cents each and heifers with calf about fifteen dollars apiece. That is what she told me to write down in the book," Sarah answered.

"That is about right," Paul answered. "Is that satisfactory with you?" he asked Victor.

"Yes. That is a right price for both Sarah and me. Your ma separated the milk, didn't she?" he asked Sarah.

"When Uncle John was alive, he took the cream to town and sold it. After he died, we quit separating and just fed the extra milk to the calves and the cats. Ma was gonna get a pig or two to feed the milk, only she got sick and couldn't walk outside anymore and so we never got one. She said I didn't know anything anyway and if Kelly brought one, I'd get stung with a runt so we never got one. That was after the second cow freshened with a calf. Now it is a good thing we did cause it would just be another thing to take care of."

Paul watched her during this exchange of conversation. He quietly told Sarah, "Your not half as dumb as your ma thought you were." She just bowed her head looking at her hands.

"Some of the young stock are older," Victor told Paul.

"Then let's just lump the young stock together and make if fifty dollars for all of them. Is that all right, Sarah? And three hundred dollars for the beef cows."

She nodded her head yes.

"Then that makes the sale of the cattle four hundred five dollars. I'll just put that figure in here. And what about the chickens?" He looked at Victor first, then Sarah.

"They're old hens," she answered. "They didn't lay much anymore. How about nothing for them? I'll just give them to the Labellas. It being fall they can be brought over here and butchered. I have to eat here too, you know."

"Is that what you really want?" Paul asked her. " The sale of the animals, the renting of the land and the living here?"

"Yes." She seemed surprised at how glad she was at the decision.

"Very well. But I do think something should be put down for the chickens. Maybe a price of five dollars. How many are there, by the way?"

"Three hundred." Sarah answered.

"Then five dollars for the chickens. That way everything is down on paper that is personal property."

"Now, I have this all filled in, so Sarah, you sign here and then after you are done, then Victor you sign here." He shoved the papers across the table. Everyone was silent as the put their signatures on the lines allotted for that.

"I should have asked you to read it first," Paul told Sarah. She looked at him in surprise. "Don't ever sign anything else before reading it first. This was read as we went along so it should have been clear to everyone. But remember that. From now on, don't sign anything until you read it first. "

"Yes." she answered. " I'll always remember what you just told me."

"Now that that is done, I want to show you a copy of the will," Paul told Sarah.

"We'll go outside," Mary said as she and Victor got up to leave.

"No, please stay," Sarah pleaded. "In case I don't understand everything. Then I can ask you after Mr. Paul leaves."

"If you are sure?" Victor told her, settling down once again on his chair.

"Yes." Sarah assured him.

"Your pa and ma had a will that is still standing," Paul

told her. " Your ma got everything when he died and then when she died, it went to you. I don't think your Uncle John had anything to leave to anyone as he never had a will that I know of. Anyway, the administrator of your pa's and ma's will was myself. Now, just a few days ago your ma had Earl Conway write me a letter that she signed and had Conway deliver it, that asked for a redoing of part of the will. She wanted me to add on the bottom of the will something changing the administrator to Conway. She asked me to bring it out this coming Saturday, tomorrow that is. I don't know why she picked out Saturday but that is what the letter said. She died Thursday, was buried today, Friday, so it never got changed. Just between you and me, Sarah, and you Victor and Mary, and I don't want this to go any further, it was better for you, Sarah, that it was never changed. You need something explained?' he asked looking at Sarah.

"What is an administrator?" she asked

"He would handle all the money, make the decisions, do the deciding. You would not have had much of anything to say about any of the money or the ranch or anything. It would be just about like when your ma was alive. You never had anything to say about the money then, did you?"

"No. I only did what I was told to do." She answered looking down at her folded hands in her lap; the other three exchanged quick glances.

"So I continue being the administrator of your estate, Sarah. The farm is clear of debts, has been for a long time. Your ma didn't spend money for much of anything, except feed for the cattle and chickens. I think she made sure they were fed good. I don't imagine she spent much for clothing or food for the house?" he asked.

"Nothing much for clothing. Mostly feed sacks that I bleached and washed for sheets and towels and other stuff we needed in the house. Every fall there was new overalls made and flannel shirts. We had our own garden vegetables and our own meat." Sarah answered, all the while looking down at her folded hands. "When ma needed anything, she asked Mr. Kelly to get it for her. She didn't know how to drive and with Uncle John gone she had to ask the Kellys to get what feed she needed or anything else."

"There used to be a lot of range cattle. Do you remember them being sold, or most of them?" Sarah was asked.

Looking up, she answered, "When my uncle got so he couldn't take care of them, they were almost all sold. One day they were there and the next they were gone. I was never told who bought them. Kelly rented the prairie pasture last year. Uncle John kept a few cattle to keep the pasture near the buildings chewed down."

"It's good pasture 'cause it has a river running through it. Always water for the animals to drink," Victor said.

"Nice to keep butter and milk and cream cold in too." Mary told them. "We never had sour cream to sell either when we sold cream, as we kept the cream cans in the river during the summer months. That spring house is so nice. You've got a good one over at your house too," she told Sarah.

"You know how much money there is in the bank?" Paul asked Sarah.

"Yes. Over ten thousand dollars."

"That's a lot of money, a lot of money. Conway would have enjoyed using that, I am sure. With the farm out of debt, you are in very good financial shape. And with you living here for five years, with the farm rented out, it will give you time to decide what you want to do with the ranch and yourself. A time to get to know what you want to do," Paul told her. "There will be hell to pay when Conway finds out your ma has died and the will was never changed. He may try to bluff his way in but as long as the will was never changed , he doesn't stand a chance. But I can't see him not trying. That's why I'm glad you're here with the Labellas and I would watch that house because he may try to find money there. He may think there is some there and if nothing else tear it apart just to get revenge," Paul told her.

A quick look of panic went through Sarah's face, then that distant look of blankness took over again.

"What time is the funeral?" Paul asked.

"Two o'clock," Victor answered. "At the funeral home. It's not in any church."

"Her ma never went to any church, the undertaker told me." Victor told Paul. "That is the way her uncle was buried too."

"And she'll be buried by Sarah's pa, out in the cemetery," Mary told him. "We're going with Sarah. Oh Sarah, we never decided on wages for you for helping me."

"I thought the use of the house was my pay. I don't need anything else. What would I have to spend it on?"

"No, the use of the house is only part of your pay. Because of use of the house, Victor and I talked about giving you forty cents an hour for the time you help me. And you have to have some money to buy yourself some clothes, or at least material to make some dresses and other things I imagine you need."

"You may find I'm not worth that."

"I think I'll find you're worth much more than that," Mary answered her.

"And now I'll drive back to town so you can get on with your work and get to the funeral home in time. Thank you, Victor, for calling me and Sarah, thank you for everything. I think this is a very good way to handle everything. And as I said, be careful for Conway because I think he'll be as mad as a rattlesnake for a while." Taking his briefcase, he went out the door. Victor walked with him to the car while Mary and Sarah started to get the noon meal.

Later in the afternoon, Sarah stood by her ma's coffin in the cemetery. She gazed out onto the prairie while the undertaker recited a few prayers. Feelings of panic rose in her throat. If it hadn't been for the Labellas, she wouldn't have been able to stand the terror that threatened to engulf her. The feeling of being a fool invaded her. How could anyone as stupid, as dumb, as worthless as she survive?

CHAPTER II

The next morning, Mary let Sarah sleep until it was breakfast time. She had been up at an early hour baking the bread, cake, cookies and pies that Victor had already delivered to Labit's. After eating, and before Victor left the house, Mary talked to Sarah about the work schedule she had worked out.

"We always eat breakfast here at nine. That way the baking for Labits is done and the men have the chores done too. I get up at three every morning. I set my bread dough the night before so it's ready to work flour in and before long work into loaves the next morning. Then I bake eight pies, a batch of cookies and a large cake. I usually make four pies of one kind and four pies of another kind, mostly raisin, pumpkin, custard and apple when I have apples. Cookies are either rolled out sugar cookies or oatmeal and raisin ones. The cake is applesauce, yellow or chocolate. When it comes to the baking, I imagine you do the same as I do, break the eggs in a dish separately, each separately in case of bloody yolks and use only coffee cups for measuring and a pinch here and a pinch there. I guess we'll just feel our way, as we bake the first time or two together. Oh, I make my own yeast cakes, I suppose your ma did too. Most of us do when it ain't always easy to get to town and saves having to buy yeast all the time. Made out of cornmeal and buttermilk and some of the yeast cakes from the ones made the time before. I see you shaking your head yes, so I see you know what I'm talking about. I bake every day, except Sunday. Some days, I bake during the day and Victor delivers this before five o'clock when they shut down. This is done when the weather don't look good for the next day. Sometimes Victor don't get there at all if the roads are so bad but we're only a couple miles out of town and with the sleigh, most times he can get it done. I started to bake when Victor and Tony quit milking so many cows. Victor quit selling cream then and we needed the extra money so I started baking for Labit's. Now, with Ma coming, I sure will be glad of your help cause Ma'll take a lot of extra time. I'll wake you when I get up or do you have an alarm clock?"

"Ma had one." Sarah answered.

"What time did she set it for?" Mary asked

"She had it set for four o'clock so I could get the cows milked before I had to take care of her."

"You went back out after breakfast and did the chickens?"

"Yes. I fed them and cleaned the barns and bedded the cows and the calves."

"Then getting up at three o'clock won't seem quite as early to you. One hour earlier, but not like you were used to sleeping until seven o'clock or later. Now that we've got that settled, when did you want to go down to Sarah's house and move her stuff?" Mary asked Victor.

" I think today we'd all better go down there and get it cleaned out," Victor told Sarah. "Then Tony can stay there at night. We'll leave a bed down there so he has something to sleep on. The stoves are already there, so he'll be warm. It's early in the fall but some nights will be chilly anyway. He can start a fire and get the chill off the rooms. I don't like to leave any of your ma's stuff there. We can't see the house and I don't trust Conway. The only thing we can do is put what you don't use in the bottom floor of the granary. When Conway finds out what he missed he'll be like a rattlesnake. He'd think nothing of going through the house and tearing everything apart."

"It'll take about ten minutes to do the dishes. Then I'll be ready. Sarah, you can get the dishpans from the pantry . The teakettle is hot and there's hot water in the reservoir too. Homemade soap is on the shelf by the dishpan," Mary told the woman.

"You got any boxes over there at all?" Victor asked Sarah.

"There are some upstairs. Ma never threw anything away. And there are gunny sacks and feed sacks there too."

"I'll see if I can find anything here that we can use," Victor said. "Tony is about done in the barn so he can harness up the horses and we'll bring back the furniture on a wagon."

"The small house has to be cleaned up, Victor, before furniture can be put in it," Mary told him.

"We'll just leave it on the wagon for a couple of days while that is done. Maybe Sarah can get that done while we get your ma . We have to get her Thursday or are they bringing her here?" Victor asked.

"We have to get her. I figured to bake twice tomorrow so we could get an early start on Thursday. It'll take us a couple of hours to drive to my sister's."

"Sounds like we had better get busy today and make sure we have all the house cleaned out before dark. I'll see how Tony is doing."

By the middle of the afternoon the Hysell house had been completely stripped. The wagon was stacked high with furniture, pots and pans, bedding, boxes of dishes and other household items that they could fit on it. The rest was packed into the car.

"Sarah, what you going to do with your uncle's car?" Victor asked.

"I don't know," she answered. "I don't know."

"I wonder if maybe next summer you should learn how

to drive it. We can leave it in the shed here, right where it is. It ain't been run for a while and it sure won't start without working on it, like getting a new battery. It would help if you knew how to drive. You could take the stuff to Labit's then instead of me."

"I can't drive. I'd never learn how to do that, " she told him, defiantly shaking her head no.

"Nonsense. You can learn how if you try. But you got to try, not just say you can't." He and Mary exchanged a quick glance as Sarah stood wringing her hands in panic.

"Never know what you can learn if you try," Mary said. "I think we got everything out of here." she added, walking around the empty rooms.

"Oh Sarah, do you know where the key to the car is so it don't get lost?" Victor asked.

"I think the keys are in the car or hanging on a nail in the shed beside the car," she answered.

"I think you got a problem there, Ma" Tony told her as they watched Victor and Sarah walking across the yard. "Seems funny too, 'cause I can remember her from school and she was smart. Got all A's. But so different from anybody else. Never talked much to anyone, only when she had to and never started doing anything until she was told to do it. 'Course I was little then so maybe I just looked at it different or something."

"No, I think you hit the nail on the head. I begin to wonder if she was allowed to think at all for herself. Maybe her ma never let her do anything without being told. Maybe her ma didn't want her to try anything. I don't know. I do know though that for now she's a life saver for me with Ma coming. I just don't know how I would have done it all."

"And here comes some more trouble. That's Conway's car coming in the yard."

"Oh, I hope Victor sees him and comes," Mary told him as they watched the dark-haired, dark-complexioned burly man him get out of his car and stride across the yard.

He was a man well remembered as being the school bully.

"I'll talk to him and you run out the back door and get Pa. And hurry," Tony told her. He walked to the door while Mary ran toward the back door. She had just left the house when Conway opened the door.

"Well, looks like I just got here in time," he said, coming into the house and looking around. "Seems like you just helped yourself to everything like you had a right to. And whatever you did with everything , you damn well can just bring it back." Grabbing the front of Tony's shirt, he shoved him against the wall. Although fully as large a man as Conway, Tony was caught for a moment off guard and reeled against the wall. Catching his breath, he crouched and then brought up a fist hitting Conway in the stomach, sending him reeling across the room. Tony pulled him up to his feet just as Victor and Mary came into the room, followed by a very scared Sarah.

"Seems Earl thinks we helped ourselves to something we didn't have any right to," Tony told them as he held the man upright. "And he was going to roughhouse me, only it didn't work out quite that way. I fought too many battles on the school yard not to remember how to defend myself," Tony told them.

"Let him go," Victor told him.

"Glad to," he said, dumping him on the floor.

Conway slowly got up, his hands rubbing his stomach. "You got no right to come in here and empty this damn house out. I got power of attorney and I'm gonna run this show. You'll regret this many times over," Earl told the group.

"No, you do not have power of attorney," Victor corrected him. "I know the papers were never signed giving you that right. Bertha Hysell died too soon for that to be done. They were never signed. Parry Paul has the power of attorney. Now you listen to me and listen well. I don't want any trouble with you but if I have to, you and me'll go to the lawyer's office so you see the papers that have been signed.

Sarah rented this ranch to me for five years. And Tony is going to live in this house, not Sarah."

"I do too have power of attorney," Earl insisted.

"No you don't and you know it," Victor answered.

"You damn well know I have power of attorney?" he asked Sarah as he walked over to her. The rest watched in amazement as she stood her ground, never answering but also not backing away as he had hoped. Perplexed, he stood for a moment looking down at her. She never looked away . Finally he walked out the door, got into his car and drove away. Only then did they notice another woman was in the car, his ma.

"Sarah, you ain't afraid of him?" Mary asked her in astonishment.

"You never show fear of anything. If you do that only makes it worse for you," was her only answer.

"Do you think Earl will come back, Pa?" Tony asked, rubbing his hand over the back of his blond head .

"You get hurt, Tony?" Mary asked. "Here, let me look. I don't see anything."

"I only got my head banged on the wall when he shoved me. My shoulder hurts a little too. I always thought he was bigger than me but guess I've grown since I saw him last. I'm as big as he is, don't weigh as much but as tall. Do you think he'll come back, Pa?" he asked again.

"I don't know. He don't know where Sarah is going and I hope when he finds out, which he will in time, he'll be smart enough to stay away from our place. Sarah, you do realize you couldn't have stayed here alone, don't you?"

"Yes," she said, only her eyes showing her fear.

"His ma is an awful woman and he's got several sisters that must be lazier than their ma cause that place of theirs is a dirty hole. Only been on the yard once to buy hay. Went into the house to pay for it and I wouldn't eat off that table. Dogs in the house and cats and dirty dishes and flies sitting all over everything. This was the middle of the morning.

The place smelled," Victor told them.

Mary shuddered, then told Tony, "I don't think you should stay here alone for a few nights anyway. If he got into the house and you didn't hear him, he could kill you or hurt you bad."

"I've been thinking the same thing. Pa, you better camp here a few more nights, whether you want to or not."

"Yeah, I think so too. Conway's a coward but if he thought he could get the upper hand, he would. Is that everything, Sarah?" Victor asked.

She wrung her hands together for a few moments, then told them, "You want to see if we can see if my uncle buried any money down in the cellar where I think it is. We got the potatoes and stuff down there and the canning down there yet. That ain't been moved yet."

"Let's take a look around." Victor said. "I think we can all go down there cause I don't think Conway'll be back. At least not today." Heading toward the kitchen door, Sarah stopped him.

"There is a trapdoor into the cellar, here in the pantry."

"There is? No one would have known that. But I think I'd rather go into the cellar from the outside. We would hear anyone that drove in that way. Let's see what we can see," he said, going out the door. Lifting the cellar trap door, he led the way into the darkness.

"Tony, go into the barn and get the lantern hanging by the door. And bring a shovel from the shed too." While waiting for the lantern to be gotten, the three looked around the dark room.

"Here Pa," Tony said as he came down the steps. "I got a match here." As he walked around the room, the rest moved empty fruit jars, heavy crocks and other items stored there into the middle of the room.

"There's a spade down here," Tony said, picking it up from where it leaned against the wall, behind some sacks of potatoes.

"That spade stayed down here all the time," Sarah told them.

"Maybe he had that spade down here for a reason," Victor told them. "Well Sarah, where do we start?"

"Right here," she answered, pointing to the ground near the door. "I'm not sure just exactly where the cans are buried."

Taking the spade from Tony, he started at the door, poking it hard into the ground every few inches. Almost around the room the first time, he suddenly hit something. Digging, he unearthed a small syrup can. And then another and then another until he had six syrup cans. Poking around with the spade he could find no more.

"Anyone want to guess what's in these cans?" he asked the anxious group.

"Victor, please open one before I go frantic," Mary pleaded.

"Rusty. I can't find my pocket knife. You got one, Tony?"

He handed his pa the knife. Victor pried on the lid several places until the cover came loose. Lifting it, he looked inside, then reached in, pulled out some paper and then some paper money.

"Where we going with these, Sarah ?" he asked .

"I don't know. The bank? Ma kept her money in the bank."

"I don't know about that. Several banks have went broke around here and I just don't know but what I wouldn't just take these back to our place and bury them just like your uncle had them. I suppose the rest has money in it too. I really think we ought to poke around the rest of the cellar floor too but I doubt if we will find any more. We can do that tomorrow. I'd like to get these out of there right now. It gives me a funny feeling to have all this money here and we down here like sitting ducks if someone should drive into the yard. A person can get killed for a lot less money than this. Tony, you grab some and I'll take the rest and let's just get home. We'll decide what to do with this when we get home. And count it too if you want it counted, Sarah. But not now and not down here. Let's go."

Later that evening, after chores and supper dishes were done, Sarah and the Labella family sat around the supper table. Supper had been a silent meal, each in their own thoughts. Finally, asking Mary for a final cup of coffee, Victor broke the silence.

"Well, Sarah, what now?"

"I think and think of Uncle John and those cans of money. And the times he didn't have a pair of overshoes to wear and rags for a jacket. He was kind to me."

The rest of them looked at each other, Mary remembering what Tony had told her when they waiting for Sarah to find the car keys. Sarah ran her fingers over the top of her coffee cup, suddenly looking up and putting her hands in her lap. Her ma had hated her doing that and had slapped her fingers many times with whatever was handy for doing it. She noticed Victor holding his cup in both hands while Tony kept his fingers wrapped around his coffee cup handle. Hesitatingly, she put her fingers on the top of her cup again, rubbing the edge back and forth. No one cared.

"Again, I think we have to come up with something to do with that money. We can't leave it out in the hay barn under some hay. It just can't stay there. And we'll be gone all day Thursday getting Grandma."

"I wonder if it could be buried until Sarah has time to decide," Mary pondered. She continued to darn the sock she had in her hand. "What do you think?" she looked at Sarah.

"I guess that's all right. I don't know what else to do with it except put it into the bank."

"I don't think it would be a good idea to suddenly put that much cash into the bank. Someone, including the banker, will wonder where it came from and then wonder if there is any more where that came from. That teller at the bank is a talker and sometimes about business he has no business talking about. And with people hard up and getting harder up every day, and knowing your ma died, they may wonder if there is anymore where that came from and really go through your ma's buildings looking for it. Besides, there's banks going broke, doors being shut tight, more and more. I finally decided to keep some money here at home too cause I just didn't want it all at the bank. I felt better about it."

"Is the bank in town here all right Pa?" Tony asked.

"As safe as any, I guess. I asked the lawyer and several others and they all felt Phillip Quilly run a good sound bank. He's the banker is town here," he told Sarah. "There are good banks, or at least everyone thought they were good banks, all over going under, so who knows?"

"Well, tomorrow, I have to bake twice for the restaurant so Sarah, please set your alarm clock for three o'clock. I thought Thursday when we're gone, you can wash the little house so you can get all your things moved in there on Friday." Mary told the woman.

"And tomorrow, that money will be counted and buried," Victor added

"Know where yet, Pa?" Tony asked.

"Been thinking about it and wondered if the end of the feed alley, ahead of the cows where the hay always lays, wouldn't be a good place. Maybe right against the wall. I got our money buried in the feed alley by the horses in the horse barn. It gets walked on all the time so it gets packed good," Victor answered. Sarah gave him a surprised look as he disclosed this information. "Sarah, I would trust you with my life. I have no trouble telling you this as I know you won't tell anyone."

"Thank you," she whispered.

The next morning, after the first baking had been delivered and the chores were completely done, Mary started the second baking while the three other nervous adults sat down with the six syrup pails. As a precaution Victor had locked all the doors. Each pail was packed the same, paper carefully put in the middle and then paper bills carefully placed flat on the outer edge on the inside of the can. Several hours later, after counting and recounting they found each can had exactly the same amount of money in it, exactly three thousand dollars in one, five, ten and twenty dollar bills.

"That makes eighteen thousand dollars, Sarah," Victor told her.

Bewilderment hung like a cloud over Sarah. She only looked at Victor. She couldn't answer him.

"Again, as I have said before, I think these cans have to be buried and right away. I wouldn't take these to any bank, the money that is. At least not for now. And this counting and this money is not to be told to anyone. I'm sorry, Tony, but I don't think even Johanna should be told, at least not until you are married. We don't want someone to get wind of this and come in here with a loaded gun and want the money. We all could be killed. People kill these days for a few bucks.. Eighteen thousand dollars would be like a gold mine and that ain't counting the money your ma and I have stacked away here."

All agreed with this. Mary didn't want to leave her baking when the cans were dug into the ground but Victor made her go anyway so she would see where they were in case something happened to the rest of them.

"See, right here is where I thought," Victor said, pointing to the ground ahead of the feed alley where the milk cows ate. Taking a shovel he started to dig, while Tony dug close by him. Down about a foot and a half, they soon had a hole large enough to hold all six syrup cans. Dirt was shoveled back and the excess was carried to the back of the barn and scattered out onto a large area of barn yard. Stomping down the ground over the cans, Victor took hay and scattered it around making it look like the ground had never been disturbed.

"All done. Now let's get something to eat. And then me and Tony are going back to Sarah's house and load up the rest of the canning and potatoes and stuff in that cellar. We left it yesterday without filling in the holes where the syrup cans were and anyway, we're going to check and see if we find anything more buried. I doubt it, but we'll try anyway. Then we won't have to worry about doing it later. It's almost one o'clock and if we're going to get it done, then we're gonna have to hurry. I've got to take that second baking into Labit's too, sometime before supper and chores."

After Mary and Victor left on Thursday, Sarah took the scrub pail full of hot soapy water, a bunch of scrub rags and a scrubbing mop with her.

"Going to clean your house today?" Tony asked as he watched her gather up the cleaning materials.

"Yes," she answered. Suddenly looking up at him, she added, "Your pa and ma and you have been so good to me. I can hardly believe that I've been so lucky to have somewhere to work that is nice like this and a place to live in that is nice and a woman to work for so nice and everybody just so good to me. I don't deserve anything like this."

"Ma's very glad for the help and Pa and me are glad for renting your ranch and you're happy here with us and I got a house to live in after I'm married, so I guess everyone is lucky. I put a ladder up there this morning so you have something to stand on," he answered. Holding open the kitchen door for her, he stood watching as she walked up the hill toward the little house. Later he told his ma about the conversation, adding, "When she looks at you with those dark brown eyes they seem to just look right through you, they get so dark. Makes yours and my light blue eyes and pa's green eyes seem like nothing."

Sarah found that the little house wasn't dirty, only extremely dusty. She started scrubbing in the bedroom and soon had the walls and ceiling done. By early afternoon, when she went down to the big house for a quick lunch, she had the walls and ceiling in the kitchen and pantry washed. And toward late afternoon, the windows and floors were also shiny clean. The odor of the homemade soap she had used made the house smell so good when she walked through each room.

Standing in the middle of the bedroom, she tried to picture where the bed and dresser and sewing machine would be put. A window on the south side of the room and another one on the southwest corner of the room limited where the bed would go and also the dresser. The only place left to put the sewing machine was in front of the window, as the rest of the west wall had hooks for clothes and the rest of the wall by the window would have to be used for the another dresser her ma had used to put all the items needed for sewing .

She was pleased to have her uncle's bed and dresser to use now. Her own bed was in such poor shape it wasn't fit to be moved and she didn't want her ma's bed, even though it was in excellent condition. The bed of her ma's had been left there for Tony to use and her old bed had been left to be cut up and burned in the stove.

She looked again into the kitchen cupboards. Her ma hadn't had kitchen cupboards, only boards nailed onto the walls to hold the dishes and the kitchen supplies she had. Nails hammered into the wall had held the pots and pans. Now she would have a cupboard to put things into. It was made out of rough boards but nevertheless, it was a cupboard and it was nice. Mary had given her some papers to line the shelves with. The stove stood against the north wall. There were three doors in the kitchen, one leading to the bedroom, one to the porch outside and one to the large pantry and storeroom. This was a luxury, as her ma hadn't had a pantry either. She certainly didn't have enough groceries, dishes and pots and pans to fill all the kitchen cupboards and the pantry shelves too. Maybe the boxes Tony had taken down from the attic could be stored in here. She had no idea what was in them, as her ma had forbidden her to ever look in them.

Going through the kitchen toward the door, she stopped a moment and looked through the large window facing the south. This was the only window in the kitchen but it was a large one and it made the room light. The kitchen door led onto a small porch on the south side of the house. It had a wooden railing and posts and pleased Sarah a great deal. She took a few moments and just ran her hand carefully around the top of the post at the top of the steps. Although the wood was somewhat splintery, the whole idea of a porch of her own delighted her.

Giving the sky a quick squint, she knew she'd have to hurry to have supper ready when Victor and Mary got home. Still she stood a few minutes just looking at the outside of the house, with the sparkling windows and the scrubbed little porch.

"Got it all done?" Tony asked as he joined her.

"Oh, you scared me," she told him. "Yes, I'm done and it smells so nice. What time is it, do you know?" He pulled out a watch from his pocket.

"Four o'clock, just a little after. Pa and Ma got home about an hour ago."

"Oh, I wanted to have supper ready for them . I better go see what I can help your ma with," she told him.

"No hurry. Ma said she got Grandma settled in bed and she was gonna lay down for a few minutes too. Ma got some canned chicken for supper from the basement," Tony replied.

"Oh, chicken... I like that but I'll be eating here from now on, at least when the wagon gets unloaded."

"Ma said you and her would have to work that out but

when you're helping her, then you'll eat down at the big
house. This is the little house and that is the big house and
your ma's house will now be called the Tony's house, at least
while I am living there. I don't know if anyone told you,
probably not, 'cause Pa was in a hurry this morning, but we
had visitors last night. A car drove in and someone got out,
quiet-like, but Brownie, that's our dog, had went along with
me and Pa last night and he was one the porch and started to
bark. Whoever it was got into the car in a hurry and drove
out with the lights off. We can only guess who it was but I
was glad Pa was there too. By the time Johanna and I get
married next fall, Pa thinks we won't be bothered anymore
with nighttime visitors. He thinks whoever it was will get
tired of the game and find something else to do."

"Your pa thinks it was Earl Conway, don't he?" Sarah
asked

"Kind of thought it was. But the dog took care of it."

"Your folks have been so good to me," she told him.

"Why not? That's only being a good neighbor."

The next day, after the baking was done and Grandma
taken care of, Mary looked to see if she had anything that
could be used for curtains for the little house. Finding nothing, Mary told Sarah that the two of them were going shopping in the next couple days in Ponta. They'd measure the
windows in the little house for curtains and also get material
for several dresses for Sarah and for three or four aprons.
Mary intended to ask Tony to stay around the buildings and
the house to keep an eye on Grandma.

By this time the men had harnessed the horses and
pulled the hay wagon up to the little house. Uncle John's
brass bed frame, spring and straw-filled mattress were brought
in and put in place. Next came his dresser, the sewing machine and the old dresser with the sewing things stored in it.

The round oak kitchen table came next, along with
the six matching chairs. Victor and Tony brought in the

small buffet that matched the table. They looked at Sarah, waiting for her to tell them where to go with it. Her eyes got large as she realized she had forgotten about that piece of furniture and now didn't know where to have it put.

"There," Victor told Tony, nodding his head toward the only place in the kitchen where he thought it would fit. "We'll just bring in the boxes now and leave them in the kitchen here. You'll have to unpack them yourself. Then the rest of the furniture will have to be unloaded in the granary."

After the men got the last of the boxes carried into the house and had left, Sarah knew moments of panic. She looked at the boxes and knew she had to decide where everything was to go. There wasn't anyone to tell her what to put where. There was no one to tell her how to do it or where to start. After a few minutes of just standing and wringing her hands, she took a deep breath and started, opening first the box with the flour and sugar in it. Where should she put it? What if it wasn't right? How could she arrange anything? No one to tell her anything.

The box finally unpacked, she took the boxes with the clothing in them into the bedroom and unpacked her few things. Going through the things that had been in her ma's drawers brought a few tears as she looked at the homemade underwear and clothing her ma had worn. She gathered them together, laying them in a heap by the kitchen stove and throwing in a few pieces at a time, she burned the pile. Going further through the things that had been in her ma's dresser drawers, she found some very nice, new sheets made out of feed sacks. There were matching pillowcases, trimmed with a edging of lace. In all the years she had known her ma, she had never seen any of this. There were also several new nightgowns, warm ones made out of flannel. And her ma had worn only the many times mended nightgowns that were so threadbare. The boxes of her uncle's clothing, she stored in a corner of the bedroom to be gone through later.

Unpacking the rest of the kitchen utensils and groceries took a little longer, as she tried to put them where she thought it handiest, realizing finally that she could move them if she so desired to another place. The old plates and cups, she stacked in the pantry. Although she had nothing to go into the kitchen cupboards, she still hesitated to put the everyday dishes of her ma's in there. That cupboard was for something better than the dishes she had used all her life.

The last boxes on the floor were the boxes that her ma had forbidden her ever to look at. These had been stored in the attic for as many years as Sarah could remember. She tried to open the twine that was tied around the first box, finally having to get a kitchen knife to cut the string. Carefully taking out the first newspaper-wrapped item from the top, she unwrapped the loveliest plate she had ever seen. It was beautiful fine china ringed with gold and strewn with pink roses. She carefully took out each piece, unwrapped it and then laid it on the table until she had a full set of twelve, including cups, saucers, dinner plates, sauce dishes, platters and dessert plates.

Another box was also full of dishes. Although not as delicate as the first set, they were good china. Small blue scrolling edged the plates in this set. The third box was full of nice bowls, a glass salt and pepper shaker set and other pieces of glass and china that were used to set a very nice table. Finally on the bottom of the box were two linen tablecloths, one quite large and one smaller, plus napkins. A much smaller box was packed with good silverware, including pickle and meat forks. Two other boxes were full of everyday dishes, many of them with chips here and there. Sarah counted eleven bowls of various sizes in the everyday dishes. These dishes were in much better shape than any her ma had used all those years.

Hearing someone on the porch, she turned to see Mary coming in the door.

"How you coming with your unpacking?" she was asked.

"I have all it put away, somehow or another, but these last boxes. I just opened them now and this is what I found."

"Oh my goodness, girl. These are lovely," Mary said as she picked up one piece of the good set.

"I never saw them before," Sarah told her.

"Where were they?" Mary asked

"Ma had the it all packed away in the attic."

"She never used them?"

"No. We only used the old dishes I put in the pantry."

"You are going to use these everyday dishes now, ain't you?" Mary asked

Sarah just looked at her. She slowly shook her head no.

"Oh surely, you're gonna use them. Land sakes, child, why not? These dishes you were using before are so bad that you should throw them out and use the ones you just found."

"I can't."

"Yes, you can. There is no one telling you that you can't. They are plenty everyday ones here on the table and you certainly should use them. Those ones of your ma's are broken and some cracked so only part of the plate can be used and some of those cups are so broken that it's a wonder you don't cut your mouth when you try to drink out of them. If you feel funny using these, then maybe use only one piece a day until you get used to them."

"What if I break something?" Sarah asked.

"The world ain't going to come to an end if you do," was the reply. " Life will go on, whether you break one piece or not. Just wash them and put them in your pantry and then use some of them. Oh, not the good ones for everyday but the dishes in those two boxes should be used. Oh, you know what? That's funny but there ain't any good glasses anywhere."

Later that night, Sarah stumbled over two small boxes that she had put in the bedroom by mistake and these produced the glasses Mary had wondered about. One box had good glasses in it, twelve large, twelve smaller and six even smaller ones. Sarah held one of the smaller glasses up to the lamp and even with the many years' dust and grime on it, it still sparkled.

The glasses in the other box were plainly not as good. Some had small chips around the edges. In all her life, Sarah had never drunk from a glass. Her ma had never allowed glasses in the house. An old broken cup was good enough.

Carrying the boxes into the kitchen, she took water from the reservoir and washed the everyday glasses, setting them beside the everyday dishes on the pantry shelves she had washed that afternoon and the old ones she had moved from her ma's. The box with the good glasses she put into the pantry setting it beside the boxes of good china she had repacked.

Taking a final look at the things she had set on the pantry shelves, Sarah thought of when she had been about five years old and when washing dishes, she had dropped an everyday bowl and broke it. She still had the scars from the beating her ma had given her.

For the first time for many years, Sarah cried herself to sleep.

CHAPTER III

"You know what," Mary told Victor next morning at breakfast. "No money was saved out so Sarah could buy some material for a couple of dresses and some aprons."

"Do I really need anything?" Sarah asked.

"Yes, you do need dresses, child. And none of mine fit you at all. You don't have any dresses of your own except for the funeral one I made the other day. You can't keep wearing bib overalls. No woman wears them, except maybe in the barn. But she changes right away into a dress. It's just plain ladylike. You need two or three everyday dresses and one more good dress. Well, maybe not a good dress but maybe a piece of lace around the neck would dress it up so it looked nice. It's so plain now."

"I'm plain, homely," Sarah answered, shrugging.

"No you're not. At least you won't be when you get dresses to wear and some of that hair cut off. Yes, that is such a mop of hair," she told her as Sarah put her hands up to her head in horror. "It takes so long to wash and dry it and I think, from the few strands that like to escape from that braid you wear, that you might have curly hair. And you need three or four aprons too. One for good and three for everyday. Why land sakes, I don't know what I'd do without an apron. Why all these years I've used aprons to wipe little kids' runny noses and their tears and to gather eggs in and carry fresh peas and garden stuff in and shoo out the flies out of the house and keep my arms warm when I stand

out in the wind and for carrying clothes pins in and a hot
pad when one ain't handy for taking off a hot pan off the
stove and just for everything. Don't know what I'd do without an apron."

"Ma would roll over in her grave if I cut my hair,"
Sarah whispered.

"Then she will have to do just that. Land sakes child,
she ain't here anymore and you can do what you want. She
ain't going to tell you that you can't."

Sarah's brown eyes got larger and larger. She couldn't
imagine herself with wearing a dress and an apron and she
surely couldn't imagine anything but long hair that was
braided to the waist. Long hair that was washed only once a
week at the most and combed only then.

"Then you can wash your hair more often and run a
comb through it every day," Mary told her. "Now it's such a
job to take care of anything that long. Victor, some money
should have been saved back for that trip into Ponta. We
should be able to get material for one dress for a dollar, not
counting the thread or rickrack for aprons or material, scraps,
remnants for aprons. Once you get used to wearing an apron,
you'll wonder how you ever managed without one."

"Then I'll just give her some money when you go shopping and it can be taken back when Sarah gets paid. When
you want to go to Ponta?" he asked.

"I think tomorrow. I talked to Tony and he said he'd
watch Grandma. And I want to get some other material too
so I can start to sew for Christmas. That is coming too,
Sarah. You want to think about that 'cause I know everyone
here will give you some little things so you have something
to unwrap like everyone else. We don't give very much, only
things needed, like overalls or shirts or material or dresses I
sewed for my daughter and her girls and I give Johanna something and also Lee, our older son and his daughter. His wife
died about three years ago. It was three years, wasn't it?" She
looked at her husband and he shook his head yes.

"I don't think I want to give anybody anything and I don't want anything," Sarah told them.

"Why not, child?" Mary asked.

Looking down at her hands Sarah finally told them, "We never had any Christmas. I don't know anything about it, except what there was at school, when I went there. I think I'll stay in my house that day. It would be better."

It took Mary a few minutes to digest that piece of information, then she slowly answered, "Then it is time you learned about that wonderful day. Was your ma against religion?"

Again, Sarah took a long moment to answer, "I don't know what religion is."

"Then we'll teach you," Victor told her. "A bit at a time. We go to church about once a month during the winter time and more often in the summer. Don't go every week, but do go some. Not the best church members, but that's how it is. As far as religion is, we'll teach or show you some and you can make up your own mind about that. As far as Christmas and presents and dinner and Christmas Eve, that I want you to join in with us. We don't give much, only things needed, 'cause there ain't any money for anything else but we do have candy and homemade wine and do play cards some and have a tree and decorations that are mostly homemade. We have some company to help us have a fun time. Our son Lee and his daughter, Cora Lee and sometimes Gertrude, our daughter and her family, sometimes the neighbors that are close to here. Depends on the weather."

" I don't know anything about talking to other people. I don't mind talking to you, all of you, cause you're so nice and have been so good to me but I don't want to have to talk to anyone else. I wouldn't know what to say," Sarah told him.

"Then you can just be with us and soak up some of the friendship that there is. The other people won't bite. As far as getting gifts, Victor and I'll give you something, not much, but something and I think Tony has something in mind to give you too. And if you don't know what to give Victor and me or Tony, then we'll just give you some ideas and you can go from there. It is a fun time, child. A really fun and nice time of year."

"And the house smells so good with chicken baking and dressing and pumpkin pie baking, and the fresh pine smell of the Christmas tree," Victor added. "You can enjoy that and you don't have to say anything. The rest of us do enough talking for everybody." Getting up from his chair, he started to put on his jacket and four-buckle boots. "Tomorrow morning, then is shopping time. I'll deliver the baked stuff and then come back and we'll have breakfast and then clean up to make another trip to Ponta. Should be home by noon for dinner. We'll drive past the place where all this baked stuff goes, Labit's, so you can see where it is, Sarah."

"Tony'll have to check on Grandma while we're gone tomorrow. I'll remind him again this noon. Now, I'll change Grandma's bed and Sarah, you can start the washing. Got to change everything when she wets it all, not like we ordinarily do it to save washing. You did it that way at your house, Sarah, top sheet goes on the bottom and bottom sheet gets washed?"

"That's always the way Ma had me do it."

Sarah pulled the washing machine out from the corner. She went onto the back porch and got the benches that held the two tubs and put them in place by the machine. Two more trips to the porch produced the two tubs that she put on top of the benches. Taking a large dipper, she scooped out water, from the copper-bottomed boiler on the stove, into a pail. This water was dumped into the washing machine. This was repeated until the washing machine was full. What hot water was left was divided between the two tubs. Sarah filled the tubs half full of water by pumping water into the pail using the hand pump that was fitted onto the edge of the galvanized sink in the kitchen. Looking around the pantry, she found a bottle of bluing. A small slug was added to the final rinse tub. Taking a small pan that had melted homemade soap and water in it, she dumped this into the washing machine. By the time she had this done, Mary had brought out bedding from her ma's bed.

"So much washing now with ma here. Such a shame that she wets the bed sometimes. Not so nice to get old when you can't take care of yourself good," Mary said, putting the sheets into the washing machine. She stepped aside while Sarah took hold of the handle on the machine and started to pull it back and forth.

"I'm saving for a gasoline powered washing machine," she told Sarah. "That will be heaven after this. My arms get so tired pulling that handle back and forth to agitate the clothes."

"I think this is nice." Sarah answered. "I never had anything like this. I always had to wash with a scrub board."

"This's better than that. My hands used to bleed when I got done washing that way. I'm going to try to bring Ma out here. I thought she'd have a wheelchair when she came but I guess I was wrong on that 'cause we'd have had to pay for one and Victor said to let it go 'cause he didn't have enough money with him and my sister said she and my other sisters weren't going to pay for it so ma didn't get a wheelchair. I'm gonna tie her into that rocker, if I can. I should have had Victor help me before he left. Maybe at noon when he's in here. Would be nice for her cause then she can see everyone. I don't know if I can handle her alone."

"I can help you," Sarah offered. " I used to carry Ma from the bed to the table, to the rocker and then back to bed .Toward the last she had to stay in bed all the time." `

"But your ma was a small woman and Ma is anything but small. And it's all dead weight, like carrying a sack of feed. But maybe we can do it anyway." The two women, one on each side, got the older woman out of her bed and into the rocking chair they put by it. After Mary tied the woman into the chair, with one of them on each side of the rocker they dragged it across the floor until it set by the kitchen table.

"There, we got that done. How's that, Ma? Better than laying all the time in that bed?" The old woman gave Mary a crooked smile and tried to squeeze her hand.

"She appreciates someone doing something for her and I think she's glad she is here instead of in the hospital. Now," Mary turned to Sarah and said, " when we get the washing done and the clothes folded from the last washing and the ironing done, that should be all I need you for today. Then, unless you want to make your own supper, you can come down about four o'clock and help me get supper. It's up to you." Sensing that Sarah was having trouble deciding, she went back to her work.

Sarah pondered the rest of the afternoon, finally deciding to join them for supper. She wanted to ask Mary something.

"Mary, do you have any scrap paper I could have? I hate to bother you and maybe I shouldn't have."

"Nonsense. I have a little. But maybe tomorrow you can buy several tablets in the dime store and pencils and a pen too, if you need them. Tony said you used to draw things in school, pretty things. Ever think about trying that again, something to do in the evenings with your time?"

"I found some crayons I didn't know we had when I cleaned through some of Ma's stuff but I couldn't find any scrap paper. There was some good paper, but I couldn't use that. That would be wasteful."

"Well, maybe after you've played around with the colors a while, you can use the good paper 'cause by then you'll be so much better. I know somewhere upstairs, there are colored chalk. I'll have to hunt for it. I sure don't use it and no body else does either. You can have it."

"That would be nice," Sarah answered, her eyes brightening.

"You want to dish up the fried potatoes?" Mary asked. "I see Tony coming and Victor too. I got stewed tomatoes with bread cut up in it too. And the rest of that cake I burnt this morning. Don't know why it had to burn. I tested the oven to see if it was hot enough and I guess it was 'cause I burnt the cake. That the way you always tested your oven?"

"Yeah. Always a tablespoon or so of cake batter on a pie plate shoved in the oven for a few minutes. You fired up the stove so soon after the cake was in this morning.. Maybe cookies would have been better to bake when it was so hot."

"But I had the cake batter mixed up and ready to go. And then had to mix up another one. It's not too bad tasting if you cut off the burnt off the bottom. Guess that's the way it goes. You all go ahead and eat while I help Ma eat." Pulling up a chair to the rocker she had the old lady tied in, Mary started to feed her with a spoon. "After I get her done, Victor you can help me get her back in bed. She's tired of sitting here and needs to lay down."

Sarah compared her ma and Mary's ma in her mind. Her ma had never weighed very much, thin and short in stature while Mary's ma was tall, almost as tall as Victor but much heavier than he was. She had a moon-shaped face that had a tendency to look pleasant. Although she couldn't reply when Mary talked to her, she answered with a somewhat crooked but effortless smile. She thought the woman found smiling came easy. Sarah tried hard to remember when she had seen her ma last smile Even when Uncle John was alive, her ma's nature was harsh and unyielding. Sarah found it best not to even think of those days, better to leave sleeping dogs lie, as Uncle John used to say.

Before nine o'clock the next morning, Victor had their Model A Ford in front of the house waiting for Mary and Sarah. As they drove along, Victor and Mary pointed out things of interest to her. They never realized this was her first time in a car, her first trip to Ponta, that she had never been farther than the schoolhouse in her entire life. Her eyes and mind tried to soak in everything as they went along.

"Now you remember the hospital, Sarah?" Mary asked, not waiting for her to answer. "And here is the high school and the grade school. Don't know how many children go to the high school. I know our kids didn't. We just didn't have the money to send them and Victor didn't think it was needed anyway. Tony is ranching with us, Lee got a job on the railroad and Gertrude got married when she was sixteen. Down in the next block is Labit's, right there Sarah. Where you gonna park, Victor?"

"Right down this here block, I guess. This here is close to the dry goods store and shoe store. You were going to get a pair of shoes, ain't you?"

"Yes. Oh yes. I have to 'cause these are so worn out I can't even tie them anymore. Can't keep them on my feet. And you'll be back about eleven for us? Right about here? If you don't see us, wait in the bakery."

"OK, I'll go to the feed mill and get some salt for the cattle and chew the fat with whoever comes in there. I'll be back around eleven." Waiting until Sarah and Mary were out of the car, he drove off.

"All right, we'll start here with the material, Sarah. I forgot to ask if you had any patterns you liked so we could know how much material to buy. No?" she asked as Sarah shook her head. "Then we'll just figure three and a half to four yards. Most of the material is only thirty-nine inches wide so we will need at least that much to get a dress and full sleeves out and a collar too. Should be able to get a dress for about a dollar." Sarah followed Mary into the store, her eyes wide as she looked up and down the store aisles. Tables full of material, buttons, rickrack and other notions, thread and patterns filled the store. Mary walked up and down the aisles looking with Sarah following, her eyes darting here and there trying to take it all in.

"This is good cotton material, Sarah. Do you see anything you like? Maybe walk around some more and see if you find anything that strikes your fancy. I'll look at the remnants they have and see if I can find anything for aprons."

It was hard for Sarah to absorb everything. She finally picked out one piece of material, a dark blue with white and yellow flowers sprinkled on it and another piece, light brown with white polka dots splattered on it. Looking around she noticed the two other women shoppers carrying the bolts of material to the front of the store where the clerks were waiting. She debated, trying to decide if she should do the same. Sensing she had found something, Mary asked her to show her what she had found.

"Oh that is pretty. And so is the other one. Those will both be fine, nice and darker for everyday. Won't show the dirt so soon. Now you really need another piece of material too. Three everyday dresses is not too many. And I found some really nice lace to put around that dress you have on, the one I made for the funeral. Did you go down this aisle?" When Sarah shook her head no, Mary took the two bolts of fabric Sarah had picked out, and motioned for Sarah to lead the way. She stopped by a bright green piece that had tiny flowers scattered all over it and looked at Mary, questioning her choice.

"Sarah, that's a pretty piece. Nice and bright and it will make up real nice."

"Maybe I should take a darker color but green is my favorite color. I never had anything green before."

"If you like that one, take it. I have a remnant that will make a nice apron to go with it. You don't need any underwear, do you?"

"No, I found some in ma's drawers that had never been worn. They're made out of flour sacks but they're fine."

"Let's just pick put one pair of good panties for you and a good undergarment and whatever else there is, oh yes, a slip. Just one good set for under your good dress. And two pair of silk stockings too. They cost sixty-nine cents apiece. And cotton stockings for everyday. We'll get those at the Penny's Store next door to here. And we've got to stop at the dime store too to get that paper for you. We won't worry about any material for any Christmas presents today for you to sew on for your presents. I don't suppose you have any idea what you would want to give anybody anyway. I found some flannel for some shirts so I got something to start sewing with. Thought I would maybe tie a quilt for my daughter. That is, if I get time."

Sarah listened to her, then quickly asked as they came toward the table where the material was measured and lengths cut, "Mary, do I have enough money for all of this? I saw a price above the material but I didn't know how big a piece of material I got for the price I saw."

"Land sakes child. I should have told you. That price is for each yard. And yes, Victor gave you enough for all of that. He gave you fifteen dollars."

While measuring the material for cutting the yardage needed, the clerk kept giving Sarah quick glances, trying to figure out who she was. Finally she asked Mary if she had a relative staying with her.

"No. This is Sarah Hysell. You know her ma was our neighbor and she died about ten days ago. Sarah is helping me out while my ma is staying with us. She's a real help."

"You still baking for Labit's?"

"Oh yes. I wasn't sure how I was going to keep up with it all but now with Sarah helping me out, we're managing very nicely. My ma has had a stroke and needs a lot of extra care. My sisters and I take turns, six months at a time."

"Oh that's nice for you to have help. My aunt has had a stroke and the family has to share that care too. It's so hard. And you have my sympathy too," she said looking at Sarah. "Looks like your going to have some sewing here to do, both of you."

"Oh, I almost forgot. I figured to use the patterns I

used to use for Gertrude but I almost forgot the thread. We need thread for all of this. And possibly some rickrack or seam binding for the aprons. You don't have any rickrack or seam binding, do you?" she asked Sarah. She shook her head no.

Several more minutes were spent picking out the extra things needed before Mary and Sarah paid for the things they had picked out. She spent anxious moments while the clerk added up her purchases. Yes, the money she had been given that morning more than covered the cost, with almost nine dollars left.

Next stop was the Penney's store. Mary helped Sarah find the undergarments, slip and stockings that she thought Sarah needed. After the first pair of panties were held up for Sarah to look at, Mary could see the woman had never even seen anything like it before, let alone trying to pick out a pair she liked. Finally Mary used her own judgment and picked out what she hoped would fit and would be liked.

Next came the shoe store. As Mary was trying on shoes, Sarah sat quietly trying to tuck her feet under her chair. The only shoes she owned for good were the ones on her feet, a very shoddy worn-out pair of black men's shoes that had been her uncle's. Her ma had used these for her good shoes and now they were Sarah's. As they were sitting in chairs toward the far side of the store, Sarah could see all over. Pairs of shoes were on the display shelves and single shoes were hooked by the heels and hanging from the boxes they came in. She looked and looked, her eyes coming back again and again to a pair of black tie shoes with an inch heel that had fancy work on the toes. When Mary had been fitted, the male clerk looked at Sarah.

"You have enough money for a pair, Sarah," Mary assured her.

"That pair up there." Without hesitating Sarah pointed toward the black shoes. "How much do they cost?"

"Let's look," the clerk answered getting up. "Price is

two ninety-eight. You want to try them on?" Sarah nodded yes. Smiling, the clerk helped Sarah untie her shoes, then got her size.

"Very nice indeed," Mary told her. The pleasure Sarah had was so obvious as she looked down at her feet. "Why don't you take them, if they feel good on your feet. Be sure and walk around a bit here so you know if they fit you and do feel good." Watching her walk in the new shoes, Mary asked her if they were the ones she wanted.

Sarah nodded yes and after Mary asked her if she wanted to wear the new ones home, the old ones were put into the shoe box and the purchase was paid for.

"Well, we'll be done after we stop at the dime store. Then we'll go to the bakery and have a cup of coffee. We'll have time before Victor comes." The dime store was another wonderland to Sarah. So many things to look at, so many things to see. Mary hurried her along as she wanted the treat of a cup of coffee so it wasn't very many minutes until they were in the bakery. More new things to see and marvel at. The glassed-in counters had shelves and shelves of cook-ies and rolls, cupcakes, chocolate and white and several fruit pies waiting to be cut and put on small plates. Sarah watched to see what Mary was going to do and when she sat down at a small table covered with a red and white checkered table-cloth, Sarah did the same. The smell of the baked things did not startle her as she smelled this every morning while help-ing Mary with her baking, but the cafe atmosphere in the building did. Someone came over and asked them what they wanted. Coffee and filled raisin cookies being brought to them was something brand new.

"I've got money to pay for my own," Sarah told Mary when she realized Mary was paying for all of it.

"Land sakes, child. This is my treat. I appreciate your helping me so much and it has been a pleasure to have some-one to take with me shopping. It's been so long since I had Gertrude to take with me. She's been gone so long already.

Just eat and enjoy." Mary looked up as another couple about Victor and Mary's age came into the bakery.

"Well hello there, Lillian, and how are you, Joe?" Mary greeted them. Glancing at Sarah, she realized she was visually shrinking in her chair. "Sarah, this is our neighbors on the south, Joe and Lillian Morshian. This here is Sarah Hysell."

"Oh, Bertha's daughter?" Joe asked.

"Yes, you knew Bertha died about ten days ago?" Mary asked.

"No. We didn't. I'm sorry, Sarah," Joe said. Lillian also gave her sympathy.

"Sarah is helping me now. I have my ma with me for the next six months and that's a lot of extra care so Sarah's helping me has been a godsend. Sarah is living in the little house behind our house and Tony is living in the house on Sarah's farm, her ma's farm before she died."

"Oh, that sounds like a nice arrangement," Lillian told her.

"It works out very well," Mary agreed.

"Don Kelly still working the Hysell land?" Joe asked.

"No. We've rented it now," Mary answered. "Oh, there comes Victor. It's about eleven o'clock and he's come to pick us up."

"Looks like you did some shopping," Lillian commented, seeing the packages lying on the floor.

"Yes. We're going home to sew, ain't we, Sarah?"

"Hello, neighbors. Wish I had time to visit but got to get home. Help Tony with some fixing on the chicken coop. Why don't you people come over and we'll really get down to a good visit," Victor said.

"Oh, and bring your scissor along for cutting hair.. My hair needs a trimming badly," Mary added. "Come on over Sunday. I don't have to bake for Labit's so I have time to get dinner ready for company."

"That'd be nice," Lillian said, "but no extra fussing, you hear. And I'll bring along the hair scissor and clipper."

"Dinner at twelve," Mary called as they left the building.

That evening , before Victor went back to Sarah's old house to sleep, he and Mary had a cup of coffee, a slice of bread and jelly and a few minutes to visit.

"You think you'll get Sarah to come down here Sunday for dinner?" Victor asked.

"I've got an even bigger job and that's talking her into having her hair cut. 'Ma wouldn't like it. She would turn over in her grave.' That woman had a terrific hold on that girl."

"I been thinking and wondering about something. You remember when Conway went over to her that day. Most any other woman would have ducked or cringed away from him but she just stood there and didn't make any move to get away."

"I would have just crumpled."

"Most any woman would have but she didn't and if you remember I asked her about it afterwards and she said that you never show fear of anything. If you do, it only makes it worse for you. I thought about that a lot. I wonder how much Sarah got hit and how hard she really had it in that house."

"She sure acts different than any of our children acted," Mary told him

"I think she had a different upbringing than our children had. We kept out children in line, they toed the mark and did their chores and didn't sass us at all and they got a paddling or two when they needed it, but it seems to be different for her. 'Course there was always laughter and loving too," Victor said. " I hope she knows how to sew with all that material I saw hanging on the lines drying today."

"She says she can sew and I don't doubt it. I know she

mended and that looks very good. What I saw when she moved. I imagine her ma taught her how as I don't think anything much was bought ready-made there. You leaving now?" she asked as Victor went to the door.

"I'm doing this until we get a good snow and then I'm going to crawl into my own bed. We haven't had any trouble since Earl was there that first day and that car came that one night when Brownie barked. I'm getting tired of this, believe me. By the way, Fred at the feed mill has a large German shepherd dog he's giving away. I thought about getting it as our dog seems to have decided he wants to stay with Tony over there."

"Oh, why don't you get him? I hope he's a good watch dog."

"The best, I was told. Maybe tomorrow morning I'll pick the dog up on my way back from Labit's. Another mouth to feed but if he's a good watch dog, then he'll be worth it."

"Oh, what has Pa got with him? " Tony asked his ma as he watched Victor coming toward the house the next morning. "It looks like a big dog and he is pretty."

"He said he was gonna see if the dog Fred at the feed mill had to give away was still there. And he must have been if you see a dog. Hello, and you did get the dog, I see," Mary said as Victor came through the door.

"Yeah. This here is Bud and he can stay outside or inside. Fred says he's a real clean dog but I think he's a little big for in here." They watched as the dog made his way around the kitchen, smelling as he went. He stopped by Sarah. She made no attempt to touch him or pet him.

"Come on, Bud, you better go outside," Victor called.

"He won't run away, will be?" Mary asked.

"I don't think so. He seems to be a really nice dog. Tony, take him with you when you go to the barn."

"Sarah," Mary told the woman, "Please, it's time to start the washing and I'll take care of Ma. Maybe, Victor, you can help me get her into the kitchen after you finish eating breakfast. I want to help Sarah cut out a dress and an apron this morning so she can start to sew it. With company coming Sunday, I want to get some of the cooking and baking done for that Saturday. So Sarah has two days to do her dress and apron. I plan to help her if she needs any help, maybe measure the hem and whatever else is needed."

Morning work done and dinner over with, the pattern was laid out on the blue material and cut. Sarah carefully folded each piece so she could carry them to the little house. Opening the sewing machine in her bedroom, she began the putting together of the dress. Before long she was immersed in the job. It was such a pleasure to be sewing on something that was brand new, not something that was half worn-out and had to be remade, as she had done so many times for her ma.

By four o'clock she was getting hungry. Although she had had baking powder biscuits a few days before with Mary's family, the thought of the warm rolls, along with the soup Mary had sent along with her for supper sounded so good. Putting some wood in the cookstove, she went into the pantry found the ingredients needed and stirred up a batch, rolled them out and put them in the hot oven. The smell from the baking filled the little house. Sarah found she had a strange feeling of belonging, something she had never had in her entire life. Here she had something that Ma had never had before. She did not have to ask Ma for anything. Ma was not there to make fun of her and make her feel like she was dumb. And Ma was not there to force her into doing something she didn't want to do.

She shuddered as she thought of Earl Conway. Ma could not force her anymore to be nice to him. And Ma had died before she could give Earl the power of attorney over her. She remembered her ma screaming at her and that would be Sarah's punishment for not obeying her. Her ma was too weak and Sarah was too big to beat anymore but she would make her marry Earl and then Sarah could see how smart she was. He would keep her in line. He would beat her when her ma couldn't anymore.

I'll show her, Sarah thought defiantly. She can't scream at me anymore or make me do anything I don't want to do anymore. I'm going to have new dresses and aprons and I have a new house to live in where no one tells me I didn't make the bed right and didn't wash the dishes clean. I'll show her. I'll have my hair cut Sunday when the Morshians come. So what if she didn't ever want me to cut my hair? She ain't here anymore to make me do anything and never will make me do anything I don't want to again.

Suddenly Sarah felt weak, so shaky she could hardly take the pan of biscuits out of the oven. Pulling the cooking soup onto the back of the stove to keep warm, it was fully an hour before Sarah felt strong enough to finally eat her supper. Another hour passed before she turned again to the sewing.

During the night Sarah heard Bud, the dog, on her porch. He barked a few times and then settled down, lying against the front door. Sleep had come hard for her. The thoughts of the late afternoon kept roaming around inside her head. But after the dog lay on her porch to sleep, Sarah's eyes closed and she drifted into heavy sleep.

Going out the door the next morning right after three o'clock, she had to push Bud away from the door to open it. Bending down she petted him, receiving a few licks from his tongue as her thank you. It was dark outside so no one could see her petting the dog. The habits of her youth were embedded in her mind. If you petted something or showed love for something, it would be taken away from you and killed. How well she remembered the kittens and the pup that her ma had hit in the head with the shovel. All had died, except the kitten her uncle had given her after the burning session. Her uncle had warned her ma never ever to lay a hand on that animal and she hadn't.

So uptight were her nerves that Sarah was almost to the panic stage as she helped Mary Sunday morning. The old hens that had been butchered on Saturday morning were cooking on the stove. Noodles had also been made on Saturday and were now put into the broth with the hens . Potatoes were cooking on the stove, minutes away from being done. Fresh buns, filled with applesauce and sprinkled with sugar, had been baked that morning. Sarah had set the table while Mary and Victor moved Grandma into the rocking chair in the kitchen.

"You got a new dress and apron on," Tony told Sarah when he came into the kitchen from doing chores before dinner. By that time she had conquered her feelings enough she was able to give him a small smile and a whispered thank you. She looked down at the large collar edged in white and yellow rickrack that matched the flowers on the blue material. Glancing farther down she caught a glimpse of her new black shoes. Sticking her hands into the large pockets of her new apron, Sarah gave Tony another quick smile as he started upstairs to change before company arrived.

"I think Sarah's dress and apron look so nice." Mary added as she surveyed the kitchen. "I think we're ready. Oh Sarah, can you run down to the cellar and bring up some pickles. Bring the dill pickles. Yes, I know, Victor, those are your favorites. Maybe bring some beet pickles too. They add color to the table. Joe and Lillian should be here anytime. I wish Johanna could have been with us today," she added, turning to Tony as he came downstairs.

"I do too but her ma and pa went visiting some relative and wanted her to go along 'cause she's old, the relative, and won't be seeing Johanna again probably."

"I see them driving in," Victor said.

"Oh Sarah won't like it that she's out there when they come. She may stay down there until they get into the house." And that is just what she did. After Morshians were in the house, coats taken, and seated, Sarah came back into the kitchen. A slight smile was given the company and she went into the pantry to take care of the pickles. While Mary was talking, Sarah drained the potatoes, mashed them and put them into the bowl Mary had set out. She then dished out the noodles and chicken into another large bowl.

"Lands sakes, child." Mary said when she saw Sarah had taken care of everything. "You got everything on while my mouth ran like water. Well, everyone just sit up and eat. I have to make a plate and feed Ma. I'll eat after that. Here Lillian, you sit here and, Joe, you sit right beside your wife. The rest just pull up a chair and set."

"I brought the hair clipper and scissor along," Lillian told her.

"Good. We can do that this afternoon, after dishes are done, while the men take their walk out to the barn. Sarah, did you decide what to do with your hair? I've been trying to get her talked into cutting it some, at least cut some of it off 'cause it's so hard to take care of."

"If it's not too much bother for you, if you want to be bothered, I want it cut like Mary's," she told Lillian, adding, "if you don't mind doing it."

"I sure don't mind, Sarah," was the reply, while Mary, for once, was stunned into silence.

Leaving the big house around three o'clock, Sarah slowly walked up the hill to home. Entering the house, she went into her bedroom and stood before the mirror looking at herself. A new dress and apron, the first she had ever owned. And new shoes and stocking, also a first-time event. And a new haircut, the first she had ever had. She could hardly believe she had the courage to have it cut. She had sat with her eyes shut tight while Lillian had cut the long reddish brown braids off. Using water and some wave set, Lillian had gotten the front hair to lie flat against her forehead and some bangs had been cut. Lillian used a little wave set to get the hair to curl into a spit curl around each ear. Both Mary and Lillian agreed that this looked the best. Sarah sat as if in shock, hardly daring to believe she had the courage to do such a thing.

Ma would be outraged, she thought. Ma would be so angry. I've went and done it, she thought, and now I have to live with it. Hearing Bud bark on the porch, she went to him and petted him. Seeing Tony in the yard, she quickly stood up, hiding her hands behind her back.

He came to the edge of the porch and told her, "You can pet him all you want, Sarah. I think he likes you better than any of us. Brownie stays with me, wherever I go and I like that. I think it's nice that Bud likes you 'cause he'll bark if anyone comes around the yard. He's sure a good watch dog. Pet him all you want. We don't care. And I like your hair. A big, big improvement over the long braids." He stood a moment nodding his head yes, then left her.

Sarah watched him walk down to the big house. Opening her kitchen door, she held it open and after a few moments, the dog walked into the house. Shutting the door, Sarah knelt down, putting her arms around the dog. She hugged him, mixing the tears into his hair.

CHAPTER IV

"Got a lot to do before Christmas, Sarah," Mary said as they baked one morning the middle of November. "Besides all the baking everyday and Ma to take care of, and sewing for Christmas, there's the butchering. We're almost out of meat. Got just a few jars of beef left and a couple of jars of chicken soup meat left and then we are out. Glad for the jars of meat we got from out of your cellar. We'd have been out by now otherwise. We'll have to butcher a few old hens to tide us through until Victor thinks it's cold enough outside for the meat to chill down good. When you butchered over at your house, I reckon you had to help with everything."

"Yes. Uncle Pete did the butchering and Ma and I helped him."

"We talked about it last night and decided to butcher two hogs instead of just one and a larger steer 'cause we got to have enough meat for Tony's house now too. An extra mouth to feed when they get married. Victor thought maybe next Monday if it's cold enough. This is the middle of November so it should be cold but it's still so warm and nice outside. I suppose when the weather turns cold, we'll get a big snow storm or blizzard and then cold. We can do without the blizzard right now. January is soon enough for that. We make our own blood and liver sausage and can a lot of the meat and fry down a lot of the pork. Make hams and bacons too. I like to have it all done before Christmas so we can have sausage for Christmas and so I can do other things after the first of the year. Like quilting and sewing and knitting and embroidering pillow cases."

"Ma always made a raw meat sausage too," Sarah timidly told her.

"Raw meat sausage. Now I'll have to mention that to Victor. You know how to make it?" Sarah nodded her head yes. "And you cleaned your own casings from the pig guts?" Mary asked.

"Yes, I had to do that," Sarah answered.

"Oh, that's not a very nice job. We have made tripe too. I don't like it but Victor does, so sometimes we do make that."

"I've made that too," Sarah told her. "Lot of work."

"Oh, I'm so glad you're here to help with everything this year. I didn't know how much extra work it would be with Grandma here. Not that I don't love her, you understand, but it's just more work. But my six months will be over the end of April so there'll be more time to work in the garden and can. With four of us girls taking turns, we have her only every other year. While we're taking care of the meat, I may have to just dry some of her bedding without washing it and use it again, even if it smells. Can't be washing while we're using the wash tubs for the meat."

"Do you butcher chickens too?" Sarah asked.

"After the other butchering is done. We do that too before Christmas, if we can. Usually do about thirty or forty old hens but this year he thought to do more 'cause Tony needs some too and because we got those extra hens from your place. Victor is anxious to get them butchered cause some don't lay many eggs but are still eating. He's got them in a different place to keep them separate. Those are the ones we've been killing and eating now, along with the culls of ours. All of them are three-year-old hens."

"Uncle John used to say you had to have young pullets and older cows to get the most eggs and milk," Sarah told her.

"And he was right about that. I been sewing at night some and got the flannel made up into the shirts for Victor and Tony and Lee and Orville. Orville is Gertrude's husband. I'll give each of them two new shirts. I had some of the flannel here from before, last winter, and that and the material I bought the day we went to get your dress material is what I used. Now I have to get some more to finish the shirt sewing. Then want to make a new dress for Gertrude and a new dress for each of her girls. And a new dress for Cora Lee. I made a pair of pillow cases for Johanna. Sewed lace on the edge and embroidered it too." Seeing a funny look pass over Sarah's face, she added, " I like to make something for all of them. I enjoy giving them each something for a gift for Christmas. That is one of the joys of that season. You wait and you will see what I mean."

The Friday before the butchering, Victor went to Don Kelly's and bought two hogs. For years Kelly had tried to talk him into buying little pigs and raising his own to butcher, but as yet he hadn't talked Victor into it. He felt he was a cow man and didn't know anything about pigs. So every year when butchering time came he made the trip to Kelly's to buy hogs.

The next Monday morning was cold enough for Victor and Tony to butcher the hogs. On Sunday, water was poured into the large iron kettle in the yard until it was about three-fourths full. Kindling wood was arranged under the kettle so first thing Monday morning, about three o'clock, the fire was lit. By nine o'clock when Victor got done with the delivering and had breakfast, he and Tony killed two hogs. After slitting the throats, Victor caught the blood in a kettle. Setting the kettle in the snow, he stirred and stirred to make sure it didn't clot. Then they worked on scalding the hogs. They had a rope hung on the tree above the boiling water. Using a single tree, they attached rope to the hogs' hind legs and hoisted it up until it was high enough so they could drop it into the water, lifting it out and then dropping it back in again several times. They scalded it until the hair was loose enough so it could be scraped off the hide. The hog was then laid out on a hay wagon. This was repeated with the other hog. Both Mary and Sarah took scrapers and helped scrape the hair off the hides. When they got done with this the skin was a nice white color and very clean. Each hog was then hoisted into the air and split open down the belly. Guts were emptied out, saving the heart, liver, tongue and intestines.

The inside of the hog was splashed clean with cold water and then the animal was split in two pieces. Tony hoisted one half onto this shoulder and Victor the other half. They carried them to the shed and hung them. The other hog was treated the same. The door on the shed was securely shut and bolted so no animals, like a cat, could get in. It would be two days before the halves were taken into the house and cut up. It would take that long for the animal to cool down and the animal heat to leave the carcasses.

Meanwhile, the heart, tongue and liver were washed and taken into the house to be washed again. These would be put in the upstairs bedroom to cool. The next day they'd be taken care of. The intestines were emptied out, washed and then also taken into the house to be scraped. To do this, they were turned inside out, washed and then scraped very carefully with a knife to get them clean. These would be used for some of the liver and blood sausage. Since Sarah had made raw meat sausage before, Victor decided to try a little of that too, and casings were needed for this too.

The next day, a beef steer was led into the yard and shot. Hanging the animal upside down using the same tree the hogs had been hung from, the men commenced skinning it, starting with the rump and back legs. By the time they were done the animal was completely in the air and the head had been cut off. Taking a knife Tony started slicing into the belly, catching the guts in a large wash tub. Pulling the tub aside, after this was done, they splashed the inside of the animal clean with cold water. It was then split in half. Then each half was again split in half across the middle of the animal. Each quarter was carried into the shed where the hogs were hanging.

Although Victor liked tripe, he told Mary that with Grandma there he thought she had enough to do without making that too, even with Sarah there to help, so the steer's stomach was thrown away. But the liver, tongue and heart were saved, washed and then taken into the house to be washed again and put in the spare bedroom to cool.

The day the beef was butchered the family had pork liver and onions for their dinner, along with some fried potatoes. The fresh meat was enjoyed by all. Sarah took the beef heart and tongue and cleaned them good, cooked them and then skinned the tongue. She made a sweet sour dressing that she poured over the heart and tongue. The next day she would bringing this to a boil and pack most of it into scalded quart fruit jars and seal it. What was left would be eaten as a special treat the next several days.

Wednesday the hogs were brought into the house and cut up. Hams and bacons were put into large stone crocks that had a water, salt and curing salt brine in it that was so stiff with salt that it would float a potato in it. The hocks and shanks were saved to be used for head cheese. This would be made on Thursday using a sour brine. Part would be canned for use during the hot summer months. Some of the spare ribs were put on the stove to cook. Sauerkraut would be added later, along with dumplings for their dinner. The rest of the spare ribs were put in the spare bedroom upstairs to freeze for using later. Time was spent cutting up pork chops and pork steak. These were placed on cookie sheets and baked in the oven after the lard had been rendered. The baked pork would be layered in smaller crocks. Hot lard would be poured over the meat to seal it so it would keep to be used during the summer. The skins from the sows and the cleaned sow heads would be used in the liver and blood sausage.

"That's all for now," Victor told the other three after the fourth half was cut up and everything done that could be done. "Tomorrow the women'll have the pork finished and then Friday we start on the beef."

" What good help you are, Sarah. It would have been so hard with Grandma here and getting the baking done and everything. You are such a blessing." Mary told her.

"Thank you," she whispered.

"And next year Johanna will be here too," Mary told Tony.

"Yes. That'll be nice," Tony agreed.

"Our family is growing, Mary," Victor added.

Thursday the lard was ground and then cooked. Sarah watched the cooking of this like a hawk. Mary kept an eye on it until she was sure Sarah knew what she was doing and then she did the washing, meals and took care of her ma. The pork chops and pork steak baking in the oven sent an aroma through out the house that made everyone hungry. Mary made sure some was done so they could have the treat of the fresh pork for dinner. Corn bread made with fresh pork cracklings added to the pleasure of the meal.

Friday, after breakfast, the first quarter of beef was brought in. The tallow was pulled out of the quarters and saved to be rendered down for soap and for frying donuts. Roasts were cut out and some steaks. As everything had to be cut and sawed by hand, only the easier-to-work-with steaks were cut. Most of the roasts and some of the steak was cut into chunks to be canned, ground for hamburger or used for raw meat sausage. All bones were kept to be cooked, meat picked off and canned for using as a base for soup later.

By supper time, all four quarters had been cut up. Saturday would be another day of canning and cooking tallow and grinding hamburger. Then the big clean up day would be Sunday. That would be the day of making sausage: blood, liver and raw meat.

The big copper bottom wash boiler was scrubbed so it would be clean for cooking everything that hadn't been canned or processed in some other way. Since this had to cook for a long time the boiler was on the stove early. These sausages would be made in the afternoon.

The rest of the morning was spent grinding the beef and pork trimmings that were used in the raw meat sausage. Spices, salt, and pepper were added to the meat mixture. Victor, after washing his hands and arms very well, put his hands into the meat mixture and mixed and mixed. In the meantime Tony had gotten the attachment that was used for stuffing on the grinder. Sarah had taken the cleaned casings and started to string them onto the stuffing attachment. Tony worked the meat through the attachment into the stuffing. When Sarah thought there was enough meat in the casing to make a ring, she cut the casing off the end of the stuffing attachment and tied it with string in a special knot. Victor, watching her, realized she had done this many times before and was very good at it.

The day before, the men had gotten the smokehouse ready for the sausage. As the rings were finished, Victor carried them out and hung them in the smokehouse. When they were finished at noon, he started a slow fire. He would have to keep this going for a good day to make sure the smoky flavor seeped through the rings. Then in about a month he would have to start the fire again when he smoked the hams and bacons.

"What's this, Pa?" Tony asked, finding several pounds of the raw meat sausage mixture in one corner of one of the containers they had been using.

"I saved that back to be fried for supper. It smelled so good. It won't have that smoked flavor but it still will taste good," he answered, grinning, as Mary shook her head and gave him a bowl to put the meat in.

Before dinner was eaten, Mary scooped all the meat and bones out of the boiler so they would cool. Dinner over with, she went through the piles of meat and bones, carefully picking out all bones and bone splinters. Victor then ground the meat, dividing it into two tubs. In one tub was dumped the blood he had gotten the first day of butchering. Spices, salt, pepper and ground cooked onion were added to each tub. Mary then put her hands into the mixtures and mixed and mixed. When she was satisfied it was enough, Victor scooped out the thick mixture and they started to stuff the casings. As before, Sarah made the rings. Victor took them into the spare bedroom to cool. Not all this meat was stuffed, as they had no way of keeping it from spoiling when the weather got warm, so some was left to be canned the following day.

Monday, after the sausage that was left was in jars and cooking on the stove for the three hours' processing needed, Sarah and Mary cleaned and scrubbed all the equipment that had been used.

"I hate to think of it, but tonight the men are going to lock up old hens and we can pluck feathers tomorrow," Mary told Sarah.

"I never minded cleaning chickens," Sarah told her. "I never really hated doing any of the meat. Ma didn't have any meat for several summers and when that happens you're so hungry for the taste of meat, that you don't mind doing the work."

"Oh yes, that makes cooking hard. Lots of potatoes to fill the space. Meals get to be tasting the same without meat to spice it up."

"And you get tired of potatoes too," Sarah told her.

The old hens were butchered the next day. Again the copper-bottomed boiler was full of boiling water. Dippers were used to ladle the water out into pails that the beheaded hens were dipped in, up and down, until the feathers were loose enough to be plucked easily from the skin. Victor and Mary were careful not to overdo the dipping, so the skin wouldn't tear. Sarah and Tony began plucking feathers as soon as the first birds were done.

The hens were divided into twelve per lot for dipping. By that time the water in the pails was getting cooled down too much to be effective. After the feathers were plucked, the birds were singed to get off the fine hairs on the skin.

Sarah and Mary then gutted the birds, first cutting off the legs and feet, then cutting the carcasses apart, they took out the insides. The livers, hearts and any eggs or egg yolks were saved. These larger egg yolks made the best noodles while the smaller ones were thrown into soup to be cooked.

As each bird was cleaned, Victor or Tony gave it a good scrubbing in cold clean water. Then the birds were put into another tub of clean water to soak. By the end of the day, every tub and the copper-bottomed boiler were full of pieces of chicken. The pieces were washed again and then taken out of the water, put on a clean oilcloth that lay on the floor of the spare bedroom. They had to cool overnight before they could be canned.

It took two days for all the chicken to be canned. The first day, the good pieces were packed into jars, salt added and water to fill the jars. The jars were then processed for three hours. Since there were so many old hens to do, it took a long time to get all the jars done. The bony pieces: the ribs, backbones and necks, were cooked the following day; the meat picked off, put back in the broth and canned for soup.

As with the meat butchering, every tub and utensil used had to be scrubbed clean. The last thing washed was the kitchen floor and that required scrubbing twice to get all the grease and grime off.

"My, I'm glad that's done," Mary told them at suppertime that night. "Now, I can get my thoughts going for Christmas. Do you know what?" She looked around at the rest. The men shook their heads no and shrugged. "We missed Thanksgiving Day. It was last week when we were in the middle of the meat."

"So much for Thanksgiving Day," Tony said. "I guess I'm just thankful we're done with the butchering and the old hens. That's my Thanksgiving."

"Yeah, Mary," Victor agreed, "so much for Thanksgiving Day. I'll bet Sarah didn't care."

" I remember it from school. No, I didn't care."

"A week to Christmas, Sarah," Mary said as they watched Victor leave the yard with the horse and sleigh. He was on his way to Labit's. "I have my sewing all done and the more fun things are going to happen now. We're gonna make candy and popcorn balls and cookies. I forbid anyone to eat those I put away for Christmas. Only the rejects are eaten now. What kind of candy do you like to make?"

After a moment or two Sarah answered, "I don't know how to make candy."

"Well, then you'll learn how to make fudge and divinity 'cause that's what I make. It's a good day today to make divinity. Has to be a sunny day, no clouds or snow or rain 'cause then the candy won't set in nice peaks. It takes a lot of beating so with you here to help me then it won't be so hard on my arm. Did you notice Grandma has taken to crying out more and more? She was so happy when she first came. Even when I have her in her rocking chair. I talk to her and then she quits. But she is so restless, specially late afternoon and evening. More than when she came. It makes for more running. So with you here to help me, I know the candy beating won't be left while I have to run to her. We'll start right after an early dinner today. I usually make about four batches 'cause I send some back with Lee when he comes and that happens to be Victor's favorite candy."

"Now," Mary told Sarah as they started after dinner,

"we cook the sugar and water and syrup until it reaches the thread stage when you hold the spoon up and let a little syrup run off the spoon. You can also test the syrup in cold water. If it makes a somewhat hard ball, not real soft and not too hard, then it is right, cooked long enough. You'll see after we do this once or so. I thought we could make a couple of batches this afternoon 'cause the weather is just right outside. Ma's sleeping, so she's quiet for now."

After the syrup had been cooking for a few minutes, Mary took three eggs and separated the yolks from the whites. The yolks she saved to use for making noodles or dumplings. The whites she started to beat with a wire whisk. After a few minutes Sarah took the whisk and continued the beating while Mary tested the syrup. In a few more minutes the whites were standing in dry peaks and the syrup made a nice ball in cold water. Sarah kept beating while Mary very slowly added the syrup to the egg whites. Mary took her turn beating after she had poured all the syrup into the egg mixture. They continued to beat until Mary tasted the candy and it had a grainy texture.

"It's ready to spoon out, Sarah. Taste that grainy taste," Mary told her. "We'll do it like this." Taking two teaspoons, she took a spoonful and with the other spoon pushed the first spoonful onto a greased pan. Watching her, Sarah did the same thing until the bowl was empty. Scraping out the sides of the bowl to get the leftovers, the two women ate the crumbs left.

"Good?" Mary asked.

" Yes. It's good." Sarah agreed.

"Now, let's wash up the kettle and make another batch, quick before supper has to be made. We'll leave out a few pieces for the men and put the rest upstairs before supper. Victor is liable to make his supper on just candy if he sees all of this."

The next day was sunny again so another two batches of divinity were made.

"Tomorrow is the day for the popcorn balls," Mary told Sarah. "I raised the popcorn in the garden so I got plenty. I usually make plenty balls so I can send some back with Gertrude when she comes and with Lee too. They keep pretty good and it gives me something I can give them to take back. I like to do that."

"Man, does this place smell good." Tony said, coming into the house the next day at noon for dinner. "I think I'll just fill up on popcorn."

"No, you won't," his ma answered. "But I might let you have a small bowlful after dinner, just 'cause I want some too." Tony's laughter joined his ma's.

"First we got to get all the old maids out of this popcorn, Sarah. Then we'll cook some syrup, sugar and water to the soft ball stage. The syrup is poured over the popcorn, let cool just long enough to handle it and then we stir it up and make balls out of it."

"Won't that stick to our hands?" Sarah asked.

"We grease out hands with butter first," was Mary's answer.

Before long the syrup had boiled to the right consistency and was poured over the popcorn. A couple of minutes later, the two women were pressing the popcorn into balls and putting them on waxed paper. They cooked syrup two more times before they had all the balls Mary wanted.

"I'll save back a few to eat tonight and the rest I'll put away in a box in the spare bedroom upstairs with the divinity. I've got to remember to send a few with you when you leave here after supper so you have some to eat tonight too. Tomorrow we make fudge and the dough for the cut-out cookies. They get baked the next day. I also want to make a filled cookie that is made out of the same dough as the roll-out cookies, but you put two cookies together with a raisin filling inside. We all like them and that we do also on Friday."

"When is your family coming?' Sarah asked.

"Lee will be here Saturday afternoon. He comes on the train, him and Cora Lee. Gertrude comes that same time. They're coming by train too. They come in on the same train. They'll be here for supper. It makes it so nice with Lee working for the railroad, they all get free passes and can ride for nothing. Otherwise, I know Gertrude couldn't come. It'll be a late supper, about eight o'clock but we open our gifts the next morning after breakfast anyway so it don't make any difference. If the weather and roads are OK, then sometime in there some of will go to church. Someone has to stay home with Grandma and, if real cold, someone has to watch the stoves. I'm just glad they're all getting here. It's been a long time since Gertrude's been home for Christmas. I don't know if Orville is coming or not. Last I knew she wasn't sure he could get off work. With jobs so hard to find, he sure better not lose the one he has. It took him long enough to get it. Just between you and me, he don't like to work that hard and he don't seem to hang onto jobs that good. Got a wife and two girls to take care of. You'd think he would worry about that some. Maybe I'm the one who does the worrying instead of him. And I guess I said enough about that, but I know you won't say anything to anyone about it."

"I wouldn't, you know that," Sarah agreed.

Four batches of creamy chocolate fudge filled the kitchen with an aroma that stirred the stomach juices. Two batches were made in the morning and two in the afternoon. Mary left a few pieces out for dinner and supper, knowing, if she didn't, that Victor would be a very unhappy man. The rest she hid upstairs. Also in the afternoon, she gave Sarah the recipe and she made a double batch of cookie dough for the cut-outs and a double batch of dough for the filled cookies. This dough was put in the coolest corner of the pantry so it would chill.

The next day the cut-out cookies were made. Instead of frosting them, Mary just sprinkled sugar on top of each batch of dough when it was rolled out and ready to be cut with the cookie cutter. Taking the rolling pin, she lightly rolled the sugar into the dough. The filled cookies took longer. Raisins had to be ground and cooked with a bit of water and some sugar. Half of the round cut-out cookie had a teaspoon of ground raisin put on it. Another round cookie was put on the top and then the edges pasted together with the edge of a fork.

Some of the poorest looking cookies were left out for dinner and supper. The rest were put away to be brought out the twenty-fourth and twenty-fifth.

While in Ponta that morning, Victor had picked up a small wooden barrel of raw herring and a large container of oysters. Mary took the herring, washed them very good and cut them into pieces. While the brine for the herring was cooking, she cleaned and sliced a bunch of onions, layering them between the herring in a gallon crock. Lastly she dumped the hot brine over it, covering the herring with the spicy, vinegar-flavored liquid. This was put on the floor in the pantry.

The oysters were put in the spare bedroom for oyster stew on Christmas Eve. Mary told Sarah that this was something they had every Christmas Eve since she was married. Victor's ma had always had it and so she continued the tradition. Along with the oyster stew were the pickled herring, deviled eggs, fresh poppyseed buns, applesauce buns and the cookies and candy they had just finished making.

"And you will be here for supper that night, Sarah?" Mary asked suddenly realizing she had just taken it for granted Sarah was going to be there.

"No. It wouldn't be right. That is for you and your family. No and please don't ask me again," she said, shaking her head.

"All right," Mary answered slowly. " I'm disappointed 'cause you worked so hard getting it all ready. How about Christmas Day? That's when we exchange the gifts and I have something for you and I know Tony has too. I wanted you to be a part of this and enjoy it with us."

"I don't know what to give you, any of you. I didn't make anything. I don't have any material to make any shirts out of," Sarah told her.

"Land sakes, girl. It's too late for shopping now. Don't you have anything from your uncles that would be all right for the men? And I don't need anything. I just like to give to everyone. I want you to come Christmas Day."

" Maybe I can find something there for the men. What or how or what do you do with it? I mean, do you just hand it to them or hold it behind your back so they don't see what you have for them?"

"You wrap it up. I'll show you what I mean. Follow me and I'll show you. I have some of the gifts in here where Grandma is. See, they're wrapped with their name on the front of it. I'll give you some paper to wrap your presents in. And some string too."

Suddenly her ma gave a series of loud screeches and grunts. They both jumped.

Mary took Sarah by the arm and they tiptoed out of the room.

"Ma is doing that more and more," Mary said. "I hate it. She can't help it, I know, but I just hate it. It's about time to start supper. Those dumplings you made out of those egg yolks sure were good this noon and I know they'll taste good fried for supper too, along with the rest of the blood sausage we didn't eat for breakfast. We have most everything done that I wanted done today. Tomorrow we'll make a couple of apple pies and a couple of pumpkin pies for Sunday. And we have to dress out those two roosters Victor has been talking of using for Christmas unless Victor decides he don't want to butcher them now. In that case I'll use the canned ones we just did. But I'd rather save those for summer."

"What are you having for Sunday dinner?" Sarah asked.

"Baked chicken, dressing with prunes and apples in it,

baked squash, mashed potatoes and gravy and two kinds of pies. Oh yes, the rest of the prune and apple rolls and bread and butter. We have to churn butter tomorrow too. Oh, there goes Ma again." she said, as she shook her head and shuddered. "I forgot one of the most important things about Christmas and that is putting up the tree. Tony's going to cut it tomorrow morning and it'll be put up tomorrow night after the family gets here and after supper. We don't get to bed very early that night but it is so much fun. We'll try to go to church Christmas morning, real early so I can make the dinner on time."

"Maybe I can work on the dinner while you're gone," Sarah told her.

"You don't want to try and go?"

"Never been to church. I'd rather get the dinner."

"I'll mention that to Victor and instead of going to seven o'clock, maybe we'll go to nine o'clock. I'll see what he says. I wasn't sure how it would work out with Grandma anyway."

Sarah took some of each kind of food with her the afternoon of Christmas Eve when she went home. Mary, realizing that she absolutely didn't want to come, had let her go. Bud followed Sarah and Mary smiled as she watched the woman let the dog in her little house. At least she wouldn't be alone. She had the dog to keep her company. She wondered if Sarah had any time to try to draw or color. She had been pretty busy helping her with the Christmas goodies.

Finally settling the little children down to sleep, Victor, Mary and their three children sat at the kitchen table later that evening enjoying their cup of coffee or glass of milk and some of the goodies Mary had put out.

"You didn't get Sarah to come tonight, did you Ma?" Tony asked.

"No. I just couldn't get her talked into it. But she had Bud to keep her company so she wasn't alone."

"Bud?" Lee asked

"The German shepherd dog I got from Fred at the feed mill last fall. That dog adopted Sarah."

"Oh, I wondered. I thought you were going to lose your hired girl, Ma," Lee told her.

"Do I remember her?" Gertrude asked. " I just can't remember that name."

"They were there when you were still in school but she is much younger than you are. She was maybe in first grade when you were in eighth." Victor told her.

"I guess maybe I do faintly remember her. A shy, timid girl, always wearing overalls. And shirts."

"I remember her some too," Lee told them. "But she was maybe five years behind me in school and I was too busy making eyes at the girls my age to worry about someone so much younger."

"You always had eyes for the girls, didn't you?" laughed Tony. "Sarah was ahead of me in school but I remember she was always by herself. Never played much with anyone else. Always alone. I don't think she had it nice at home and the more I see of her here, I think I was right."

"She has never had a Christmas, except what she saw at school. There was never any candy or cookies or popcorn balls made there, nor a Christmas tree. I don't know what she'll think when she sees the one we have. It ain't decorated so fancy but it went up with love. And that's what counts. And she's never been given a present before and didn't know how to go about giving one back. Nor did she know how to wrap one — a present, that is," Mary told them.

"She never was at the Christmas program at school. She always had a part in it but she never showed up the night of the program. Do you remember, Ma, the night Jim Lasey's daughter had to read the part Sarah was supposed to have? After that, the teacher always made sure Sarah had something on the program that when she didn't show up, it didn't make any difference," Tony told them.

"Will Johanna be here tomorrow?" Gertrude asked her brother.

"You betcha. She's coming tomorrow morning. I'll bring her back after church. I hoped the roads would be good to drive on but they ain't good enough for that. So guess we're going to have an old-fashioned Christmas, going to church in a sleigh and wrapping up good in blankets and quilts and soapstones for the feet."

"Better to snuggle, little brother," Lee told him, as laughter circled the table.

"And how is the wedding plans coming and I hear you're going to live in the Hysell house for now?" Lee asked Tony and from there on, the rest of the evening was spent talking of many things.

When Sarah went home the afternoon of the twenty-fourth, she spent a few minutes petting and hugging Bud. Looking at the wrapping paper and the string she had laid on the table, she still had no idea of what she was going to give the people in the big house. She regretted sincerely ever hearing the word Christmas. Dragging out the box she had her uncle's clothes in, she laid them out on the bed. Most of the few clothes he had were not anything to be given to anyone as a present. She had seen the new shirts Mary had made and they looked so nice. These were not. At the bottom of the box she found a pocket watch her uncle had that was like new. For some reason he had kept it in a box in his dresser drawer instead of wearing it. This would make one present. Going through the clothes again, she shook out a pocket knife. It wasn't new but was a very good one. Uncle John had bought it in town not many months before he had died to replace the one he had lost. Her ma had scolded him without end for spending the money on it. If he hadn't been so careless, he wouldn't have lost the first one, her ma had told him. Sarah remembered that her ma had hollered about this for days until Uncle John had told her he had used his own money and she could just shut her mouth. He was tired of hearing about it. Her ma didn't mention it again but meals were more unpleasant for a long time after that, with the banging of the pans on the table and the disagreeable look on her ma's face.

Holding the knife in her hands for a long time, Sarah knew if she could find something else, she would keep the knife herself as a keepsake of her uncle's. He would have wanted her to have it. Pulling out the box she had packed the things of her ma's she didn't know what to do with, she started going through it. And found a shaving mug, a nice shaving brush and a good straight razor. Sarah thought these must have been her uncle's shaving things that had been packed in a hurry with her ma's stuff but looking closer at the mug, she found the initials M.H. on the side. She suddenly realized this had been her pa's, the man she had never known. He had died when she was only a baby. Her uncle had told her his name had been Marvin Hysell. She held the shaving mug in her hands several moments, finally deciding she would keep the mug and give the shaving brush and straight razor to Victor. His straight razor had several nicks in it. He had to be extra careful when he shaved so he wouldn't cut himself. This razor was in excellent shape.

Now all she had to do was find something for Mary. Suddenly she knew that had been solved too. Going into the pantry, she went through the box of her ma's with the good bowls in it and took out several. Minutes were spent deciding which one to give away. The one she finally decided on had a pattern on it that she knew would match the good dishes Mary had used the day Lillian and Joe Morshian had been there for dinner.

Many more minutes were spent trying to wrap the presents. She had never wrapped anything in her life and it took her a while to figure out how to do it without all ends sticking out where she didn't want them. After all three had been wrapped, she laid them on the table, side by side.

"Now Ma, I have my Christmas presents wrapped to be given away and if you don't like it, you can just... just... just..." she said aloud, finally spreading her arms out and unclenching her hands with the fingers open wide. Bud gave a quick bark. Sarah grabbed him in a hug, dragging his head in her lap as she sat on the floor by him.

Used to getting up so early in the morning, Sarah was awake before four o'clock. Rolling around in her bed, she finally got up, knowing she wouldn't sleep any more. Since Gertrude was with her ma, Sarah didn't think she was needed at the big house so early so she spent time before breakfast cleaning her house. Her little bundle of clothes to be washed, she would take down the next morning to be washed with Mary's. Having to wash every day, Mary could see no sense in Sarah's washing with a scrub board at home. So she washed her few clothes down there, bringing them back up to her own house to be hung on the wash line she had strung back and forth in the pantry. Although the proper way to dry clothes in the winter time was to hang them outside first and then finish drying the frozen articles in the house, both Mary and Sarah opted to just hang them inside to begin with. Mary didn't like the frozen fingers that came with hanging wet clothes on an outside wash line in the middle of the winter.

Shortly before breakfast, she had a visitor. Sarah immediately could see the woman resembled Mary and knew Gertrude was standing at her door.

"I don't think I remember you and if I don't remember you, you probably don't remember me either, but I'm Gertrude. Ma wondered if you could come down this morning and help me get dinner."

"I didn't want to barge in on your family get-together," Sarah answered.

"You won't be barging in on us. I told Ma I'd come and get you 'cause she has her hands full with Grandma today.

She's really unhappy and Ma don't know what to do with her to get her settled."

"I'll just put some wood in the stove and then get my coat on and come," Sarah answered.

"I don't know where anything is anymore. Used to but been gone too long from home to remember where anything is and since Ma can't seem to get Grandma happy this morning, every time I have to ask where something is, it just makes Ma more nervous. She said she was glad there wasn't any baking to do today. But it has been extra hard this morning with Grandma. So she wondered if you could come earlier than the eight o'clock she told you first. We're so glad you're here to help. She would have had it real hard without you. I know what she writes to me and it is all gratefulness. You've even got some presents here. Are they for today or somewhere else?"

"No, they're for your ma and pa and Tony. They've been so good to me."

"You've been so good to them," Gertrude told her.

"Come on Bud, it's time you went outside too," Sarah answered, going to get her coat.

"I like your hair," Gertrude told her as they walked down the yard. "It lays so nice to your head and I'll bet it's easy. My husband don't like short hair so I don't have it cut. He couldn't come yesterday. He works at a men's store and they were so busy that he just couldn't get away. Last time we came for Christmas he came too. He had a different job then. Anyway, I like your hair."

"It's real easy to wash," Sarah answered, finally adding, "Your ma has her hair this way and she thought it would be nice for me."

"Was your hair long before?"

"I braided it and it came down to my waist. The first time I washed it, after it had been cut, I thought there wasn't any hair there anymore," Sarah told her, surprise in her voice as she realized it wasn't hard to talk to this woman.

"I got some help, Ma," Gertrude called as they went in the house. "Oh dear, listen to poor Grandma. This here is my daughter, Irene, and this is my daughter, Dorothy. One is three years old and one is four. They look like twins but they ain't. Both look like me and I look like my ma, and Tony looks like her too and so does Lee. Blonde hair and blue eyes. My husband is dark with dark green eyes. He's thin and tall while I'm shorter and again, like ma, a bit heavier. Tony is taller and built like a bull, like Pa would say, and so is Lee, only Lee's not as stocky as Tony is. Oh my, does Grandma always act like this?"

"No. When she came, she was all smiles but now she's been getting more uneasy and some crying and screaming but not like this," Sarah answered. "What's been done toward dinner?"

"I got the chickens out and then didn't know where she moved the roaster to and Ma is nervous enough this morning without me coming in there and asking her questions all the time. Lee suggested I get you cause Ma said you were going to be here while we all went to church anyway. All of us except Ma, that is."

"I'll get the roaster and get the chickens in and then peel the potatoes and get the squash ready to bake. The pies are done," Sarah told Gertrude as she went upstairs to get the large roasting pan. "Oh!" she exclaimed as she saw the man at the top of the stairs.

"Come on up. I'm Lee and I'm glad you're here 'cause Ma has her hands full this morning and with us all leaving for church, Ma needs help."

She went past him into the storeroom. He looked after her a moment, shrugged and then went downstairs. Bringing the roaster downstairs, Sarah wiped it out, put some water in the bottom of it.

"I made the bread dressing," Gertrude told her, bringing the bowl to Sarah so she could stuff the chickens. "Got your coats, girls? We're about ready to leave and you'll have to hurry. Run to the toilet quick cause it'll be cold in the sleigh even wrapped as good as we'll be with the extra quilts and horsehide and warm soapstones. Glad it ain't far to church."

"If it was, we wouldn't be going," Lee told her. "Cora Lee, ready?"

Sarah stood quietly in the corner of the kitchen watching as everyone finished getting their winter clothes on. Lee finished buttoning up the coat of a little girl who looked enough like Gertrude's daughters that she could have been their sister. When Victor came down the steps, followed by Tony, they went out the door and were on their way.

Using the bread dressing Gertrude had made, Sarah made fast work of stuffing the chickens. Rubbing them down with salt and pepper, she put them into the roaster. Onion slices were added and the roaster was slipped into the oven.

"Is Grandma this way all the time?" Lee asked Sarah when they got home from church.

"No. She's been getting more and more restless and uneasy. She screams a little sometimes and grunts some, but not like this. Lots more restless at night, starts middle of the afternoon but never this early in the day."

"I feel sorry for Ma if this is how it's going to be from now on. How long does she have yet to take care of Grandma?" Gertrude asked.

"Mary said something about six months altogether and that would be the end of March when that time is up," Sarah answered.

"I'm glad you're here. We all are," Lee told her. "Ma'd have had to quit her baking otherwise and I know they need that money she gets for that."

"Sarah, I forgot you don't know Johanna," Tony said, presenting a good-looking woman with dark hair. "This is Johanna." The smiling young woman, about Sarah's height, put her hand out for Sarah to shake. She had dark brown hair cut in a bob, dark blue eyes and a smiling, happy face.

"Tony has told me such good things about you," she said. "He also said you were the best cook. I hope I can do as good when we are married." Tony laughed as he put his arm around her shoulder.

"Grandma still having problems?" Victor asked, coming down the steps after changing into clean barn clothes. "What you wrinkling your nose for, young lady?" he told Gertrude. "You smelling the barn clothes? Don't bother me to have a little barn smell in the house. In fact, I'm mighty proud of it."

"Guess it's been too many years since I lived where there was that smell and I'm just not used to it anymore," Gertrude answered him. "Too bad there ain't a separate place where they can be hung so that smell ain't in the kitchen where the food is."

"There is but then the clothes are ice cold to put on and that ain't no good either," Victor answered. "Ain't many kitchens on a ranch that don't smell like manure in the winter time."

"Oh well, you got to put up with it. I don't and like I said, too many years being away from that smell."

"Just a city slicker," Tony told her.

"Yep, just a city clicker," Gertrude answered with a grin.

Glancing at Sarah, Lee was surprised to see a whisper of a smile on her face.

"Oh Sarah," Mary said, coming into the kitchen. "This has been an awful morning. I just can't get Ma happy."

"Ma," Lee asked, "have you had anything to eat yet today?"

"I don't think I want anything," was the answer.

"You got to eat," Victor told her. "You can't go without. I can't see any difference if you're in there or out here, she is just as noisy either way. Take a cup of coffee and, Lee, shut that bedroom door. Mary, you eat. And I mean it. She screams whether you're in there or not. You haven't been able to stop her yet. Now I mean it. Eat."

"Do you want me to go to her?" Sarah asked.

"You can if you want but I don't think it's going to make any difference," Victor answered before Mary could. Sarah went into the other room, softly closing the door behind her while Mary ate a quick breakfast.

"Getting old can be quite hellish," Victor said, looking around the room. "What's those presents doing out here?"

"Oh those are the ones Sarah brought down with her." Gertrude answered. "I was going to put them under the tree only I didn't with the commotion about getting to church. I'll do it now."

"Good for Sarah. I didn't know if she would give any presents or not." Mary said. "It sounds like Ma is quieting down. "

In about five minutes Sarah came out, shutting the door behind her. Mary looked up at her questioningly.

"She's sleeping," Sarah told her.

"She was always such a good sweet woman, always happy with an easy smile and now it's like all the demons or devils in the world are coming alive," Mary said. "All them coming alive. You got the potatoes peeled and the squash is in the oven and I can smell the roosters baking. So we're going to open our presents while Ma is quiet and before the rest of dinner has to be made. Ready, everyone? You girls have been so patient," she said putting an arm around Irene and the other arm around Dorothy.

"We were playing with our dolls. Our other grandma made us some doll clothes and we're playing with them. Ma said we had to be real quiet."

"She was right. I didn't want any crying around here this morning more than what I already had. And here we are. Christmas morning again and everything looks so nice, the tree. I just love to just look at it." Mary told everyone. Victor smiled and patted his wife on the shoulder. "And

Johanna, it's so nice to have you here with us."

While everyone was getting settled in the parlor, Sarah found a chair near the far end of the room, as far out of the way as she could get. Looking at the Christmas tree, she tried to think back to her school days and if she had been taught the meaning of a tree at Christmas time. She couldn't even remember why there was a celebration at Christmas, let alone what the tree meant. Sometime she would ask Mary, when there was no one else around.

What was so different to Sarah was the liking everyone seemed to have for each other. And Tony's Johanna was greeted so nice and seemed so nice. It wasn't like when Earl had come to see her ma and her. He came into the house cussing and swearing and her ma had answered him the same way.

And she had seen Victor pat Mary on the shoulder. What would it be like to have someone touch you like that? The only touches Sarah had ever felt hurt, had been in anger and hatred. She realized she was wringing her hands and she also realized she was being watched... by Lee. She glared at him and when he started to grin, she looked away quickly.

That evening, Sarah looked out the bedroom window, watching Tony ride his horse from the barn across the yard. He was going back to her ma's house to sleep. She saw Brownie trotting alongside the horse. The moon shone so brightly that it was like a pale version of day and she could see them quite plainly. She watched a cat creeping along the big house foundation and wondered why it wasn't in the warm barn curled up in some straw sleeping.

It had been such a different day, nothing like she had ever experienced before.

The opening of the gifts, the delicious dinner, the warmth of the family toward each other and toward her, a stranger. And the presents she had given were so well received and appreciated. And her gifts, the pearl necklace and matching pearl earrings Johanna and Tony had given her, and the beautiful black purse she had gotten from Mary and Victor. She had never had a purse before, let alone earrings and a necklace. What her ma would have thought of that! Why in the world would anyone as witch-homely as Sarah need anything like that? You didn't need anything as fancy as that to do the chores and ranch work and anyway, where would anyone as plain and useless as she was have need for those things. Frowning, she fingered the presents until she felt Bud behind her. Kneeling, she hugged and petted her friend.

CHAPTER V
January 1931

The men spent the winter months after the first of the year doing chores and getting ready for spring. Hours and hours were spent after the one major blizzard, shoveling paths around the yard so the animals and chickens could be fed. The path to the hen house was through one of the deepest drifts and after hours of shoveling, Tony had it wide enough so they could carry one pail of water at a time and one pail of feed at a time. And with animals down at Tony's place, there was an additional set of buildings that had to be shoveled out. Cold freezing weather required an ax and a fork to break up and clean out the ice from the water tanks so the animals could drink.

The men hitched up a team of horses and, piling rocks on top of the drag, cleared the roads as best they could. Tony had seen a snow plow hitched ahead of a team of horses that the highway department used and he told his pa that before another winter came, they were going to make one like it.

"Have at it," he answered. "But are you sure it wasn't for a truck?"

"They got some of them too, but the one I saw was for horses and, by golly, we're gonna have one too. Enough of this. Why, you can't hardly get out of here with the sleigh every day."

"It's bad 'cause the snow is so hard, but one of these day we'll get a Chinook wind and then it'll be better."

Perhaps the most time-consuming task was pumping water by hand to fill the water tanks when the wind didn't blow so the wind mills ran. After several days of hand pumping, the men were fit to be tied.

"Either it's blowing snow like crazy or it ain't blowing at all," Victor said, rubbing his tired arms.

"What's a motor cost to put on the pump?" Mary asked, adding, "or maybe I shouldn't ask."

"Too damn much. Sure, I could take some of the money we got stashed away but that's for emergencies. And I don't want to touch that."

"Could I say something?" Sarah asked, very quietly and timidly.

"Say whatever you want, everybody else does," he answered.

"Aside from what I used to buy material with and curtain material with, I got saved what you have paid me for working here. Could I give you that money for the motor?"

"Land sakes, child. That's for whatever you need for yourself. You'll need some more summer dresses and that's what that money is for," Mary answered.

"By the time I need summer stuff, I'll have some more saved up. I don't buy much for myself. I even get groceries from here to feed myself supper. And if you use the motor down at my place, then it'll be used for something of mine. And if I don't have enough, then take some from one of those pails."

"All right. I'm going to take you up on the offer. I ain't gonna turn you down. My arms ache so bad these past nights that I ain't been able to sleep good. I keep getting catches in them. I'll get a motor first thing tomorrow morning when I take in the baking, but Sarah, the motor is yours and we're only using it," Victor told her.

"I'll get the money down here when I come in the morning," Sarah answered. The rest of the day seemed to be brighter, even with the cold weather seeping in through the cracks of the windows and walls of the big house and later, her little house. She realized lying in bed later, that the nice feeling she had came from doing something for this family that had been so good to her.

There were many more days that winter and winters to come when the motor on the windmill was a big asset to the men. So many days there wasn't any wind at all and without the motor, the men would have had to pump the water by hand.

Although the one large blizzard that winter made extra work, by spring they were glad they had that much snow. The rest of the winter had very little moisture. Talk at the feed mill and in town was of everyone hoping for many spring rains to make up for the lack of winter snow.

While the men spent the rest of the winter taking care of the animals on both places and getting ready for the spring work, Mary and Sarah worked on various projects suitable for that time of the winter.

Sarah had finally made the curtains for her windows. The fabric Mary had helped her pick out for her bedroom was a fine lacy white material. Four basic panels were cut for the main parts of the curtains while another long ruffled valance was added to the top of each window. The kitchen window had the basic short panels across the bottom with ruffles on the middle of each top panel, gathered with ties on each side. These were made out of off-white colored feed sacks Sarah had brought with her when she moved. Trimming them with red rickrack and seam binding and by starching them heavily, Sarah had made her kitchen window very attractive. Although she liked her kitchen curtains, she was entranced with the billowy bedroom window coverings. Never had she ever dreamed of anything that lovely.

To clean up her uncle's threadbare old clothes she had brought with her when she moved, Sarah had cut and sewn the rags into long strips that she braided into rugs. One small rug went by her bed, while another larger one was put in the kitchen by the door going into her bedroom. She cut the old overalls into thin strips that she crocheted into a round rug that was put by the kitchen door. Mary told her to keep the strips thinner, so she would be able to wash this rug when she had too. This addition to her home made the floors in her little house so much warmer and made the rooms feel homey.

One job she put off was the unpacking and putting in the kitchen cupboards the good dishes of her ma's she had found when she moved. She had unwrapped them all that day, looked at them and then packed them away again, putting the boxes in the pantry under a shelf. Mary had asked her about it when she had come up to see the hung curtains and again when she had looked at the rugs.

"Land sakes, child. Still haven't put those good dishes in that cupboard?"

"No. I did the curtains first and then worked on the rugs and I've did some drawing and worked with those colored chalk you gave me. See, this is what I have done," Sarah answered. She quickly gathered together some papers to show Mary, disrupting her train of thought.

"These are pretty. Look at those colors. I sure couldn't do anything like this," Mary told her, going through the sheets. Some were of animals, horses, kittens, landscapes of snow-covered hills and several very good pictures of Bud.

"You've got a knack for this, Sarah. You know what I'd like. This picture of the snow-covered hills, another picture of spring and everything getting green, one of fall when everything turns brown and the garden has pumpkins and squash and, oh, I skipped summer. One of summer. I'd put them in frames and hang them in the parlor. Maybe make them using colored chalk. And don't say you can't do it 'cause I see that you can. And I'm in no hurry. 'Cause you've got to have the seasons changing to do this, so see what you can do. Both of these of Bud are very good. It's too bad you can't take drawing lessons, then you'd get the real learning of add-ing the touches to make them extra good."

"I just do it when I get tired of sewing," Sarah told her.

"Sure, I understand," Mary replied. "And while you do such a good job on these drawings, just don't you forget to wash up those boxes of stuff in that pantry too. It's such a shame to have that beautiful stuff just in boxes. They stayed that long all those years, time for them to be seen and you've got the cupboards here to put them in. For some reason you hate to even think of them but it just seems a shame to keep them in those boxes any longer. I just love that bowl you gave me for Christmas. I'm going back now. Grandma was sleeping when I came up. Oh," she added as she put on her coat, "The men want to play cards this evening after supper. And I was to ask you to come on down and play with them."

"I don't know how to play cards," Sarah told her. "And I've told Victor that before."

"And he ain't going to take no for an answer. Says you know how to do lots of things and you'll learn this too. Can't hardly play five hundred with three. Need four."

"Three that know how and one stupid me," Sarah an-swered. "I'll come down and then he'll know how dumb I really am."

Eating the one meal a day that Sarah ate in her own house, she thought about the card playing. Victor and Tony often frequented the taverns in Ponta if they happened to go into town in the afternoon. There was always someone there that they could play pitch with. Mary didn't mind them hav-ing a few hours of fun. Having a choice of anything they wanted to drink, it sometimes was a glass of beer and many times a cup of coffee. And now they wanted to teach her how to play. Sarah cringed at the thought of learning how to play, 'cause her ma had been so against anything like card playing, beer drinking, dancing, anything that was in that common vein.

"Well Bud," she told the dog lying on the kitchen floor,

"now I'm going to join the heathens that Ma hated and try to learn how to play cards. Someday, she may raise out of the grave and haunt me for all of this."

Looking back on that first attempt at card playing always brought a smile to Sarah and the other three. She found out, as did the rest, that she wasn't so dumb at learning the difference between aces, kings, queens and diamonds and clubs. Because five hundred needed four players, this was the first game they taught her. Several evenings later she was quite good at it. Also taught to her was solitaire and rummy. The Sunday afternoons Tony spent with Johanna's family, the three left at home spent playing rummy. Sarah soon realized she was as anxious as the rest for free hours to spend shuffling the cards.

The last thing Sarah did before the long winter ended was to empty the boxes of dishes in the pantry that Mary had urged her to take care of. The Sunday morning she did this the roads were frozen, so the rest went to church. Sarah had stayed with Grandma but when they came back she excused herself and went home. After stumbling over one of the boxes the night before, she had finally made up her mind to do it.

When Mary came up after dinner and a nap, she found Sarah holding open the cupboard doors, looking at the two sets of good china and the bowls, platters and glasses she had washed that day

"Oh my goodness child, you did unpack all those boxes. You've got fine china here that is better than most women have that live in town and got money for fine things. Not many have anything like this," Mary told her, taking out one of the plates.

"I didn't know how I wanted it placed. I put it in several times before I finally left it like it is now."

"You can always change it again if you want to, you know. What's these in this here box?" she asked, looking into a box sitting by the kitchen door.

"The old dishes that we always used at home." Sarah answered, adding, "I just decided to get rid of the them."

"That's fine. You got plenty of everyday dishes out of those boxes that your ma had packed away. You still got all the pots and pans your ma used. They're in bad shape. Maybe sometime, you can take some of the money Victor pays you and get some new ones. Although the heavy cast-iron fry pans are good ones. They last forever. Are you done now? The men are ready to play cards." She put her knuckle against her left jaw and, rubbing, added, "My teeth hurt today like hell. And I don't often swear but they're bad today. You know that hard ribbon candy Gertrude brought at Christmas and left, well, I got to chewing on some of it this morning and chewing that hard stuff just don't make my teeth feel good. I guess I got to stick with the softer stuff."

"Your teeth are like Uncle John's were, probably got pyrorrhea in them. He would have had to get store teeth if he hadn't died first," Sarah answered.

"That's what Victor says too. His teeth are good but mine are getting loose and the gums are red and sore. I brush them good too with salt and soda but seems like it don't do any good."

"Uncle John didn't brush his much."

"Victor says when I get a bad enough toothache then I'll let him take me to the dentist. I'd rather have another baby than go to a dentist. Hurts awful and he'll just shake his head and want to pull them all out. I know that's what he'll want to do and then I'll run around, with my mouth all puckered up waiting for the gums to heal and dry up and then try to put a mouth full of store-bought make-believe teeth in them and chew. Yeah, I think I'll just stick to the soft food and forget all about the dentist."

"I've never been to one, " Sarah said.

"Stay away from them as long as you can. Let's go play cards. That way maybe I can forget about my toothache and dentists."

"You got any more homemade soap upstairs?" Sarah asked that same evening, as she was cutting up soap to put in a pan with water to melt for the next morning's washing.

"There's more up in the storeroom, ain't there?" Mary answered.

"I can't seem to find any."

"I'll go up and look," Mary said, heading up the stairs. In a few minutes she came back down. "I guess I'll have to have Victor get me some at the store tomorrow morning. We've been using so much, with washing all the time, that it's all gone. I thought I'd have enough to last all winter until next summer when I can make some in the iron kettle out in the yard."

"I've got a little of Ma's left. Ma used to make it in the winter. She had a recipe for cold water soap."

"You know how to make it?"

"I made it lots of times. You just use lye, cold water and tallow. It's better left for a while before using, but Ma used it right away. Got to be careful so the lye don't burn you."

"Anyone that uses lye knows that. You got the pans the soap was made in?"

"Sure. They're in the attic in Ma's house, or Tony's house now. I can have him get them when he goes back tonight."

"Do that and then make some soap. I've got plenty of tallow. I don't like the soap you buy. It ain't nearly as good as homemade soap and costs money besides."

"What does it cost?" Sarah asked.

"Six bars for a quarter. That's Crystal White laundry soap. And that soap sure ain't what homemade soap is."

Tony brought the pans for the soap making. Before long there was a supply of soap big enough to last the rest of the winter until larger batches could be cooked in the big kettle in the yard.

Every Saturday or Sunday for past winters, that winter and many winters to come, the family enjoyed ice cream. Unless they brought home ice from town in the summer, which once in a while they did, winter time was ice cream-making time because they had a plentiful supply of ice on the stock tanks. The wooden ice cream freezer was brought out when the weather got cold in the fall and soaked in one of the water tanks so the wood would swell. Mary or Sarah took eggs and cooked a rich vanilla pudding with lots of vanilla in it for flavoring. Putting this into the metal can on the inside of the wooden ice cream freezer, they inserted the paddle into the metal can and fastened on the top. Ice was chopped fairly fine and put around the metal can, filling up the space between the medal can and the wooden holder. Salt was run onto the ice and the turning of the handle attached to the paddle commenced. After it was hard to turn, the paddle was taken out and the ice cream was covered. The ice cream freezer was put outside in the snow and wrapped with a sheepskin jacket until dinner or supper time. Many dishes of this treat were enjoyed during the long winter months. For Sarah this was extra special, as she had never tasted anything as good as this before.

As usual in the winter after Christmas, Mary tried to do many of the things she enjoyed doing during the winter months like embroidering, sewing and making rugs, but soon found her ma's illness too stressful. A few minutes with the needle and the embroidery floss or at the sewing machine, along with listening to the noises her ma was making, made her so nervous she couldn't continue. It was most stressful to listen to the old lady and not be able to ease her problems.

"If only she would quiet down at night, at least I could sleep and get some rest but toward evening is when she really gets stirred up and during the early part of the night," she told Sarah over and over. Victor had resorted to sleeping at Tony's house so he could get some rest. Mary was getting so tired out, Sarah and Mary decided that Mary would have to sleep every other night in the little house in Sarah's bed while Sarah spent that night with the old lady.

And when the six months were up and it was another sister's turn to take care of Grandma, Mary found out the other three sisters had decided as long as Mary had hired help she would have to keep their ma. They were not going to take their turn.

Asking Sarah to stay with Grandma, Victor and Mary spent one Sunday the first part of April visiting the other three sisters. A rousing family argument followed, with the result being a very upset Victor and a weeping Mary. So angry was Victor that he walked out of the family discussion, slamming the door behind him and vowing to never speak to any of the others again. As the days and weeks went by, his attitude never changed.

"My wife has been used and trod on by three selfish women and their equally selfish husbands," he told Gertrude and Lee when they were home for Easter Sunday. "It's too bad Grandma ain't got some money 'cause I'd charge the rest of them and then they would have a fit."

"You would not," Mary told him.

"Try me," was the answer. "It's good enough for you to listen to that screaming and to take care of her and to wash the bedding, day after day, and try to make her eat which she don't want to do now. That's good enough for you but not for them. They're too good for that. It makes me so angry I'd like to put my fist through the wall. I'm better off not thinking about it. Dear brother-in-law Will was in town yesterday," he told the others, because Mary had heard the story the night before. "They must be here for Easter at his sisters and Will and his brother-in-law were in town for something. I didn't see him soon enough or I would have crossed the street before I got to him but I ran almost into him. He tried to talk to me but I just kept right on going, like I didn't know him and had never seen him before. No, I ain't forgiven them for what they did to Mary. Not by a long shot."

"I don't know what I'd do without Sarah," Mary said.

"But if she wasn't here, then they would have taken their turn at keeping Grandma," Gertrude told her.

"I don't think so," Victor replied. " I think they'd have found some other reason for not taking her back, for not taking their turn. Sarah was just a good excuse for them. Look at 'em. One is married to a rancher but they live in town now since their son took over the ranch so she belongs to how many card clubs and society clubs and church clubs. Has she got time for a sick woman? And another one is married to a banker and likes the same clubs her sister does. And another is married to a man who owns a hardware store and she helps him there all the time. She is his unpaid employee. No, I don't think they'd have taken Grandma back. I think when she was brought here last fall, they just washed their hands of the whole thing. I think they had talked it over between them and asked Mary to take the first shift of taking care of Grandma and that way they got the old lady here and I don't think a one of them intended to do anything for her. They just said that to get Mary to take her first and then they were just going to leave her here and that's what they did. Do you think any of them want to listen to that old lady's screams or change bedding how many times a day? It makes me so spitting mad cause they wouldn't even consider coming up once in a while to help Mary out. Don't get me wrong, I feel sorry for Grandma. She can't help what she is doing. It just makes me mad I'd like to kick out a wall or something, maybe their heads."

"I wish I were closer so I could help you," Gertrude told her ma, giving her arm a squeeze.

"Thank you. But you got your hands full where you are what with Orville gone so much of the time at the store," Mary answered. "I'm so thankful he has a job earning some money. Just look at the men who don't have any jobs and families to take care of. No work or money. What do their families do for something to eat? "

"And getting to be more and more that don't have any work," Victor added.

"I hope I can hold onto my job," Lee said, smiling at his daughter as she climbed onto his lap. "There are lots of men laid off from the railroad. So far everything's all right so I hope it stays that way for me."

"Cora Lee likes staying with her other grandma, don't she?"

"Yeah, I guess," Lee answered, shrugging his shoulders. "It's nice for me with them living in the next block, then I can send her down there and go to work. If I was on the trains, like conductors or firemen, then I don't think it would work 'cause then I'd be gone for days at a time and they don't want her at night at all or weekends or holidays. I'd have to send her back here to stay with you. They only keep her 'cause she's their daughter's kid and I don't know how much longer that's going to work either."

"I didn't see Sarah go," Gertrude said, looking around the room. "She go back to her house?"

"I think she went to lay down and maybe sleep. She's staying here tonight while I go and sleep in her bed."

"How can you stand that screaming, Ma?" Gertrude asked.

"You just do, you just do," she answered adding, " I've never missed housecleaning my house in the spring but even with Sarah here, I don't know how I'll get it done this year. Ever time I think about it and listen to Ma, I just get a sick feeling in my stomach about how it's supposed to get done and..."

"Forget it," Victor told her. "Just forget it. You can do only so much and so just leave it go."

"I hate the dirty feeling that the house has in the spring. Just look at the greasy walls from the cookstove and the same in the parlor but I just don't guess it can be helped this year," Mary said. "Guess Ma's being sick is getting to me."

"You got all you can handle right now and I don't want to even hear of you worrying about a dirty house. You follow me?" Victor asked.

Sighing, making a motion like bowing to the master, Mary shook her head yes while the rest laughed.

"Dirty house. Don't know how we'll stand it, " Tony said, adding, "But the master has spoken."

Fry cakes were a treat. Sarah had never heard of them so Mary made them one Sunday morning when the roads were too muddy to go to church. After mixing the dough, she rolled it out and then cut it with a donut cutter. When she figured the lard and tallow were hot enough, Mary slipped a few into the hot grease to fry. One side brown, she flipped them over and fried the other side. Laying them in a cake pan to cool, she continued to fry the rest. Rolled in sugar, the spicy fry cakes were certainly a treat to be enjoyed.

The following Sunday, again very muddy, Mary made another batch. Only this time, hurrying to check her ma, she fell over a chair and turned her ankle.

"Lucky Sarah was here. Don't know what would have happened to that hot grease otherwise, maybe a fire." Mary moaned, as she soaked her foot in a pail of hot water. "I sure didn't need this along with everything else."

After several days Mary still wasn't able to get around. Even wrapping the ankle with strips of cloth and using a cane she didn't have the support she needed to be able to walk. She tried to sit on a chair and help push the handle back and forth on the washing machine but had to give that up when her arm gave out on her. Tears of frustration were streaming down her face as she moaned to Victor.

"Can't do anything. And Sarah's got her hands full without Ma and the extra washing and everything. If I only had enough money saved for a gasoline wash machine. But I don't."

"But I do," Sarah told them, somewhat shocked at herself for being so vocal.

"Land sakes child. I don't want you using your money for that," Mary answered.

"Why not? If I don't have enough saved up at the house, then you know where to get what money I'm short. With Grandma being here all the time and who knows how long, it sure would be nice. Please Victor, go and buy one, maybe today," Sarah pleaded. "I'll go up to the house and get my money from there and if that ain't enough, then you go get some more, get whatever more you need."

"It'll be your wash machine," he told her.

"OK. So I got a wash machine but we'll use it here. Please?"

"This afternoon?"

"Yes, if you can," she answered. He thought a moment, looking first at his wife, then Sarah and then Tony.

"What you smiling for?" he asked Tony.

"Might as well go, Pa. Seriously, I can't think of anything Ma and Sarah'll get more use out of, what with Ma laid up right now and Grandma here and sick like she is."

"All right. You can get your money and I'll go into Ponta this afternoon. I don't know what they cost but I'll pay the rest of it, if Sarah ain't got enough money and then she can just pay me back out of her wages. That way she don't have to take anything out of the cans." When he got back with the machine in the back of the truck, he and Tony unloaded it into the kitchen. Next morning, after the water was poured in, he showed the two women how to start the gasoline motor. Victor stayed with them until they had the first load washed and put through the wringer.

"Imagine, just imagine. Pure magic. Touch a knob and it washes by itself and touch another knob and the wringer works by itself," Mary sighed.

"Just make sure you don't get your hands in that wringer," Victor cautioned them. "'Cause it won't stop until the knob is shut off, even if you've got your hand in up to the elbow. And I'm glad that neither of you got long hair 'cause if any of that got in there, you'd lose your scalp before it could be turned off. But it will save a lot of hard work."

The warm spring sunshine in May warmed the hearts and souls of Sarah and all the Labellas. Tony and Victor set the alarm clock nightly, taking their turn checking the ewes when the lambing season started. They didn't want to lose any of the mothers or babies. Although none of them liked to eat the meat, they raised them for the wool they sheared off the animals in the late spring and for the money they got when they sold the lambs in the fall. Victor didn't know how long that would last either. With the price of fall lambs down so badly, it hardly paid to put the feed into the animals.

The yards and pastures were dotted with little calves bawling for their mas and also several young colts. Watching the brood hens setting on their nest of eggs, they knew that before long there would be fluffy yellow chicks following those mother hens around the yard. Someone had come into the feed mill and left some duck and goose eggs, so Victor had brought them home. They were supposed to be fertile. Brood hens were found and nests made. Nobody was sure how many days the hens had to sit on the eggs before they would hatch, so everyone was watching this with interest.

The flower bushes and plants around the houses were showing signs of coming alive. Little green sprouts and shoots were sticking out of the ground here and there, promising colorful flowers when their turn came. The lilac bushes were starting to bud, promising tiny bunches of purple color.

Mary and Sarah walked around the unplowed garden after supper one evening. They talked of what would be planted and where. One of the men always plowed the garden and then worked it down so it was fairly level and all the dirt clumps broken up into moist soft dirt. An iron garden rake would finish the job, making the ground nice for the little seeds that were to be put in the rows. They could see the strawberry bed getting green and tiny buds coming.

After the spring wheat had been planted, Victor promised the garden was the next job. He had checked the calendar and the dark of the moon was coming. The potatoes had to be planted then. Sarah knew all about planting in the dark and light of the moon as her ma and uncle had always planted that way. The dark of the moon meant planting everything that grew under ground and the light of the moon was time to plant anything that grew above ground.

The second week in May became the potato planting time; Sarah spent time cutting up the old potatoes that were used as seed. Each piece of potato had to have several eyes on it so she was watchful as she cut. After she had several five-gallon pailsful cut up, Mary thought that should be enough.

Victor had picked up a few small pails of onion sets that morning from the onions left in the basement. These and some radish seed would be the first planting in the newly worked ground.

By noon the garden was worked down to a dark, crumbly, easy-to-work-with substance. At the end of each row a small wooden post was put with a long wire running from one post to the other. Using the wire as their guide, each man took a shovel and commenced digging holes about six to eight inches deep. Sarah came behind and threw a hunk of potato in each hole. The men then covered the hole with the rich, dark dirt. This continued until every potato in the five gallon pails was used.

"That's a lot of potato, Pa," Tony told him.

"But you've got to have some too this coming winter, what with you getting married. And if we have any extra ones, we can give them to Gertrude and to Lee too and his mother-in-law. Maybe that will make her feel more like keeping Cora Lee for Lee."

"Just think of all the potato bugs to pick off," Tony told Sarah.

" I'm thinking and I don't like that job,"

"Nobody does," Tony agreed. " Onions next, Pa?"

"Yeah. Got the hoes? I'll dig the trench and you and Sarah can put them in. And then we'll both cover them when they get all planted. We've got to put in those radishes too. Can't hardly wait for the first of them. With a piece of bread, they make a mighty fine sandwich."

"I'd rather have a sweet onion sandwich," Sarah told them.

"Say, that's something you forgot to get, Pa, sweet onions."

"Those are little seeds, I think," Sarah told him.

"Right," Victor agreed. "Hi Mary. Come to check on us."

"I come to help. It don't make any difference if I am in the house with Ma or not, she's gonna holler and I can't stop her so I guess I'm just going to have to let her. I thought I could help a little out here. Potatoes done already?"

"Yep. Now you make a list of the other seeds you want 'cause I'll pick them up when I stop at the mill next time," Victor told her.

"Carrots and rutabaga, beets, peas, green beans and yellow beans and parsnips which should have been planted with the radishes. I wonder if I haven't got some of that seed left from last year. I'll look before the radishes are planted. We've got sweet corn and popcorn from the cobs we saved last summer. Even got them shelled. Land sakes, I'll have to write all of this down and then think about it some. You think of any I missed, Sarah?"

"Cucumbers for pickles and dill," Sarah added. "I think I saw cucumber seeds in the cellar."

"And Ma's got dill that comes up every spring down by the strawberries," Tony added.

"We'll have to just write this all down. Maybe I'll go down and check my canning and that will give me an idea of what I missed. Don't want to forget to plant something. Oh, got to have squash, hubbard and the little ones, individual ones and also pumpkin for pies. Although squash will do for pies, if I have to. I've got a lot of those seeds saved from the squash and pumpkins last fall. Same with yellow and green beans and northern beans for baked beans and kidney beans for chili and lima beans too. It's so good just to be out here in the dirt," Mary told them.

"When the warm weather comes, the wanting to dig in the dirt is always there," Victor said. "Getting dirt under the finger nails is a good feeling."

The hatching of the duck and goose eggs produced eleven yellow fluffy ducklings and fourteen equally adorable goslings. Everyone enjoyed watching the parade of ducklings, goslings and chicks as they followed their mothers, the old hens. All too soon, the downy softness turned into little white feathers with the fluffiness gone.

Although there was only one bad blizzard during the winter to give some moisture, the rains that usually came in spring were few and far between. Everyone was worried about the hay and wheat crops. Tired of waiting for the rains that never seemed enough when they came, Victor and Tony laid irrigation pipes to the garden and also the large hay field that lay on the other side of the river. Many days were spent running water to keep the vegetables and hay field growing.

The first radishes were enjoyed by Victor while the rest of the garden grew, at first in little fine rows of green and then in larger rows of vegetables. Sarah spent many hours hoeing and pulling the pesky weeds. She and Mary alternated between picking strawberries and picking off potato bugs. These they threw in a small pail and then dumped a little kerosene on top of the crawling mess. But in a short time, they could repeat the whole process again. Wood ashes were sprinkled on top of the small squash, pumpkin and cucumber vines several times a week to keep the little striped bugs from devouring them.

Starting with strawberry jam and sauce, the jars in the

basement continued to fill. Hours were spent shucking peas and canning them. Green and yellow beans were picked, cleaned and cut to be put into jars. Beets were pickled with a sweet sour brine. Soon jars of dill pickles, bread and butter pickles and sweet pickles were carried into the basement. One smaller crock was filled with cucumbers, brine poured over the dill and cukes and left covered for a few days until Victor could stand it no more and he started eating the not-quite-ready pickles. When the wild chokecherries were ripe, they were picked and made into jelly, along with wild plums for jam and also cobbler. What wild gooseberries could be found were picked and canned. By now, the tomatoes were ripening, the first ones eaten and enjoyed by the family. Later pailsful were picked and canned as vegetable and strained juice. Before the fall was over, piles of squash and pumpkin would be in one corner of the cellar while another corner would have sacks of potatoes in it. Down along the river were several apple trees growing wild. The family never knew what kind they were but they did supply enough to keep everyone in canned applesauce and canned apples for pies.

Just as the garden was planted to keep the family in food for the coming months, hay and grain had to be harvested for the animals. The hay that had been irrigated was cut first, dried, raked and then, using the hay stacker, piled into huge stacks. Water from the river was then run over this land. Victor wanted another crop of hay from it as he could see the prairie grass that was always cut for hay wouldn't give as many stacks this year as he wanted. What they mostly would get would be tumbling tumble weeds that would have to be cut while they were green with some buffalo and wheat grass mixed in. Mary cautioned them again and again to be careful for angry rattlesnakes being brought onto the hay stack with the hay the stacker threw onto the top. The snakes did not appreciate being taken along with the hay onto the stacks and many a man had been fatally bitten this way.

"This extra work and time we spent this summer hauling around those water pipes and running that pump paid off in the amount of hay that was harvested off that piece we irrigated," Victor told Mary.

"The same with the garden. I don't think we'd have gotten much of anything otherwise. I know what some of the neighbors I talked to at church Sunday said about their gardens. I hated to say anything about our having the jars in the cellar full when some of them hardly got half what they usually got of garden stuff to can. So I just kept quiet about it."

"Smart thing to do," he agreed. "We'll have enough hay to get us through the winter. Got a lot more than others have. If we start to run short , I'll just get rid of most of the sheep. And the wheat ain't much to brag about, not like some years. We got that little bitty shower that one day or we'd have nothing there too. That made the difference between something to thresh and nothing to thresh. Some didn't even have the threshing rig come in, just cut it for feed as was."

"I walked down to Tony's and looked at the geese and ducks this morning. They're making out fine down there. Shame to have to keep them fenced in but I don't think we'd have had any left by now if they had gotten into the river."

"Too many turtles. They'd have eaten them all. We don't want to get too many of them just 'cause we can't let them run loose. But they'll make a mighty good Christmas and Thanksgiving dinner, that is if we remember it is Thanksgiving Day this year." Victor answered.

"That was funny last year. I remembered it days after it was over. Oh well, we lived anyway," Mary told him as they both laughed. "I've said it over and over, but I don't know what I'd have done without Sarah this summer. Like that threshing crew. What would I have done? We worked those long hours preparing food for the extra twelve men that were there for dinner and supper that day. So glad you decided to set up the tables in the yard under the trees for the men to sit at to eat, rather than have the men come into the house with Grandma. And suggesting that the food be served on the porch from a table there. The men could come through, pick up a plate, help themselves to the food that was there and then sit down at the tables. That worked out so good. There didn't even seem to be too many flies and we just covered up the food with towels to keep off the ones that were there."

"I don't think there was any choice. Men don't want to go into a house where there is that constant screaming and hollering. It went for this year and we'll take next year when it comes," he answered. "'Long as there was plenty of food, the men can put up with not being served at a fancy table."

"Mary, the circus is coming to Windsor. I saw the flyers posted in town. It'll be here for Labor Day," Victor said.

"Oh my goodness. I ain't seen one of them for a long time. But how can I go with Grandma here? We'll all want to go," she answered.

"We'll just have to think of something so we all can. Sarah, you got to go too 'cause that's something to see. The elephants and lions in the cages being pulled down the street and the clowns. It's just something to see and the wagons all painted up fancy being pulled by horses all decked out in fancy gear. We're going, that's all there is to it. Pack a lunch for dinner and spend the day, get there early. Have to figure out what to do with Grandma but we're going." And they did. Tony was going with Johanna. For two dollars, Don Kelly's wife would keep Grandma at her house. They didn't want to go, had just seen a circus the year before when she visited their daughter. Mary and Victor thought this was very expensive but when they found out Sarah intended to stay home with Grandma so they could go, they told the Kelly's they would take them up on the offer.

Not knowing what to expect, Sarah was overwhelmed with the day. Getting Mary's ma from the house into the car and then into Kelly's house was an undertaking. Victor's carrying her each time she needed moving proved to be the easiest part. Mary had to take along many blankets and sheets to put under the women in the car and at Kelly's. She also had to take along extra nighties. Sensing something different the woman seemed more uneasy than usual, muttering and crying all the time. Mrs. Kelly had been a nurse, something Mary didn't know, so she took this all in her stride. When Mary came back in the afternoon to get her ma, she and Mrs. Kelly came to an agreement on her taking care of Grandma the day of Tony's wedding. Although Mary and Victor had thought two dollars a lot for keeping the old woman the day of the circus, they knew she got good care. Sometimes there just wasn't any other choice.

Taking a noon picnic lunch of fried chicken made that morning, buttered bread, oatmeal cookies and water, they left early. After dropping Grandma off, they drove to Windsor and staked down a good place to watch the parade, taking with them their lunch and several blankets to sit on, along the curb. They could have opted for going to the field and watching the big tent being raised and walking around seeing the animals like many people were doing, but decided the parade was the better thing to see. At noon, they ate their lunch and waited. At one o'clock the circus band came marching down the street followed by the brilliantly painted wagons pulled by the horses, decked out in their finest harnesses. The wagons had animals inside them, among them lions and tigers. One wagon had a woman playing a calliope. This fascinated Sarah. But she soon had something else to watch as the elephants came, surrounded by circus people, some riding the animals and some walking beside them. Clowns, in their clown suits and painted faces, frolicked and scampered down the streets. All too soon it was over.

"Well, what'd you think, Sarah?" Victor asked while they were picking up the blankets and ready to leave.

"It was just great. Thanks so much for bringing me. I enjoyed it all so much. I'll see the whole thing again when I lay down to sleep and for many days to come. Thanks again."

"Our pleasure," Mary answered.

"I think we've got time for a break here, Pa," Tony told him the next day. "The threshing's done and we've all been to the circus so we got that out of the way. It's to early to pick corn and dehorn calves. And my wedding ain't until a month from now so let's go fishing. Hell's bells, we ain't been fishing all summer."

"I thought that was what you were leading up to," Victor told him with a grin. "I'm all for that. Sarah you ever been fishing? Mary don't like to. Says it's too slow and she can think of lots of other things she would rather do than fish. Likes to eat them but not catch them."

"I've been fishing lots of times," Sarah told him.

"Then get your work done this morning and we'll go fishing after dinner," she was told.

"Where do you go? There ain't no deep holes here for fishing. When me and Uncle John used to go, we walked about three miles along the river to where that small dam is on Ma's land."

"That's another place to go, Pa. Sarah can show us where the best place is there. Otherwise, we drove down to the bridge, down along the schoolhouse. You got a cane pole?"

"There's several out in the shed where Uncle John had his car."

"Then I'll run down there this morning and pick them up," Tony told her.

"And I'll dig some worms and catch some grasshoppers. Shouldn't have any trouble finding plenty of them — grasshoppers, I mean. Worms we'll find down near the river where it's wet. Too dry anywhere else. Throw in the spade right away, Tony, so we don't forget it. And find a gunny sack for the fish we catch." Victor said, adding, "And a jar of water in case anyone gets thirsty."

"How come you know how to fish?" Tony asked Sarah when they were driving to the fishing hole after dinner.

"Ma liked fish a lot. She didn't fish herself but she never cussed when Uncle John and I went fishing. We went many times in the summer, starting with early spring and going until late in the fall."

"Pa, why haven't we went before, a whole summer and first we go now? We always went more other years too."

"Might be we didn't go 'cause we've been busy. We used to go between planting and haying but this year we spent it irrigating," was the answer.

"What you looking at, Sarah?" Tony asked after they started to get their lines into the water.

"It's so peaceful here I wouldn't mind if I didn't catch anything. I just enjoy looking and looking at the birds and the wild flowers that're still blooming. Ain't many flowers blooming though, must be cause it's dry and late in the summer. It's still nice, even so."

"But a few fish would make it even better," Tony told her. "Hey look at your bobber. You've got something on there."

"A big carp," he told Sarah as she pulled the fish onto the bank. "It could at least have been a bullhead or a crappie or something else but a carp."

"Carp are good," she told him.

"No they ain't," he answered as he started to throw it into the bushes.

"Don't you throw that away," she said as she scrambled after it. "I'm gonna take that home and pickle it."

"Pickled carp?" Victor asked.

"That's good. If you like head cheese or pickled pigs feet and you like fish, then you should like carp pickled. If not, then I'll eat it all myself."

"You'll be eating a long time. That's a big one."

"I'll can it if I have to. That's my fish. And where is

your bobber?" she asked Tony. He grabbed for his pole as the bobber went under and the line went tight. A few minutes later he had a very nice bass.

Driving home later that afternoon, they had a good meal of fish in the sack besides Sarah's carp. Golden fried fish, along with freshly baked bread made up the supper menu. Sarah took some teasing about her carp but the pickled fish didn't last long after she made it that evening.

"Got to go again before long pa," Tony told Victor. "You gonna go again, Sarah?"

"I'd like to go again , if you don't mind taking me," was her answer. She enjoyed eating the fresh fish but most of all, the peacefulness of the river always enchanted her.

"You think it's gonna freeze tonight?" Mary asked Victor. It was the second week in September and the wind coming from the northwest blew cold. The temperature during the day had been going down.

"Wouldn't be surprised," he answered.

"Then I'd better get ahold of Sarah so we pick what tomatoes are left and green peppers."

"Any of those watermelons left?" he asked. "Sure glad we were given those seeds to plant. I sure enjoyed them this summer. Hate to see them come to an end."

"Just a few. I'm gonna get Sarah so we get picked what's left, just in case it does freeze." An hour later, three baskets of green tomatoes, a few green peppers and about six watermelon stood on the porch.

"We'll take some of those tomatoes and wrap them and put them in the spare bedroom to ripen. And make green tomato preserves out of some and fry some. You ever make those at home?" Mary asked Sarah

"Yeah," she answered. "But I liked green tomato pie the best."

"Green tomato pie? I've never had that. How is it made?"

"You mix together green tomatoes, sugar, flour, cinnamon and salt. Put it into a pie shell and cover with another pie shell. Bake about an hour. It's good. Ma always had me make some in the fall, even before the tomatoes were gonna freeze. We fried green tomatoes too, rolled them in milk and then flour and salt and pepper. But the pie was the best."

"Tomorrow morning you're gonna make us a pie of tomatoes so we can taste it." An extra crust was made in the morning and Sarah made the green tomato pie. They all took a small piece to taste and then finished up the pie for dinner. Mary cooked up some green tomato preserve and, for several suppers, green tomatoes were fried. But some of the tomatoes were kept separate so fresh green tomato pie could be enjoyed day after day until they were gone.

One morning soon after that, Victor hitched the horses to the potato digger that stood behind the shed and dug the rows and rows of potatoes. Sarah and Tony, with Mary helping when she could, took pails and picked up the potatoes as they came through the digger, over the grates and onto the ground. Pail after pail was picked up and then dumped and scattered onto the flat wagon racks to be dried and then put into sacks to be stored in the cellar for the coming winter's eating. There were many sacks full, but as Victor had told them at the time they were planted, they could always give some to Gertrude and to Lee.

After the potatoes were safely in the cellar, the men picked up all the squash and pumpkins, piled them onto one of the flat wagon racks and hauled them to the cellar. The last thing that was picked was the cabbage. As soon as there was time, the cabbage shredder and a wash tub were scrubbed. The shredder was put on top of the tub and Tony and his pa took turns shredding the cabbage that Mary packed firmly into large washed crocks along with salt. Large pieces of wood were placed on top of each crock as the cabbage was left to ferment into sauerkraut. After this had fermented, some would be packed into jars and canned while the rest would stay in the crocks for eating during the long winter.

Sarah had never been to a wedding, had no idea of what happened, what it was all about. As the big day drew near, she found herself more and more wanting to stay home with Grandma. Mary wouldn't hear of it. Victor had checked again with Mrs. Kelly to make sure she remembered she was supposed to take care of Mary's ma that day so Sarah would have no excuse for staying home. He had also found a couple in Ponta that would stay at the two places while they were gone. The woman would stay at Tony's house while her husband kept an eye on everything else. That way they didn't need to worry about coming home to milk their couple of cows, feed the chickens and gather the eggs. And they didn't have to worry about anyone coming in and stealing because it was widely known there was a wedding coming.

Mary had taken Sarah into Ponta several weeks before the wedding and helped her pick out a pattern and material for a new dress, a light blue soft fabric with tiny dark navy and white stars sprinkled over it. White lace had been bought for trim. The pieces of material Sarah had bought last fall for dresses had been three yards for a dollar. Sarah was horrified to see the material Mary had helped her pick out cost sixty-nine cents a yard. And the lace cost almost another dollar.

"Now you got that material, you need shoes and a purse to go with it," Mary told her, marching her down the street to Penney's to pick out a navy purse for seventy-nine cents. Sarah remembered the shoe store they went into next. But these navy shoes cost her four dollars and ninety-nine cents instead of the two dollars and ninety-eight cents she paid for her black shoes.

"You like them, they fit you and they look good," Mary told her looking down at the shoes. "They got a nice inch heel so you won't feel tottery in them and they got that strap across the front leaving all that foot showing between the strap and the lower part of the shoe, across the front by the toes. Yes, you'll get a lot of wear out of them."

"I don't go anywhere to wear them," Sarah told her.

"You're gonna go to a wedding, for a start," was Mary's answer. "And the pearl necklace Tony and Johanna gave you for Christmas and the earrings will look nice with that dress. And I got a navy coat, nice material, that's too small for me upstairs that I'm gonna get down when we get home, and give it to you to remake so you have something to wear in case it's rainy or cold that day. And no arguing 'cause that coat has hung up there forever 'cause I didn't want to cut it up cause it was too good for carpet rags. Now let's pay for this and then see where Victor is so we get home."

After they got back, Mary went upstairs and got a navy blue light weight coat and also found a pattern for a coat for Sarah to follow.

"Land sakes, child. You gave Victor the money for that motor last winter. Now I'm giving you a coat to remake, kind of like an exchange. Only you got to get it done before the wedding, just in case it's cold or rainy. And there should be enough material left from that coat to make a matching hat of some sort 'cause you got to have a hat for church."

After the afternoon spent shopping, Sarah laid out the material, the purse, the shoes and Mary's coat on her bed. She couldn't imagine herself wearing anything that fancy. And the pattern wasn't like anything Sarah had ever seen. Johanna had on a dress made something like that the last time she had been here, but then she was pretty and it looked nice on her. Not in her wildest imagination could she see herself wearing anything like this. Ma would say she was really putting on the dog, going way out of her reach. Why, anyone as ugly as she was couldn't expect to wear anything nice like this. Overalls, a flannel shirt and men's shoes were good enough for the likes of her.

"I don't know about that neck on that pattern. It seems too low. I don't want anything that ain't right up to my neck, "Sarah told Mary when they were ready to start cutting the next morning.

"If you want, we can make a collar that's up high, instead of no collar and a V-neckline like they got here. We can cut the neckline higher and put a collar on the edge of the V-neck. I know you even wear your summer dresses up that high. Don't know how you stand it when it's so hot outside and you got on long sleeves and you're buttoned right up. It ain't hard to put a collar on here, I got a pattern that would work fine for that kind of a collar."

"That lace would go on the edge of the collar, wouldn't it?" Sarah asked.

"Yep. Instead of going around the plain neck and V-neck in front it goes around the collar. And the pearls can go under the collar and you'll see some of them, instead of all of them. Should work out fine. Johanna had a dress like this one the last time she was here. No belt or waist, with the skirt joined to the top around the hips. On you, thin as you are and about the same height, this should look real good. And that material will lay just fine for this kind of a pattern. Now you want to cut it out here and then sew it at home. Then you can try it on as you go to fit it. Although I think with this size pattern it should fit good. Same size as the other dresses you've made."

"You got to show me how to sew the lace on before I go," Sarah told her.

"All right. It goes like this," Mary said, showing her she should do it when she got far enough to sew the lace on the large collar.

Before supper, Sarah had the dress done except for hemming. After giving it a final pressing, she put it on and taking her straight pins with her, she went down to Mary's for her to measure for hemming.

"All done?"

"Yeah. Do you think it's all right?" Sarah asked, slowly turning around.

"It looks fine, just fine. My, that made up nicely. I'll

get the yard stick and pin it for you. Now stand still and I'll go around you," Mary said as she knelt on the floor. "You're going to have a nice hem, just right."

"Your ma must be sleeping," Sarah said.

"Yeah. You know she has to be or you'd hear her. At dinner this noon, I told both of them that it's gonna seem funny having just Victor and me to eat. Although you eat some meals with us, you usually eat supper at your house and then we'll be all alone, just us two, except for Ma and she don't eat when we do 'cause I feed her first. When you have a family, the table seems always full. Then it slowly gets fewer and fewer as the kids leave until finally the last one is gone and it's just back to a man and his wife. Lonely, but I'm so glad Tony found a good girl like Johanna."

"She is nice," Sarah agreed.

"You bring down your everyday dress too?"

"No."

"I'm almost done with this. Why don't you go back and change and then come on back down and eat with us? With sewing all day, you probably didn't eat much for dinner. I know you didn't take much with you when you left here this morning. I'm done and I'll get started on supper now. Run back and change and then come on back down. I see Victor starting for the house. 'Course he don't mind too badly waiting a couple of minutes for supper. Tony ain't here yet anyway."

Grabbing the heavy cast-iron frying pan, Mary spooned in a few tablespoons of lard and then sliced the leftover potatoes from dinner into the frying pan, adding some finely sliced onion and the pieces of leftover beef chopped in fine pieces. Fearing there wasn't enough in the pan to feed the four of them, she cut several slices of bread into pieces and threw them in the pan too.

"Smells good, Mary," Victor told her as he hung up his jacket.

"Got your dress all done?" Tony asked as Sarah came back into the kitchen.

"No, it's got to be hemmed yet."

"It turned out real nice. Sarah is going to look really good in it," Mary told them.

"I'm glad you got a new dress. I wouldn't want you to miss my wedding, " Tony told Sarah.

Sarah glanced at him quickly. " I didn't think it would matter if I was there or not. There's gonna be lots of your friends and Johanna's friends and relatives. I have trouble talking to strangers."

"You make out nicely with us," Mary told her. "And you'll do fine with everyone else too. This is a smaller wedding, just our family that you already know and, of course, Johanna's family. Just her brothers and sisters and her ma and pa. And her two grandma's. That's all that's gonna be there for the wedding. There is the dance in the evening and there'll be more people there. People can't hardly wait for a chance to get together and visit and dance and have fun."

"If you don't have something like that then you can plan on a shiveree."

"A what?" Sarah asked.

"Shiveree. That's where the neighbors take pots and pans and saws and hammers and sneak up on the bride and groom's house, after they are sleeping, and bang and holler until they come out. Then drinks and food are set up and there's a party," Victor answered.

"Johanna's pa and ma figured a dance at the school house would be the better way to go than a shiveree," Tony told her.

"Since we got some place for Grandma to stay and people to keep an eye on everything here we don't have to worry about coming back for chores. I let it be known when I played cards last time, that someone would be here and stay all day and during the dance too. Everyone knows we never leave the place alone, there's always someone here all the time so with the wedding, especially the dance that everyone knows about, it'd be a good time for us to have visitors snooping around," Victor said.

"I know I feel better about it." Mary told him.

"You never know, Earl Conway might get it into his head to try to make trouble, get his revenge for being cheated out of that ranch and money," Victor added.

"He has a girlfriend," Tony told them. "She's from over by Windsor. He was driving around town with her last weekend. Someone said that was his girlfriend. She's fairly good-looking."

"I feel sorry for her," Mary said.

"Do you think Earl would do anything the night of the dance?" Sarah asked.

"You never know," Victor answered her.

"I never thought any of my children would get married without my sisters being there to celebrate with me. But then I never thought they would turn on me this way either," Mary said looking down at her plate.

"I know, Mary, but we ain't inviting them and that's all there is to it. And you know why."

"I know. They wouldn't come anyway and there ain't any of the other aunts and uncles on Johanna's side invited, except to the dance. But it still makes me feel sad."

"The whole thing makes me feel fuming mad, not sad, but mad as hell yet," Victor answered.

Sarah had never been in a church before that she could remember. Seated four seats from the front pew, she looked around her in wonder. It was beautiful, the most beautiful thing she had ever seen. She didn't begin to understand what it all meant, the colored glass pieces that made pictures in the windows that shimmered as the sun's rays hit them, the statues on the side altars and the large altar in the front of the church. She jumped as the organ began to play softly. The only time she had ever heard any music played had been on the old piano in the schoolhouse when she was in school.

As the organ continued to play, Gertrude, her two daughters and a man Sarah had never seen sat down two pews ahead of her. All had on their very best clothes. Then Lee and Cora Lee came in, sitting directly in front of her. They were also dressed up, Lee in a dark brown suit and Cora Lee is a obviously new dress. The pews on the other side also had people in them, also wearing their very best suits, dresses and hats. These Sarah guessed were Johanna's family.

Victor came down the middle aisle with Mary holding onto his arm. He looked so elegant in his dark suit and white shirt and Mary so lovely in her new dark green dress, made somewhat like Sarah's dress before the collar was added. She had on a necklace of pearls, a gift from her grandma on her pa's side many years ago.

Tiny tears came to Sarah's eyes as she watched them. A feeling of yearning griped her so tightly that she bit her lip to keep the tears from rolling down her cheeks. There was so much she had missed out on from all those years of living with Uncle John and her ma. So much everyone else did that she had never heard of before. No wonder Ma had called her dumb. She was stupid and ugly.

For a moment she couldn't think what was different and then she realized the organ had stopped playing. A moment later it began again, very loud as Tony and Johanna's sister came down the middle aisle followed by Johanna and her brother-in-law. As the priest began the mass, Sarah watched what the others did and slowly began to do the same. It was better doing that than sitting there and feeling conspicuous for doing nothing. At least now, she looked the same as the rest, although she didn't have a glimmer of an idea what it was all about. The language used for the service wasn't in English and Sarah didn't understand a word of what was said. And the priest faced the altar so she couldn't see what he was doing, not that she would understand what was happening if she could see the front of him. When the rest went up to communion, Lee whispered to her not to go up there. While he was gone, Cora Lee crawled in beside Sarah, whispering that she couldn't go up there either, 'cause she was too little. In spite of herself, Sarah had to smile.

When they were outside after the wedding was over, Lee spoke to Sarah, "What religion are you supposed to be?"

"I'm not any religion. I didn't have any idea what was going on," she answered indignantly while he roared with laughter.

"I think they're gonna have pictures taken at the studio while the rest of us go out to Johanna's folks' house for a bite of breakfast," Lee said. "I'm ready for a bite to eat too. Hungry and I'm sure everyone else is too."

"That's what your ma said yesterday, about the pictures and the eating," Sarah agreed. "Johanna looks so beautiful. Her dress is so pretty." Standing close to Sarah, she could see the dress in detail, the cream-colored material shimming in the sun. A lower rounded neckline was held together with two strands of pearl beading. The entire edge of the neck was filled with lace, the same lace that went around the bottom of the gathered sleeves. A sash gathered in the waistline. Sarah had never seen a hemline like the wedding dress had. There were two layers, the bottom one was the same length all the way around, while the top layer was cut in pointed pieces and completely edged with the same lace as the neckline and the sleeves. Johanna had cream-colored shoes and cream-colored silk stockings that showed from under the hem line that came about six inches above her shoes. Her sister's dress was made exactly the same except it didn't have the extra pointed layer on the skirt and was light blue in color. Both carried large bouquets of red and white roses. Tony, standing beside his bride, looked so handsome in his navy suit and starched white shirt with the rounded collar and navy tie. He sported several red roses on his lapel, as did his groom's man.

The rest of the day passed in a haze of uncertainty. Sarah was glad to share a table with Lee and Gertrude's family at the wedding dinner. After the dinner, the gifts were opened from the two families. Sarah had asked Mary about this and had been told she could do what she wanted to about the gift. If she wanted to, she could go into town with Victor and buy something at the dime store or hardware store. Sarah finally gave them one of Ma's bowls. Ma had kept them wrapped in a box all of her life, so she guessed Ma wouldn't miss this one either. Johanna was thrilled with the gift.

The dance in the evening was another learning experience for Sarah. She was sitting quietly watching the four band members coming in when Lee sat down beside her.

"Well, how much of what went on today did you ever see before?" he asked

"None. My life with Ma and Uncle John was very different. One you wouldn't understand."

"You never went anywhere then?"

"No. Ma didn't believe in going anywhere. You were put on this earth to work and you damn well better do just that." He raised his eyebrows at her. "I'm just telling you what she always said. And I ain't saying no more about how we lived." They sat a few more minutes in silence as the band tuned up.

Lee finally turned to Sarah and said, "I don't understand how your family lived or thought. It had to be very different, how your ma thought." A frown crossed his face as he watched a tear slowly trickle down her cheek.

"Can you dance, Sarah?"

"No. I'm going to just watch. But you don't have to feel sorry for me. Heavens, dance and have your fun."

"I will," he answered. "Uh-oh. Tony looks mad as hell. Who is that?"

"Earl Conway," Sarah whispered, watching the big man and his girlfriend come into the schoolroom.

"So that's the famous Earl Conway. I think I'll just stay here a while and see what happens. That his girl, you suppose?"

"Tony said he had a girlfriend. I feel sorry for her, real sorry." Lee, looking at Sarah, could see she meant every word of it.

Lee stayed by Sarah for a long time. Like her, he watched the dancing, explaining to her as the different polkas, waltzes and schottisches were played. The circle-two-step fascinated her.

"Wish you knew how to do all this?" he asked.

"Yes. It would be fun," she answered, not realizing how the yearning came through her voice. As many times before, Lee wondered at her previous life.

When Gertrude begged Lee to dance with her, Orville took his chair. She realized then the family wasn't going to let her alone to be tormented by Earl. Later that night she would shed tears for the thoughtfulness and kindness this family gave her.

CHAPTER VI

The first day of November, Victor brought Gertrude and her two girls when he came back from delivering to the bakery. They had come in on the train that morning. A letter several days before had told of their coming. This was not a usual visit. They had come to stay for a while. The letter also said Orville was not coming with them and that he wasn't working.

"Land sakes child," Mary greeted her, giving her a hug. "And Irene and Dorothy too. I'm so sorry to hear about Orville's not having a job anymore. Do take off your coats and then have some coffee and breakfast. Milk for you little girls."

"It's been a hard time, Ma. Harder than you think. I'll tell you about it later," she answered, throwing her coat over the rocker Grandma used to sit in.

Her ma looked at her with concern. Gertrude had dark circles under her eyes and they looked puffy. She had been crying. Victor gave Mary a shake of his head indicating she shouldn't ask.

"Holy cow, Gertrude," Tony said, coming into the kitchen. "You must have packed up the whole house and brought it along."

"I did," she answered. "And how is married life?"

"Good. I'm on my way home now for breakfast. It only takes about five minutes to walk back there. Johanna expects me back about this time every day. You want me to carry in some of the stuff in the car? It's starting to snow."

"I'll come and help you," Victor told him. "It won't take long with both of us working at it."

"Pa tells me as long as we're staying here that the girls'll still go to the old schoolhouse I went to. I'll have to think about talking to the teacher soon so she knows they're coming. Maybe a couple of days from now, but first I want to go with Pa in the morning and stop at the hospital, if Pa has time, and see if I can get a job there. I thought maybe that would be the first place to start to look for a job."

"Maybe I shouldn't be here and you could work with your ma," Sarah told her.

"No. I want a job in town. I don't want to work here with my ma or stay here either. I want a place of my own. No, not even the little house you have, if I can help it. No, this is just right for both you and Ma. You're the best tonic she can have, the best helper. You get along so good."

"You're going to look for a place to live here?" Mary was confused.

"I want a place by myself. That's why I want to find a job first, then get a place to live and then get the girls into the school by where I live, if I can get a job, that is. Depends on how long that takes. Living two houses from the school was the nicest thing before. I didn't have to worry about them walking a long ways or getting wet when it rained or snowed or anything."

"You're going to live by yourself, just you and the girls?" Mary slowly asked. "I don't understand. Where is Orville going to live?"

"I don't have any idea, Ma, where Orville's gonna live. Yes Ma, just the three of us. Girls, you done eating? Why don't you go and find the sack that your dolly clothes are in and take them and your dollies into the parlor and play with them? Nice and quiet." She waited until the girls were gone, then continued, "Orville has run off with another woman. Ain't that just something else? I don't think it really has sunk in yet. Ma, how can you stand that noise Grandma makes?"

"You just do," Victor answered, settling back down in his chair. "You just do."

"I'll go home and come back later," Sarah told Mary. "Then I can get the washing started."

"No, stay here," Gertrude told her. "I almost feel like you're part of the family and I sure don't have anything to hide. I didn't do anything wrong except feel like a fool. I didn't even have a hint he was doing this. That he had been seeing this woman for about a year now. She's young, about eighteen or so, I guess. His brother said she's a good-looker, got a good shape, not like mine, fat. His brother sneered at me that I must have been a dumb one not to have known that he wasn't working all those hours and he didn't work at Christmas or those other times when I came back here and he didn't come with me. Said he couldn't because of work. He thought I was the dumb one."

"What you tell him?" Victor asked.

"That I loved Orville and trusted him and believed in him. Wasn't that what you were supposed to do? And he never answered me. I think I gave him something to think about. Anyway, Orville's gone with the woman. Just ran off with her. Took the car, his clothes, all his clothes and left. I got the furniture and the stuff in the house 'cause he felt I'd need it for the girls. That's what the note he left said. He left the note with his brother. He brought it over for me. After I told him that I trusted Orville and all that other stuff I believed in, he helped me pack up the stuff. I brought what I could with us, some was sent in boxes by freight on the train, like bedding and quilts and pots and pans and dishes. And the furniture I sold to the neighbor woman and her husband. Didn't get much for it but it wasn't worth much either. Got twenty dollars for it all. I figured I could use the beds you got stacked in the attic when I got a place to live. And I think there's a couple of old dressers up there too. And I can use the money I got for the old furniture to buy some old stuff here, if I have any money left. Maybe I won't find a job very soon but I'm gonna try."

"When did you find him gone?" Mary asked.

"When I came home from staying with my neighbor lady who's in the hospital. I stayed with her 'cause she had surgery and her husband couldn't go 'cause he had that stroke. I went to the hospital after the girls left for school and stayed all day. She was so sick. I had asked the other neighbor lady, next door on the other side, to watch the girls when they got home from school so I could stay at the hospital until the lady's daughter and son-in-law came that night. Her daughter was going to stay with her all night and then the rest of the time, until she went home. She couldn't get there the day she got her surgery 'cause he couldn't get away from work any sooner. They drove about a hundred miles. When they got there, the son-in-law brought me home. I went to the neighbors and picked up the girls. When we went into the house, it was cold and no one was there. The fire had went out. I lit the lamps and thought it was so funny that Orville wasn't there. Then I heard his brother at the door and he had a funny grin on his face and he gave me the note Orville had written. I think he thought it was kind of cute. But he did come back the next day and help me pack up the stuff and found someone to buy the furniture. And I got enough money for it for it too 'cause I know what Orville paid for it when he bought it. It was old then so I think I got enough. Anyway, I wasn't in any position to haggle about price. I was just glad I found someone who had some money to buy it 'cause I didn't know how I was going to get it here. Anyway, Orville had bought it and I figured I didn't need the furniture to remind me of him."

"Oh my, oh my," Mary said, looking down at her cup of cold coffee, trying to digest all the information she had been given. "'Course your welcome here and you can stay as long as you want. There are those bedrooms upstairs and there's extra furniture in the attic you can have. Some of it needs fixing but Victor'll fix it up for you."

"I'm sorry Ma, but I didn't know where else to go,"

"'Course we'll help you and Irene and Dorothy. 'Course we will."

"I knew you would Ma." Gertrude answered as she put her head down on her ma's arm and cried.

There weren't any jobs available at the hospital, nor anywhere else in Ponta. Victor asked and Gertrude tried but there just wasn't any to be had. But there was a job available on one of the ranches east of town. The son and his ma lived there alone. She had dizzy spells causing falls, was on a cane and needed someone to be with her. There had been several women there before but it hadn't worked out. Word of Gertrude's job-hunting had come to the son and he drove out to Labellas.

The women in the house had no idea who he was when he knocked at the kitchen door.

"I've been told that there is a woman here that's looking for a job," he told Mary when she opened the door.

"Yes. That's right. My daughter Gertrude is. You can come in if you don't mind the noise coming from the bedroom. My ma is under the weather, has been for a while. Had a stroke. I'll get Gertrude."

He looked around the room, noticing Sarah.

"You're not the woman looking for a job?' he asked. She shook her head no as Gertrude hurried into the room.

"I'm Gertrude Lugwid and I've been trying to find a job."

"I'm Hugh Epperson." he answered, offering her his hand. "My ma has dizzy spells, has taken several falls and a bad one recently and is using a cane. She has a hard time getting around. But her mind is sharp as a tack, not like what I am hearing coming from that room. I know what that is 'cause my aunt was that way. No, Ma has a good mind but her dizziness gives her troubles, bad troubles. I

can't be in the house with her and outside too. I need someone to watch her and help her and do the cooking and the
washing. Ma and I are fussy what we eat. I have the wife of
one of my hired men come in and clean for me once a week.
But she ain't no cook and I would rather fry us an egg or two
than eat what she fixes. So I need a cook and someone to
watch Ma some. Not take care of her cause she is too inde-
pendent for that. Would that be what you could do?"

"I think so. First off though, you have to know I've
been to a lawyer and am going to divorce my husband. If
that puts you off, then that is the way it is. He decided another woman was better than me and just left with her."

"You didn't know anything about it?"

"Not a thing. Just came home from taking care of a
woman at the hospital that had surgery and he was gone.
Left a note, that's all," she answered, shrugging. "So I packed
up everything and came back to ma and pa."

"I don't think that would be a problem. I think my ma
will agree to that."

"Another thing and a big thing. I have two daughters,
age five and six years old. And they go with me."

"Oh, well... let me think a minute. I think Ma and I
can put up with them but can they put up with us? I'm a
bachelor, used to my own peace and quiet when I'm in the
house and Ma is used to that too. Girls can giggle a lot and...
well... it would be different. Why don't you come out to the
ranch and we can see if we can stand each other, if we think
we can get along. By the way, how good a cook are you?" he
asked.

"A good one, if I do say so myself, " she answered.
"What about school? Is there a school near there or where do
they go?"

"There's a school about a half a mile from me. And a
good teacher, I've heard. That's not so far that they couldn't
walk on good days and otherwise, we can work out something on them getting back and forth if my ma likes you and

your children and you like my ma. I guess I never told you I own a ranch just east of town. Do you have any way of getting out there?"

"My Pa can bring me out. He will, if I ask him. How about tomorrow morning, about nine o'clock as he delivers baked stuff to Labit's. Ma and Sarah, there in the corner, bake every morning for Labit's. Pa takes it into town most mornings, except when the weather's too bad to go."

"Fine. Ma and I'll be waiting for you. Oh, tomorrow is Saturday, is that all right?"

"Yes. And I'll bring the girls with me."

Gertrude stood by the door watching him go. A smaller man, wiry, definitely someone who fitted the description of a tough rancher. She hoped the trip out there in the morning would solve her immediate problems.

"I left them there," Victor told Mary the next morning. "Good thing Gertrude took along a change of clothes for all of them cause they stayed. I'll bring out the rest of their clothes Monday morning. Mrs. Epperson is quite an old lady. I think she said she was seventy-six, and sharp with the tongue. Not sassy or nasty but just a good sense of humor."

"What's the house like?" Mary wondered.

"It's an old one but fixed up pretty nice and it was clean. I guess he has someone coming in to clean so Gertrude don't have to do that. All she has to do is cook the meals, bake for them, bread and sweet stuff — I guess they like sweets — and make sure the old lady has someone to help her when she gets up so she don't fall. She can get around some by herself with her cane but Hugh don't want her alone, in case she falls and he's outside, 'cause that's what happened the last time she fell. She lay for a long time before he found her. Oh, Gertrude has to do the washing too, but Hugh said he had a motor on the washing machine. So that ain't so bad."

"I hope it works out for Gertrude, that she's happy there."

"I don't know how soon she'll be happy, Mary. She's still mad about Orville and that'll take a long time before she gets over that. But it sure seemed funny, the girls don't seem to miss him at all."

"If he was gone as much as Gertrude said he was, then they didn't see him much anyway. Does Gertrude have any time off? Will she be able to come back for Christmas?"

"Yeah. Hugh said he'd bring them back Christmas Eve day and I could take them back the twenty-sixth, in the morning. They won't be here for Thanksgiving but we never make anything of that anyway. 'Cause there never is anybody but us. And sometimes we're butchering about that time anyway."

"What's she getting paid?" Mary asked.

"Fifty cents a day and room and board, so that ain't half bad. She'll have it better money-wise than if she worked at the hospital."

"But it won't be a home of her own," Mary told him.

"No, but it's a roof over her head and I don't know how long she would have stood it here with Grandma. That drove her crazy."

"That's true. Ma made her nervous, even before this. That's why I wondered if she could take this job 'cause she ain't much for nursing somebody but I guess she'll have to try it and I hope she likes it, 'cause there sure don't seem to be anything else for her to work at."

Sarah was more prepared for Christmas this year. She knew what to expect and had planned what she was going to give as presents. With it looking like Lee might lose his job, Gertrude's money so tight and Tony and Johanna just married, Gertrude wondered if it would be all right to throw everyone but ma and pa's name in a bowl and draw out that name and just give that person a gift. She knew she didn't have money to buy or make everyone a gift, even a small present. Lee thought that would be fine, as did Tony and Johanna. This was done one Sunday noon when Tony and Johanna came to eat with the family.

"You want me to draw a name too?" Sarah whispered in surprise.

"Sure. We wouldn't have put your name in if we didn't want you to. You gave to me last year, didn't you?" Tony asked.

"Well, yes."

"Then draw one out and make sure it ain't your own." Peeking at the name she drew, Sarah was pleased to see it was Cora Lee's. Mary had just given her several larger pieces of red material to use for quilting and she thought there was enough so she could make a real pretty dress for the little girl. She thought she even had lace or some rickrack to trim it up with and maybe there would be enough scraps to make a dolly dress to match. The pleasure she got out of thinking about making the two dresses surprised her. She finally gave up trying to figure out why it pleased her so.

This year she had bought denim and flannel and made an overall jacket for Victor. She knew the one he wore to Ponta was in poor shape. The gift for Mary took more thought. There was a lovely piece of linen in Penney's that she had looked at both times she had been in town shopping for her Christmas needs. One day when Mary was tending her ma, Sarah had quickly taken a tape measure and measured the length of the dining room table. She added inches on each end and allotted for hems. The tablecloth Mary had used when they had company was an old one, frayed with some darned holes here and there. Sarah didn't think Mary had any other one or she would have used it, as Mary had a great deal of pride when company came. So the last trip made into Ponta, Sarah had bought the linen. Evenings after that were spent pulling threads to get an even edge and then hemming and pressing the large piece of material.

Sarah gave even more thought to the next part of Mary's gift or even if she should give it as a gift to Mary. During the previous winter, she had showed Mary a winter picture she had colored, using crayons. Mary had told her she would enjoy pictures, colored with colored chalk, of each season of the year. Thinking about it for several days, Sarah had finally gotten courage and started a winter picture. When done, about a week later, she had been very happy with the results. Later on, during the rest of the winter months, she had drawn several more winter scenes, each one depicting the season in a different way. She did the same with the other seasons, always drawing three of each, again having a different angle and view in each picture.

Laying the pictures side by side on her kitchen table, she asked Johanna what she thought and the woman had been ecstatic at the beauty and the quality. She asked if Tony could see them too. Sarah asked them to pick out a set for Mary. She had looked at them so long that it was impossible for her to decide anymore. Tony thought there were frames in the attic that would fit the pictures he and Johanna had finally picked out. One morning, when Mary was shopping with Victor in town, he and Sarah hunted and found four matching frames. Helping her, they framed the four seasons. Both Johanna and Tony urged Sarah to continue the art work. Johanna also told her that she hoped that Sarah would get her name the next year for Christmas.

Because of the warmth of the fall and early winter, the butchering got put off until close to Christmas. They were glad for the extra help from Johanna. Mary knew her ma had had several more small strokes and she required a lot more time than before. She couldn't be tied in a chair anymore so she had to be turned regularly so she wouldn't get bed sores. Mary needed extra help with the changing of the sheets and bedding. Sometimes they had to wash twice a day to keep clean bedding available as it took so long to dry the bedding on the wash lines strung in the parlor. They finally had to give up pressing the sheets everyday, they had no time and it didn't pay to try to keep them ironed. Mary had decided this after she had just pressed a pair of sheets, put them on Ma's bed and then the woman had promptly soiled them.

Mary had to take extra time to feed her ma now, as it was very hard for the woman to swallow. Everything had to be soft food, sometimes just bread soaked in milk was all Mary could get her to eat.

With all this extra work, they were all glad when the last of the butchering was done and the tubs, wash boiler and floors washed up. The old hen butchering was put off until after Christmas. Victor could see that Mary was looking strained, very tired and getting irritable. He just felt it better to wait with that. It would be enough to just get the extra work done that came with Christmas. And anyhow, he wasn't feeling that well himself. For several days, his throat had been hurting and it wasn't getting any better. He hadn't said anything to Mary, feeling she had enough to handle as was. But when he got up the next morning, he knew he wouldn't be able to do anything outside today. Swallowing even water was a painful trial. Everyone knew he was sick when he went back to bed and stayed there the whole day. A soft-boiled egg and a little chicken broth were his meals. Mary fixed him a hot toddy with hot water, sugar and brandy later that evening. This brought on a lot of sweat but no relief for the throat.

The next morning when Tony took the baking into town, Mary told him to swing around Doctor Larson's office and ask him to come out. Victor had trouble talking this morning, his throat was so bad. She could see white and ugly red blotches in his throat when she had looked. She feared he had quinsy and there wasn't any relief for that except lancing the tonsils. And if it got bad enough the person having it could die from not getting any air into their lungs.

The doctor confirmed her suspicion. Asking Mary to hold a basin in front of Victor with the edge below his chin, he took a sharp-pointed knife and poked a hole in the swollen tonsil. Pus and blood squirted into the pan.

"That should give him relief ?" Mary asked.

"Should help a lot. It'll drain for a while and, Victor, you'll have a bad taste for a while in your mouth from it but that should do it. Now if it don't get better soon, let me know and I may have to lance it again," the doctor answered. "Bad thing, quinsy. Painful and deadly if not lanced. The throat swells so shut that the patient can't get any air and he suffocates and dies. Probably feel like staying in bed a couple more days, Victor."

"Thank you for coming," Mary told Doctor Larson. "I'll pay you before you go."

"You know what I'd like for pay, instead of money. I'd take a couple jars of canned beef and a couple dozen eggs, if you have them. That canned beef is better'n anything I can get in any store. I never know when I'm going to get to supper and with my wife dead now and alone I just open up a jar of that beef and have some bread with it and I enjoy. I heat up the rest of it the next day." He left there with three quarts of canned beef, two dozen eggs and a loaf of fresh bread.

Johanna came over several days with Tony after breakfast the week before Christmas and helped Sarah with the baking and candy making. She was excellent help. Having picked up a pail of peanut butter at the store, she taught Sarah how to make peanut butter fudge, something that Sarah could have made herself sick eating, she liked it so much. They made the divinity and fudge that Victor liked so much. Filled cookies and rolled-out sugar cookies were baked. Popcorn was popped and the syrup cooked for the popcorn balls. Johanna also showed Sarah how to string popcorn so the strings could be hung on the Christmas tree.

"How much longer do you think Grandma will live?" Tony asked his pa at dinner one of those days.

"I don't know. She's lived longer now that I thought she would. I think some of that is because Mary gives her such good care and I guess she's got a real strong heart. It's been a long time now that Mary and Sarah have taken turns staying here at night. And with it cold outside, Mary just hates to have to go out in the cold and up to the little house to sleep but there just ain't much sleeping here with all the noise and that never seems to quit. You'd think Grandma would get a sore throat."

"I don't know if I could have done for Mary what Sarah has done," Johanna told them.

"She's been a blessing and don't feel funny about being told that," Victor said, as he looked at Sarah, who was looking down at her hands. "It ain't everyone that can take care of someone who's like that. I doubt if I could. Oh, I've helped Mary turn her but to be around that constant noise would just drive me up a wall."

"I know I'm glad when I can go home to my own quiet house. Not that it will always be so quiet cause we're going to have a baby next fall," Johanna told them.

"Oh how nice," Sarah told her, somewhat surprised how glad she was for the woman.

"You can help me take care of it," Johanna told her.

"Oh no. I don't know anything about a baby, nothing at all. I've never held one and I'd be afraid I'd drop it or something or choke it or I don't know what," Sarah replied, visually shrinking in her chair.

"I think we got the message, Sarah but then you never know what you can learn if you want to," Tony said, laughing. "You staying here all day, Johanna?"

"The only thing that's left is to butcher the old hens or roosters and I'm going to leave that up to Sarah. My stomach ain't up to that job right now. Otherwise we got everything done that we can get done before tomorrow. When is

Gertrude coming? And Lee?"

"The twenty-fourth, which is tomorrow, ain't it? I can't believe it's almost Christmas. Yes, both of them will be here tomorrow. Lee and Cora Lee are coming in on the train that gets in early that afternoon and I don't know what time Hugh is bringing Gertrude," Victor answered her. "She and the girls'll be here for supper that night. It don't seem possible that's tomorrow. I'll chop the heads off those roosters right after dinner and then you can clean them up, Sarah. I'm glad I got the herring and oysters this morning. The weather might keep me from getting into town in the morning. It's snowing real hard right now."

"We've got the snow plow ready to go, Pa," Tony told him. So when it quits it won't take so long to clear out a road for you and the sleigh. Just hope it don't get so awful cold. Honey, I'll take you home before it gets too nasty outside."

"Making that snow plow sure was a blessing. Now I only hope it works as good as it's supposed to," Victor replied.

"Hope so too. We looked good at the one the road guys use to clear the highways with and the old ones they used for horses. We'll see soon enough how it goes. Ready, honey?"

"Thanks for the help, Johanna," Sarah said, as she put on her coat. "I know Mary's glad for your help too."

"You're welcome. That's just part of being in the family. I'm ready if you are, Tony."

When Sarah came into the house the next morning, she stopped inside the door and stood trying to figure out what was different. And then it struck her, the house was quiet, so quiet it was frightening. Taking off her coat, she hesitated before finally going over to the bedroom door and peeking inside. The old lady lay very quietly, something she hadn't done for months. Hearing a sound behind her, she whirled around to see Mary standing behind her.

"I think ma's had a hard stroke. She quit screaming about four o'clock this morning and she hasn't made a sound or moved since then. She ain't dead. She's warm but I think she's in a coma or whatever they call it when you ain't of this world anymore but still ain't dead."

"She will die now though, won't she?" Sarah asked.

"Yes. I can't feed her anything so I suppose everything will just come to an end and quit working. I haven't any idea how long that'll take. I wish we didn't have the baking this morning to do 'cause I just don't feel up to it. I thought when it snowed so hard last night, there wouldn't be any baking for town but I guess there is, besides what we need here. I feel like — I don't know what I feel like."

"Like the end is coming," Sarah answered. "I remember how I felt when I could see the end coming for Ma, when she lay so still and I just knew she was dying. It's a funny feeling, like no other."

"Yeah, it is. Well, I suppose we had better get at it and then we need extra baking besides so we have for us tonight and tomorrow. I'm glad Johanna helped you those couple of days. I just couldn't do it anymore. And we have the herring to do too and the oyster stew, eggs to cook."

"The herring's done. I carried the keg up to my house last night and I did it then. My house smelled so nice and spicy and vinegary all night. I liked that smell. And I took eggs with me too and cooked them so I'll go back and get them later this morning and devil them. Oh, look at this dough, it's ready to make into the loaves."

By the eight o'clock deadline, the baking was done and ready for Victor to deliver. Shortly afterwards, they could hear the sound of the horses and the sleigh coming. Bundling up, Sarah helped Victor carry out the baking. He told Mary that, as soon as he got back, he was going to go with Tony on horses and cut the Christmas trees so they could be set up in the parlors before dinner instead of after supper that night. He didn't care when Tony and Johanna decorated their tree but he wanted theirs trimmed that afternoon, or at least before late at night so they could visit with everyone being home without the extra work of the tree, and also they just never knew how it was going to go with Grandma now. Mary was agreeable to this change. Her mind was on her ma and the other work just came automatically, without much thought.

"You know I miss that herring brine smell in the house but I sure am glad you got it done," Mary told Sarah early that afternoon. "It would have been just one more thing to squeeze in, the cooking of the eggs too. My heart ain't in Christmas this year."

Mary was like a bundle of nerves waiting for her family to arrive. She went to the window in the front door on a regular basis trying to catch a glimmer of either Victor, Lee and Cora Lee or Hugh Epperson bringing Gertrude and the girls.

"I'm not sure what I'll do with my time after Ma is gone," she told Sarah as she stood looking out the window. "So much of my time was spent with her that when she ain't here anymore, I'll be lost."

"You'll probably get done the embroidering that you didn't get done last winter and the sewing and there's still the old hens to butcher and can. And the pork hocks and shanks are still frozen upstairs to be made into head cheese. But it'll be different. It's different already with being so quiet."

"And such a big change you had when your ma died."

"Bigger than you ever know," Sarah told her. A few moments later she added, " I've so many times wished I could tell you how much I think of what you people did for me. I could never have gotten out of that house without your help. I wouldn't have known where to start. And with Earl Conway being around, I'd have never gotten out of there by myself. You took me under your wing and helped me, taught me so many things and were so good to me."

"You came at the right time 'cause I needed your help.

You needed us and we sure needed you. So we were good for each other. And here comes a sleigh. It's not ours so it must be Gertrude."

"And I see the other sleigh coming too, so your family is all home."

"We're gonna decorate the tree now," Mary told the three little girls after they were all settled in the house. Their eyes dancing at the thought.

"When did you say, Grandma?" Irene asked.

"Now before supper. Grandpa's gonna do the chores and we're gonna do the tree. Then we'll eat our Christmas Eve supper that's always special. We've got it all ready, just to finish up, last-minute stuff."

"That's right, girls. Then after supper and dishes are done, we'll see if Grandpa will light the candles, for a minute or two, so we can see how pretty they are. Then we'll visit and eat some of that candy and cookies Johanna and Sarah made. There won't be anyone going to church tonight with the wind starting to blow again hard and it starting to snow so we can just eat the treats and visit," Mary said. "I already asked how you liked being at the Eppersons. I want to hear what it really is like."

"I don't think she believed me when I said it was fine," Gertrude told Lee. Three excited girls danced around the table and around the house until they were told to go sit in the parlor and be quiet or there wouldn't be any tree decorated until they had gone to bed. Minutes later, the boxes that held the few decorations were brought from the attic and opened. Strings of popcorn were hung around the tree and the last thing put on, by Lee, who was the tallest, was the angel that had been given to Mary by her ma the first year she and Victor had been married. Sarah watched Lee put his arm around his ma. The tears trickled down Mary's cheeks as she looked up at the white silky angel.

Cora Lee broke the spell as she said, "Now Grandma, now it's Christmas."

Lee laughed as he stroked his daughter's hair, then said he was going to play some cards with the girls to keep them quiet until Pa came in from the barn and Tony and Johanna had arrived.

"I've got the coffee pot on already," Mary said. "And there's gonna be cocoa as soon as it gets hot. I made the chocolate and sugar and water before so all that was left was to put in the milk and get it hot. There's just the table to set and food to be set on. Here's Johanna now. Looks like she's got Tony's clean clothes with her. And I see Victor and Tony coming across the yard now."

"Ma, you wanted to know about the Eppersons?" Gertrude asked as they were eating supper. "Well, Hugh is real nice to work for but my real boss is his ma, Nellie. She's seventy-five years old, has a mind that works like a forty-year-old and is a real nice lady. I have to do the cooking and baking and I do the washing. They appreciate everything I make to eat, especially the chicken noodle soup and lots and lots of pies. Nellie has a hard time getting up out of a chair, has arthritis some but when she gets up she has to stand a few minutes until she gets over being dizzy. Then she can move around pretty good, but with a cane."

"Do the girls like it there?" Mary asked.

"Seem to. They like school and have made friends there. Hugh takes them in the morning and gets them at night. I think he's real glad there's someone in the house that his ma likes and can get along with. She could see why I'm getting a divorce and Orville leaving with another woman really got her goat. I got the idea, from what she said, why the two women Hugh had hired first were not suitable, in her words. The first one was downright lazy, in her words, did a sloppy job of dishes and washing and just didn't have an ambition. The second one was the other way, did a good job of everything only, I think, from what Nellie said, that she would have like to moved in permanently, in other words, marry

Hugh, and she didn't last long after Nellie decided that. If she don't like the woman Hugh hired, she don't last long."

"I would think that you getting divorced would put you in the position of looking for a husband," Lee told her.

"She knows that another husband is about the last thing I want, next to a rattlesnake bite, at least right now."

"How does Nellie get along with the girls?" Victor asked.

"She likes them, both of them. They read to her and show her their papers from school and she reads to them and they all have a great time. I'm so lucky to have gotten this job 'cause it gives me time to think and plan and decide what I want to do. Besides not having found anything else, it's a job. I don't think, right now, it would make any difference what I'd like to do, there ain't no money to do it with anyway. I guess what I'd do if I had the money would be to go to school and then teach but I ain't got any money and need to feed the girls so that's out of the question anyway."

"You gotten any further with the lawyer?" Mary asked.

"That'll take a while, at least a year, Mr. Paul told me. Nothing goes in a hurry there and if Orville can't be found, then it takes longer yet. I wrote a letter to the neighbor who lived next door to me on the right side and I got a letter back. She said her husband heard from Orville's brother that Orville and his girl friend are living down near Omaha, living together like man and wife and telling everyone they are married, got wedding rings on and everything."

"Shameful! Just shameful!" Mary said shaking her head.

"Neither of them got any pride," Victor added.

"Well, as long as we're in the telling the story of our life, then I'll add mine," Lee said. "Ma, you still got those spare rooms ready 'cause I guess Cora Lee and me are moving back here. I got transferred so I won't be home much and Anne's ma just don't want to take care of Cora Lee anymore. She told me flat out to get somewhere else for her. She don't want to keep her for the days and days I'll be gone at a time. She don't want to. I'm just glad I still got a job. They laid off some more just the other day so I'm lucky to have a job at all."

"You're welcome here anytime and you know that," Mary told him. "Will your relatives still be able to ride the trains free, get passes?"

"I think so."

"Will Anne's ma feel bad when you move away?"

"Some, I suppose. It ain't that she don't like her, she just can't keep her for days and days at a time. I know Annie's pa don't really like having any kids around so maybe he's the reason for her not wanting Cora Lee around for days on end. When she kept her during the day, he was gone and when he got home, Cora Lee was gone. She liked the money I paid her, I know that was what she used to buy a few things around the house. My transfer is for the first of the year so I'll be moving New Year's Day and have to start the second of the new year. No time in-between for getting settled but I'll have most of the packing done ahead of time and ship it on the train so it'll be here before we will, at least most of it and the rest'll come when we do. Maybe it can be stored in the attic, I don't know where else but there ain't gonna be any furniture cause I'm gonna sell that. I don't want to have to pay anyone to bring it up here. It ain't that good anyway."

"Another year coming. Wonder what the new one will bring?" Mary pondered. "The past one brought Tony's wedding and such a nice addition to our family, Johanna. It brought Gertrude a new home, something I never expected, and it also brought Lee and Cora Lee back to us."

"And the new year will make me one year older," added Victor. "Just another birthday."

"That reminds me, Sarah when is your birthday?" Mary asked.

"Why? What's the difference?" Sarah wondered.

"'Cause I want to know so we can wish you a happy birthday, like everyone else gets. And 'cause I want to bake a cake for you. I don't give any presents for birthdays but everyone gets a cake at least 'cause I know they all enjoy the stuff, I guess." Mary replied.

"My birthday," Sarah said and shook her head no, adding "I don't want anyone to worry about it or ask me or remember it. Now I think it's time I went home 'cause you don't need me anymore tonight, Mary." Putting on her coat, she added, "What time do you want me down here in the morning, Mary?"

"About ten o'clock is just fine. Good night, Sarah," Mary said.

"Good night then. You going somewhere?" she asked Lee as he put on his coat.

"I left a bottle of wine out on the porch. I was just going to get it," he told her, holding the door open.

Before she could step off the porch, Lee grabbed her arm and asked her, "Why do you always fight Ma on everything. You just got to be difficult. What the hell is the difference if she knows when your birthday is?"

Try as hard as she could, she couldn't shake Lee's grasp of her arm. Taking a deep breath, she finally spat at him, "'Cause my ma told me that I was a curse when I was born. That she wished that day had never come and that she hoped that I'd die, only I never did. She told me so many times that she hated me and that the devil gave me to her. She hated me. You understand that. She hated me. I never had any of the love you have in this house. I don't know what that is. And by the way, my birthday is Christmas Day and that's tomorrow and that's why we never had anything for Christmas when she was alive. Because it was my birthday and she hated my guts." As Lee let go of her arm, she whirled and ran down the steps and up the hill toward the safety of the little house and Bud. The expression on Lee's face as he watched her go was of shock, dismay and discovery wrapped up in one. He opened the wine bottle and took a couple of slugs before he replaced the cap and went into the house.

Sarah was sobbing by the time she opened the kitchen door. She slumped to the kitchen door, wrapping her arms around Bud.

"I've finally said what there's to say about my birthday and about my ma and about how she felt about me. I finally put it all together and said it," she told Bud as he licked her face.

Lee glanced at her when she came into the house the next morning. She gave no indication that she had seen him. After hanging up her coat, she took her gifts into the parlor and put them under the tree. Seeing everyone coming into the room, she found herself a chair in the corner out of the way. Sensing Lee watching her, she ignored him as best she could. Turning, she looked at the excited little girls. Tony appointed himself "the hander out of the gifts" so before very long everyone was unwrapping their presents. Sarah looked at the two gifts she had been given. The first was from Mary and Victor, a warm bathrobe made out of heavy flannel in a soft shade of pink. Sarah rubbed the flannel against her face, savoring the softness. The other gift she saw was from Lee and instinctively she looked at him. He had been watching her and knowing she had found him, he raised his eyebrows at her. Immediately looking down, she unwrapped the present finding a beautiful pin and earring set.

"What did everyone get?" Gertrude asked. " We have to tell everyone what we got before we go to finish getting dinner. Irene, why don't you start and we'll go around the room."

One by one, the presents were shown and the thank you's said, along with a few hugs from the children. Cora Lee was elated with her dress and matching dolly dress. Sarah was rewarded with a huge hug. When it came time for Sarah to thank Lee, she looked at him a moment and then distinctly said her thanks, giving him a tiny smile. Only Lee knew how much courage it took to give him that little smile.

"Time now to get dinner cooked," Mary said. As she

went past Sarah, she was asked if Grandma was any different. Mary shook her head no and told her she was still warm, alive and no different.

As Lee went past Sarah he leaned down and whispered, "My daughter gave you a very big hug as a thank you. I hope that wasn't the first hug you've ever gotten,"

"None of your business."

"That's sad," he answered.

"That's the way it was. Just the way it was," she flatly answered.

The morning of the twenty-sixth Mary's ma passed away. Victor stayed with Mary during those hours. Sarah, coming into the house at three o'clock, knew she'd have to do all the baking by herself. She wished they could have shut the bedroom door so she wouldn't hear anything, nor be a part of the death. But when the door was shut there wasn't any heat in that room so it had to be kept open, at least a little. She was glad she had the extra work to do for. This somewhat occupied her mind as it kept racing back to the day her ma had died.

Waking early, Lee came downstairs to get a cup of coffee he knew was already brewed on the stove.

"Pa ain't outside?" he asked, seeing his barn jacket and four-buckle boots still by the kitchen door.

"He's in your grandma's room with Mary. They think Grandma's very close to dying." Sarah answered.

"Oh," he answered. "The stove is getting low on wood. Can I fire it some more or don't you want any in there right now?"

"I was going to put some in when I finished making these pies. If you would, please put some wood in. Then I can just keep on with this and don't have to wash my hands."

After he was done and had taken a cup of coffee, Sarah asked him, "Lee, would you like to live in the little house I'm in? I could move somewhere else and with Grandma gone, Mary won't have the extra work she had before and she probably won't need me like she did with her ma here."

"Do you want to move?" he asked.

"That's not the idea," she answered. A moment or two later she continued, "Yes, I like it here. Why wouldn't I? Everyone's been good to me. I've got it better than I have ever had it before but sometimes that has to come to an end, just like Gertrude's living before had to end and you have to do other things then. It won't be like living alone to live here with your ma and pa."

"Put your mind at ease. I don't want to live in your house. I'm taking a new job on the railroad, it's going to make me be gone a lot more and what would I do with Cora Lee while I was gone? If we moved into your house, I'd have to leave her here with Ma most of the time anyway. Have to pull her out of bed early in the morning to take her down to the big house, so it's much better to just be living here in the big house all the time to start with. Besides," he continued after taking a sip of coffee and helping himself to one of the filled rolls that was a reject, " I know pa has talked to the hospital about baking for them and it sounded like they might be able to work something out. So there'll still be plenty of work for both of you. Besides, Ma wants to go and visit her cousin a few days this summer and she also has a very good friend, Frances, she wants to see. And she'd have to go by train both places. It makes it nice for everybody that they can go by train and it don't cost anything with me working on the railroad, free passes. Pa sometimes went with her when she visited before but with Grandma here last summer nobody could go. Maybe Pa'll go along with her, I don't know. And when she goes, Cora Lee has to have somebody to stay with. She could stay with Johanna but I know she likes you, so it works out good. I think you'll be needed, unless you want to leave here."

"No. Maybe it's bad but I think of this as a safe place to be. I never thought about it before but this place is like a hole to a rabbit, a place to crawl into and feel safe. Where no one can get me." Realizing how much she had revealed of her previous life, she clamped her lips together and her face flushed.

"And anyway, what would Bud do without you?"

Lee thought she wasn't going to answer him when she finally spoke softly, "I'd miss him terribly." She looked up as Victor and Mary closed the door to the bedroom.

"I'll go to the undertakers when I take the stuff to Labit's, Mary. And when he comes to get Grandma, then you can talk to him. And I'll also talk to Father at the church. The funeral mass will be said here at church. And I'll send wires to your sisters after all the arrangements have been made."

"They won't like it that the mass is here, Victor," Mary told him, wiping away the tears that were streaming down her face.

"That's too bad. But your ma made me administrator several years ago, so I got the right to do as I want on this. She'll still be buried by your pa. You're leaving today?" he asked Lee.

"Yes. I have to be back at work tomorrow morning. There's no way I can get to the funeral with starting here the second and having to move over the New Year's holiday. It just won't work. They'll never let me off, not even for my grandma's funeral."

"While I'm in town, I'll call out to Eppersons. They have a phone. I sometimes wished we had one too," he told Mary as she looked up in surprise. "Maybe Hugh will bring Gertrude in so she can go to the funeral. You and me will accompany the body back to be buried. I'm going out now and help Tony. I'll be back in about an hour from now, yeah, the baking should be done by then. Have to change clothes before I go, seeing as how I have to stop at the undertakers and the parish house."

By noon, the arrangements had been made. Mary's ma

would be laid out at Mary and Victor's house until the morning of the funeral. At that time, the casket would be moved to the church. Because of the distance and inconvenience, none of Mary's sisters would come to the funeral mass. They had wanted another mass to be said at their own church but the parish priest said he would be gone during that time. Victor felt if they had wanted to they could have come to the church here. Trains were running and it could have been worked out, but because of the hard feelings the sisters didn't want to try. They would be at the grave site when their ma was buried.

"That was the hardest thing, that funeral and the burial," Mary told Sarah after it was all over and they were back home. "My sisters all stuck together, wouldn't even talk to me, just like I was an outsider. On the way back from the cemetery, the undertaker asked Victor and I what had happened and so we told him. He said that they'll live to regret it 'cause that sort of thing generally comes back to haunt. He said he had worked so many years with people and it usually works that way. He knew I was hurting from the way they acted. But time will heal, I guess, and maybe someday things'll be better. I'm glad this year is done."

CHAPTER VII
Spring 1932

On the advice of the lawyer, Parry Paul, Victor and Sarah took all their savings out of the bank in Ponta. Paul had watched banks in other towns around the state being closed by the State Department of Banking and he felt the financial position of the bank in Ponta was no better then the banks that were just closed.

Victor, Mary, Sarah and Parry had talked at length many hours one day early in April about what to do with the money when it was drawn out. During the course of the conversation, Sarah told the rest that she had saved a lot of what she had earned helping Mary and she didn't feel comfortable just having that in a bowl in her house. Checking and studying the banks in the surrounding towns, Paul advised them to divide up the money and put some in each bank and maybe keep some at home, buried somewhere.

After Parry left that April day, Victor and Sarah decided the next day to withdraw their money from the Ponca bank and deposit it into three other banks in three other towns. Three days in a row, they made a trip to these different towns, opening savings accounts in the bank in that town. The money Sarah had saved from working for Mary and the money from the renting of the farm, she put into a syrup can and Victor buried it, along with a syrup can of his and Mary's extra money in the dirt floor of the chicken coop. Scratching loose straw over the disturbed dirt covered it so no one ever knew the dirt had been disturbed.

This spring Sarah watched the coming of the new lambs, calves, and baby chicks, goslings and ducklings with a lift in her heart.

The arrival of a sow and her seven little pigs one morning fascinated Sarah. She had never seen pigs before. Someone had given them to Victor when he had gone to the feed mill. The man had to either give them away or kill them because they weren't worth any money and he didn't have grain to feed them. The squeals they gave when Sarah leaned down to touch their backs made her giggle and laugh. Victor told her they were born with their noses in the ground rooting. He put rings in their noses to keep them from destroying the fence the men had put up to keep them penned in. From then on, the potato peelings and any other scraps from cooking were given to the pigs.

Even with the extra baking the two women did now that they supplied the small hospital, there was time for Sarah to be outside some afternoons. Several times she had taken the fishing pole and gone fishing by herself at the dam over at her ranch. It was a three-mile hike each way but she enjoyed the walk and was elated when she was able to bring home several messes of fish to be fried golden brown for their suppers. Seeing her pleasure, Victor and Tony got the hankering to fish too so they took a few afternoons and evenings off and the three drove to the river by the schoolhouse.

One afternoon, Joe Morshian brought over several saddle horses for Victor to try out. He wanted to buy a new one as the one he generally rode was getting too old. He just wanted to turn it out to pasture to live out the rest of its life. Sarah was outside when Joe came.

"Hello, Sarah," Joe told her as he tipped his hat her direction. The pretty brown mare he was leading came up to her and nuzzled the hand she stretched out to her. "She's a nice little horse, gentle. A nice horse. Got a pretty white marking on her forehead, and four white feet. Otherwise she's all brown. Hi there, Victor. My mare has taken a hankering to Sarah."

"Have you ever ridden?" Victor asked her. She shook her head no. "Like to?"

She looked at him with wide eyes, then looked to the height of the horse and amazing herself, answered, "Yes."

"You've got some money saved from working here. Maybe you'd like to own her. I think she really has taken to you. How much for her and the other horse here, Joe?" The men dickered on the price for the two animals, finally coming to an agreement of thirty dollars for the two horses.

"I think that's a fair price, Joe," Victor told him. "Well Sarah, I'll pay Joe for both of them and then you can pay me."

"But Victor, what'll I feed her?"

"She can eat what the other horses are getting. She'll be just fine."

"I mean, you and I'll have to come to an agreement on the feed. You just can't feed my animal for nothing."

"I think we can work that out," Victor told her. "We'll talk about that at supper time. I'll go and get Joe the money and then you and I are proud owners of some new horses."

"She has to have a name," Joe told her. "You just can't continue to call her the mare you got from Joe."

"Bonnie. She'll be called Bonnie," she answered. A cat she once had was called Bonnie and she had a special place in her heart for the name and the animal. If anyone wondered why she picked out that name, they never asked and she didn't tell.

After Tony had found a saddle that fit her, she learned the pleasure of riding. The first times, she had a mighty sore body but with determination and the love of the freedom it gave her, she soon overcame that problem. Many afternoons she explored the ranch, finding each ravine and gully, even going all over the ranch of her ma's. This was all new to her, as she had never been allowed to roam as other children did.

Following the river one day, she came upon a larger lake at the end of Victor's land. She had heard everyone talk of the lake on the ranch but this was the first time she had actually seen it. She watched in awe as the wild ducks and geese rose in startled flight as she and Bonnie rode up to them. They circled above her and then slowly came back, floating down onto the lake's surface. She had never seen anything so beautiful. Bonnie stood patiently as she absorbed the picture before her. Later, describing what she had seen to the family, Victor told her there were fish in that lake but that kind of fishing would be harder because it was shallow on the edge of the water and it required the fisherman to wade into the lake about twenty feet before it was deep enough to put out a line. Many times Victor, Tony and Lee had fished this way, but Sarah decided she would stay with river fishing.

She did spend some time evenings putting down on paper, with colored chalk, the picture she had in her mind of the lake and the ducks and geese. In the far distance she drew cattle and hills with a few clouds floating in the sky. When done, she showed it to the family, finally framing it with a frame Mary found in her attic. Waking every morning, she had the pleasure of looking at it as it hung on a wall in her bedroom.

Garden planting this year was so much easier than the year before. After the men worked it up, Mary and Sarah, with Cora Lee's help, spent several pleasant afternoons planting. Mary was anxious to get the garden planted, for she was planning a visit to her good friend, Frances. It had been several years since she had seen her and with Sarah here she could go and everything would be taken care of at home and Cora Lee would be watched.

When Lee moved in he had told everyone that he would be gone much of the time working and he had been right. He was gone sometimes for three to four weeks at a time.

He, nor anyone else in the family, complained as more and more men were getting laid off. Railroad cars were full of hobos and bums hitching a ride in the boxcars. Times were tough and getting tougher every day.

Cora Lee enjoyed the move to the ranch. Every day she tagged the men, finding new things to look at and different bits of information to bring back to the women. The first day she discovered one of the barn cats sitting by Victor as he milked their cow. She tried to pick it up but Victor told her to leave it sit and just watch. She gave a delighted squeal when he squirted milk at the cat and the cat opened its mouth and drank squirt after squirt. Lee laughed when she told him and remembered when he was that age and had watched his grandpa do exactly the same thing.

She also was fascinated with the sheep shearing. Tony and Victor put all the sheep in a small pen and then, one by one, took out the ewes and the sheep buck, sat them on their butts and hand-clipped off the fleece, starting at the top of the head and neck, working their way down. the greasy fleece was stuffed into a very large burlap bag that Victor took to town the next day and sold. Cora Lee told Mary that the sheep had gotten undressed for the summer and that the baby lambs didn't even know which ones were their mothers, only the mamas knew by how the babies smelled which ones were theirs.

One evening shortly after the sheep shearing, two coyotes found their way into the pasture where the sheep were kept. Because of the warm evenings, Bud now slept outside on Sarah's porch. The sheep pasture was beside Sarah's house and the dog, hearing the fuss, raised such a rumpus barking that he scared off the coyotes and brought Victor outside to see what was the problem. Standing right outside the fence, the dog continued to bark until Victor got a lantern from the barn and checked the sheep.

"Two dead ewes and one lamb dead," he told Sarah, as she stood on her porch. "Damn coyotes. Now we'll have to watch for them 'cause they'll be back. They won't be satisfied until they kill all of them."

"They didn't get a chance to eat any of the meat, did they?" Sarah asked.

"No. From when Bud started to bark and I got out here, I would guess there was more than one of them. Probably a pair with little ones. Think we'll take horses tomorrow and look and see if we can see a den anywhere. Don't suppose we'd be lucky enough to find them and kill them."

As it turned out, three lambs were orphaned from the killing. Mary found baby bottles and from that day on until they were big enough to eat grass, they were bottle-fed. Cora Lee was given the job of holding one of the bottles. She made such pets of the three lambs that they followed her all over, even trying to come into the house after her. Victor finally had to lock them in a pen by the barn to keep them out of the garden.

Tony and Victor scoured the prairie for several days, finally coming upon the coyote's den. They shot the two adults and several puppies. Beside the den was a half-eaten very small baby calf, rabbit furs and pheasant feathers.

Victor brought news back from town one day early in May of the closing of the Ponta State Bank. He wondered how many of the good people in the town and surrounding area had lost money and, in some cases, their life savings when the doors were closed.

After Joe and Lillian Morshian attended a wedding in the neighborhood west of them, Joe told Victor of running into Earl Conway and his bride. The couple had run away and gotten married in Wyoming by a justice of the peace about a week before that. According to the bride's aunt, who also was related to Joe, her parents had been very much against her going with Earl so the couple decided not to ask her parents for a wedding but had eloped.

"He was strutting like a banty rooster," Joe told Victor.

"He also let me know how lucky he was not to have ended up with Sarah Hysell. Her old lady had been dead set on him marrying the daughter but he sure got lucky with that, that it didn't work out cause the old lady died before it got done. He also let me know he knew that whatever money that old lady had was in the Ponta State Bank and it had all gone with the closing of the doors."

"Well, I've got news for him. Sarah's ma's money wasn't in that bank so she didn't lose it."

"Wish I could say the same," Joe answered. " Just glad we didn't get the last money we were saving into the bank too. We always saved up just so much and then made a deposit of that amount but we weren't quite to that amount so that much didn't get in there. We lost some but not as much as some of them did around here."

"Earl's in-laws ain't so keen on him then?" Victor asked.

"Must not be. Just glad it's not my daughter that married him. Wonder how long it'll take before the rest of his family moves in with Earl and his bride. If they think she'll feed 'em and wash their clothes, they'll be there. Lillian's sister used to live in the same neighborhood as they did and she always said they were the laziest bunch you ever saw and also the meanest."

"I'm glad it ain't me," was Sarah's only comment when Victor told her later that day.

Mary took on spring housecleaning with a vengeance. She had two years' dirt to scrub and she and Sarah tackled it together, doing first the big house and then Sarah's little house. Ladders were gotten so the ceilings and walls could be scrubbed in each room. Several days were spent scrubbing in each room. The grime and grease from the wood stoves came off hard, even with using the good homemade soap and scrub brushes. Victor never took the huge heater in the parlor out in the summer to a shed, like many men did, but he did take the stove pipes down to clean them and in the process they came apart and soot was dumped on the floor in the parlor and kitchen. The women were not pleased, even when he apologized and tried to help them clean up the sooty mess.

Throw rugs were washed and the ones too large to wash were taken outside on the clothes line and pounded with a broom. Windows were washed with vinegar and water, polished with old bed sheets until they were sparkly clean. Straight curtain panels were washed, starched and stretched on curtain stretchers while bedroom and kitchen curtains were given the same treatment, only they were ironed because of their many ruffles. Doilies were carefully washed and then put into a heavy sugar water and laid on a sheet in the parlor with each point pinned down with a straight pin.

Furniture was polished, closets were emptied and clothes aired on the line. Bedding was washed and straw mattresses taken outside and beaten and aired. Kitchen cupboards were washed and everything wiped clean and rearranged.

Even Sarah's brass bed was cleaned and polished. A mixture of salt and vinegar was mixed with flour and enough water to make a paste. This was brushed on the brass, left ten minutes and then washed off with soapy water and rinsed well. Sarah and Mary polished the bed with old wool cloths until it had a high sheen.

The men sighed with relief when the spring house-cleaning was over while the women walked through the rooms enjoying the clean smell of the hours and hours of effort.

"So damn dry this spring, lots worse than last year," Victor told Mary and Sarah as they ate dinner one day soon after the cleaning was over, toward the end of May. "The spring wheat barely came up, just had enough rain to make it sprout and come up but hardly enough to make it keep growing. And now the wind's blowing, sucking the little moisture out that is left in the ground. Sky looked funny this morning so maybe we'll get some rain before the day is over. They say farther west and in Kansas and Oklahoma and Texas the dust storms are already bad Be hard to get much hay this year if this keeps up, except what we irrigate. Tony and I were wondering about irrigating the flat south of the river at Sarah's. It would make a lot of extra work but maybe we'd save some of the hay there if we did. Otherwise we'll have only hay from the irrigated land east of the river and tumbling tumble weeds and what buffalo grass and wheat grass grows from the prairie. Unless we get rain soon, won't be much hay on the range."

"Not enough snow last winter either to help," Mary added.

"Nope. Hardly any snow and most of that we got around Christmas. Made it nice to get around with the ground froze but sure is hard this spring. Heard tell of different ones out on the gumbo just packing it up at night and leaving. Turning the cattle out and just leaving. Ain't got any money to pay taxes that were due first of the year and no money to even feed the family, let alone make a payment at the bank. So they just leave, sometimes in the middle of the night. I heard tell at the feed mill this morning about two different ranchers out on the gumbo that did just that."

"They don't try to sell the cattle for what they could get out of them?" Mary asked

"They don't own them, the bank does in most cases. And if they do own them and sell them, the bank has first dibs on the money anyway." Getting up and heading out the door, he added, "Guess we'll look over the flat down there and see what can be done. The garden is wet enough now that it can go for a few days."

Toward evening, the sky got dark and the clouds angrily churned. All the adults stood in the yard watching.

"Suppose we're gonna get a real storm now," Victor said. "Hardly any rain all spring and then all hell breaks loose when it does come." As the storm got closer the lightning stretched from way up in the clouds to the ground, bolt after bolt. Thunder could be heard, rumbling in the distance. The closer the storm got, the more quiet the air became.

"Don't like this," Victor said. "Won't be surprised if we all end in the cellar. This sure don't feel right."

"Hope Tony and Johanna are keeping an eye on this," Mary said.

"They are, I'm sure. Tony went home early because he didn't like how it looked."

Suddenly the stillness ended and the wind started, bringing with it blasts of rain that was full of hail. Mary grabbed Cora Lee's hand and they all ran toward the cellar under the house. Victor could hardly close the cellar doors, the wind was so strong. They stood on the dark steps listening to the hail and rain pound.

"Where's that lantern?" Victor asked, feeling his way down the steps, stumbling and swearing. "Here it is, I found it." Using a match, he soon had it lit, giving the people down there some rays of light.

They had hardly gotten settled to waiting before the storm was over. The pounding of the rain and hail stopped abruptly. Victor cautiously opened the cellar doors to peer outside and saw the sheets of rain and hail across the prairie east of the buildings. Blowing out the lantern, he returned it to a shelf in the cellar before joining the women out in the yard. Small branches from the trees were strewn over the yard, as was anything else the wind could pick up. A thin layer of large hail stones were lying white on the ground.

"Too dark now to check and see if there's any more damage," Victor told them. "Have to do that in the morning. Might as well go to bed now."

A check of damage in the morning found several range cows dead from a lightning strike. As Victor found out in town the next day, they were luckier than a lot had been. A tornado had touched down east of town and done considerable damage. And south of town hail lay inches deep, destroying what wheat and hay fields had endured the drought and doing considerable damage to cattle and horses.

"So I guess we're lucky at that," he told Mary later that day. "Sure wished we could have gotten more rain than we did. Water in that can on the yard looked like about a quarter of an inch. That sure won't go far."

"How can you wear those long sleeves?" Lee asked Sarah when he was watching her pick over some strawberries the end of June. "It's hotter than hell in here and you got on a long sleeved shirt and bib overalls. Woman, what is wrong with you?"

"I was picking strawberries and I crawl around while I pick."

"But you always wear long sleeves."

"I'm used to it," she answered.

"But why? Ma wears short-sleeved dresses and she even got brave enough to have some that are sleeveless. Pa wears flannel shirts in the summer but they're almost worn out and Ma's cut off the sleeves. And here you are, dressed like it's middle of the winter, dressed up like you're afraid to show your arms."

Grabbing hold of her arm, he added, "Why, you're wringing wet." Sarah jerked away from him and the old shirt started to tear around the collar, with that part of the shirt and the sleeve coming off in Lee's hand.

"Oh, I'm sorry, Sarah. I didn't mean to wreck your shirt. What the hell?" He hollered as he caught sight of her arm and shoulder. A long series of deep puckery scars started below her elbow and extended as far on the shoulder as he could see. "What the hell?" he repeated as Sarah tried in vain to get away from him.

"Where did you get those from?" he asked, giving her a little shake. "And how far do they go anyway?"

"Let go of me," she screamed.

"Not until I get some answers."

"Let me do," Sarah screamed again, wriggling until

the worn-out shirt finally came apart. She grabbed the front of her shirt, stretching it as best she could to cover the front and side of her that was now exposed. Tearing out the back door, she left Lee standing with the remnants of the shirt in his hand. He strode to the back door and watched her run across the yard to her house. Tearing open the door, he ran after her, managing to just get the edge of his foot in her kitchen door before she got it shut. Wildly she screamed again and again. Lee grabbed her and held her tight.

"Shut up. Quit that screaming and shut up. I'm not going to let you go until you do." He held her as she sobbed, until she finally went limp in his arms. "That's better. You know me well enough by now to know that I'm going to find out what happened to you. Something awful happened and I'm going to find out, even if we have to stay like this the rest of the day."

"Your ma will be wondering why the berries ain't done," she told him, in between the final sobs.

"Here, use my hankie," he told her as she tried to wipe her nose on the shoulder of what was left of her shirt. A few minutes later, after wiping tears, shuddering with the last of the tears and several times of nose blowing, Sarah heard Lee say again, " Sarah, you might as well tell me what happened 'cause I won't quit until I know."

"I need another shirt," she answered, going into the other room to change.

"That's fine, but I ain't going anywhere until I have some answers. So if you don't come out very soon I'm coming in there," he threatened. He was very surprised to see how quickly she came back out and after a moment of thinking, he realized she instinctively reacted as if the orders had been given by her ma. She had acted as she had when she was a child. Easier to obey that not to and be punished. His mouth tightened and his face looked like thunder when he understood this. Taking a deep breath, he asked again, softly this time, "Sarah, I want some answers. I didn't mean to tear your shirt or scare you or hurt you. I wouldn't do that. God knows, it looks like you've got plenty of hurting already in your life. I only want to know what happened."

Sarah raised head and looked at him for a long moment. Suddenly her knees felt weak and she groped around for a chair, sitting down. Long minutes passed while he waited for her to get her bearings. Finally she began, so softly that he came close to her so he could hear what she had to say.

"Ma wouldn't like it that you saw some of my body. You're not supposed to show anyone any of your body."

"I didn't mean to see any of your body. I didn't mean to tear your shirt. It was an accident and it happened 'cause the shirt was so old it just tore. And you were covered up, I didn't see anything much anyway. And anyway, covering your arms right down to the wrists is what I objected to, couldn't understand. There ain't nothing wrong with someone seeing your arms. And nothing wrong with dressing so you're comfortable when it's so hot outside. Nothing wrong. And remember this, your ma ain't here anymore to tell you it's wrong. She had a lot of funny ideas of what was right and wrong and not all of them are the right or good ideas. She had some strange ideas. Just remember that. All right?"

She shook her head yes.

"I want to know what happened, Sarah. And I'm gonna know what happened if we have to stay here a long time. And Ma will wonder what happened but she'll just have to wonder cause I'm stubborn enough to stay here a long time."

"I feel so weak that I don't know if I could walk down the hill to the big house right now. I feel sick all over, even sick to my stomach. Lee, my ma was different than your ma. And I don't want to talk about it, to you, to anyone. Ever." Looking up, she shook her head as she saw the determination in his face and eyes. As if beaten, she finally started to softly tell the story.

"All right, I'll tell you since you won't be satisfied until you know everything. I got those scars from my ma. When I was fourteen. She took an iron, you know one you iron clothes with and she took the edge and used it on me."

"Oh my God," Lee said, his voice shaking with shock. He whispered, "Why?" as he pulled out a chair close to her and sat down, leaning his arms on the table. He watched her as she continued.

"Because someone told my uncle that I was talking to a boy in school and he told her."

"And she took the iron to you. You must have been big by then, fourteen you said. Why didn't you run away?"

"She knocked me down and knelt on me and I couldn't get up. She tried to put the iron on my face but I got my face down so she couldn't and it made her so mad that she started on my arm and shoulders. She still intended to do my face but my uncle came into the house and dragged her away. He heard my screaming and he figured she must be doing something 'cause she was so mad when he told her about me talking to a boy in school. When he heard me, he came running but she had already done this much. He saved me from getting my face all burnt too. He always was sorry he ever told her anything but by that time it was too late."

Lee sat down on a chair, shaking like a leaf. He had never seen or heard of anything like that in his life.

"How far does the scarring go?" he asked.

"All across both shoulders."

"You say you were fourteen and in school. How could you go back to school after that?"

"I didn't. My uncle took care of me for a long time. I was too sick to even get out of bed. That made her even madder 'cause she told him that if I couldn't take care of myself and do my work then I might as well die. It would be good riddance. My uncle told her if she laid a hand on me, he would take a board to her and bash her head in 'cause there wasn't any sense in it anyway and he meant it. He washed my shoulders and arm when it got all pus and bandaged it and made me something to eat and fed me. I couldn't do anything myself. I would have died if he hadn't and she'd have been glad. It took months before I got out of bed and it was a long time after that before I was well enough to really work again. Ma never talked to me or had anything to do with me after that until my uncle John died and then she just went wild."

"Wild?" Lee asked.

"Then he wasn't there to protect me and she was boss again. Only by that time I was older and would do my chores and the work and not listen to her. And then she got sick and she was in bed so much of the time, finally bedridden all the time. She met Earl Conway then too."

"How? When she was in bed, how did she meet him?"

"He came to the house trying to rent the land."

"And I can figure out the rest. He was nice to her and she got taken in by him."

"No. He wasn't nice. He was loud and rough talking and slammed doors and swore as hard as she did."

"And she decided he would be good for you?"

"She thought he would be the boss, 'cause I didn't listen to her anymore. But Earl was strong and mean and he'd take care of me. He'd show me who was boss and she'd laugh her head off every time he gave me a black eye or two. And if he gave me some more scars on my back, she'd laugh for days and days."

"My lord. I can't imagine anyone thinking like that, let alone doing what she did to you."

"After I was good enough to get out of bed, Uncle John brought me in a kitten from the barn for my very own. Ma had never let me have a pet. When I petted a kitten or a puppy, she'd hit them with a stick of a shovel and kill them. So I never petted anything cause I knew she'd kill it. Uncle John brought me this kitten for my very own and told Ma that if she as much as touched it, he would take a board to her and she knew he meant it. I called that kitten Bonnie."

"That's what you called your mare," Lee said.

"Yes. Bonnie, the cat, lived ten years. I buried him behind the house under the lilac tree. Ma laughed when he died and made fun of me for burying him. Uncle John died not too long after that."

"So you lost your two friends one right after another."

"Yeah."

Getting up, Lee went to the screen door. He stood looking out onto the yard for minutes.

"How would your ma have liked having Earl's family move into her house 'cause Ma and Pa thought they would have done just that?"

"She never gave that a thought. She'd have had a fit but it wouldn't have done her any good 'cause she was too sick in bed to kick them out so her hard-earned money would have supported them and she wouldn't have liked it one bit."

"I just can't get this all through my head, how anyone can treat their child like that. I see Ma and Cora Lee coming across the yard toward the house. Do you feel good enough to go back to cleaning the berries?" She shook her head yes. "And rest assured, I won't tell anyone about anything you've just told me. You know that, don't you? That's our secret, yours and mine. I wouldn't hurt you any more than you have been for the world." She shook her head to let him know she understood. "I'm gonna slip out the door and go around the back of the house toward the barn so Ma and Cora Lee won't know I've been in here." With this, Lee left.

On her way out the door Sarah picked up the torn sleeve Lee had carried in his hand. She opened the lid of the stove and threw it in, watching it fall into the ashes.

"Well, Ma. I finally told what happened. Only you and I and Uncle John knew and now someone else knows. You threatened to kill me if I told anyone. Well, you ain't gonna kill anyone from where you're laying and if I drop dead walking down toward the big house, then I just do. So be it."

Lying in bed that night, she thought and thought about the talk with Lee. She wondered if Lee knew how lucky he was to have been born into a family like the one he had. And how lucky Cora Lee was having Lee for a pa. She wondered what she had done wrong to have had a ma like the one she had. She didn't think she was such a bad person, but she must have been because why would her ma have hated her so? She could see how a ma loved her family from watching Mary, so there had to be something wrong with her. The talking with Lee went round and round in her head until finally she dropped off into a troubled sleep.

With Lee gone so much, there wasn't any other opportunity for another talk with Sarah. It seemed like every time he was home, there was always something going on or work to do. Cora Lee missed her pa but found plenty to do on the ranch. Having lived in town all her life, this was a brand new world for her and she enjoyed each and every cat, dog, and lamb she could catch. They soon learned to make a fast getaway when they heard her coming. Grabbing them around the neck was not a good way to carry any animal. After Tony and Victor gave her a few lectures on how to handle the animals, she calmed down enough to start to make friends with them

"Now you finally got it right on how to handle a cat," Mary told Cora Lee as she watched her on the porch petting one. They could see Sarah on Bonnie, coming into yard after having had a very enjoyable afternoon of riding.

"Grandma, when am I going to be old enough to have a horse to ride?" Cora Lee asked.

"Long time before you are big enough for a horse, but maybe a pony sometime. We'll have to ask your pa if he ever gets home long enough to say more than hello and goodbye." In a few minutes, Sarah came across the yard toward the house.

"You had a good afternoon?" Mary asked.

"The best. That horse rides so nice. 'Course, I never rode any other one so I don't know the difference. The prairie is so brown and burnt up from no rain. Big cracks in the gumbo. The lake sure has dried a lot. Still lots of ducks and geese up there but it's down a lot."

"We're lucky to have it and the river. The cattle can get water both places to drink. I know Victor talked this noon about changing pastures for the cattle 'cause of dried-up pasture and dried-up water holes. Sarah, I've been thinking about going to visit my cousin, Ida. It's been five years since I seen her and I'd like to go there before fall work starts. The garden is caught up. Tomatoes ain't ready yet and the rest is pretty well caught up with, the canning, that is."

"How long you going for?" Sarah asked.

"About four or five days, probably four or maybe even three. I don't like to be gone too long 'cause it's a lot of extra baking for you. Your afternoons'll be spent baking some of the stuff for the next morning. Sure can't get it all done in the morning by yourself. Sometimes I wished I hadn't got that extra baking at the hospital. Nice to have a little more money, helps out here with it being so dry, at least we got that much money. Some people have eggs and cream to sell so they have money for the groceries. I try to make up that difference by the baking. I hate picking eggs and Victor hates cleaning out the chicken coops."

"I always hated that job, cleaning out the coops," Sarah agreed. "You want to go, I'll be glad to do what has to be done so you can. Won't we, Cora Lee?"

"There's a car coming," Mary said, frowning as she got up to see who it was.

"It's Lee," Sarah told her, as she watched Cora Lee jump up and down. "I've got to change clothes. Get into a dress. Mary, before you go, I'd like to go into town and get some thread and buttons. Want to do some sewing before very long. Those feed sacks I bleached and washed out are really nice and white and I've got enough for a nightie from the flour sacks you gave me, only I don't have any rickrack to trim it with and I'm almost out of white thread."

"I got a letter from Ida yesterday and that's what gave me the yearning to go and see her. I just got lonesome. We were such good friends when we were little. She lives on a ranch too so she don't have her nose in the air the way my sisters do."

They watched as Cora Lee ran across the yard to throw her arms around her pa's legs. He picked her up and hugged her, squeezing her until she squealed with joy. Sarah watched a few moments and then turned to go to her house and change clothes.

"Hi Ma," he said, giving her a hug too. "I see not everyone's happy to see me. Sarah sure didn't worry about saying hello."

"She's been riding and wanted to change her clothes. Put on a dress. Lee, how long you staying this time?"

"I've been transferred back here. The depot agent at Windsor had a stroke and can't work anymore. Had it last week and so they asked me if I'd like the job. I said I sure would, 'cause that's what I used to be at Hennison. Windsor is only seven miles from here so I figured I could probably drive some of the time and go in on the early morning train some of the time and come home on the later train at night. My hours'll be from seven in the morning until five at night. I checked train schedules and that'll work out. I'd like to leave Cora Lee here. Not have to move to Windsor and find someone to watch her and have to find a house or whatever. I don't have any furniture anymore 'cause I sold it so I'd have to find some of that too."

"It'll be nice to have you home so much more and we'd all miss Cora Lee if she left," Mary told him.

"That's a six-day job, ain't it? Just like it used to be at

Hennison?" Victor asked him at supper that night.

"Yeah. I got to work Saturdays, all day until four o'clock. Get off one hour earlier. I figured some of the time I could drive but when the weather and the roads got bad, then I'd go by train and keep a supply of clean clothes at the depot for times when I couldn't get home. I'd have to find a place where I could board when I had to stay there overnight. Somebody said there's a hotel close there so I'll check that out."

"It's so nice to have you home," Mary told him again.

"And it is nice to be home. And to see Cora Lee. She's growing so fast."

"That she is and she's having such a good time on the ranch. Everyday is a new adventure for her. She's finally learned how to pet and carry the dogs and cats around without strangling them. And she's careful for getting cactus needles in her feet and watching for rattlesnakes. Oh, Lee, she needs new clothes too. All of her dresses are too short for her, both in length and from the waist up to the neck. She's growing so fast that I don't think we can wait until Christmas to make her something that fits her."

"Get whatever you need, Ma, and I'll pay you for it. I don't know what to buy."

"I didn't think you did. I'll make some dresses cause I'm sure I got remnants. Victor." Mary looked at him. "I know I went to visit Frances this spring but I'd like to go and visit Ida."

"I wondered when I brought that letter the other day if you wouldn't be wanting to do just that. Thought maybe that letter would bring this on," he answered.

"I talked to Sarah and she's willing to do the baking and do everything that has to be done while I'm gone. The garden is caught up some and the canning is done as far as we can go. It'll be a month or so before Johanna's baby is born."

"How long you going for?" he asked her.

"Four or five days. Maybe only four or even three."

"You gonna write her first and then wait for an answer back?" Lee asked her.

"I thought maybe I could call her from town. She don't have a phone but the neighbor does and she gave me the telephone number. I never used a telephone in my life but there's a first time for everything."

"I could call for you Ma, if you want me to." Lee told her. "Where'd you intend to call from? What phone were you going to use?"

"We can go to the telephone company office and use a phone there. You have to pay a nickel for the call. That's why it's not done very often but in an emergency, then that's where you go," Victor told him. "You want to go, then you can go into town with me in the morning and we'll make that call," he told Mary.

"Thank you," she answered. "I'm so excited already, I can hardly wait."

The following month was a full one. Mary came back from her cousin's, bubbling with enjoyment.

"I take it you had a good time," Lee told her.

"Oh, we did. We talked and talked and talked, hardly slept at all. And I got some new dress and apron patterns and some new quilt patterns and some new recipes and... and... I just enjoyed it all." Victor shook his head and then grinned. It was nice to have his wife home.

Lee settled down to his new job with ease. The transfer, from one area to another and from one job to another was done with a minimum of problems. Not having to relocate his household helped a great deal.

One evening Tony woke Victor to tell him he was taking Johanna into the hospital. He wasn't home the next morning. Everyone waited and waited until finally they saw the car come back toward evening with the news that their little daughter Marion had been born that afternoon. It would

be a full ten days or more before Johanna would be allowed
to come home.

For Sarah, this month had been an especially busy one.
When Mary had been gone, she spent most of her days baking for the household and the commitments in Ponta. She
had the washing and ironing to keep up with, plus the cleaning of both houses. She found it a bit stressful having Lee
home so much more of the time but he made no mention of
their previous talk that hot summer day. After Mary came
back, she spent some afternoons with Bonnie, did a bit of
fishing and, with Lee's comfortable presence, she was able to
slip into the most contentment she had ever had.

"Sarah, you want to hold the baby?" Johanna asked
when Mary, Sarah and Cora Lee had walked down to see the
baby after Tony had brought her home from the hospital.

"Oh no. I maybe would drop her. I'll just look at her
from here," she answered, backing off.

"She don't break. Here, sit down." Johanna said, grabbing her arm " Hold out your arms like this and I'll put her
here for you." Before Sarah could object again, she was holding the baby. Afraid to move, she sat stiffly looking down at
the little face sticking out from the blankets. So tiny, so delicate and so helpless were her thoughts as she finally carefully
ran a finger over the soft cheek.

"See, I told you that she didn't break," Johanna said.
"You hold her while I warm up the coffee and slice one of
the coffee cakes you brought for Tony and me to eat." As
she got the lunch ready, Cora Lee hung over Sarah looking
at the little baby.

"What you think of her, Cora Lee?" Mary asked. "Pretty
little, ain't she? And you were just as small as that when you
were born."

"And now I'm so big," Cora Lee answered, stretching
her arms out wide.

"So big and getting bigger every day."

"Here, let me take her so you can have your coffee," Johanna told Sarah taking the little baby from her arms.

"She feels warmer than she did when you gave her to me," Sarah answered.

"Oh, I'll bet she wet herself. I'll change her quick. Pull up a chair and start drinking your coffee. I sure have a lot more washing now than I did with just Tony and me. And Ma says I got to be real careful this winter so Martha don't chill when she wets at night."

While the two other women discussed the problems of the cold weather and little baby's wetting, Sarah thought of the minutes she had held the baby. She had once been that tiny and that innocent. What had she done to make her ma hate her so? What can a little baby possibly do to bring on that kind of hatred? Her thoughts were so far away that it took a moment for her to realize Mary was ready to go home. Somewhat in a daze, she thanked Johanna for the lunch and followed Mary home.

"Sarah, you never did get to Ponta for your thread and other things you needed for sewing, did you? I never thought of it until now that you didn't get there. What with my going to see Ida and leaving right away."

"No. I still need some things before I can sew anything."

"Maybe you and I can get Victor to go into Ponta tomorrow afternoon. It's Saturday and it would be a nice break for all of us. Lots of people go to town on a Saturday afternoon and visit with their neighbors. The women get dressed up in their best clothes, fix their hair the best they know how and the men put on their best bib overalls and white shirt. Take the cream and eggs into town and trade them for groceries. We never did much 'cause Victor never liked the idea of getting a set habit of doing that 'cause he was always afraid, if everyone knew we did that every week, then someone would come in and steal, and I guess this has happened too. But

maybe once in a while would be all right. We'll take Cora
Lee with us. Right now she's down at Johanna's. She sure
loves that baby. I'll ask Victor when he comes in for supper
tonight. I think we're all done here, so if you want to leave
you sure can. What you gonna do? Go riding?"

"I thought I'd go fishing for a change. I'll ride Bonnie
to the fishing hole. I'm hungry for some fried fish or maybe
some pickled carp. Whatever I happen to catch, if anything.
Got to catch some grasshoppers 'cause I sure can't dig any
worms. Ground's like a rock from being so dry. Say," she
said before leaving, "I saw some tomatoes that were almost
ready to eat last night. Did you happen to notice them?'

"No but I haven't been down to the garden for a while.
Good, I'm hungry for them. Lots of canning when they
really get started. Got to can lots of jars of tomatoes this year.
We ran out this summer. But the fresh ones don't have as
good a taste as when they are rained on. That irrigating sure
don't give as good a taste only I best not complain 'cause we
wouldn't have any if the men hadn't run water on them. I
think the beets are about ready to make pickles out of too."

"Bye now," Sarah told Cora Lee as she started down
the steps. Going home, she changed into a shirt and bib
overalls. Picking up her cane pole off the porch, she and
Bonnie with Bud trotting alongside, started walking toward
the river and an afternoon of enjoyment.

Before long the fall work was going in earnest. The
many quarts of tomatoes that Mary needed soon lined the
basement shelves along with the other jars and jars of canning. There wasn't much wheat threshing because of the
drought but enough straw was gotten to fill the mattresses
with fresh straw for another year. The men began working
on getting the cows and their calves closer to home to be
soon dehorned, branded and whatever else had to be done to
get them ready for the winter months. This included separating them from their mothers, a very noisy job of cows and

calves bawling several days until they got over the being apart. Days were also spent getting the corrals and the fences of the pastures closest to the barns ready for the winter months. Haystacks had to be fenced around to keep the animals out of the hay until they were needed for feed. Many, many jobs had to be done, making these busy days.

Victor and Tony counted cattle and looked at the stacks of hay and feed they had and wondered if there would be enough to make it through until spring next year.

"If it hadn't been for those two fields we irrigated, we'd never begin to have enough. I don't know now if we will," Victor said.

"Bad enough with the drought, but the grasshoppers sure didn't make it any easier either. Last year we had them only by the edge of the fields and the fence lines but this year there were lots more of them and they eat lots, into the fields all over," Tony answered.

"Lee said everyone that came into the depot says the same thing. Everyone hopes for a winter that'll kill their eggs, 'cause if it don't, then there'll be more next year than this year," Victor answered.

"Sarah'll just have to fish lots and lots more to use up more of them," Tony answered. "And the ducks and geese just love them. They eat until they can't hardly walk."

"Don't think Sarah can fish that much. I'd like to get rid of a few head of sheep and cattle at the sale barn, only it don't pay to take anything into the auction barn 'cause they can't even give cows and calves and sheep away. No body wants them so they just finally take them out and shoot them. I was down there yesterday afternoon and the place was full of trucks. Saw lots of ranchers I hadn't seen for a long time there, they brought in cattle 'cause they don't have feed for them anymore. Also saw lots of men I never seen before, wondered where they come from and someone said off the boxcars. After the sale, they just find another boxcar to crawl into and are on their way again. Someone else said that they wondered if some of the animals that didn't sell and were going to be shot weren't given to them and they went alongside the tracks somewhere and cooked some of the meat. When I said this at the supper table last night, Lee said he wouldn't be surprised. Sees lots and lots of boxcars with men in them going by every day. Some of these men go to the churches in town there and ask for food, and some chop wood or do most anything just to get a meal."

"I wondered if we ever could sell some to the meat market in Ponta, maybe one a week or two. That would thin them out and be less to feed. Wondered if maybe they'd take any lambs 'cause we've got a really good crop of them this year. When we ain't got any feed then, we've got a lot of them. We didn't lose hardly any this summer, only the ones the coyotes took," Tony told his pa.

"Worth trying, I'll stop tomorrow morning and ask." Victor made an agreement with the meat market to sell them a steer, a cow and two sheep each week starting the first of January until he had as many sold as he thought he needed to. He would get paid a cent a pound for the beef, the cow and for the sheep. All were pleased to see this agreement made. At least there would be a little money for the ones sold and less to feed by spring. Victor knew that some ranchers had taken to shooting some of the stock and just leaving them lie for the coyotes and birds.

October soon faded into November with the extra job of butchering. This year would be easier by far as there wouldn't be any more early-morning baking for the restaurant or the hospital. Labit's daughter and her husband had come home to live. Their son-in-law had lost his job and Labit's had offered both of them a job working in the restaurant, he as a cook and she doing the baking and also waiting on tables. And since there were two more at the Labit's collecting wages, they went to the hospital and offered to do the baking for that establishment too. Mary and Victor could see the reasoning behind it all. They knew it was going to hurt them financially although neither minded the extra three hours' sleep in the morning. After Christmas, Mary intended to go after some seamstress work, for both herself and Sarah. Victor intended to continue stopping at the restaurant so the Labits would know there were no hard feelings. Too many years of friendship were there for it to be lost.

For a change Sarah looked forward to Christmas. The sewing she had done she had enjoyed doing. The name she had drawn this year was Gertrude's and when inquiring of Mary what she thought Gertrude needed, Mary had thought nighties. These were made from feed sacks and trimmed with rickrack and even embroidery. Sarah had done this in the evening, listening to Bud's snoring. Victor had broadly hinted he could use another denim jacket, so that was his present. And Mary had so treasured the linen tablecloth she had gotten the year before that Sarah had picked up another piece of linen, only this time to fit the table with as many leaves as Mary could put in it. With the family increasing Sarah knew that before long Mary would have to spread the table out larger and use the bigger tablecloth. Johanna had told them just the other day that another baby was on the way.

Lee had brought word of an incident and accident that he had heard about at the depot. Earl Conway's wife had been brought into the hospital suffering from a fall, or so he said. Her leg was broken and she had multiple bruises all over. She had been six months along with a baby and had lost it in the hospital. When word got back to her parents, they came to see her, talked to her and took her home with them. Conway was furious. A fight with his brother-in-law and father-in-law had resulted in him landing in the hospital. The minute he had gotten out of there, he had gone to the sheriff and demanded his wife's relatives be put in jail. Nothing was done as the sheriff put him off, knowing how Conway was and figuring he had it coming to him. Leaving the sheriff's office in furious rage, he had driven too fast on a turn, lost control of his car and had gone over the embankment. Bud Hucker, a neighbor who had left town right after him, saw how he was driving and saw him go over the bank. He stopped and went to help him, only there was no helping him as he was dead.

After Lee told the story, he glanced at Sarah. She had intently watched him telling what had happened. After the others had commented on it, she added, "I can't feel sorry for him. His wife is lucky. Now her hell is gone." Never one to swear much, they all looked at her surprise. She meant every word.

Mary got up Christmas morning feeling worn out with no ambition. She was also tired of having her mouth hurt. She had finally made the decision to go to the dentist and have her teeth pulled after the first of the year. The pyrorrhea had finally rotted her gums and her teeth ached every time she ate. She envied Victor his good set of teeth.

Christmas Day she was content to let others set the table and get the meal. As Mary was never a shirker, all wondered why. Victor thought it was probably a let down from the heavy load she had been carrying. All the baking and then her ma, the baking for both places, even with Sarah helping, had been a chore. The squabble with her sisters had worked on her and their attitude at grandma's death and funeral had not helped make it any better. Then the letdown of all those years of baking for Labit's and Labit's going after the hospital baking too, he felt had worked on her. She had kept going as long as there was the butchering work and then getting ready for Christmas. But with that over now, he felt she would probably need a little time to just rest up.

The next day Mary was in bed sick.

"Can't keep nothing down and she's got the chills," Victor told Gertrude when he went upstairs to get her out of bed before he went to the barn. "Suppose it's the flu."

"Good thing you've got Sarah here, Pa, as I got to go

back to Eppersons this morning."

" I know you're supposed to but a snowstorm is brewing out there and getting worse all the time. I don't know if I'll be able to go with you or not."

By breakfast, the decision not to take Gertrude and her girls back had been made. It was snowing so hard and the wind was starting to blow so that it was hard to see to get from the barn to the house. It was like looking into a sea of white. Tony had hurried home and Victor told him not to try to come back until it was better. He had the stock over at his place to take care of and Victor said he would do whatever had to be done here at home.

"Mary ain't any better?" he asked Gertrude at noon.

"No. Sarah ain't come down yet and when she does, I'm going to tell her she can go home if she wants to. As long as I'm here, she can stay up there. We don't both have to be here. I don't think there was much planned for doing today anyway."

All that day Mary was sick. The next day she wasn't any better. The third day her stomach was settled but she had a full chest, a runny nose and the sniffles. By the fourth day she had a full-fledged head and chest cold, along with chills, fever and a hacking cough.

By this time Sarah was doing the doctoring as Victor had taken Gertrude back with the sleigh after he and Tony had gotten the roads opened with the horse-drawn snow plow. Sarah got out the goose grease, warmed it and Mary put this on her chest, while Sarah greased her back. A warm towel was wrapped around the woman. These were alternated with a mustard poultice, a mixture of dry mustard and warm water spread on a cloth and also applied to the chest. Victor had made her hot toddies with whiskey, sugar and hot water. All this made her sweat so much that Sarah was changing the bed several times a day and Victor once during the night. The sixth day, with Mary no better, Victor went into Ponta and asked the doctor to come out. He confirmed what they had feared. Mary had pneumonia. He left some bottles of medicine to go along with what Sarah and Victor had been doing. He told Sarah to make some chicken soup and feed Mary the broth.

Nothing seemed to help. She was getting weaker and weaker. Her chest was full and her breathing could be heard across the room. Fear gripped the household. This was a dreaded thing. Pneumonia was a killer. If you lived through it, it took months to recover. Victor lay by her side those nights listening to her breathe. Terror gripped him. He feared his Mary was dying and this finally became a reality. Eight days after she came down with the stomach flu, she was dead.

"What a hell of a way to begin the new year," Victor told the family as they gathered together waiting for the casket to be brought back to the house for the wake. "Who would have thought a year ago when her ma was laid out here, that Mary would be dead the next year."

"Her sisters and their families are coming?" Gertrude asked. "You got ahold of them?"

"I telephoned them," Lee answered. " I only called Aunt Tillie. She was going to let Aunt Bertha and Aunt Fern know. They know when the funeral is and the wake. I waited for a call back if they needed someone to meet the train or what they intended to do. They never called so I don't know what they decided."

"Maybe they'll just come to the church," Tony said.

"That could be. They ain't very welcome out here, not since Pa and them got into that fight over Grandma." Lee answered.

"I worry some about Sarah too," Johanna said. "Mary was just like a ma to her."

"Better than her own ma but far," Lee told her. " I talked to her some and I know Pa did too. He wants her to stay here and keep house for us. So she's going to. She really don't know where else to go."

"She'd have to get a job like I have if she left here so she might as well stay here," Gertrude added.

"She's got some money," Tony told her. "And she knows how to hang onto it too but she ain't got the word, what is the word I want to use....."

"Experience," Lee interrupted.

"That's a good word. I think she'd have a hard time She has trouble talking to strangers."

"She's staying here," Lee assured them. "You wouldn't have wanted to go through what she did as a child."

"I figured she must have had it hard," Johanna said. "She don't say nothing about when she was a child."

"You wouldn't have wanted to live it," Lee told her as the rest looked at him in surprise.

"What happened to her?" Tony asked.

"It ain't my story to tell," Lee answered.

Tony had guessed right about Mary's family. They came by train and went immediately to the church. When the immediate family followed the hearse to the cemetery, they went back to the depot and soon after were on their way back to their homes.

"It will be a long time before I forgive them for that," Gertrude said when they sat down to dinner after the burial.

"They ain't worth the worrying over and fretting about," Victor told her. "They ain't worth it. Best forget they ever existed."

CHAPTER VIII
1933

The days were very busy for Sarah as she tried to keep up with the housework in both houses. Many noons, she'd set the table for Victor and then go home to fire her stove, taking enough food for Cora Lee and herself on a plate and they'd eat it at her little house. Victor wanted to be alone. He appreciated her understanding. She knew he wasn't sleeping as well as he should have been. He worked long hours outside and in the barns. Tony sometimes complained that Pa was looking for extra things to do when there already was plenty to do but he realized that the man was trying to fill in every hour, trying to make up for the void in the house. Victor had told the family he was so thankful for the company of Cora Lee and Lee those long evenings. Cora Lee's chatter and Lee's steadiness helped fill the emptiness.

"There is a pattern for everything, I guess," he told everyone one Sunday morning late in January. " Sarah and Grandma come, Grandma dies, the baking ends in town, Mary gets to visit Ida and Frances for the last time, only Mary didn't know that. Gertrude has a new home and Lee comes home. Everything that happened we wondered why but as time goes on, the pattern gets clearer."

"Almost scary," Tony added.

"Somewhat, but that's how it is. Mary was so glad for Sarah's help and I sure am too. I don't know how you feel about everything, Sarah, but you doing the work here in the house has been a godsend for me and for Lee too with Cora Lee."

"You and Mary helped me when I badly needed help and now I'm returning the help," Sarah answered. Before she looked down at her plate, Victor noticed the tears in her eyes and knew she missed his Mary too.

Sarah spent her spare time sewing many things from the bleached feed sacks such as pillow cases and bed sheets, nighties and underwear for Cora Lee and herself. The nighties she trimmed around the neck, hem and sleeves with pieces of dress remnants. She had debated and finally getting courage had asked Lee if she could make Cora Lee some other clothes the little girl needed. Mary had made a few things last fall but she was growing so fast that she was badly in need of almost everything. He gave her money and she and the little girl went shopping when Victor went to Ponta. He even treated both of them to dinner at Labit's. It was the first time either had eaten in a restaurant, something Sarah wouldn't forget for a long time.

"Imagine," she told Johanna. "You ordered what you wanted. They had several dinner specials written on a blackboard, you picked what you wanted and they had it cooked and brought it to you, you ate and then they cleaned up after you. No dirty dishes to wash or nothing. You just got up and walked out the door, oh after paying for it of course. Sure couldn't do that many times. Costs too much."

Sarah enjoyed the sewing she did for Cora Lee. Using several patterns, she made her one good and three everyday dresses for summer, two winter jumpers with blouses and a lightweight coat for spring and fall. She also made her several pair of overalls and long-sleeved flannel shirts for cold weather use. Having enough flannel and using an old overall yet from Uncle John, she made her one pair of lined overalls for really cold weather. Victor thought that idea was the best thing she had made the little girl. It kept her nice and warm when she followed the men outside the rest of the winter. Other items made included two new slips and a garter belts to hold up her long brown cotton stockings.

After long thought, Victor hesitantly asked Sarah if she could, maybe, line him a pair of overalls like she had done Cora Lee's and also make him a hood to wear over his head for blizzards. The hood would tuck under his jacket collar, go over his head and button under his chin. He had seen someone wearing one in town and would like one too. Talking this over with Johanna, they came up with a pattern for the head hood and also, using a pair of bib overalls for a pattern, they lined a pair of bib overalls for Victor and one for Tony. The men were very thankful for the hoods and lined overalls the rest of that winter and coming ones.

This again was the winter for small snows, only one good snowstorm but many days of wild cold winds, followed by Chinook winds. The big blizzard, the end of February, came with such a blast that the barns were hard to see through the whirling snow. Days were spent scooping out paths and trying to keep a bare road open to the main highway. Those nights Lee was forced to stay at Windsor at the boarding house. He found he didn't like this. He missed the ranch and the companionship of the people there. But he was so thankful for his job. He had heard of many others that had worked for the railroad that had been laid off. One man in Windsor worked with Lee at Hennison and was now working at an oil service station for fifteen dollars a week and mighty glad to have a job at all. He didn't see anybody riding the boxcars during the cold of the winter but knew that summer would bring plenty of that. Most of these men were good hard-working men, if only the jobs were there for them to do. The Depression was hard on everyone.

By the last days of March it looked like the end of the long winter. Days were getting warmer. A day of warm rain hastened the advent of spring. The gumbo was a sea of mud, gooey sticky mud. Four-buckle boots were caked thick and it wasn't very long before everyone was as sick of that as they were of the winter months.

The only good thing the men could see about the mud was the hope that this was the end of the drought. There had already been two years with enough dryness and poor crops and everyone sincerely hoped this had come to an end. The lake on the far north of the ranch was once again full of water and the river also was full.

All longed for the flowers, green grass and baby animals. And these came too. By the middle of May, there were baby lambs, calves and even a colt as Bonnie had become a mother. As often as she could find a few moments free, Sarah had been checking on her mare and each time she was greeted with a neigh as the horse came to be petted. Victor waited until she was done with dinner dishes one day before telling her she would probably find something if she went to check on Bonnie.

"And you didn't tell me until now," she accused him as she flew to get her jacket on.

"I knew I probably wouldn't have gotten any dinner, if I had," he answered, laughing as he watched her run out the door.

"You're right, you probably wouldn't have had any either," she answered. Victor and Cora Lee joined her. A wobbly little colt stood by his mother, getting his first dinner. "Ain't that a beautiful little animal?" Sarah asked them.

"It is a fine colt," Victor answered. Watching a few minutes more, Sarah took an excited little girl to the house for her nap. Sleep was hard coming that afternoon.

And when her pa came home that evening, Cora Lee dragged Lee down to the corral to show him Bonnie's little baby.

"Bringing her back to the ranch was the best thing I ever did," he told his pa later.

"And Mary and I were so glad you did."

"I got to go down to Hennison." Lee said. "Anne's pa

died this morning and the funeral is day after tomorrow, Saturday. I got a wire this afternoon at the depot. I'll go down by train tomorrow after work and come back on Sunday."

"You gonna take Cora Lee?" his pa asked.

"Yeah. I'm glad Sarah made her some new clothes. I asked her to pack up some things for Cora Lee and I'll take her along with me in the morning. It'll be a long day for her but I can take her to the boarding house for a while. She's got a little boy about the same age and they can play and also take a nap so she won't be so tired. "

"She'd probably sleep on the train if she don't happen to nap," Victor told him.

"I'm really dreading going back there," Lee said. " I don't know what Annie's ma is gonna do with him gone... Always closed-mouthed about money but I know they own the house but her pa was the one bringing in the paycheck every week and her ma's so scared of staying alone at night that I don't know what she'll do now. Everything seemed to scare her at night. Daytime, when she could see outside, then she was all right but night was something else. John used to get so mad at her 'cause she'd have him running around outside trying to see what was making this noise or that sound. I don't think she's gonna handle losing John very well. I understand Selma's there now. She sent the telegram."

"That's Annie's sister's name? For the life of me, I can't remember her ma's name," Victor said.

"Her ma's name is Frieda and her pa was John. Selma's a school teacher. Anyway, I'm not looking for this to be a nice time. Selma's a very nice person but not at all like Annie. She always liked to be alone, by herself, liked to be away from the family. Far away, not one to run home for anything. Annie was so happy and made you feel good. Selma was different, hard to get to know 'cause she never said much or told you much about herself."

"Annie was a nice-looking woman but if I remember

right, Selma was the good-looker of the two, looked like her
pa. Dark black hair and dark eyes, thin and tall, real thin
while Annie was like her ma, shorter and more stout, brown
hair and not as good-looking," Victor said.

"Selma's still good-looking."

"Not nice to have to live with afterwards, death that
is," Victor told him. "Once in a while you wait for it to
come 'cause it gives the person rest, like Grandma, but most
of the time, it's hard to find any peace with yourself after
someone you love goes and leaves you. Kind of like to blame
them for going and leaving you here alone and behind."

"Yeah, I know Pa," Lee answered. "I went through it
too."

"I'm so happy to get back here," Cora Lee told Sarah
as she stormed in the kitchen door. "And I've got to go and
see that little colt. He's got to have a name, you know, Sarah,
you can't always be calling him the little colt."

Sarah grinned as she watched her bolt across the yard.

"She didn't even change her clothes, did she?" Lee asked
as he came into the house, carrying their baggage.

"No. The chicken soup's ready so if she don't come
back right away, we'll have to call her and then she can change
before she goes back out again." Sarah finished getting the
food on the table, while Victor went back outside to fetch
the little girl. Soon they were sitting down to enjoy the hot
supper.

"You've got to give him a name," Cora Lee told Sarah
again.

"I have."

"Oh. What is it?"

"My uncle John had a horse that looked like Bonnie's
colt. He called it Stormy. And so that's what I named him.
His horse had the same dark brown, mixed with black color-
ing, so much darker than just brown, and all one color too.
So he's Stormy."

"Oh, I like that name. Will he be wild like a storm is?"

"I don't know. I don't suppose so, 'cause he gets plenty of petting and really is spoiled," Sarah answered.

"And how was the funeral?" Victor answered.

"Awful," Cora Lee answered before Lee could. She got quite a look of reprisal from her pa. "Well, it was, Pa."

"That ain't very nice to say though," he told her.

"But when grandma died here, it wasn't like what it was down there."

"I know, Cora Lee but there's a difference in people. Some handle things like that better than others. You done eating?"

"Yeah, and I wanna go back outside and see the cats and the dog and Stormy."

"Then go," Lee told her. Waiting until she got outside, he told them, "She was right about it being awful. It was. Sit, Sarah. I want you to hear all of this 'cause I'm afraid we're gonna have company out of this, company none of us want. I tried to talk Frieda out of coming here. I don't think I got the job done. I told you, Pa, before I went that I didn't know what Annie's ma was going to do with John gone. Frieda's been in a panic ever since John died. Selma is about fit to be tied. Frieda latched onto her like you wouldn't believe. She wants Selma there every minute and especially at night. I said she was scared to stay alone and that ain't changed. And to make it worse, Selma lost her teaching job. When she told the school board that she had to go home for her pa's funeral, they told her they had a man, with a family, that needed her job worse than she did 'cause she could go home to her ma's. So she ain't got a job now. So Frieda latched onto her and told her she had to stay with her from now on. And Selma ain't one to want to be hung onto."

"Ain't there some other children there?" Victor asked "I thought Annie had another brother or sister."

"She has a sister who lives in California and a brother that lives in Ohio. Neither came to the funeral. Her sister didn't have any money to come with and the brother has been out of a job for about a year now. His wife cleans in a hospital to keep them eating."

"So what happens now?" Victor asked.

"I don't know. Selma was going to look for a job, even a housekeeping job somewhere but she don't want to live with Frieda. Selma wanted me to move back and live with Frieda. She said I owed her ma that for taking care of Cora Lee after Annie died."

"You paid Frieda for taking care of Cora Lee, didn't you?" Victor asked.

"Yes. And am I ever glad I did. Selma quit throwing that in my face when I told her I paid her ma for taking care of Cora Lee. She didn't know that and she shut up after that. Frieda asked how you were getting along now with Ma dead. I told them about Sarah keeping house for you and living in the little house. And that was a mistake cause Frieda put it together that maybe something could be worked out for her to keep house for you. I tried to get it through her head that you wouldn't go for that but I don't think I got it done. So I wouldn't be surprised to see them come on the train here. I thought about it coming back, that maybe they'd decide to come here and see if something couldn't be worked out for Frieda to come here."

"No, that ain't gonna work. This is my house and my ranch and they ain't going to tell me what to do. Annie's ma would drive me right up a wall."

"But what I'm afraid they'll do is try to make Sarah feel guilty about being here and get her to leave, then Frieda could say that you need a housekeeper. See what I mean, Sarah?"

"Yes," she answered slowly.

"You think they'll come and badger Sarah?" Victor asked.

"I don't know. I thought about it on the train and it just could happen. I hope not but I can see it happening. I just wanted you both to know how it was and what could happen and how Frieda could get nasty to Sarah. I don't think Selma would be but Frieda just might. 'Course Selma is desperate to get out of her ma's clutches so I'm not saying that she won't push too."

"Hell's bells! No wonder Cora Lee said it was awful. They ain't gonna shove Sarah out the door though. We've got a lease agreement," Victor said, adding, "I don't want them here and if we all stick together, then we'll be all right. They'll have to leave cause there won't be any room for Frieda here. I don't owe them anything and neither does anyone else here."

A week later Selma and Frieda arrived. They had sent a telegram to Lee, only he didn't get it as he left the depot before it came Saturday afternoon. When they got off the train at Windsor Sunday afternoon there wasn't a soul in sight. Setting her ma down on the bench by the wall, Selma walked several blocks past a lumber yard and a creamery until she came to some houses. No one was home in the first house, nor the second, nor the third. The local doctor and his family lived in the fourth house. Noticing a car parked in the driveway, she pounded and pounded until she finally roused him from a Sunday afternoon nap.

"You want something?" he asked.

"I'm looking for some help. And nobody seems to be home anywhere. My ma and I came in on the train. We were supposed to be met by Lee Labella but there's no one there when we came in. My ma's sitting on the bench by the depot now. Do you have a telephone I could use to call the Labellas?"

"They don't have a telephone, I know that for a fact," he answered.

"Oh dear. You real sure of that?" Selma asked.

"I'm very sure of that. Lee and I just talked about it the other day. The only thing I can see is for you to go over to the hotel, about a block west of the depot and take a room for tonight until the depot opens tomorrow. Then you can talk to Lee yourself."

"And who are you please?" Selma asked.

"I'm Doctor Druga, the doctor here in town."

"Would you know of anyone I could pay to take us out to Labellas? Could you take us out to Labellas? I'd be glad to pay you for the trip."

"I'm not taking anyone anyplace this afternoon. As I said, go to the hotel and get a room. They serve food there so you'll make out all right." Turning slightly as he heard his wife call, he told Selma good-bye and shut the door.

Sighing, Selma walked back to her ma, helped her up and then carried their luggage the block west to the hotel.

"You left me all alone sitting there in a strange town, and now you're gonna make me walk to a hotel and we're supposed to pay for a room and food," her ma complained. "I'd of thought that you could have found someone to take us out to Labellas seeing as how Lee couldn't put himself out to be here to meet us."

"It didn't hurt you to sit there and wait for me. And I told you before, the doctor said there wasn't anyone to take us out to Labellas and I'm tired and want a bed to sleep in and I'm hungry and the hotel has beds and food, he said, so that's where we're going. I can't do any better than that, Ma.".

"All right. All right, already. Let's not squabble. It's just that we ain't got much money and now we got to spend some more on a place to sleep and get something to eat."

"I would have liked it better if I could have spent some time looking for a job and after finding one, find someone to stay with you instead of going on what could be a wild goose chase here."

"I don't want anybody else staying with me. You're my daughter and you should love your mother enough to want to spend the rest of her time on this earth with her."

"Ma, we'll drive each other crazy."

"Well, that's why we're here. If I could keep house for

Lee and his pa and live with them, then you can go back to living alone since that's what you so badly want to do. I still don't know why you can't stand being with your ma, after all she's done for you."

"I know Ma, I know. I've heard it all before. But if we can't talk Lee into moving or his pa into letting you stay there and keep house for them, then you may have to have someone else stay with you. Just wait." She held up her hand to stop the flow of words she knew was coming. "I don't know where I'm going to find another job and it might not be close enough so that I can come home every night."

"Knowing you, probably won't try to hard to find one in town either."

"If we could get Lee to move or his pa to let you keep house for him, then you could rent your house to someone. Then you'd have the income from the rent plus having free room and board, plus maybe a little for your wages. That would be the ideal setup. But we may have a hard time to get that done. If we can get rid of that housekeeper of Lee's pa's, whatever her name was, then we'd have a chance to get you in there."

"We're gonna have to work hard to get something done 'cause I don't want anyone else staying in my house with me but you and since you're bound determined to be alone somewhere else, then we've really got our work cut out for us to get something else done here. It's either get Lee to move or get that woman out of there."

Lee had the two women on the depot doorstep early the next morning.

"And why weren't you here to get us yesterday?" Frieda asked.

"I didn't even know you were coming," he answered.

"Selma sent a telegram Saturday afternoon."

"It didn't get here before I left or I'd have sent one back to you not to come," he answered. "At least not for a while until you get everything settled at your house."

"You know we need your help, Lee," Frieda whimpered.

"Did you try to get a job, Selma?" Lee asked her.

"There ain't many of them to be had," Frieda quickly answered.

"I looked a little but I didn't have much time," Selma answered.

"I'm afraid she won't find anything there," Frieda said. "Ain't you even going to invite us out to where you live?" Frieda asked.

"I can't go home until this evening. I got to stay here all day and be here when the trains come through. You better go back to the hotel and settle down there for the day. The train leaves at five fifteen this evening."

"I don't want to go home," Frieda told him.

"I take the train back to Ponta and then I drive home from there."

"Oh, I see. Then we'll go with you when you leave this afternoon."

"I'm afraid so," Lee answered with a sigh. "Leave your luggage here."

Pulling her ma by the arm, Selma helped down the steps and up the street toward the hotel.

Victor, seeing more than one person in the car that evening, knew immediately what had happened. Going toward the car, he went to greet them.

"I see you brought some company back with you, Lee," Victor told his son.

"I found them this morning at the depot, Pa," he answered.

"We came in yesterday, Victor," Frieda told him. "Selma sent a telegram but Lee said he didn't get it Saturday, so when we came in yesterday, there wasn't nobody there to meet us. The local doctor told us about the hotel and we stayed there last night."

"Good thing there was a hotel," Victor told her. "You would have spent a long night otherwise. Come on in, I think Sarah has supper ready. Don't know if she has enough for two more but there's always bread and butter."

"We ain't fussy, you know that, Victor," Frieda told him.

"Sarah, we've got company," Victor said, "This here is Frieda, Mrs. Strode, and her daughter, Selma Strode. This here is Sarah Hysell."

"I'll just get two more plates," Sarah said.

"Oh, I hope we don't make too much extra work for you," Selma told Sarah. "Is there anything I can do?"

"That's her job," her ma told her. "That's what she gets paid for, 'course if it's too much extra work, then I'd be glad to help you. Some people just ain't fit to take on extra work like some of the rest of us."

"It's all ready now," Sarah answered, lifting her eyebrows as she looked quickly at Lee. A slight smile crept on her lips as she noted the thunderous expression on his face. Before anything more could be said, Cora Lee bolted into the room. Stopping before her pa, she looked at the two visitors and then slowly went to Frieda's open arms and allowed herself to be hugged and kissed.

"Then let's eat," Victor said, gesturing for the rest to find a chair while Sarah poured the coffee and got milk for Cora Lee.

The next morning, Selma made a point of getting up earlier enough so she could talk to Sarah in the kitchen while she was getting breakfast. Baking powder biscuits were cooling on the cupboard while the canned blood sausage was heating in the oven. Coffee was perking on the corner of the stove.

"Hello, Sarah," Selma told her. "Anything I can do?"

"It's all ready, waiting for Victor and Cora Lee to come in," Sarah answered her.

"Lee's gone already?" she asked

"Yes. He leaves early to get to the train," Sarah answered.

"I got a problem I want to talk over with you," Selma said. "That coffee smells good. Any chance of getting a cup?"

"Sure," Sarah answered, pouring her a cup of the fragrant brew.

"Like I said, Ma and I have a problem. Pa was the one who brought home a pay check every week and now he's gone. And I got laid off from my teaching job when I came home for the funeral so now I have no income either. And with jobs so hard to find and Ma feeling Lee owes her a favor, we hoped Lee would find a place to stay where he works, not have to come back here every night. Then Ma could stay and keep house for him. But from what he keeps saying, he isn't going to do that, so the only other solution Ma and I could see is for Ma to stay here and be Victor's housekeeper. There isn't any money coming in when I don't have a job. And when I do find one, it maybe away from here. Ma needs security now and being here, with other people and relatives, would give her that security she needs with Pa gone. Only one problem, you would have to leave so Ma could have the job you do. Lee owes Ma many favors and the family here don't owe you anything. They gave you a job but now someone else needs that job so I hope you understand you may have to move on."

"Lee said you were a teacher," Sarah said.

"I've taught for twelve years now. The school I taught at now has a man teacher as the school board felt he needed the job worse than I did so they gave him my job when I came home for the funeral."

"That must have been hard for you."

"Yes it was. Would it be hard for you to go back to your own home, to your ma and your family? It's hard to tell someone else how difficult it is to lose your parent. I have to find another job and I don't know where that will be. Ma is so afraid to stay alone and working here as the housekeeper would be just right for her. She wouldn't be alone, 'course she'd have to move into the house here. She'd be afraid to stay alone in that little house up there, where you stay . And with Lee and Cora Lee here in the house, no one would talk about her being here. What are the chances of you being charitable enough to do that for her? You do understand what I mean?"

"I understand real well," Sarah answered. "My ma is dead and so is all my family. And I'm not leaving here," Sarah told her.

"But if you were told to, then you would." Selma told her "If we work this out with Lee's pa, then you'd have to. I'm sorry but that's how it is. I have never been one to push things onto other people but sometimes it's a case of having to look out for one's self. I hope you understand that I don't like to have to do things like this but I have to look out for Ma and myself."

"It ain't that simple," Sarah said. "The ranch Tony's living on is mine. We signed an agreement, lease I guess you call it, for a number of years. That included my living here and working for Mary and now with her gone, then working for Victor. It also included Tony and Johanna's living in my house and me living in the little house. Those years aren't up yet and I'm not leaving, breaking that lease."

"You mean you have money?" Selma asked her eyebrows raised in disbelief.

"I own the ranch and have some money besides that, if that's what you mean." Sarah answered.

"That lease included your living in the little house you live in?"

"It does. Yes."

"Oh, here's Victor for his breakfast. Where's Cora Lee?' Selma asked.

"She's coming soon. Just staying with Tony until he goes home for his breakfast," he answered.

"That's better that's she isn't here. Can I talk to you quite frankly right now?"

"What's on your mind?" Victor cautiously asked.

"Sarah and I were having a talk before you came in. I think Lee probably told you about Ma being so afraid of staying alone. I never saw anyone so scared of being alone at night. We hoped to talk Lee into moving into Windsor and having Ma being his housekeeper but he don't want to leave the ranch here. We wondered then if Ma could be the house-keeper here. Sarah could find a job elsewhere. But Sarah says there is a lease or some agreement and she wasn't able to leave because of the agreement."

"Sarah works here. Lives in the little house. Tony and Johanna live in the house on her ranch... I repeat, *her* ranch and we rent the ranch she owns. If that is what she told you, then she told you right 'cause that's how it is."

"That kind of makes it hard to work out something for Ma here," Selma answered, obviously defeated.

"There ain't nothing to work out here for you and your ma, Selma. I'm mighty fussy who I let come into my house day after day. Mighty fussy. And me and Sarah get along. She gets along with Cora Lee. She got along with Mary and Tony and Johanna and with everybody. She has her own home, she goes home when the work is done."

"Victor, I wouldn't have come here at all and asked anything of you but there's problems to be worked out with Ma and I really don't know how to correct them."

"Lee tells me that you want very much to live by your-self," Victor said.

"Yes. I told Ma that I have to find a job and it might not be close by so I'd help her find a roomer to stay with her, or an older lady that needed a home so she wouldn't be alone. She's not afraid during the day but nighttime is something else. She had me outside looking to see if there was some-thing by the house. There was. A cat. Crying out loud. I don't know how Pa stood it all these years. Now the other night at the hotel, she slept like a baby. I don't know the difference but there were noises in the hall but they didn't bother her. I tell you, Victor, if I have to live with her I'll go crazy. I like to live alone, by myself. I don't like living with anyone. I'm a fussy old maid and that's the way I like it."

"She don't want a roomer or an older lady with her?"

"No. She can't understand why I don't want to live with my Ma."

"How much is Frieda gonna hound Lee by telling him that he owes her for taking care of Cora Lee, 'cause he paid her for doing it?"

"I didn't know she was paid."

"Well, she was." Hearing someone in the stairway, they turned to see Frieda coming down.

"Victor, I can't imagine anyone like you having a son like Lee. You seem to be a man that when he owes a debt , he repays it." Frieda told him.

"And what do you mean by that?" he asked.

"Lee owes me plenty for taking care of Cora Lee when Annie died."

"He paid you every time you took care of her and you know it."

"I don't remember," she answered.

"Oh yes, you do. And he did pay you so he don't owe you anything. As far as Sarah is concerned, we have a written signed five-year lease with a lawyer drawing it up. It's legal. I think Sarah told Selma but I'll tell it again. After Sarah's ma died, Sarah inherited the ranch. We had a lawyer draw up a lease. We leased her ranch. Part of the lease said that she, Sarah, lives in the little house here and helped Mary at that time and now with Mary gone, she still works here. Also in the lease is the agreement of Tony living in Sarah's house on her ranch. This agreement is for five years."

"It can be broken," Frieda told him.

"It won't be broken," Victor told her. "Get that through your head. You're not coming into this house," he told her.

"I know the panic you feel, Frieda. Mary ain't been dead that long, you know. It's a terrible thing to have to be alone."

"But you're not alone. You have Lee and Cora Lee living with you," she told him.

"Yes, for now. But someday Lee probably will marry again and then I'll be here alone. And it don't make any difference how many live with you, some days you still feel like you're alone. Selma said you don't want anyone else living with you but Selma. Maybe you'll have to have an older lady live with you, or a couple that need a home. I don't think it would be hard to find someone that needs a place to stay these days. Or a roomer that would work during the day and pay you room, board too, if you fed her. That way you'd have a little money coming in. If I remember right, that's a big house you got so maybe you could take in several roomers. That money coming from them would take the place of the money John was bringing home. And you'd have someone in the house at night."

"I always was afraid at night," Frieda whispered. "Would you take us back town, Victor? I can see we ain't gonna get any help from here, so the sooner we go back the sooner Selma can start to look for a job and maybe someday we'll get this all settled so she can live by herself again, since she's bound determined to be alone. I can't stand being alone and she can't wait until she's alone."

"It will never be the same again, Frieda," Victor told her. "But maybe if you get tough enough in your thinking, it will be livable again. We'll eat first and then I'll get the car out so you can be on your way."

"And who has a birthday?" Lee asked

"I do," Cora Lee answered. "I do, Pa."

"And how old are you going to be?"

"Four years old," she answered, holding up four fingers.

Sarah and Victor watched with amusement.

"One more year and she'll be in school," Victor said.

"One more year, Grandpa?" Cora Lee asked

"That's right." he answered.

"Do you suppose if we ask Sarah she would bake a cake for this birthday and we can have a little party with Tony and Johanna and Martha too?" Lee asked Cora Lee.

Her eyes danced with anticipation. "Would you?" she asked Sarah.

"You bet and you can watch," was the answer.

"What about a present?" Victor asked when she had run outside to play.

"Nothing. A cake'll be enough and with everyone here to party with her, that'll be enough. I'm going to get her some crayons today so she'll have something to open."

"Would you buy her a tablet too, and I'll give you the money to pay for it," Sarah asked him.

"And pick up a couple of pencils from me," Victor told him. "She loves to take one of mine and draw on paper."

"All right. I'll pick this all up today, at noon and then she'll have some presents too.

"You ever given a birthday present before, Sarah?" he asked

"No."

"Ever been given a birthday present? Or had a party?" Lee asked.

"You know the answer to that. I don't have to answer it," she replied.

"Well, maybe we'll have to change that this year," he answered.

"Best to forget it," she told him. "Get it right out of your head."

The next day the cake was baked. Several tablespoons of the cake batter were put on a small pie plate and baked to see if the oven was the right temperature. After the sample was baked the rest of the batter was baked. Cora Lee was excited. She jumped and clapped and run and sang until Sarah told her she had to be quiet so the cake wouldn't fall in the oven and be a very flat cake that no one could eat. Then there wouldn't be any cake at all because there wasn't time to make another.

Johanna had suggested to Lee that she and Sarah combine their food and have a birthday supper instead of a party in the evening. Shortly after Martha had her nap, Johanna brought over freshly baked buns and a jar of canned peaches that went well with the canned chicken and broth Sarah intended to thicken for gravy and the potatoes already peeled to be cooked. Between the two women they had the table set and everything ready, waiting for Lee to get home and the rest to finish their outside work. Sarah had sent Cora Lee to watch for Lee.

"She sure is excited," Johanna told Sarah.

"Has been all day. You should have seen her when I baked her cake. The sample I baked to see if the oven was hot enough I gave to her to eat after it baked and she was so excited that I was afraid she'd choke on it," Sarah answered. "Here are the men. We don't even have to see them, I can hear Cora Lee."

While Cora Lee blew out the candles on her cake and opened her gifts, Sarah watched with a funny feeling inside her. She hadn't felt this way for a long time, as if she was missing something, like something was lacking. Chiding herself, she plunged into the dish washing with vigor. The sooner she got over that feeling, the better off she was.

But that feeling came back to her again that night while she lay in bed trying to sleep. She had so much to be thankful for. She had a nice home now, a loving dog lying right outside her porch door, a good place to work and nice people around her. But what happens when the five years are up? What if there are changes? What if Lee marries and moves his wife in here? The thought of never seeing Cora Lee again made her suddenly ill to her stomach. The thought was terrifying. The thought of never seeing the family again gave her shudders.

"Got to get out of here for a while. I can't sleep anyway," she told herself. Dressing, she silently let herself out the door and, with Bud on her heels, headed toward the corral and Bonnie. She needed to ride again, needed to get on Bonnie and see the hills and the valleys and the lake. She needed to think about something else but what drove her out of her bed that night. Standing by the corral fence, she picked up and stroked one of the cats from the barn that had found her in the night. Bud gave a quick bark, startling her into dropping the cat, getting scratched in the process.

"I scared you. I'm sorry," Lee told her, coming up beside her to stand by the corral fence.

"You did scare me. I thought everyone was asleep," she answered.

"So did I. I finally got Cora Lee to sleep. She was so tired, yet too excited to even think of sleeping. Then I talked to Pa a while. He went to bed and I thought I would walk outside and have my cigarette out here. It's so nice tonight."

They stood in silent companionship for a few minutes.

"When you going to learn to drive that car of your uncle's?" Lee asked.

"I thought everyone had forgotten about that," Sarah answered. " I remember your pa saying he was going to leave it down by Tony's until I could learn how but that's been a long time ago and I sure don't have any more urge to drive now, than I did then. The few times I have to go to town, I just ride along with your pa. Whatever would I need to learn for?"

"One thing, you could take lunches up to these guys when they are working away from home. A hot meal, instead of a jelly sandwich. And another thing, Cora Lee starts school next fall, a year from now and I won't be able to take her, with my working and I don't want to move away from

here. But I'd have to rely on Pa taking her, or Tony and I
hate to give them another job. If you drove, you could take
her some of the time."

"I'm dumb, Lee. Too dumb to ever learn that."

"I thought you were over that by now. Hells bells,
woman. You are so far from stupid and dumb it's laughable.
You talked to Selma, told her just how it was. You sew like a
dream, have taken care of Martha for Johanna, take good
care of Cora Lee and she adores you. You do so many things
and do them so well. What's dumb about you? I don't want
to hear you say anything so stupid again."

Sarah looked at him and then felt the tears coming in
her eyes. Turning away she leaned her head on the fence
post, feeling the tears streaming down her face. Sensing he
had made her cry, Lee tried to turn her face to his. She re-
sisted, forcing him to take both her shoulders, turning her
body toward him. Seeing the crying, he put his arms around
her and held her tight against him until he felt the sobbing
was done with.

"I'm sorry Sarah," he murmured. "So sorry, I wouldn't
hurt you for the world."

Rubbing her head with his hand, he sighed. "I won't
ask you about driving again but when you're ready to think
about it, let me know and I'll teach you. As for being dumb,
you are one of the smartest women I know. And don't you
ever forget it." With that he left her, going into the house.
By this time Bonnie had found her and stood silently while
Sarah stroked her face and petted her neck. In about an hour
Sarah left her and went into her little house, while Bud settled
down on the porch right outside her door.

CHAPTER IX

It was so hot. The chickens spent most afternoons lying under the shed, trying to stay out of the sun. Some days there were hardly any eggs to gather. Milk for the house was also down. The cows stayed in the shade of the trees by the river, hardly bothering to eat at all. Victor was irrigating the gardens late in the evening trying to keep everything alive and growing.

Waking up at night, they could hear the coyotes howling. Victor thought they were coming to the river at night to get water and to hunt. The men had moved the sheep closer to the buildings because of this. Several range cows had freshened late in the season and the coyotes killed one of those calves for food.

"I don't care how many rabbits and jack rabbits they eat," Victor said. "They ain't fit for humans to eat anyway with the boils they got in them. But they could stay away from the cattle and sheep we got."

"Guess you can look at it this way, Pa. That many less to feed when there ain't much hay on the range to make."

"Still makes me sick to see a torn-up calf or sheep. They can go eat prairie dogs, they ain't good for anything but making holes that horses can break a leg in."

"I checked the wheat this morning, Pa, and I wonder if the grasshoppers are gonna leave anything at all. They've hatched good this year. Winter sure didn't get rid of any eggs. There's scads of them, lots and lots of them. The place is just hopping wild with them, alive with them, every step you take. The ducks and geese can hardly waddle these days, they eat them until their crops are so full they can't hardly walk."

"I heard at the mill this morning that just south of us, they're eating everything up, leaves off trees, branches. Thick enough in some places that the fence posts are hanging thick with them. And Hucker, Bud, said the other day that someone in Kansas had written his cousin that they ate the eyes out of horses and cows down there."

"Maybe we ain't got so much to complain about, they ain't that bad here. I don't think we'll get any wheat though, at least not much, although I suppose we'll have to thresh just to get the straw, at least we can feed that along with hay and get the range cattle through the winter. Need some for the mattresses too. Ours feels like a flat pancake."

Sarah was tired of the heat and sick of her long-sleeved dresses. They felt so warm when she put them on in the morning, she could hardly tug them over her arms. She stood in front of the mirror, hot and irritated. Pulling the dress back over her head, she looked at her scarred arm in the mirror, turning first forward and then backward. Defiantly she took the scissors from the top of the sewing machine, and poised, ready to cut. She just couldn't. Years of habit were too strong. Once more she slipped on the dress, tugging it into place.

"You have no guts," she told herself. "Lee told you that you were as smart as anyone else. But you're not 'cause you'd cut those sleeves off otherwise. You'll just have to suffer 'cause you have no guts." Almost to the porch door, she swung around and nearly running, went back into the bedroom, grabbing the scissors and pulling the dress off, slammed it down on the kitchen table. Hardly measuring to get the same length cut off each sleeve, she whacked off the material above the elbow. Another cutting got it even on both sleeves. Holding the dress up, she shuddered.

"Can't quit now. Got to hem the sleeves and then I'll see what I've done." Hemming done, she pulled the dress back over her head and, walking back to the mirror, looked at the results. It didn't look that bad. Her scars showed but not as much as she thought they would.

"Well, you done it. You went and done it," she told herself. "And if anyone says anything, I'll just make like I didn't hear them. But if Lee says anything, I'll hit him. I just will. Maybe, just maybe, one of these days, I'll show him and learn to drive too. Look out Bud," she said pushing the dog aside as she came out the door. "Move it 'cause I'm late to work now."

Although Victor knew something was different about Sarah's dress, he really didn't figure out what was it was. Tony had other things on his mind. This hot weather was making Johanna miserable. One little baby to take care of and another one on the way was almost more than she could bear. Cora Lee noticed the scarred arm and started to ask Sarah but realizing the little girl was going to say something, Sarah turned her attention to something else and the Cora Lee didn't mention it again.

Sarah knew she should have made something hot for Lee for supper but just couldn't bring herself to firing the kitchen stove to cook anything. It was hot enough in there yet from the baking she had done early that morning and from their noon meal. Running last minute to the cellar, she grabbed a jar of pickled carp and a jar of head cheese to go with the fresh bread. Lee was in the kitchen when she came back in. He looked, squinted, raised his eyebrows and then walked around Sarah.

"Not one word or I'll hit you," she told him.

"I didn't say anything," he answered.

"And if you're smart, you won't," she replied. Then astounding herself, she added, "And I'm ready to learn to drive too."

Lee whooped with laughter. It rang all over the house. Victor came in and wondered what was the matter.

"Better look out, Pa, Sarah's ready to take on the world." Lee answered, grabbing Cora Lee as she ran to him. "Hi, little one. Just one quick hug cause it's too hot for anything else."

Victor agreed and the rest of the meal was spent talking about the weather, its effects on the animals. For the second year in a row, there wouldn't be much wheat to harvest and a scanty hay crop.

After supper dishes were done, Lee looked at Sarah and asked, "You ready to start that lesson?"

"Now?"

"Just as good a time to start as any. And we'll use my car. I don't even know if your uncle's runs. It ain't been ran for a couple of years or so now. It'll need some work done on it so we'll just use mine. It's the same as your uncle's, a Model A Ford. Come on now, or were you just talking for the fun of it?"

"I ... you're sure..." she stammered. Catching the mocking look on his face, she stalked to the door, calling to him, "Come on then. I'm ready." Lee shrugged and looked at his pa who was grinning from ear to ear.

"Now this ought to be something," Victor told Lee as he headed toward the door.

"She know anything about a car?"

"I'm sure she don't," Lee answered. And when he asked Sarah, she shook her head no. He motioned for her to get in and he spent time explaining how to start the car, the brakes, the shifting lever, first, second, third and reverse gears, the clutch and the gas pedal. He started the car and showed her how to shift, how to get from first, to second and to third gear and how to use the brake.

"Now it's your turn," he told her, getting out and going around to the passenger side. "You're in this too deep to back out now, Sarah," he said, seeing her hesitation.

Swallowing back the panic, she moved over to the driver's side and started it, carefully pushing down on the gas pedal to keep it running.

"Now, push in the clutch and shift to first. Then let out the clutch carefully and at the same time press down on the gas pedal. Good girl. You've got it moving. Now press down on the clutch and shift to second. Good. Now push down the clutch and shift to third. Very good. Now drive around the yard. When you come to the gate, drive through it and drive down the lane. When we get to the highway, we'll stop and turn around and drive back. That way you'll learn how to shift into reverse."

By the time Lee thought she had driven enough for one day, Sarah was exhausted but jubilant. Her first venture at driving had been a success. Climbing out of the car, she threw her arms wide and hollered,

"I did it. I did it, Ma. I can't believe I did it."

Lee grinned as he watched her. "And you did a hell of a good job, too," he told her. "Now we'll try to drive some every night and then before long we'll drive into town and you can learn how to drive there. By the way, Sarah, Cora Lee told me about your cutting the sleeves off your dress and she wondered about the scars. I told her that you had gotten hurt, I didn't know how, and that you didn't like people talking about it. I don't think she'll talk about it to you. I don't think Pa or anyone else will say anything at all to you. Going back to Cora Lee, she might try to pet your arm or something like that 'cause she still remembers how her arm hurt when she cut it and she really thought you had a bad ouchy."

"Thank you," she murmured as Victor walked over to where they were standing.

"She's a natural," he told his pa as Sarah walked away.

A week more of driving on the dirt lane, and then early Saturday morning Lee and Sarah made the drive into Ponta.

Sarah learned how to meet another car and how to park. She soon realized a whole new world had been opened for her. It was only two miles from the ranch to Ponta, so she knew she could do the shopping now that had been Victor's job before. And she knew he wouldn't mind at all of being relieved of the burden.

Several more weeks of driving Saturday mornings in town and then Lee took her to get her driving license. She passed with flying colors.

"See," Lee told her when they were driving back home. "I told you that you weren't dumb."

"But I have such a hard time telling myself that. You've never been told that from little on that you were stupid and dumb and ugly. Cora Lee is lucky. She has such a nice family that take such good care of her."

"We love her," he answered. "Say that word, Sarah, say love. Say we all love her."

"You... all... love... her."

"Such a little word that means so much. Got a new problem. It just came to my attention yesterday. You remember Selma and her ma Frieda?"

"They ain't easy to forget."

"Selma got a job at Hennison. She got a job working in the clinic there. As a receptionist and answering the phone and keeping books. And I guess she got a room near the clinic, close enough to walk to. And Frieda did take in a couple of roomers. Anyway, one of the nurses at the clinic has a sister, Eliva Veroff, living in Windsor. She and her husband, Clyde, own a grocery store in Windsor. I don't think Frieda meant to start any trouble for anyone here, in fact I am sure she didn't but she did tell one of her roomers about coming out here right after John died and them thinking maybe she could keep house for Pa and me. The roomer must have taken what Frieda said wrong and since one of them is a sister to one of the nurses at the clinic, this roomer talked to her sister, the nurse about it . By the time the story came back to Eliva and Clyde it sounded like Frieda and Selma were thrown out the door by that old man Victor and some hussy who lives there and they say keeps house for them. She made it sound like you and Pa were having something shady going on. You had better park the car while we talk about this. You're driving all over the road. Here, drive down here. This here road runs along the river and we can get home from here."

Sarah looked at Lee with tears and hurt in her eyes while he continued, "Clyde Veroff came down to the depot to collect some freight and asked me about it. I told him that Selma was related to me and how. And I told him what happened and that I don't think Frieda meant to make anyone any trouble.

"He thought it was real fair of me to tell him all this and he figured I told the truth. He had met Selma once and had told his wife she seemed real nice. He said they would make sure his sister-in-law got the story straight. And she could talk to Selma about it too, which I guess nobody did. Anyway, when he was ready to leave, and I had helped him load up his freight, I told him that I intended to marry you but just hadn't told you yet."

"Are you serious?" she asked, staring at him.

"Very serious. I've been for a long time but I knew you weren't ready to even think about marrying a man or going anywhere with a man, even to a school program or to a movie in town or anything. And of course, there's another problem, when you're ready to consider marrying, and that's church."

"I don't know what to say, Lee. I don't know anything about being married. I don't know anything about being a mother. My own ma sure didn't teach me anything good or how to be a good ma. I don't know if I ever want to get married. I just didn't ever think further than working here for your pa and keeping house and living in the little house. I know that I'd miss all of you people so bad if I left. I never gave a thought to what would happen if your pa married again."

"You've had a lot to get used to. A different sort of life. You've done real well. You're a good cook and a good house-keeper. Cora Lee thinks the world of you. You've become the ma she don't have. Think about that. Anyway, that's the story that's been going around the hospital so now you know. And I'm dead serious about getting married. You can have all the time you want to think about it but don't just put it out of your head. You think about it serious. Now let's head for home and you can tell everyone you passed the test."

"What's that shiny golden line across the prairie, Grandpa?" Cora Lee asked Victor as she stood looking out the west window one afternoon the middle of August. They had come into the house when it looked like there might be a rainstorm approaching. Thunder and lightning, with wind swirling the dust in clouds, was the extent of the storm.

"I don't know," he answered. "What you say you see?"

"Come and look then," she urged. Getting up from his chair, he went to satisfy her. Looking into the distance, he could see the line had grown into a full-fledged prairie fire that lightning had started.

"Oh, that's a fire and with wind out there yet, it'll spread like crazy. Got to get Tony and we'll have to get word out so we get some help fighting this." He ran out the door, got into the car, and headed to Tony's house. After talking to him, he took off for town to get help. Before very long, wag-ons with large cattle tanks filled with water were being hauled toward the fire. Cars and trucks, filled with men, crawled across the dry prairie. By this time, with the help of the wind, smoke and flames filled the sky. Tony had hitched up a team of horses onto the single bottom plow and was head-ing that direction.

"What's Uncle Tony gonna do?" Cora Lee asked Johanna as the women watched.

"He's gonna plow ahead of the fire to try to keep it contained in the burnt-out area. And the men going out there have shovels to pound the flames out and some have gunny sacks they're putting into the water tanks, getting them wet, and pounding on the flames."

"It's scary," Cora Lee said, grabbing hold of Sarah's leg.

"Yes, it is," the women agreed. The men didn't come back at chore time, so with Cora Lee's help and direction, Sarah went to the barn and milked the cow. Everything else seemed to be all right. Sarah had Lee check before he went after work to fight the fire too.

About seven o'clock, Tony came back and asked if the women could put together something for the men to eat.

"Just some sandwiches, bread and jelly'll do fine. We've got water to drink but nothing to eat. I think Leon Rumney, lives west of here a ways, went back for food too. And so did Joe Morshian's kid. And there's food coming from people in town too. Got about fifty men and kids out there and we've got all we can do to keep it from going out of control. We're all hoping the wind'll die down now with night coming on."

"Do we have to worry about the buildings here?" Johanna asked.

"Not right here as long as the wind stays where it is, but it could burn everything south of the buildings if the wind continues the direction it's going now. And that puts it plenty close to Ponta." He watched as the women sliced bread and smeared jelly on the slices. Putting them together, they made up all the bread they had on hand in both houses. Tony thanked them, kissed Johanna quickly and rode back toward the smoke.

Toward nine o'clock, the wind died down and with the fire break that had been plowed, the fire was under control before midnight. Most of the men stayed close, lying down on the hard prairie dirt to rest during the rest of the night in case it started to burn again. For some of the men, this was the month of fighting fires. Almost every day the trains had made fires along the railroad tracks, sparks flying from the wheels onto the dead dry grass ignited into fires, some small but some large and dangerous.

Johanna was angry, very angry. She had been telling Tony that the fence along the house wasn't very good. The posts looked like they were slanting and when she touched them, they rocked from side to side and that they had rotted off right under the ground. She had reminded him of the fence that very morning and he had told her one of these days, when he had time, he'd get around to fixing it and, anyway, it wasn't that bad. She was the only one getting up in a roar about it. The cows were still in the pasture, weren't they?

A couple of cows this very morning — after he mocked for her reminding him of the fence — got into a fight, leaned too heavily on the fence and broke it down completely. It didn't take long before they and a dozen more cows in that area had walked over the top of the barbed-wire fence and to freedom. This freedom included the washing Johanna had started to put on the clothes line just an hour before that. The first cows through took down the clothes line, the next ones through went over the clothes, trampling them down into the ground. As Johanna came out the front door carrying more clean clothes to be hung, the first cows ran past her. Setting her basket down and screaming at them, the second batch of cows ran past. She couldn't see anymore cows coming but she did see her freshly washed clothes lying in a dirty mess on the ground.

About that time, she could hear Martha toddling behind her. Scooping her up, she took her back into the house, shutting her in her bedroom where she couldn't get into trouble. She gave her a piece of bread to eat and went back to pick up the dirty clothes she'd have to rewash. Dumping the dirty mess on the floor, she let the bawling Martha out of her room and just stood, hands on hips, and wished she had

Tony there to tell off.

Just thankful she hadn't washed the new flannel she'd bought for more diapers and sleepers, she finished the rest of the wash and then carrying out the water, she filled the machine with fresh clean water she had heated after she could see she had to wash again.

"Not done washing yet?" Tony asked as he came in for dinner. "Don't look like any hanging on the line drying yet? Have a bad morning or something?"

"Let me show you something," she said, taking him by the hand. "You see that fence? That's what it looks like when it ain't fixed up properly and cows lean against it and get out and trod all over my clean washing I had on the line. And past the house. I don't know where they're at now, I suppose over by the big house somewhere 'cause they didn't go down the lane. And let me tell you something, after dinner you're going to take over the washing to the big house so I can hang them to dry and your gonna fix that fence good... You understand? Good. And also my clothes line. Now let me show you what clothes look like after cows have trampled over them"

By evening, the fence was fixed with new posts and new barbed wire, the wash line was up again, tight and sturdy and the clothes dry from hanging on the wash line by the big house. Some of the clothes would never look the same as they did before the cows found them as the stains never came completely out. After Johanna cooled off, the family had a good laugh about the cattle and her washing.

The end of August, Martha had a baby brother, Harvey. Cora Lee loved the little baby. She had taken to sneaking over there to see him, a habit the rest did not appreciate. They didn't want her making a pest of herself.

"Oh, I don't mind her coming. When I don't want her here, then I just send her home. She sits real good and I give her the baby to hold and usually he stops crying until I can take care of him. And she's taken Martha outside and played with her too. Really, she helps me a lot," Johanna assured Lee when he scolded her.

"You're sure?" he asked.

"I am and if I don't want her here, I'll just tell her she'll have to go home."

"You do that."

Sarah knew Lee had watched her as she sometimes held the little baby. He had said nothing more about wanting to marry her but she knew he was only biding his time. Most days she just put the thought out of her head. To marry and have children of her own was something so farfetched, so unbelievable. Her ma would have said she was too dumb to have any babies of her own. Yet as she held little Harvey, thoughts of her own baby whirled through her head. To be responsible for such a tiny thing was a fearful thought.

During this same time, Lee got a letter from Frieda. She wanted to see Cora Lee. She asked if Victor would let her stay one night. She would await Lee's return letter as to how to proceed.

Lee talked to his pa and Victor agreed that Frieda certainly could see Cora Lee. Lee wrote for her to come. He did ask that she come on a Saturday so he could bring her home when he came from work and would be home the next day, when she was here. The visit was set for the first weekend in October.

"Well, how did it go?" Tony asked Lee after they had gotten back home that afternoon and Frieda was sitting on the porch talking to Cora Lee.

"Pretty good. Sarah had everything done and was gone when we got here. I suppose she's in the little house."

"No, she went riding with Bonnie. I guessed you told her you would take Frieda out for supper in Windsor. They ate supper early here so Sarah could have dishes done and be out of the house when you came back with them. She felt

Frieda should have as much time with Cora Lee as she could have."

"We got something to eat in Windsor before we left town. She hadn't had anything much to eat since she ate the lunch she packed for the train ride."

"Frieda looks good."

"I think so too. When she wrote she said she had some things she wanted my advice on. She hasn't told me yet what they are."

"Cora Lee is growing so fast. And she talks a mile a minute," Frieda told the men, when she joined them.

"She's happy here," Lee told her.

"Selma still working at the hospital and living alone?" Tony asked.

"She's still living alone. I walked over to see her the other night. She keeps her place spotless clean. Another reason why she didn't want to live with me. I didn't keep everything as spotless as she wanted everything to be. One of my roomers is a nurse at the hospital and I asked her how Selma did at work and she told me, kind of on the sly 'cause she ain't supposed to be saying anything about anybody. Anyway she said Selma did her work perfectly and kept everything she touched clean as a whistle."

"You think she's happy working there?" Lee asked.

"No. She's found a teaching job again about sixty miles east of here. The teacher got sick and someone down there knew Selma was out of a job and knew she was a good teacher, which she is, and so she got called. She's moving next weekend and starting to teach the Monday after that."

"You'll miss her," Lee said.

"Yeah, I'll miss her but she won't miss me. Lee, I wondered if you would help me. I need some information and then if it looks like it would work, I need somebody to just tell me if I'm doing the right thing."

"What's on your mind?" Lee asked.

"One of my roomers is a nurse, guess I told you that

before. Her sister and brother-in-law own a store here in Windsor. They told her that the Windsor Hotel is looking for a housekeeper. There is an apartment that goes with the job, a nice one, I was told, upstairs on one corner of the building. The hotel is nice. Selma and I stayed there that one night when we came out here last time. I want to know if you know anything about the people who own the hotel and also go with me to see what kind of a job it would be."

"This job would be for you?" Lee wanted to know.

"Yes. The nurse I was telling you about, she'd like to buy my house, keep on working and keep roomers too. I gave my roomers room and board but she'd set up the rooms so they could cook in them and do their own cleaning."

"Sure, I'll help you."

"Another reason why I'd like to live in Windsor is that my other children live so far away, so Cora Lee is the only family I got here and living here, I'd see her once in a while."

"You told Selma any of this?"

"I told her and she thought it would be a good idea. "

"I see Sarah coming. She must have been riding," Lee said. " And here comes Pa too and Tony."

"Where is Cora Lee? I forgot about her."

"She ran down to Tony and Johanna's when you were talking to me. They have a new baby and she really likes her. She helps Johanna by playing with Martha, her little girl, and when Johanna don't want her there, she sends her home."

"She's got it nice here."

"We all have," Lee answered.

"I know there's pie there for lunch," Victor told them. "As soon as Sarah gets her horse put away, then we'll go into the house and have some lunch before we settle in for the night. Sarah took the last of the canned pumpkin and made pie and I can't hardly wait for a piece."

The rest visited quietly as Sarah bustled around the kitchen, getting plates on the table for the pie and coffee cups for the hot coffee perking on the stove.

"You ready to sell your house then?" Victor asked Frieda.

"I think so. I guess it's time to move on and do what I have to do. I know I can't keep on with the roomers forever 'cause the house needs fixing here and there and I can't do and John ain't here to do it anymore. So it would be a good time to sell it. And with Selma moving again and anyway she don't want to be bothered by anyone, even her mother, I'd like to be near Cora Lee and see her once in a while 'cause the rest of my family are so far away and no money to go visit them and they ain't got money to come and see me. I never in my life had to make any decisions about anything until John died and I knew I had to get someone in the house with me 'cause Selma sure didn't want to stay with me, and I got my roomers. I finally started to make decisions of my own. First time in all these years and now with thinking of selling the house, well, I thought about this plenty after I was told of the job here and there was someone to buy my house. I've did things I have never had to do since John died, like carrying out the ashes, buying wood for the stoves, paying the bills, deciding what had to be paid when I got the money from my roomers. John took care of all of these and then I suddenly had to. I guess that's why I went into such a panic after he died cause I never had to do any of those things. And here I am again, an old lady going to start something else in my old age. That's why I wanted you to help me, Lee, 'cause I need someone to get behind me and give me the final push, if you think it's a good idea." Glancing away from Victor, she caught Sarah watching her with the funniest look on her face. "Well, what's on your mind?" she asked Sarah.

"I think you are really, really great. I admire you. I have an awfully hard time making up my mind about anything," Sarah answered.

"Sometimes you got to take the bull by the horns and do it," Frieda told her. "I didn't have any choice after John died 'cause I finally got it through my head that Selma wasn't gonna help me with anything. Selma takes care of Selma and that's all she takes care of,"

"Then I guess if you can do it then I can do it too and take the bull by the horns," Sarah told them. Saying each word very slowly, she repeated, "Take the bull by the horns," and, in a rush, she finished the sentence with, "and tell you all that I'm going to marry Lee, I don't know when yet but I am going to marry him."

"Good girl," Lee told her "Good girl."

Victor reached over and took hold of Sarah's hand and asked, "You really are going to marry Lee?"

"Yes."

"I'm glad. As glad as Cora Lee will be. And when that comes, I'm gonna move into the little house. You'll have to keep it clean for me, but I'm gonna move up there."

"I don't want to shove you out of your home," Sarah protested.

"After you get married, this house will probably be filled with babies, bawling at night while I want to sleep. No, I want my peace and quiet and that's where I am going."

"Do you think I'll be a good ma?" she asked Victor.

"I think you'll be good. Look at Cora Lee, she thinks you're great and she's a pretty good judge of character."

"And so do I," Lee told her. "So do I."

"And so do I," Frieda said. "Cora Lee will be well taken care of."

The next morning Frieda and Lee went into Windsor and talked to the owner and his wife. The hotel was looked over, the unfurnished upstairs apartment inspected and what the housekeeping job involved discussed. The present house-keeper intended to work until the end of the year when there was room for her to move into her daughter's home. This suited Frieda very well as she had to finish the selling of her own home, decide what she wanted to keep out of the house and what had to be sold.

It was decided Frieda would move her belongings into the apartment between Christmas and New Year's Day. She would start work on the second of January.

"I hope I've did the right thing," she told the family when she was ready to leave Monday morning with Lee.

"I hope so too," Lee told her.

"It ain't like it was before, Frieda. It just ain't," Victor added.

The ranch had more visitors in October, late in October. A car drove into the yard one evening about six o'clock. An older man and a woman got out. Both medium built with graying hair, he with a dark suit, white shirt and tie, and she with a light weight coat and hat. Sarah didn't recognize either of them, nor did Victor.

"We're looking for Sarah Hysell," the man told Victor when he went to see what they wanted.

"Sarah is here standing on the porch." He waved for her to come. The couple watched her walk toward them.

"You wanted me?" she asked Victor.

"These people are looking for you," he answered.

"We stopped down at the place where you used to live and we were told you were here. I don't suppose you know who we are. You were only a little baby when we last saw you. I'm your ma's sister. I'm Lorna Bowser and this is my husband Leroy."

"I didn't even know Ma had a sister. You don't look like Ma but you look some like Uncle John."

"Your ma didn't look like any of the rest of the family. John and I looked like our ma. There were two other sisters but they're dead now too. The last one, Ida, died about a month ago. When the letter came back that the lawyer sent to your ma and to John that they both were dead, we decided to come and try to find out what happened to you.

"And now we found you. There is a fairly large inheritance that'll be divided up between Ida's sisters and John, only he's dead too, and their children."

"How many sisters did Sarah's ma have? "Victor asked

"There were five of us. Gert, Ida, Bertha your ma, myself and our brother John, I'm the only one left of the five. John never married? " she asked Sarah

"No," Sarah answered shaking her head.

"And Ida never married. Gert has two sons and I have ten children. We live about a hundred miles east of here, in a town called Sandy Mount."

"I know where it is," Victor said. "We're ready to eat supper and you're welcome to stay."

"We'd like that," Leroy answered. Finishing supper preparations, Sarah had very little time to visit. Victor kept the conversation going with the two people, something Sarah was very grateful for. Lee was coming in the door as she was just ready to dish up. Cora Lee followed him, giving the screen door a slam.

"Careful," Lee warned her. "You know better than come in like that."

"This here is another son, Lee and that is his daughter, Cora Lee. Cora Lee's been down to my other son's house, Sarah's house, what used to be her ma's. They live there. Lee's wife died a few years back and they moved back here when he was transferred to Windsor as a depot agent. He rides the train back and forth every day to work. This here is Lorna and Leroy Bowser. Mrs. Bowser is Sarah's aunt, her ma's sister." Lee went forward to shake their hands, giving Sarah a quick look of surprise as he did. She shrugged slightly.

During the supper meal, Sarah responded slightly to the couple. She asked a few questions about her ma's family, offering very little information when asked in return.

"Your ma never told you that she had sisters, did she?" Lorna asked Sarah.

"No."

"And John never told you either?" she asked

"I never knew there was any other family but them," she answered.

"I don't know how your ma treated you or John and I hate to say anything against her, but when we left here the last time we saw her or you or John I felt very sorry for you. I don't know how to say this, and maybe I'm very wrong, but your ma was a cruel woman. At least she was to all of us, just like she had the devil in her." Lee and Sarah looked at each other. "I often wondered what kind of a life you had."

Sarah shrugged her shoulders.

"When did you move over here?" her aunt asked.

"Sarah moved into the little house right after the funeral. And my son Tony moved down to her house and has lived there ever since. Sarah lives in the little house back of this house," Victor answered.

"I'm glad you found somewhere nice to go. I'm very glad 'cause everyone wants to be treated nicely. How did your ma and John get along?"

"They understood each other." Sarah replied.

"I often wondered why he stayed with Bertha. Why he worked there and maybe it was because he wanted to make sure you didn't get hurt too badly," Lorna told her.

"You were about a year and a half when we saw Bertha and John the last time," Leroy told Sarah. "We had come as a surprise 'cause she never invited anyone. We took one look at you and I got sick all over. I went behind a shed and threw up. You were so bruised and beaten from a fist, I suppose, that it just made me sick. Lorna and I didn't know what to do, so we went to the minister in Ponta and he came out and talked to Bertha. It made her so mad that she told us to never come back again and I doubt if she went to church again. John never did go to church but Bertha used to. Her husband, your pa, Marvin, was a minister's son, " Leroy told Sarah.

She didn't answer, only made a movement of her hands.

"Was there anyone else in your family that was like

that?" Lee asked.

"No. I don't know why Bertha was like that. She was the oldest one," Lorna answered. "But it just seemed like Bertha had a mean streak in her. She was the one that killed the kittens and the puppies and even a calf, only she seemed sorry for that. Pa never knew what killed the calf, but she did with a club. She hit it on the side of the head and then tried to make sure Pa didn't see what happened. When he found out she did it, she got a beating for that. She got beatings for the kittens and the puppies she killed too, but not so bad as she did for the calf 'cause the calf was a heifer and it was to be raised for a milk cow. Milk for the kitchen, you know."

"Sarah's ma was bedridden for a while before she died," Lee told them. "Sarah did all the chores and took care of her. John died before her ma did."

"And we never knew, any of us, that John died either," Lorna answered.

"Sarah and I are going to get married next spring," Lee told them.

"I am so glad for you." Lorna answered. "Not a nice thing to say, but it is a blessing for all that Bertha is with her maker. She and the devil. I wonder who'll win the fight."

Two weeks later Lee took Sarah to see Father Weller at St. John's Church in Ponta. He had been the priest at this church for many years and knew something of the people in the area who weren't his parishioners. Some of Sarah's background and her coming to the Labella ranch were familiar to him. He asked Sarah and Lee to come Saturday mornings, as often as possible, so he could go over the teachings of the church with them. He also gave Sarah a book to read because he knew how unpredictable the roads were in the wintertime. The decision whether to become a church member was to be hers in the spring, before the date of their marriage. Although he pushed for her joining the church, he could see no reason why they couldn't be married, if she did not.

Many evenings, Lee sat with Sarah and they went over the teachings in the book the priest had given her. Lee realized he was also getting an update on his own religion. There were many things he had forgotten.

It was a busy fall following a very hot summer. Soon the bitter cold would fill the sky again and winter would be upon the prairie.

CHAPTER X

Gertrude wrote her pa that she was coming home for Thanksgiving. They would be there that morning as early as possible. Johanna, Tony and their two children would also be there for dinner. Sarah sat down on Monday, after Victor brought the letter home, and figured out how many that would make and how much food she had to prepare. Johanna sent word with Tony that she would make the pies and also come over early Thanksgiving morning to help with the peeling of the potatoes and the many other things that needed to be done.

"I'll help you kill and dress several ducks and a goose on Wednesday," Victor told Sarah on Monday.

"That'll help a lot," she answered. "And I'll set out some old bread to dry for the dressing. I think there's some prunes here yet for it. And next time I go to the cellar I'll bring back a couple of jars of pickles. Get everything done so it's not all left for Thursday. I'll make a bread sponge on Wednesday night after supper and then finish bread and make some sweet dough the next morning. It should be done good by the time the ducks and goose have to go into the oven."

"I don't want you to get up so damn early that morning. 'Tain't necessary. Make the bread the day before and everyone sure can eat bread that's a day old," Victor answered. When Sarah looked at him, he added, "I'm just glad you're here to get the meal for everyone and I don't want you to work so hard doing it. Don't know what we'd have done without you these past months."

"Thank you," she whispered. "Thank you."

By Wednesday night, the geese and ducks were stuffed and ready to bake. Loaves of bread had been baked and thick applesauce made, ready for the sweet dough Sarah intended to make early in the morning. Those were always best when baked and eaten the same day. She had brought up jars of several kinds of pickles and also the potatoes for peeling and cooking the next day. Several small squash were lying on the floor in the pantry to be baked when the fowl baked the next day. Looking around the kitchen, Sarah knew everything was as far as she could go that night.

Early the next morning the alarm clock rang, prodding Sarah out of bed. She laid out on the bed a new dress and apron she had just made several days before. She intended to slip back before dinner and change her clothes. Got too much pride, her ma would have said. She almost put the dress back on the hook before she got hold of herself and dismissed the thought. Ma wasn't there anymore to tell her what to do and maybe, just maybe there wasn't anything too wrong with having some pride in how she looked. Looking at the time she knew if she didn't hurry, the applesauce biscuits wouldn't be done by the time the fowl had to go into the oven.

By seven o'clock the sweet dough was raised, ready to be rolled out and cut into round biscuits. Remembering the time schedule Mary had, Sarah knew she would have them baked before nine o'clock when the fowl had to go into the oven. Victor peeked into the bowl of dough when he downstairs and shook his head.

"Just what time did you get up this morning?" he asked "I thought I told you to bake bread yesterday."

"You did but you didn't say anything about sweet dough. This ain't so bad, not like baking bread too. I got up at five-thirty, only a little earlier than I usually do. There's coffee made if you want a cup quick. I made that first thing, after getting the dough finished." Taking a cup out of the cupboard, she poured Victor a steaming cupful. He took a quick sip, then put a little cold water in it to cool if down.

"That's hot," he said. "I think if I remember right there's some cookies left in here." Reaching into a tin setting on the cupboard, he took out several roll-out sugar cookies to eat with the coffee. "Much as I'm glad Gertrude is coming home, today will be lonesome for me."

"Because Mary ain't here," Sarah agreed.

"You're one of the few I can talk about Mary to. Most people don't want to even hear her name. Like she never was there. It's like when she died, you never mention her again. Thank you for listening."

"I liked her too." Sarah told him. "She was good to me and she did like her family."

"She so liked it when her whole family was around her. We never made much of Thanksgiving, but most times we did have a good meal that day. Even forgot about it one year when we were butchering," Sarah laughed when she remembered, as that was the first year she had been with them. "Christmas she really liked. She liked to sew for the kids and give everyone something for a present. I'm not looking forward to Christmas at all. I don't know what to give everyone, except some money, and she'd say that was a cold gift. Giving money don't go far enough, she always said when I told her she had enough to do without sewing half the night. She felt she could buy material and make the money stretch a lot farther with shirts and dresses and stuff like that."

"Most everyone can use some money," Sarah told him as she cut out the biscuits with a cookie cutter. "But if you wanted to, you could pick out some shirts for the men and little shoes for Harvey for next summer. The women, Gertrude and Johanna could use material for a dress and maybe a little doll for each of the three girls."

"Maybe tomorrow you and me can sit down and see what kind of a list we come up with. But I don't want you sewing nothing for them from me. We'll see about taking a morning to shop early in December. I ain't one to want to wait until right before Christmas to do that. Mary liked to have the bustle of doing some things the last night or so but not me. I want to know it's done in case of bad weather and roads. Now got to go down to the barn. I hear Cora Lee talking to Lee, so they both must be up."

"Sarah," Cora Lee called as she bounded down the stairs. "You got everything ready for today?"

"No, but I'm getting there. Sweet dough is all panned out so it'll smell good in here before long." Giving Lee a quick smile, she told him good morning also.

"You'll have everything done before Johanna gets here," he told her.

"She's got two kids to get ready and I don't," she answered. "She'll be here, I suppose, by ten o'clock and then we'll have the potatoes to do and set the table and have a cup of coffee. Anyway, she baked the pies and that helped a lot. You gonna help grandpa?" she asked the little girl.

"I'm going to see my cats and the dogs and grandpa," she answered, starting to get on her warmer barn clothes.

"You enjoy having Johanna around, don't you?" Lee asked after Cora Lee left the house.

"I like her. She's nice and I don't feel like I'm dumb around her. Raise your eyebrows, but I don't. Some people I do feel that way."

"We all do at times," he answered her. "A guy I knew before I got married, used to run around with him, moved back to his pa's ranch about four miles from Ponta, south of town. I ran into him at Windsor the other day. He invited us down to his place and I'd like to go, both of us go. I don't know his wife, he married her while he worked at Richfork. He asked us to come Sunday afternoon. I told him we'd try. You caught up now. Bring a cup of coffee and sit down for a minute."

Sarah brought two cups filled with the hot brew. He

recognized the hesitancy in her manner .

"You can do it, you know. And there's a first time for meeting everybody."

"Sunday afternoon. We going to church first?"

"I thought so and then eat a big breakfast and then go there afternoon. Leave here about one o'clock and come back about five o'clock. It would be nice to visit with Roy again. I think he said he has four children, three around Cora Lee's age and one a baby. We'd take Cora Lee with us."

"I'd rather not. But if you want me to, I will," she answered slowly.

"We'll get it done, Sarah. I'll probably have to push you every inch of the way, but we'll get there. I see Pa coming toward the house so I suppose he's ready for breakfast. A little one today with a big meal at noon, I suppose?"

"Fry down bread," she answered. "I saved back a little of the sweet dough and the lard's getting hot on the stove."

Cora Lee, coming into the room with her grandpa said, "Oh, fry down bread. Yum, Yum. I love it rolled in sugar."

Sarah punched down the sweet dough once again and then breaking off small pieces, she dropped it into the hot lard and tallow. When it was brown on one side, she took a slotted spoon and rolled it over to brown on the other side. As soon as this side was done, she scooped the hot dough out and put it into a pan to cool. Before long the small cake pan was full of the browned pieces of bread dough. Putting some sugar into a small bowl, she set both on the table.

Sliced bread and currant jelly were put on the table, along with some hard-boiled eggs Sarah had cooked that morning.

"What you got left to do, Sarah?" Lee asked.

"Got to put the applesauce on top of the biscuits now and then they're ready to bake. The goose and ducks are ready to go into the oven so I only got to get the squash ready to bake with the fowl. And then peel potatoes. I figure

Johanna'll be here by then."

"I helped Sarah churn butter yesterday, Pa," Cora Lee told him.

"We made a big bowl of butter, nice and fresh tasting from the cream we skimmed off. Cora Lee helped a lot when she helps with the churning," Sarah added.

"She should help, she's getting big enough to. You got the feeding and some barn cleaning to do, Pa?" Lee asked.

"I got some feeding to do yet. Tony was going to do the barn cleaning before he went home so when he came back he could have on clean clothes. I said I would finish what he didn't get done. We done some extra stuff yesterday so we wouldn't have to be so long out there this morning. I'd like to be done by the time Gertrude comes."

"I'll help you this morning and then you should be done, "Lee told him.

"That would help."

"I want to slip up to the house and change clothes," Sarah told Johanna later. "I think we've got most everything done, just to set the table yet."

"You made up that new material?" Johanna asked.

"Yes. And I want to wear it today,"

"Run then. I'll watch everything," she answered. Taking plates from the cupboard, she started to set the table. Sarah had debated yesterday about using a tablecloth until Victor settled it by telling her to use Mary's, whichever one Sarah had given Mary that fit the table. Cups and glasses were put on, along with silverware. Going through the china cupboard, she took out bowls for the potatoes, gravy, dressing and squash. She looked at the beautiful pickle dish Mary had treasured and finally put it back and found a white bowl instead.

"Harvey, you picked a good time to want to eat. I got time now, so let's get it done. Oh, Sarah," she called from the bedroom when Sarah came back into the kitchen, "I'm going to feed Harvey. I think I've got the table set right."

Victor hurried into the kitchen, stopping to wash up in the wash basin in the kitchen sink. Right behind him was Cora Lee and then Lee.

"Hope you were done in this sink," Lee told Sarah as he started to wash.

"We are," she answered.

"Oh, that's a pretty dress. New?"

"I just made it and so I put it on for today," she answered. "Actually, I hurried to make it so I could wear it today. See, I'm getting better." He grinned and kissed her forehead.

"You'll do fine. Cora Lee know what she was to put on?"

"I set out a dress for her earlier. She'll just throw the dirty clothes on the floor but I'll worry about that later."

"OK. I'm going to change then. Want to be changed too before Gertrude and the girls get here."

"I see a car coming up the lane," Tony said as everyone gathered around the kitchen a few minutes later. "I don't recognize it at all." They watched as Gertrude, the girls and a strange man, tall with red hair, got out of the car and came toward the house. Victor went to the door to greet them.

"Hi, Pa," Gertrude said, kissing his cheek. The two girls echoed the greeting.

"Here, I'll take your coats," Sarah told them while gathering the coats up in her arms.

"Pa, and everyone, this is William Farr. Will, this is my pa, my brother Tony, his wife Johanna and little Harvey and Martha is somewhere. I don't see her now. This is my other brother Lee and this is Sarah. Oh, here is Cora Lee and little Martha. That is my family." Hands were extended and greetings made.

"Actually... Pa... Will's now a member of this family too... 'cause we got married a week ago. Will is Nellie's grandson, Hugh's nephew. He lives near Westfield and owns a ranch there. We both live there now. I moved last week, after we got married."

"I didn't know the divorce was final, had been finished. The last I knew, nobody knew where Orville was," Victor told her, somewhat stunned.

"It was, Pa. It was finalized three months ago. I went to court August twenty-fourth. The papers were signed then. Orville didn't come, his lawyer came instead of him. He lives in Denver, Colorado now, still with the woman he ran away with. After the lawyer finally caught up with him, he was ready to get the divorce finished so he could marry her. I guess they've got two children already and her ma wanted them to get married."

"Who married you?" Victor asked.

"A judge. I can't get married in church 'cause of the divorce and so a judge married us. We went out of state to have it done, took a train, and got married there. I'm sorry Pa, if you don't like it, but it's done and I feel good about it and I hope you can give us your blessing or at least accept it."

"It's a surprise, a shock," he slowly answered. "I guess you know what you're doing , at least I hope so. I think if you had written I wouldn't have been so surprised, that's all. How come you didn't write?"

"'Cause I wanted it all done with before you knew, any of you knew."

"Well... it's..." Victor shrugged his shoulders and then added, "It's over and done with and we'll just accept it. You got to live with it. I hope you're happy. And if you are, it'll be a different way than what you were brought up. I hope you're happy... guess I said that before. It'll just take a while for me to accept. Why don't you dish up the food, Sarah and Johanna, and we'll go into the parlor and get out of your way while you're doing it."

The two women hurried with the finishing touches. The potatoes had to be drained and mashed, the goose and ducks taken out of the roaster and carefully carved while the dressing was taken out of the cavities of the three birds, the gravy made and the squash dished up. Bread was sliced, the pies were cut and the applesauce biscuits put on a plate.

"We got it all on," Johanna told Sarah, "at least I think so. Oh, we got to have another setting, another plate."

"I'll get it and also another chair You want to call them, while I get it done?"

"Come and eat, it's all on," she told Victor. Standing in the parlor door, she could see the conversation was strained.

"Let's eat then," Victor said, getting up and heading for the table. "Where you want everybody to sit, Sarah?"

"You sit where you usually do and the rest can just fill in. I'll sit here so I can pour the coffee."

"I'll sit here by the highchair and Martha will sit here by me," Johanna said. Tony took a place and the rest followed suit.

"Pass the potatoes, Lee. And Tony, get the meat started," Victor said. Lee handed him the potatoes and the meal progressed. Slowly the silence started to fill until the room was full of conversation and gradually there was laughter.

"That was a shocker," Lee told his pa and Sarah that evening after Gertrude left.

"That is was. Mary would have been most unhappy. For the first time, I'm glad she wasn't here to be a witness to it. It would have hurt her terribly."

"It helped that Will's a rancher. At least we have something in common with him. And it'll be better that they live near Westfield and do their business there. He just bought that ranch there, got it for a dollar and a half an acre. Bought it from the government, I understand. It's gumbo and dry but he's going to put in some dams to catch the rain for water for the cattle," Lee answered.

"Yeah, that land's going cheap. Nobody wants it with this drought. Can't find feed for the cattle nor water for 'em to drink. I wondered where he got the money from to buy it. So many are just packing up and leaving their land, like packing and pulling out during the night. Turning the cattle loose to fend for themselves and not telling even their neighbors they're going," Victor said. "You still got to have some money to pay for what you buy, even if it goes cheap, or to at least have enough so the bank will finance the rest," Victor answered.

"He got financing from Hugh and his ma Nellie. He told me that's where the money came from. I guess Hugh had his eye on this land and knew it could be bought from the government. He figured dams could be made to catch what rain there was and also figured to irrigate some for hay. I don't know where he thought to get the water from to irrigate, but Hugh's not dumb by any means so he must have something figured out. Will said Hugh didn't want any more work or land so he and his ma talked about it and they knew Will wanted to get out of the ranch where he was working so they helped him do it. Gertrude said the buildings on the place are quite good. She also said that Hugh was gonna help them out with feed and money, if they needed it to get started. Hugh ain't got any kids of his own so I guess he thinks a lot of Will," Lee answered. He added, "I hope Gertrude's happy. She had a bad deal the first time. I never did like Orville or really trust him. And she said the girls needed a pa and she needed a husband and Will is a good man and will be a good pa. "

"When did she say that?" Victor asked.

"When they were ready to go home. I walked out to the car with her."

"I hope she's happy. It'll take some getting used to," Victor said. "You leaving, Sarah? I would think you'd be tired. You've been up early with the baking and everything. It was a good dinner. I would have enjoyed it better if Gertrude's announcement hadn't come right before we ate. But supper was better. I guess she ain't coming back here for

Christmas. Too far and too many chores for them to make it. You tell her about you and Sarah getting married?" he asked Lee.

"Sure did. She wasn't surprised. And she's glad for both of us. As far as Gertrude is concerned, things change, Pa. I'll walk you up," Lee said taking her hand. "Night, Pa."

It was several days before Victor asked Sarah about Christmas gifts. They sat down at the table and put ideas for everyone on a piece of paper, sifted through the thoughts and finally came up with a shopping list. The men would get bib overalls; the women, material for a new dress; and the little girls, dollies. Using Victor's list as a guideline, she soon had her own shopping list finished. She had drawn Johanna's name for Christmas and knowing her broom was badly worn, Sarah thought this a good present for her. She added a whisk broom. Remembering how much Johanna liked the four scenes of the seasons Sarah had colored and given Mary, Sarah picked out four for her and found frames in the attic at Victor's, and added this to Johanna's gift. Cora Lee would get a few new dolly clothes, plus a new winter coat she intended to make out of an old tweed overcoat of Lee's. She thought it would look nice after she had trimmed it with brown braid. Lee proved to be harder to buy for. She knew, from ironing his shirts for work, that his work shirts were badly worn and she also knew he had no decent good shirt. She finally decided to make him several work shirts and buy him a good white shirt to go with his good suit. She had priced them in Penney's a while ago and she could get a nice one for fifty cents. She hoped he would be pleased.

Their visit to Ray and Molly Parpin's went as planned on Sunday. Sarah had thought and thought on Friday and Saturday about the upcoming visit until it grew to great proportions in her mind. Lee talked to her on the way over and, along with Cora Lee's chattering, the drive proved to be more pleasant than she had ever thought it would be. Seeing them coming, Ray came onto the porch to greet them. He was a big man, the woman that soon stood beside him seemed so tiny by comparison. Her smile was warm and soon she had Sarah at ease. Cora Lee was in her glory. She had three others somewhat her age to play with. They tore outside and soon had a game of anti-anti-over the woodshed going, something Cora Lee had never played before.

"She's going to like going to school." Lee told Ray. "Having kids her own age to play with is going to be great. She's having a good time today."

"She's not bashful, is she?" he asked.

"Not at all," Lee answered. "Can't you tell?"

"Well, let them play and let's go in and visit and catch up on old times and what has happened since those good days." The next hours were spent doing just that. Sarah found those hours went fast for her too. Molly loved to sew and make rugs and quilts and they spent time looking through her patterns and materials. From there they went to recipes and cooking and baking. They were both surprised to see it was almost four o'clock and time for a quick lunch.

"Enjoy the afternoon?" Lee asked as they drove home.

"Yes. She's nice. So tiny next to him. And they got nice children. We looked at sewing and patterns and cooking and recipes and it was nice. Thanks for making me come."

"They both love to play cards so sometime soon maybe we can get together for a game."

"I like to play cards. We spent many hours playing when your ma was alive. Haven't played since then. I think it's hard for Victor to do now. I play solitaire sometimes at home."

"I wonder if pa plays cards when he goes into Ponta afternoons. He used to play in town, enjoyed the conversation and an occasional glass of beer or a cup of coffee. I enjoyed this afternoon. Ray and I had a good visit. All in all, it was a good day, a good day."

Before-Christmas work included the annual butchering of the meat for the following year. The last Monday in November Tony and Victor butchered the pigs, doing three this year instead of the usual two as they had run out of hams and bacons long before the year was up.

"Pigs ain't worth anything when you sell them, can't give them away, so we might as well eat them, now we got our own," was Victor's comment. "And I sure like a good ham sandwich with plenty of good spicy homemade mustard."

The next day was the butchering of the beef. Before they had even gotten everything cleaned up, snow started to fall and by evening there were inches on the ground. Victor looked out the window that night at supper, watching it come down.

"Those flakes are big, huge," he said. "I sure hope we don't get a wind with this. We'll have enough to shovel and plow now without wind piling it up for us."

But during the night when he woke, he could hear the wind starting to howl and feel the draft coming through the window frame. He snuggled deeper under the quilts. Tomorrow would be a hard day.

The wind was still blowing when Victor got out of bed the next morning. He looked out onto a blizzard-covered yard with snowdrifts piled across the driveways and ahead of the barn doors. He was glad Lee had stayed in Windsor last night. At least he didn't have to try to get to work this morning through the blinding snow. He always worried about getting lost when you couldn't see where you were going. Although the horses seemed to have such a sense about finding their way home, more than one person had lost their way during a blizzard and frozen to death. He could remember different times when his pa had tied a rope to the house door and then to the barn door so he could use it as a guide to find his way back and forth. There hadn't been many build-

ings on his pa's yard and the wind and snow whipped through
with a fury.

Sarah came into the house as he was opening the door
to go outside. She stomped the snow off her overshoes.

"You should have stayed up there until I shoveled for
you," he told her. "Looks like you got snow in your overshoes too."

"It's deep out there just in one place where the drift is
so bad between the porch and the washline. We gonna be
able to start on the pork today?" she asked.

"I hope so. We won't do much for plowing this morning 'cause it'll just fill up again so maybe we can get some
done anyway. Enough so you can start on the canning and
the fry down meat. It'll be hard for Johanna to get up here.
Suppose Tony will have to get the sleigh out. Hard to take
babies out. Have to cover them good. Sure could have done
without this," he added, going out the door.

"I told Tony not to bring Johanna up today," Victor
told Sarah when he came in for breakfast. "Not unless it
quits blowing. Ain't no day to drag little babies out so they
catch cold and get sick like Mary did and it ain't no day to
leave wood stoves unattended. I think that house down there
is warmer than this one. I fired your stove before I came in."

"Good. I was gonna run back and fire it right after we
ate breakfast. If you did, then I won't have to do it until right
before dinner. The little house ain't bad for drafts. Seems to
help with it being against the hill that way. The only thing I
worried about with the house that way was rattlers coming
down the hill and crawling under the house."

"There has been one or two that did just that," Victor
told her. "Rattlers have a habit of always being where they
ain't wanted. After Tony gets back, we're going to do just
what we have to for chores and then start to cut those pigs.
Get done what we can and if we have to, then it'll just take a
day or two longer than we figured. It's cold enough now that
the meat will keep good. The only thing that could be bad is

Dummer

if it warms up with a Chinook wind, then we'd have to work on it until it was done, regardless of how tired or late it was. Right now it's damn cold out there. Meat'll freeze now."

The wind quit after dinner. The men cut up several halves of pork and then spent time shoveling and plowing snow. Without Johanna's help, it took Sarah the rest of the day to take care of the meat. After supper, although they were tired, the men cut up another two halves of pork, leaving the other two halves for the next day. What meat she couldn't take care of that night Sarah carried to the spare bedroom for the night. Looking at the frost covered windows, she knew it would be all right.

The next day the men cut up the last of the pork and, with Johanna's help, the pork was completely taken care of.

When Victor came in before supper, he thought the sky looked like some more snow and they woke the next morning to another snowstorm. The only good thing about it was the lack of wind.

"I don't think we were supposed to do the butchering this week," Victor said at breakfast. "It's snowed about six inches already and coming down full blast. Tony figured to bring Johanna over anyway this morning. Wrap the kids in quilts on the way over. We thought we'd try to get at least two quarters of the beef cut today and if we couldn't get anymore done, then the rest tomorrow. We'll have to shovel again, thought maybe we could put off the plowing until tomorrow. Worst is, we have to open one of the hay stacks some time today, one of them close to the barn. Figured to use up another one out farther but we can't get to it without plowing a hell of a lot of snow, so we'll just open the fence on this one for the beef cows. Sure could have gotten along without this snow, at least until next week. Only good thing about it is that maybe some of the water when it melts will go into the dams."

It took two days to cut up the beef, instead of the usual one day. Sarah and Johanna finally got the last of it taken care of Monday evening. Early Tuesday morning, Sarah scrubbed the wash boiler and filled it with the ingredients for the liver and blood sausage. It had turned warm during the night with a Chinook wind blowing over the prairie. All were glad this hadn't happened a few days earlier. The meat had stayed cold until they could get it taken care of. Later that night, after Sarah and Victor had carried the last of the jars of canned sausage to the basement, they stood a moment and looked at their supply of meat for the next year.

"You put this along side what Johanna took home and there's a lot of good eating here," Victor told Sarah.

"Yes. And I'm glad it's done. I hate to ask but when do we do the old hens?"

"In a couple of days. I'm tired of feeding them for nothing. They're only getting fatter and fatter. Be lots of chicken grease for cookies from them though. Much as I hate to even think of another mess, I ain't got any extra feed to waste on them. So guess that'll be Thursday and Friday's work. Give you a day to wash clothes and catch up a little and for us to catch up some too. Hope we don't have any more snow until we get that done. We ain't seen Lee since last Tuesday when the blizzard started. Been a week today. Maybe he'll try to come home tomorrow. Lots more work on the railroad with the blizzard too."

One afternoon the following week Sarah, Johanna, Tony and Victor went into Ponta to do some shopping. The men had worked the day before clearing out the lane to the highway. They dropped off Cora Lee and the two little babies at Johanna's sister's in Ponta, as Tony had stopped there several days before and asked her if she would watch the children while they shopped. For sure, they knew Cora Lee couldn't be along. She didn't miss a thing and by Christmas Day everyone would know what they were going to get. It was hard for her to keep any secret.

Each went their own direction to shop. By now, Sarah

knew her way around the town and where to find the things she needed. Johanna was born and raised on a ranch south of Ponta, so the stores was very familiar to her. Victor had told them they had two hours to get all their shopping done. He didn't want to be late with the chores. Along with her list of shopping, Sarah also had some of his list of Christmas presents to buy. He would take care of the bib overalls but she had to buy the yard goods. He refused to go into that store. The broom and whisk broom for Johanna, Victor would have to get another time.

The most fun was looking in the dime store for the dolls for the little girls. Sarah ran into Johanna also looking at the dolls. When she found out that was what Victor was giving them, she picked out a doll buggy for Martha and also one for Cora Lee, as Tony had her name for the exchange present.

"Are you almost done?" Johanna asked.

"I think so. I looked and looked at this little broom and dustpan set and wondered if I should get it for Cora Lee. She is my daughter, almost. I wondered if I should get her something from just me, besides the sewing. You give your daughter and son something special."

"Yes. 'Taint much but it's something just from us. Why don't you? I know Lee would like that too."

"Guess I will. What time is it? Where is that clock they have hanging on the wall?"

"It's time we paid for all of this and then went to meet the men. It's past the time we were supposed to be there. It's nice in the summer time when you drive and we don't have such a deadline."

"I like going into town with the car but these roads sure ain't what I want to drive on. I hope I got everything right. I don't know if I'll get back into town again before Christmas."

"Someone has to get the herring and oysters," Johanna said, adding "But Victor usually does that, don't he?"

That night Sarah took out what she had bought and spread them out on the kitchen table at her little house. She put Victor's presents in one pile, carefully keeping them folded just right. He wanted her to wrap it all for him. He had looked at them when she showed them to him, right after they got home. But being a man, he wasn't very interested in material for dresses. She was impressed at how good a job he did picking out the overalls for the men.

Looking through the scraps of material she had, Sarah picked out some for the doll clothes she had to make for Cora Lee. As she picked up the dolls Victor intended to give to his granddaughters, she thought how lucky these little girls were. She had never had a doll in her life. And, she thought, if I ever have a little girl she's going to have a doll, the doll I never had. She hugged the two rubber dollies for a few moments and then, thinking she was silly, put them down.

The next ten days were busy sewing. The last week before Christmas was the week of candy making, cookie baking and popcorn balls so there wouldn't be much time then to sew. Some days Sarah came back to her little house to sew in the afternoons. And some evenings she sewed until it was long after she should have been sleeping. But she had the satisfaction of seeing the shirts done. The little doll clothes were a joy to make, seeing the pretty dresses and matching bloomers, along with even a coat for each one from the remnants of an old pair of pants that had been Uncle John's. The winter coat for Cora Lee turned out nicer than Sarah had originally thought it would. The brown braid trimming gave it a finished look. It would be warm and that was important. When she had it done and pressed, she hung it on a hanger and stood back looking at it. She felt very proud of how nice it looked.

This year Tony's family decided to have their own

Christmas Eve at their house. He knew it would be different than it had ever been but the next day they would all be together and with the two little ones, it was just easier to stay home in the evening. Victor thought this was a fine idea. He suggested to Lee that he and Cora Lee go up to Sarah's house after supper and have their own Christmas Eve party.

"I don't want to leave you here alone," Lee told him.

"Maybe I'd like to be alone," was the reply. Finally Lee agreed to this, seeing this is what the man wanted.

"We never opened the presents on Christmas Eve anyway," he told Lee. "That was the time for getting the family together and now with Tony's little ones, it's better they stay home and get them to bed. We'll be all together Christmas Day and open presents like always. As you said once to me, after Gertrude married, things change and I'd like to spend the night by myself, so you all go."

Early Christmas Eve morning, Lee and Tony had gone to the hills and cut down three Christmas trees. One was for Tony's house, a large one for Victor's and a small one for Sarah's. Victor had set his tree in the stand that afternoon and Sarah and Cora Lee had decorated it. Lee put Sarah's in a stand later that day and they would decorate it after supper that night. Besides the popcorn strings she and Cora Lee had made and a few homemade stars they had also made, she had no other things for the tree. She had told Lee this when he said she was going to have a tree but he told her that maybe he would surprise her with something. She wondered if he had anything left from when he and Annie were married. But when he put several small boxes in her hands, she knew he had bought some new things. Opening them, she found the prettiest shiny brand-new round ornaments, silver, red, gold, blue and green.

"Oh Lee, they're so pretty, I'm afraid to take hold of one."

"Take it out, they don't break that easy." He watched her as she carefully took hold of one, hanging it by the hook.

The lamplight caught the bright new surface and made it shimmer. Cora Lee sat on a nearby chair, thoroughly entranced.

"Pa, I never saw anything so pretty," she said.

"Let's see how the rest of them look," Lee told them, hanging on another one.

"The tree looks so nice and it fits just right here in this corner. And it's big enough too 'cause this house is small. A tree like your pa's would have been too big here. Tony could use a big one cause the rooms are big down there, but here, a small one is better." Cora Lee put on the homemade stars she and Sarah had made with Lee putting on the ones toward the top where she couldn't reach. The popcorn strings came next.

"Where'd your pa go?" Sarah asked the little girl. She shrugged her shoulders, then they both watched as Lee brought in one more box, putting it into Sarah's hands. She looked questioningly at him.

"Open it and then you'll know." Inside the box was the prettiest white and gold angel Sarah had ever seen. She was so overwhelmed she just stood and stared, tears running down her cheeks. Carefully taking it out of the box, Lee put it on top of the tree.

"I saw it there in the store and before I left I went back and picked it up and bought it. I thought it was something really special for our first tree." Cora Lee hugged him and Sarah timidly went to him, putting her arms around the two of them. She looked at Lee when she pulled away and saw a glimmer of tears in his eyes.

"That oyster stew hot that you brought up from supper?" Lee asked.

"I think so and we'll have some of the candy and cookies I brought up this afternoon for us to lunch on tonight. I know the coffee's ready cause I could smell it cooking."

"You left Pa some oyster stew?" Lee asked

"Oh, yes. I left him a bowlful and also left him some

herring. I put away a small jar of it for tomorrow, hid it in the pantry. I knew if I didn't that he'd eat it all, all that was left. I don't know why he don't get sick, eating that much herring with all those raw onions. You'd think his belly would get upset."

"He does like it," Lee agreed. "And he never gets sick from it."

After a quick breakfast, after the chores were done the next morning and after the dinner was in the oven baking, everyone opened their presents. Sarah had wrapped the whisk broom and pictures for Johanna, and after she had opened it and thanked her, Sarah went into the other room and brought out the broom for her.

"Oh look, Tony. Boy, do I need this. And I thank you so much," she told Sarah. "And I'm so glad you remembered that I liked those pictures." Cora Lee was equally as impressed with the little broom and dust pan Sarah gave her. She wanted to immediately sweep but was told by her pa to wait until everyone had gone home so she wouldn't hit anyone in the head with her vigorous sweeping.

Sarah's gift from Lee was a lovely necklace and earring set, made of ruby- and diamond-colored stones. She held her breath while Lee took the presents she had wrapped for him. Smiling at her, he opened them, one by one.

"I'm glad for this warm shirt," he said holding up the first flannel shirt, then opening the second package, he found another flannel shirt. "And just as glad for this one. It's cold at the depot, even with wood there to fire the stove, there's lots of cracks for the cold air to come in, especially on a windy day. And this one's not a work shirt," he said, holding up the good white shirt Sarah had bought. "I'm saving this one for our wedding."

Sarah's gift from Tony, who had her name, was a nice piece of flannel for a nightie.

"I sure hoped you wouldn't come into the store material shopping until I was done getting your gift from Tony," Johanna told her.

"It's such a nice piece of yardage, so warm," Sarah answered, stroking the soft green material.

"And I've got something for each of you," Victor said, handing both women a small box. Opening it, they found a lovely brooch. "I know Mary would have wanted you both to have something of hers. I sent Gertrude hers last week. I don't want to keep them, someone should have them and wear them and who else but my favorite women."

Both thanked him with tears in their eyes.

"And now I suppose we've got to get the rest of dinner going," Johanna said. Before long the table was set and everyone seated, enjoying the good food. Dishes done, cards were gotten out for a card game. Johanna chose not to play as she had to feed her baby. More candy and popcorn balls were eaten, washed down with a glass of homemade chokecherry wine.

"Still seems funny without Mary here and also Gertrude not here with her girls," Victor told them during the afternoon. "Not the first Christmas Gertrude has missed being with us. And this year she didn't want to even draw names with anyone here so I suppose she won't ever be home again at Christmas time. Living farther away and on a ranch with cattle, it's so much harder to get away. I hope she can come once at least in the summer time so we get to see the girls some. But this is the first time Mary ain't been with all of us and it sure seems damn empty."

"That is does Pa," Tony and Lee agreed.

Later that night, long after supper was over and Cora Lee tucked in bed sleeping, Lee helped Sarah gather her things together and walked with her back to her little house.

"Now I've got another gift for you," he said, after they got there.

"I got this lovely necklace and earrings," she protested.

"This is something extra," he said, pulling a small box

out of his pocket. Opening it, she found a small diamond solitaire setting in a high gold setting. Her mouth went open and she was speechless.

"Just to let the world know that you and I are getting married," he said, as he took the ring from the little box and slipped it on her finger. Sarah looked at sparkling ring, looked at Lee and burst into tears.

"Tears, Sarah?" Putting his arms around her, he held her tight until the sobbing quit. And she went for a hankie.

"Thank you, Lee. I don't know if I'll ever be a good enough person to deserve a man like you. And a sweet little daughter like you've got," she said. "Such a big job I have ahead. Being worthy of the two of you and the trust you put in me."

"We love you and you'll be just fine," Lee assured her.

Later, she watched him go down the hill toward the big house. She wondered if she'd ever would be worthy of him. She'd been so blessed to have him want her. Lying in bed a little later, she thought back to her ma and Uncle John and the old life. It seemed so long ago and she had come so far since then.

CHAPTER XI
1934

Aside from the one big blizzard and the following snowstorms in November and December, the winter had very little snow. Ranchers were in a panic, fearing this next summer would be a repeat of the previous summers. Many had already sold off cattle to pay basic bills until they hadn't anything left. Depression prices, along with another summer of drought, would drive many more into losing their ranches and the only means they knew for taking care of their families. They remembered well the dust storms and grasshoppers.

The only good thing about the lack of snow cover was the ease in getting around on the frozen dirt roads and lanes.

Victor and the family got to church often that winter. Several Saturday mornings Lee and Sarah went to St. John's to see Father Weller and continue Sarah's religious education. There were things she didn't understand but the priest patiently answered her questions and explained until she grasped what he meant. They also set the date, the first Tuesday in May, for the marriage which was going to attended by only the immediate family and Frieda.

Lee and Victor had talked at length about the changing of houses for the families. Victor knew that he was going to live in the little house. He had made that absolutely clear to everyone. Since Tony worked on the ranch with Victor, they wondered if it wouldn't be better for Johanna and

Tony to move into the big house and Lee and Sarah move back to her ma's house. Since Sarah went back to her ma's house as little as possible and had never gone into any other room except the kitchen, Lee wondered if the house had too many bad memories there for her. He finally decided the right thing to do would be talk to her, feel out her thoughts on it.

"I don't know," she answered. "I don't like going back there 'cause it just seems like ma's in every room."

"It's going to be up to you. Tony and pa ain't pushing you to do it. They want you to go back there only if you think you can. I don't care. I'll be happy in either house." He thought a moment, then added, "We could get paint and wallpaper some of the rooms, that we live in at first. I don't think we can do them all, not enough money. We've got to buy some furniture somewhere, from an auction or someone moving away and that'll take some money."

"If we moved back there, Lee, I'd want it all different, otherwise it'll be just like going back to when Ma was there. I have some money, you know. I got that inheritance from my aunt and I've got that money buried. If we had to use some of it, then we would. I got over four hundred dollars from my aunt, you know. I can't think of a better place to use it than to put into that house."

"That's right. I forgot. Well… then if we're going to spend money, how about making it a lot different. How about tearing out the wall between the kitchen and the little bedroom and making the kitchen bigger? There's two entryways into the kitchen from the back porch and one of those could be closed up and made into a pantry with shelves and hooks for the pans. And the little room back of the parlor could be added to the parlor and it would make it a decent size room instead of two little bitty rooms. I don't know what to do about the bedrooms except paint or wallpaper them and maybe new linoleum, maybe closets instead of hooks for clothes."

Lee thought a few more minutes, then added, "New curtains would help. And there's wood floors in the bedrooms and parlor."

"If we have to move," Sarah told Lee, "things would have to be different."

"If we have to move?" Lee said, "Tain't nobody forcing you to move into there, Sarah. We'd just like you to try. Let's take this a little at a time. You told me once that Molly has a closet in their bedroom that is big enough so she can even put bedding on the shelves. We'll go and see Molly and Ray before we start so I know what it looks like. And maybe put some kind of a closet in each of the bedrooms. And there's several shacky buildings on the yard that I'd tear down and use for firewood. They ain't good for nothing."

"One was used for sheep. The other one ain't good for anything but snakes. I never went into either of them if I could help it. I was always afraid of snakes," Sarah told him.

"Good ones to tear down. You know, your ma's, no, it's your house and not hers anymore. Anyway, your house is larger than Pa's when I think about it. There's a full upstairs and cellar, better than the one here at home. How many bedrooms downstairs?" he asked.

"Four. Ma used one for a sewing room. She had one room, Uncle John another one and I had the other one."

"That's a bigger house than Pa's."

"The upstairs ain't finished at all. Just one big empty room," Sarah told him. "I won't sleep in Ma's room, Anyway, Uncle John's room has the best view of the yard, which is why he had that room. He could look out at the yard at night and see if everything was all right. The room Ma had would be the right size for Cora Lee. But I won't put Cora Lee in there to sleep. It's close to Uncle John's room with just that little storeroom in between."

"That little room would make a good nursery, Sarah."

"I ain't thought that far Lee. I'm trying to get through the wedding and now you've given me this house changing and I got to work that through my mind."

"And I think you're doing real well," he assured her. "Tony and Johanna are going to be gone tomorrow visiting her sister. I'll ask Tony if we can go down there and walk through the rooms and see how it will go. All right?" Sarah slowly nodded her head yes. She could see the sense of Tony and Johanna moving into Victor's house. She just didn't know if she could face moving back into that house. She didn't think Lee even began to understand her feelings about her ma's house.

"That's what's different," Lee told Sarah as they watched Cora Lee chattering and laughing as she pranced through the rooms.

"What you mean?" she asked, frowning.

"The laughing and happy talking of a child. That's what's different in here. There wasn't anyone laughing here when you lived here and you only talked when you had to. I want the changes in the walls like we talked and the painting and wallpapering but the thing that will make this house different is the happiness from Cora Lee and things like that."

"I hope you're right. Lee, I don't know about this. I really don't know," Sarah told him, suddenly angry. She walked into the room that used to be her ma's bedroom and pounded her fist against the door several times. Lee stood behind her. This sudden anger took him by surprise. Frowning, he watched her as she leaned against the door frame.

"The bedroom looks different than it did when your ma was here, Sarah. Just by Tony and Johanna living here it has changed. They brought smiles and good times into this house and we'll bring smiles and laughter and happiness here when we move in. Even if we have bad times and we will, it won't be like it was then 'cause we're different people from your ma and your Uncle John," Lee answered. "Do you want to walk through the other rooms or wait until another time?"

Instead of answering his question, she asked, "Will we

get all of that done before the wedding?"

"So if we don't get it all done before the first of May, Johanna won't mind if she has to live with Pa for a little while before he can move into the little house. I can't start tearing down walls until they're moved out. It'll be a mess for a while in both houses until I get this done. I know Pa and Tony will help all they can too."

"How much do you think it'll take to redo all we want done?"

"It won't be very much we're spending, although when I look at the windows, I think they should be replaced while we're in the mess. Some of the panes are cracked and the wood is rotten. The tearing down of the walls don't cost anything. It'll take a little plastering to patch up here and there but I know how to do that from working for a plasterer before I got the job on the railroad. Besides the windows, mostly the only money spent will be paint and wallpaper and curtains that you're gonna make. And doing the closets won't take much to do either and the pantry."

"And new linoleum in the kitchen."

"We're lucky there's such good hard wood floors in the rest of the house. Maybe it's in the kitchen too. If it is, then just stripping the floors and sealing and varnishing them would take care of it, like we'll have to be do in the other rooms. I'll bet it will be the end of the summer before this all gets done though. What with working everyday except Sunday and getting home later at night, that don't leave much time in a week to work here, but I'm sure Tony and Pa will help when they can."

"I don't know about all this, Lee," Sarah told him. "Maybe after it looks different it will be all right but right now, all I can see is my ma and Uncle John, but mostly Ma. Maybe when it's all done, I'll just stand in the middle of the house and yell out to Ma that we're gonna make this a happy home, instead of the one she made it." Lee put his arms around her, holding her as he realized she was crying. He comforted her a long while before they went out the front door toward home.

Victor asked Lee how it went that day and he replied, "Not as good as I had hoped. She went back to that house and helped clean it out, didn't she? After her ma died?"

"Yeah. And since then to see Johanna after the babies were born. But from what Johanna says, she never went any farther than the kitchen. Johanna asked her if she wanted to see the other rooms and she said no. Maybe we're asking too much of her to go back there. Her ma was a witch and we only know the half of it."

"I know a lot more than anyone else and there's lots I don't know," Lee answered.

"Like how she got the scars on her arm," Victor said.

"You wouldn't want to know. It would shock you and there's lots more scars than that," Lee told him.

"I had hoped that tearing down walls and painting and papering would make it different and easier for her," Victor said.

"I think there's got to be new windows and I wonder even about changing where some of them are. It would change the shape and look of the rooms. Maybe we're gonna have to do a lot more there than what I had first thought. I wonder about getting in a carpenter or two for a few days to get it done 'cause I don't have much time and you and Tony certainly don't either."

"Well, that's an idea. We probably could tear down walls but windows and making rooms where rooms weren't before would take a long time. Maybe tell Sarah that if she didn't want to live there after it was redone, then she didn't have to. Maybe redoing it will help her get rid of the boogies the house has for her, " Victor told Lee.

"I asked my sister if she'd watch my little ones while you and I went shopping for material for our dresses and Cora Lee's," Johanna told Sarah the following day. "She said

she would and keep Cora Lee too. She said she really liked
her the day Cora Lee spent there when we went Christmas
shopping. Said she got a real big bang out of her. But she
cautioned, never tell her anything you don't want told around,
'cause there ain't no secrets with her."

"That's for sure," Sarah agreed. "I suppose we should
try to go tomorrow or this week anyway, before it snows or
something else comes up. The roads are good enough so I
can drive. I don't seem to be able to get my ideas together
enough to even want to sew carpet rags or sheets or anything. I don't have the slightest idea of what I want for a
dress. I'm still trying to get everything in order in my head,
Lee and Cora Lee and a new dress for her, the wedding and
yesterday didn't help. It's been... just everything. Trying to
figure out material and a pattern is almost more than my
head'll hold. "

"You're happy with going back there, ain't you?"
Johanna asked.

"I don't know. I thought about that and thought and
thought and I don't know.."

"There's nobody gonna make you go there if you don't
want to," Johanna told her.

"I know that. I know it would be best all the way
around, for you and Tony and for Lee and me, but I guess
I'll have to see after it's been worked on." Sarah answered.

"I don't know what to tell you," Johanna said. " I do
think though with all my heart that you and Lee and Cora
Lee and who knows how many other babies, you'll make it a
happy home."

"That scares me too."

"Having babies?" Johanna asked.

"No. Taking care of them. Most anyone can have a
baby, It don't take much in the head to make a baby. It's the
taking care of them afterwards, that's what counts."

"Lee loves you, Sarah. And so does Cora Lee. And you
love both of them. You ain't your ma. And you know what's

really nice," she added, " your driving. We don't have to wait until one of the men have time. We can just get in the car and go unless the roads or weather are a problem."

"I'm glad I can drive, yes I'm glad of that. Although I had to get pushed to learn to drive, it's been another good thing I've done."

The two women did get to Ponta later that week. After leaving the kids at Johanna's sister's, they spent an afternoon looking at patterns and materials and lace and shoes and purses, finally settling for a plain cream-colored silky material for Sarah, a plain light green silky material for Johanna and a flowered blue cotton material for Cora Lee. Coordinating shoes and purses completed their shopping.

"All shopped out?" Victor asked when they got home.

"I am. My head won't hold any more looking. You know what. I wish that it was all done with, that the wedding was over and the house torn apart and redone already."

"You ain't looking forward to it?" he asked.

"No. You know the worst part?" she asked.

"What?" Victor asked, curious to see what she would answer.

"Going into that house and trying to see what Lee wants done. Having to make decisions. Having to make up my mind what I want, what kind of wallpaper I want or what color room I want. All I see when I think of it all is the house with Ma in it and I can't get any farther than that," she answered.

"I think you got to first get the walls torn out before you worry about papering and painting. See how every room looks first Can't decide much of anything until you see how it all looks," Victor advised.

"Maybe you're right cause I sure can't even think that far."

"First get the wedding over with, the dress making and all of that. The other comes after that, 'cause nothing can be done down at that house until after Tony and Johanna move out of there," Victor told her.

"Someone else always made the decisions before. Ma did or Mary did. I do some, make decisions, when I pick out material for a new dress but lots of times Johanna helps me decide. And I decide what we're gonna eat, but there's a whole lot of deciding to do the rest of this summer and I dread it. I know Lee'll want me to decide some on the house, like wallpaper, that's not for a man to know. Having to make up my mind, I don't know what I want 'cause I never made any them kind of decisions. That's what's hard. That's why I wish it were all done and over with. That it was just the garden to put in and the washing to do and the cooking. I can decide what to cook and bake. Washing is done on a certain day and Tuesday is ironing and Saturday is extra baking and Friday cleaning and that don't have to be decided. It's just done then. Maybe I'll just put in way back in my head and forget about it."

"Well, get the wedding over first and maybe after this is all over, you'll be much better at knowing what you want and being able to decide," he told her.

"I hope so. I'm afraid Lee's gonna get tired of putting up with someone who don't know nothing," she answered.

Sarah pressed the last seam on the wedding dress and hung it on the hanger. It was nicer than anything she had ever had. She ran her fingers over the smooth silky material, caressing it. Hanging the hanger on a nail in her bedroom, she stood back and looked again. The dress had no waist, just hung from the shoulders down past the hips, a sash joining the top to the bottom part. Pearl buttons ran down the front to the sash. Matching buttons were on the bottom of the long sleeves. A lovely large cream-colored lace collar accented the top of the cream-colored dress, giving it elegance. She could see why Johanna told her she needed a nice lightweight coat to go over it. Maybe someday soon she would invest in material and a pattern and make one. The next hurdle she had to get over was the sewing of the clothe hat she was going to make to match the dress. Johanna had given her a pattern to use, so tomorrow she would start on that.

The days were flying by and she was anxious to get the sewing done and over with. Before doing her own dress, she had sewed Cora Lee's, much to the little girl's joyful excitement. This had been easy. The dress front was one piece, as was the back, simply gathered from a round neckline. Short puffed sleeves had a half-inch gathered white lace edging, the same edging that went around the neckline. A simple cap that tied under the chin made of the same material, also trimmed with lace completed the outfit. Although the pattern was very simple, the blue material with the white flowers looked very dressy.

Sarah knew Lee had been talking to Tony about how soon they were moving into the big house and it was decided the move would be after the wedding. Not for the first time, she wished it were fall and all of this behind her.

The first Tuesday in May was full of sunshine and warmth. Since the wedding was planned for eight o'clock in the morning, the family was up early. Chores were done with a rush and babies dressed in a hurry. Lee dressed and then woke Cora Lee. Once she woke up enough to realize what the day held, she bounded out of the bed and into her new clothes that Sarah had laid out for her the night before. Her next stop was to wake Frieda, who had stayed overnight. To say Cora Lee was excited would have been an understatement.

Sarah dressed with care. She put on the new store-bought underwear, silk stockings and slip Mary had helped her buy so long ago. The feel of the silky material against her skin was so foreign to her. Sliding the new dress over her head, she smoothed it against her body. The pearl necklace and earrings she had given her one Christmas looked so nice on the new dress. Sliding on her new shoes, she ran a comb through her hair and fit the new hat over her head, careful not to disturb the hairdo.

Almost to the bedroom door, Sarah turned around and came back to stand in front of the dresser mirror.

"Ma would never recognize you," she said to the image in the mirror. "She would tell you to get out of those clothes 'cause they're too good for you, that you're too dumb to wear such a dress. Not good enough, she would have screamed. But Ma ain't here to say that and you can do as you want now... At least do what Lee wants and Cora Lee and Victor and everyone wants... And you do, too. Admit it, if you ain't too scared to say it. And if you don't admit it, then you're like Ma said you are." Realizing she was twisting her hands together and rubbing her engagement ring round and round, Sarah turned and almost ran out of the room. Stopping in the middle of the kitchen, she shouted, "Yes, I want to get married. So there, I said it."

Gertrude had written that it was impossible for her and Will to get away to come to the wedding, so Victor, Cora Lee, Martha, Harvey and Frieda were the only people in the church pews. Lee and Johanna led the way down the aisle with Tony and Sarah following. A few minutes later, Lee and Sarah took their vows. Victor stole a glance at Cora Lee and was surprised at how intense she was listening and watching. For the first time, he realized she was not a little baby anymore.

As a wedding treat for the family, Victor had ordered breakfast at Labit's Restaurant. A private back room had been fixed up that was used for these kinds of occasions.

"Imagine," Johanna had told Tony when she heard about the breakfast. "It'll make the wedding extra special. And Lee has hired a photographer to take pictures. That'll be really nice." These pictures were to be taken right after church at the photographer's studio.

By ten o'clock the wedding party was seated and being served scrambled eggs, freshly baked and buttered bread, ham slices and just-baked applesauce and poppy seed biscuits with lots of coffee and milk.

"Not nearly as good as the biscuits you and Mary used to make," Victor whispered to Sarah after taking his first bite. She softly laughed and answered, " Mary would have loved that compliment."

"You and Sarah going to take off now?" Victor asked when they came out of Labit's.

"Going to go over to Windsor and maybe further on to Garens. Sarah's never been there. Just spend the day doing what we want to. We'll be back tonight 'cause I've got to be back at work tomorrow. Just glad I got off today and I didn't want to push for anymore. Sure don't want to lose my job now. See you," Lee told them, as he took Sarah's hand and they went toward his car.

"Come on, Cora Lee,' Victor said. "We've got to head back home and see how Bud and the kittens and everything is back there. You'll see them tomorrow."

Looking back on the day, Sarah's thoughts were of enjoyment and pleasure. Just for the fun of it, they looked at furniture in the stores in both towns. It was too expensive. Lee knew of a family, a local banker, who was moving his family to the west coast soon. He had told Lee he thought about selling some of the furniture and just buying out there. He hated to think of packing and trying to move everything. So on a whim they went to the bank and talked to the man and then went to his house and asked if they could look at whatever furniture they weren't going to move. The house was well kept, everything in it of good quality. Sarah hoped they would be able to buy enough furniture to fill the rooms they had no furniture in, like the two bedrooms and the parlor. The man's wife told them to come back after supper. She and her husband would have decided by then what they were going to sell and what they were going to keep.

"Another meal out," Sarah told Lee. "I'm gonna be spoiled from all of this."

"You had breakfast that Pa bought and a strawberry ice cream cone for dinner and now this meal. And that'll probably be the last one eaten out for a long time. Better enjoy it. I hope we can come to some kind of an agreement on furniture we can use, like bedroom and parlor and a bed for Cora Lee. Maybe a couple of rockers too for your parlor. Let's hope this works out 'cause they got good stuff there. I just hope he don't want too much for it. And it's clean in that house so I don't think we got to worry about bedbugs."

"Thank goodness. That would be awful to buy mattresses and then have to burn them when we got them home. And it's our ranch now, not my ranch. I don't want to hear 'my ranch' again," Sarah told him. "And we're going to go to Mr. Paul and get it down on paper and signed that way."

"Thank you, Sarah," Lee answered, visibly moved.

Luck was with them. The man had found out that very afternoon that he had just ten days to get moved and find a house for his family. Lee and the man reached an agreement of forty dollars for the furniture. Lee thought this was quite high in price until his wife told Sarah that there would be lots of other things she would leave her because it would be easier to just buy when they got out to California. They would pack whatever they wanted to take with them in boxes and ship them out by train and travel that way themselves. Her brother was leaving tomorrow, driving their car out so at least they would have a car when they got there.

"My dear wife," Lee told her going home," you got a husband, a daughter and a house full of furniture and other things thrown in, all in one day. How's that for progress?"

"I hope the other things she's leaving for us makes up for the cost. And it's gonna take a week before my head takes all of it in," she answered.

Remodeling of the house was put off for several months. Victor and Tony had their hands full with the ranch work, plus the constant moving of the irrigation lines. They didn't feel they would have any extra time to help. And Lee had extra work tacked onto his schedule at the depot, so he was forced to work until Sunday noon many weeks. Because of this, several carpenters were contacted to do the actual remodeling, once the walls got torn down by the family.

The only thing that had gotten done was the moving of the furniture and the other things Lee had bought from the banker the day of the wedding. After the banker and his family moved, Lee hired a truck from Windsor to haul everything to be stored upstairs in the house Johanna and Tony were still living in. Sarah had peeked into the boxes and after finding cooking supplies like oatmeal in several boxes, she pulled out the groceries and took them down to the big house.

A constant worry for everyone was the extreme dryness of the hay fields, pastures and newly planted wheat fields. This was the third year in a row for the drought and it was taking a very large toll on the ranchers. Victor came home from town telling about water witching. He had never seen it done, but he had heard of it. He explained that a dowser claims to be sensitive to the changes in the earth. They also claim to have a sixth sense, gut feeling or whatever. Using a small forked branch, the dowser walks along the ground, pointing the fork upwards. When the branch feels the pull of water, it points downward. Although skeptical, several ranchers were going to have somebody's relative who lived in the south come up and try it. They were desperate enough to try most anything.

The dry weather brought an abundance of rattlesnakes to the buildings. Cora Lee was warned to be very watchful as she scampered outside playing. Bud's barking brought Tony to the hen house to see what was the matter and he found the dog standing just outside of the range of a rattlesnake's striking distance. Several days later, the dog was having a barking fit by Sarah's porch and investigation found several rattlers curled up under there. Victor took a gun and shot both of them. Using a pitch fork, he managed to drag the dead snakes out from under the porch. The women were especially careful in the garden, picking vegetables and hoeing. One had been found there also. Everyone took to carrying a heavy stick with them when they walked outside and even at night, care was taken.

Grasshoppers were a bigger problem this year than in any previous years. Some areas they flew in in droves, literally covering the fields in thick layers, eating everything in sight. When they flew on, there wasn't anything left. Victor and Tony felt they were lucky. They had plenty of them, especially on the prairie and in their wheat fields, but around the buildings they didn't seem quite so bad. Evidence of the hoppers could be found in the garden, but after listening to others talk, everyone decided they were extremely lucky.

When they knew the remodeling of the house was going to be put off for a while, Sarah thought of clothes for Cora Lee for school. Lee told her to go through the boxes upstairs before she started sewing anything and she was very glad she did when she found plenty to get her through the whole school year. When she finished digging and reshuffling, she told Johanna that there were a lot of clothes in those boxes to be sorted, kitchen towels and linen towels and kitchen items and just everything imaginable. But it would have to wait until the house was finished before she was going to do anything about any of it.

Before they could start tearing down walls in July, the first thing that had to be done was to move Tony and Johanna and family into Victor's house. This was done one Sunday. Before they quit that day they moved out the old cookstove

in the empty house. Tony didn't think it was safe to use anymore, as the firebox was showing extreme wear on the bottom. It took all the three men could do to get it out of the
house. The next morning Victor hooked a chain onto the
stove, hitched up several horses and dragged it into one of
the sheds.

It was the next Sunday before the three men began
work on the house. Several evenings after that were spent
tearing down and cleaning up the mess they had made.
During this process Sarah had kept herself busy with other
things. If Lee noticed she hadn't been over to see what had
been done, he made no comment.

The following Sunday, after church, there had been
various other jobs to be done or finished, so not too much
had been accomplished in the house. Lee, after supper, had
felt so tired he didn't plan on going back to the house but,
noticing he had forgotten his cigarettes there, sent Cora Lee
after them. After a little while she was still not back.

"I wonder where she is," he said, taking another look
at the clock. "I hope she don't take it into her head to snoop
around cause there's lot of nails on the floor for her to step
in"

"Or go upstairs and look around," Victor added.

"I'll go over there and get her," Sarah told them, heading out the door. In a few minutes Cora Lee was back with
the cigarettes. She said Sarah was looking around and told
her to go back alone. She'd be back in a few minutes.

"That the first time she's been there since we started to
tear everything apart?" Victor asked Lee.

"I think so. Unless she's gone over during the day."

"I haven't seen her go then either," Johanna told them.

After Lee finished his supper, had his cigarette and
another cup of coffee, he visited with Tony and Victor. Glancing at the clock, he was amazed to see it had been over an
hour since Cora Lee had come back.

"Guess I'll walk back and see how Sarah is doing," he said, getting off his chair and walking out the door. When he got to the kitchen door of the house, he could hear what sounded like wood being smashed. He cringed as he heard glass splintering again and again. Hurrying, he came upon Sarah with a maul smashing the windows and wood framing the windows in her ma's bedroom. He stood shocked as again and again she swung, glass and wood splinters flying in all directions. The walls in the room had been completely demolished, along with the doors and the windows. Nothing had been spared.

Even the outside walls were damaged. When she made one last swing, Sarah saw Lee standing in the doorway.

"What are you doing? If I had known you had that much ambition, I'd have had you over here before helping us," he told her.

"I'm rid of it. I'm rid of this room, this room that has haunted me since I was born. It's gone. I don't want those windows back in the same place. I don't want the walls back in the same way. I don't want this room to be a bedroom again. Let's make it a different room, like a kitchen or something else. But not a bedroom again. Never. Never. Never.

"I don't care what room you make this. It ain't gonna be a bedroom again," Sarah shouted.

"OK. Here, give me that maul. I think you've made your point." When he took the maul from her, she left the room and the house. In a few minutes, Victor came into the house and surveyed the mess.

"I saw Sarah running to the barn. She saddled Bonnie and rode off toward the south pasture. I wondered what happened, so thought I'd come over and see. She do this?"

"She did. She had everything smashed including the windows when I got here. Swore this would never be a bedroom again, that the windows were not to go back in the same place again but most of all, again and again she said this was not to be a bedroom again," Lee answered.

"Well, maybe she's got it worked out of her system now. Maybe now she can live with this house. Sure as hell made a mess to clean up anyway. When a woman gets worked up, look out."

"What kind of a kitchen this make, Pa? Sarah said it ain't gonna be a bedroom again. And she's got enough of the wall into that other room knocked out that we might as well finish that up too. Then we've got a good-sized room that would make a nice-sized kitchen. And the hole in the wall here could be the doorway."

"Yeah, we've got a whole new game to play now. Let's take a good look around, carefully for this glass, and see what we've got. Maybe after we clean this all up, we can take a tape measure and get the size of rooms and see how we're gonna make this into a kitchen and maybe a dining room too. See how we're gonna make the other rooms into bedrooms. Maybe only several bedrooms down here, now that two of the bedrooms have just become a kitchen. I just hope this takes care of the demons that have haunted Sarah for so long. I just hope."

When Sarah came back that evening, she found Lee sitting on the porch of the little house waiting for her. She walked up to him and he held out his hand for her. Sitting down beside him, she lay her head on his shoulder and cried. Gathering her up to him, he held her until the sobs subsided and she had control of herself.

"I'm sorry, Lee. I just couldn't help it. I saw the maul there and I thought of the hours my ma sat at those windows and watched and when I came into the house, how she screamed at me for doing everything wrong. I picked up the maul and once I started, I couldn't stop until I had it all done in. Glass and all. I'll go up there tomorrow and start to clean it up."

"You wait until tomorrow night 'cause I'll help you, we'll all help you. Pa came up tonight and we looked around and we'll take a tape measure, after the mess is cleaned up and we're gonna measure everything and figure out where we're gonna make rooms over there. Have to be careful for supports and that sort of thing but we think it will be a different house, altogether different when we get done."

"I'll come up and help."

"Your ma watched the work being done outside from those windows. I never realized those were in the front of the house and the kitchen had always been in the back. You know what, that may make a hell of a good kitchen."

The next evening was spent cleaning up the mess. Several wagon loads were hauled into a ditch that was used as a dump. Then measuring was done and several evenings were spent figuring things out on many pieces of paper until, finally, the inside house plans were complete. Yes, ma's bedroom and the next bedroom were now the kitchen and dining room. The kitchen door was put where one of the windows had been and since it was so close to the end of the room, a very small part of the kitchen was to be made into a room where the outside clothes would be put. One side of that room would have a galvanized tin sink in it built into a cupboard with a slop pail underneath.

On the other side of the wall, the kitchen side, there would be a kitchen sink, also of galvanized tin, built into a cupboard with a slop pail underneath. Kitchen cupboards were planned, to be built by one of the carpenters. Besides a pantry, there were built-in cupboards, with one built somewhat like the little house had, for good dishes.

There were to be two bedrooms downstairs and a very small room that could be used for a baby's bedroom, if the need be. Lee allowed for a closet in each bedroom, somewhat like the one that Molly had in her bedroom. And along the one side of the house was a large room that would be the parlor.

Checking with the carpenters, after the final gutting of the house, Lee found that the plans that had been put together were feasible. One other thing that was included in the plans were different windows, in different places in each room and of different sizes. Certainly a much larger project that originally thought of, but one that Sarah seemed to be able to live very well with.

As Victor said," Her demons seem to be gone."

From the day of the smashing, Sarah helped with the house whenever she could. She learned to hammer, strip old varnish off floors, wall paper and paint.

The only new thing they bought for their home was the cookstove for the kitchen. Lee had tried to find a secondhand one but everyone he looked at was in about the same shape as the old one they had thrown out. Victor finally told him to think of a new one, since the cookstove was one of the most important things they would own. He went to work one Saturday morning on the train so Sarah could drive down and meet him in Windsor when he got done with work. They went to the large hardware store there and picked out a black Acme Sterling Steel Range that cost a little over thirty dollars. Sarah had never seen a stove this fancy. It had a reservoir that held at least fifteen gallons of water. There was a thermometer on the oven door so she would know when the oven was hot enough for baking. A warming oven on the top of the stove was full length. The nickel-plated ornaments and decorations all over the front of the stove and oven were highly polished. It was to be delivered the last week in September.

"Do you want an ice cream cone?" Lee asked Sarah when they were getting into the car to go home.

"We got any money left to buy one with?" she asked. "You know we spent almost as much on that stove as we did on the rest of the furniture and stuff for our entire house."

"I know. I think we need a cone to celebrate this day, the day we bought the first anything new for our home. Here's the creamery. You want a chocolate?"

"Yes. They're the best. And a double one as long as we're spending the money today."

"Yes ma'am. Ten cents for a double cone and a chocolate one at that," he answered, laughing as he went into the creamery. Coming back with a large cone for each, they slowly enjoyed the creamy coldness on their way out of town. The family agreed that the stove was an elegant addition to their house, one of the finest they had ever seen.

There was one more thing that had to be taken care of in August and that was registering Cora Lee for school.

One week before Labor Day, the head of the school board, Leon Rumney, stopped by. He drove into the yard and, finding Victor, had a very nice visit with his old friend. Next he came to the house to see Sarah and Cora Lee. Introducing himself, he told her what he was there for. Cora Lee was thrilled.

"I need the full name, address, date of birth. Her mother's name and father's name." After Sarah gave him this information, he told her about the schoolhouse cleaning that was coming up Labor Day.

"Everyone that has children in the school is asked to help that day. The women clean up the inside of the school, scrub the desks, floors, windows and whatever else needs to be cleaned. The men fix the merry-go-round, the swings, repair the roof, siding and everything else that needs fixing and make sure the grounds are mowed and checked for rattlesnakes."

"The women bring scrub pails and their own soap?" Sarah asked.

"Yeah. Water is brought by the closest neighbor there, Edith and Hank Snazzle. They get there early enough so they get some heated on the stove. That's where the water comes from for the school. They board the teacher and take her over fresh water every morning and they get the fires started. They get paid to do this. Usually everyone is there by ten o'clock to clean and most everything is done by noon. Then there's a picnic dinner. Everyone brings something for this, your own plates, something to drink the coffee out of. Edith makes a pot of coffee. Those that don't like coffee drink water. It makes it nice for everyone, the cleaning gets done and the outside work done and then everyone can have a few hours to visit and catch up on the news and how the work is coming and just have a few hours' enjoyment. The kids get a chance to play and the new kids get to meet the others. And the new people get to meet the teacher."

"This is Monday, Labor day?" Sarah asked.

"Yes. Do you think you'll be able to come?"

"We can go, can't we?" Cora Lee pleaded.

"We'll be there," Sarah assured the anxious girl. "Then you'll meet the teacher and the other children. Lee'll be home that day and I know he'll want to come too."

Knowing his pa would enjoy the schoolhouse cleaning and the picnic dinner afterwards, Lee asked him to go along. The day proved to be a good one for all.

Swallowing her fear, Sarah walked into the school, scrub pail in hand. The first person she ran into was Betty Rumney, the school board president's wife, who introduced her to the others. Although they were busy scrubbing and cleaning, the words flew around the room. Sarah found the conversation easy to listen to and before long, she found herself adding a few words.

It was extra hard cleaning this year with all the dust and sand that the winds had driven into the room, but by noon the school room had a clean homemade soap smell. The last thing Edith Snazzle did was sprinkle an abundant amount of sweeping compound on the floor to help pick up the fine dust that the women couldn't get swept up. Memories overcame Sarah. That oily odor had been one of the last things she smelled, the days she left school before the Christmas programs were held, the ones she had never been allowed to attend. She quickly went outside and, standing a moment, watched the men finish oiling the merry-go-round. Betty Rumney joined her on the steps.

"They'll finish sweeping all that compound up. Only so many can sweep anyway. Being we're on the other side of the district we lose track of what people on this side are doing. That's one nice thing about these functions at the school house. I was shocked when I heard Mary had died. I always liked her. I never knew Lee's wife."

"He didn't live here. He lived at Hennison when he was married to Annie," Sarah answered.

"I remembered Lee some but I knew Tony better 'cause he ran around with my youngest brother. Lee used to be good friends with Ray Larpin. He don't live around here anymore."

"Ray and his wife, Molly, live south of town now. We go to visit them sometimes. We were down there about a month ago on a Sunday."

"I didn't know that. That he'd moved back. Got any children?"

"Three lively youngsters about Cora Lee's age, next year they'll have one in school and they've got a baby. Cora Lee has a good time when we go there."

"She's over there playing on the swing?" Betty asked.

"Yeah, that's her. She enjoys herself. She never has any trouble meeting new people."

"Sounds like they are done sweeping. That's my one child I have left in school yet over there. She's in eighth grade. Wants to go to high school next year. I don't know where we are supposed to get the money from to send her. Have to board her and we don't have the money for that. She may have to work for room and board where she stays if it can be worked out and she wants to go bad enough. We'll see. She'd like to be a teacher so maybe Leon will try to find the way so she can go. They're coming out now so we'll get dinner set up. I think the men are about done too."

"Where's the dinner set up?"

"Inside on the teacher's desk and the kids' desks. Some eat out here and others try to fit into the student's desks. Flies ain't so bad in there," she answered, going to get her contribution to the picnic. Sarah waited a minute until she could see how it was going to be done. Then she went to the car and got the apple coffeecake she had baked that morning. As Lee had told her, the food brought to be shared showed that some of the families didn't have much to offer. Rolled-up pancakes, greased inside with lard and then sprinkled with sugar, cold cornbread and dark syrup, bread and jelly sandwiches and cold cornmeal mush were some of the offerings. Betty Rumney and Edith Snazzle had brought three large loaves of bread and four quarts of canned beef and beef gravy that they had heated on the stove. Sarah's coffeecake and the rolled-out sugar cookies another woman brought were the only desserts. It didn't take long for the beef and bread to disappear. This was a far bigger treat to some of them than the cookies. Sarah wondered how long it had been since some of them had eaten a good meal of beef.

As she was eating, she counted ten couples besides Victor and the teacher, Miss Florence Schmitt. She came up with sixteen children for a count. Lee verified this on the way home when she asked him.

Later, when Cora Lee was outside playing, Lee asked her what she thought of the teacher.

"I didn't talk to her much. From what the others said, they like her. They talked about her some when we were cleaning 'cause she didn't come until it was time to eat dinner so she wasn't there to hear them talk. They said she is strict and makes everyone mind. They seemed to think she was a good teacher. She's sure a little bit of a woman, can't be much over five foot tall but they said she keeps law and order."

"I talked to her some. She used to teach in Hennison so she knew the town real well. Says she's going back after this year to get married. So we'll have a new teacher next year. Unless her fiancé loses his job, then she thought she had better hang onto the one she had. I asked Leon later what she gets paid and he said seventy-five a month. She told me her fiancé likes his job but don't know how long he'd be working at it. There must have been two men working there before and they laid off one. He fixes cars, an auto mechanic. Gets fifteen dollars a week pay."

"You knew most everyone there, didn't you?" Sarah asked.

"Some of them, but it's been a long time since I had seen the ones I did know. Pa knew them all. He enjoyed the day. They talked a lot about the dust bowl in Kansas and Texas and the grasshoppers. We didn't have it near as bad with dust or hoppers like some areas in South Dakota and Kansas and Texas. Had it dry, but Leon's brother wrote him that the wind blew the dust and dirt so bad in Texas where he lived that the sand drifts came to the top of the fence posts. And grasshoppers ate eyes right out of animals and horses, just ate them out. We'd heard that before."

"That's awful. Those poor animals. They must have had to kill them then."

"They did. Sure hope next year is better. We've had enough of this. Time for some rain and green prairie grass. You get along all right today?"

"Most of the time. It passed, the bad part. And guess who had it the best today?"

"Cora Lee," he answered. "Who else?"

The first Saturday afternoon in October they moved the furniture out of the little house back to their new home.

"Don't you think I should clean this first before you move in?" Sarah asked Victor when she learned he intended to move in as soon as her things were out of the little house.

"Clean what?" he asked. "You've kept this place as clean as a whistle. There ain't nothing to clean. I'm moving in this afternoon, my bedroom furniture, my kitchen table and chairs and that daybed. I got everything I want moved today all together and ready to go. Oh, there's my old rocker too and that set of pictures you made for Mary. I want them. All of Mary's dishes and stuff that's still in the pantry and Johanna's been using, I want to go through and pick out what I want and then the women can divide what I don't want. Some of that has to be done yet. Tomorrow. Then Johanna can unpack her stuff and put her own stuff out to use."

"And probably house clean, if I know my wife," Tony said.

"I'm gonna do some, but with the cold weather coming and the wood stove being used again in the parlor, I don't see much sense in doing a great deal of wall and ceiling washing. And I did the curtains and all that kind of stuff, like mattresses last spring when we moved, so I'm going to limit what I'm gonna do until next May, "Johanna answered.

"And with me in my little house, you can think of doing whatever you want to do. As much as I think of Tony and Johanna and those kids, they need to be alone and I need to be alone. We've had all the togetherness we need for a while."

"I think the little kids have gotten to Pa," Tony said, laughing. "Methinks there's a message of needing peace and quiet."

"I'm looking forward to being up there alone. When I want to nap I can do it and when I want to eat I can do it, providing I remember to take something along from Johanna's after supper. So you see, you've ain't got rid of me completely, you got me for meals every day and my washing, Johanna gets to do that and that's enough. And once in a while, I hope Johanna or Sarah remember to clean my house 'cause there I draw the line. I never cleaned a house in my life and I ain't a gonna learn now. And like I said before, I'm gonna move this afternoon, so let's eat and then get to it."

After his things had been moved, they could see Victor seemed content and happy. He settled down to unpacking and putting away things that were in the boxes he had packed to be moved that day.

"You look tired," Lee told Sarah.

"I am tired, but we got to set up the beds yet so we can sleep tonight before I say I've had enough. Tomorrow is another day," she answered.

"Then let's go set up the beds and Sarah can make them and by that time, Johanna should have supper ready for all of us," Tony told them. "Pa has his work all cut out for him and after supper, there's some chores yet to do. Got to milk the cow so we got milk for the table again so let's go get those beds done. I agree with Sarah, it's been a long day of moving. And we've still got all that furniture in your upstairs to move down as soon as possible."

"And the boxes of stuff I moved here when I left Hennison. That's still upstairs in the big house."

"Tomorrow," Tony told him. "Tomorrow."

Shoving aside boxes and dressers, Lee and Victor set up the beds, first Cora Lee's and then Lee and Sarah's.

"These closets in every bedroom sure are different than the nails we're used to," Tony told them as they walked out of the bedroom into the kitchen. He ran his hand over the top of the kitchen table. "And stripping and varnishing this table and those chairs sure made them look nice. They don't look like the same furniture. And that bed and dresser you did, Sarah, made it look like new furniture. Maybe sometime we can do the same. I know Johanna liked how it all looked."

"I didn't know if my hands would ever be the same when I got done, but I'm glad it did it. No, it don't look the same at all. There'll probably be some stuff from here for your family too, when we get through all of that upstairs," Sarah told him.

"You'll be working the rest of the winter before you get through it all," Lee told her.

"My word," Johanna told Sarah as she looked at the many items Sarah had laid out on the parlor floor the next day.

"I've found clothes that'll fit me and a lot that'll fit you. You're a lot smaller than I am now. I've put on some weight after I started eating with the Labellas. The wife of that house was my size, so where these others came from I don't know. And Johanna, they're all nice. No holes and not faded from washing at all. And the stuff is all mixed up. Bedding and sheets and blankets on top of boxes with clothing in the bottom. Just like they took a box and threw in whatever they found first."

"You want me to take this box home and try them on?" Johanna asked

"And keep them 'cause they won't fit me, no matter how much altering I would do with them. I'm just a bigger size than that."

"Thank you for the boxful. I hope they fit, and even if I have to alter them, I'll get a lot of wear out of them. My goodness, Sarah. Look at this nice coat and hat."

"I know. There's a lot of winter clothes here. I guess they thought that it wouldn't get cold in California, so there are boxes of winter clothes here. I didn't know it at the time but Lee gave him an extra ten dollars for whatever else they wanted to leave us, besides what they had told us at first, and he thinks that's why we got more boxes. I asked him why he didn't tell me and he didn't want me to think he was foolish and wasted the money 'cause he didn't know what they were going to give him for the extra money."

"I would say he did very well," Johanna told her.

Sarah spent two more days sorting. She found clothes for Martha and Harvey that had obviously been packed away for a while, as they smelled musty. Three large boxes were full of men's clothing that Lee shared with his brother and pa. There were some very nice warm jackets for all the men. Several good suits fit Lee. He wondered when he would ever wear them. Another suit, he gave to Tony for Johanna to alter. One box produced very large-sized men's clothing. Sarah put this away for future tearing apart and remaking. The only thing they didn't find were men's shirts, not a single one. Nor were there any men's or women's underwear, plenty of children's underwear, but none for the adults.

"It's so funny how these were packed," Sarah told Lee. "Carpet rags and cleaning rags and underneath was little kids' clothes. On top of this box was old towels that still have plenty of wear in them and some sheets, not made from feed sacks either. And this here box of jewelry. Why didn't she take this with her? Just look at it." She took out earrings, necklaces, brooches and small pins and laid them out on the table. "I got enough of this I could go to church everyday and not run out too soon."

"I haven't any idea why she would have left that. But you found other clothing that didn't fit either of them. Like that box of larger men's clothing and those clothes you gave Johanna. Somebody must have given them clothes, maybe some relative, and she just packed it away. What you gonna do with this?" he asked, holding up some of the jewelry.

"Keep it, I guess. Johanna has some jewelry she got from her grandma so she has some. I asked her to pick out something from here today when she was here and she did. If she needs something to go with a dress sometime, she'll come and borrow and use it when she needs it. But we ain't that kind of people that need fancy jewelry. Johanna said she never ever saw anything like this before. Well," she said, taking the box and putting it in one of the dresser drawers," I guess this just goes along with everything else that is different. I guess there's a first time for everything."

"You all done sorting now? Got every box sorted through?" Lee asked.

"Yep. What I couldn't use, I asked Johanna to look through and then I just packed the rest in boxes and it's back upstairs. Did you see the nice set of pots and pans I found?"

He shook his head no as he followed her into the pantry, where she showed him the heavy cooking ware.

"That costs a lot of money," he told her. "That's good heavy stuff."

"It is heavy. I took one old pan I had that's pretty big and put it out for water for Bud and took the pan he had water in before and put it in the barn for the cats. This one holds so much more. The rest of the pans I don't want now I'm gonna take up to the dump. These pans are so nice. I gave Cora Lee a couple of pans I found in these boxes that leak and a couple of baking pans that also leak and several old spoons, 'cause I found silverware too for everyday, so Cora Lee has something new to play with and I haven't heard much from her today. She's a cooking and baking to her heart's content."

Still holding up things for Lee to look at, Sarah showed him boxes of patterns.

"And look, Lee, here's something else I found, patterns, lots and lots of them. Johanna and I won't have to buy many patterns for a long time. Nightie patterns, dress patterns, little and big girls' and boys' patterns, not many men's patterns though. All of the men's clothing was bought, so she didn't make many of them."

"I don't think she sewed at all. There's several ladies in Windsor that do a lot of sewing for other people and she probably had them do the sewing for her," Lee answered. "I think I got my money's worth when I gave him that ten dollars for whatever they didn't want to take with them."

"I would say," Sarah agreed. "Tomorrow I'm going to wipe down all that furniture up there and then we can move it down Saturday afternoon after you get home from work or else Sunday. I don't know if I can lift it or not so you may have to get Tony to help you."

"Tony figured to help and Pa too. Then it'll really look like our home," Lee said.

"And I'll be glad it's all done. I dreaded this summer so

much."

"You think there's enough curtains to remake for all these windows?" Lee asked.

"I doubt it. I won't know until I get at making them this winter. I probably will have to buy some material. That curtain I made for the bedroom in the little house was so nice. I brought that one along, your pa didn't want it. He wanted a plain curtain. I'm gonna try to get material to match that and put them in our bedroom. But that has to wait until winter."

"When you gonna make some hominy for me?" Lee asked.

"As soon as I get a recipe for it, I suppose. I put if off as long as I can."

"Good. But first I got to get the recipe for it. I really liked it and I ain't had it since I left Hennison. I know you need ripe corn, got to cook it for a long time in some kind of lye water until it starts to crack open and swell. Then it's got to be washed and washed and washed until the hulls or husks come off and the black piece on the inside of the kernel. After that it's cooked for a long time again and then canned."

"After all that work, it had better be good," she answered shaking her head. " And there are apples to be canned from those that we picked this fall. Those haven't been looked at since we picked them but they keep pretty good. I'm just so glad this is done and we're moved."

"So am I," Lee agreed. "So am I. And we've got a home to be proud of. Now when I got time, it's that yard to clean up."

"Maybe that'll be next summer's job."

During the night Lee got up for a drink of water. The moon shone bright enough so he could see where he was walking as he went from room to room. Even though he knew if he started to think about this past summer, he would have a hard time going back to sleep, his mind zeroed in on it. His thoughts went back to when the three men had talked about painting and papering the house, hoping Sarah would be able to live here with that much done. From that it went to a few wall changes to a final complete remodeling job, aided by Sarah's rampage with the maul. She had certainly put more money into it than he had imagined they would, but they now had a fine home. And from the soundness of her sleep, she knew she could now live here without anything too much haunting her. Maybe it helped that the bedroom they now had once had been her Uncle John's. Lee wished he could have met the man who loved the same woman he loved.

Sunday evening after supper, the adults sat in Johanna and Tony's kitchen visiting. Victor had brought up from the basement a two-quart jar of the wild grape juice Sarah had made the fall before. After getting glasses, Johanna had poured each of them some of the treat.

"We've got to decide on the chickens and ducks and geese that are over at your place Lee," Tony told his brother. "Do you want them to stay there or come back here?"

"You don't have room here, do you?" Lee asked.

"Not really. But we could cull some on the old hens. Have to anyway when the pullets start laying."

"I'd like to keep some over there," Sarah said. " I don't mind taking care of them and it saves coming back here for eggs. Why don't we buy them?" she asked Lee.

"That's what we wanted to decide. You want to buy them, then we'll sell them to you real cheap 'cause they're old hens and ain't laying much and ain't worth much."

"But I'd have them for canning," Sarah answered. "Is there any pullets we could buy?"

"Not here," Victor answered. "But I think I can pick up about fifty for you. Joe Morshian's neighbor left during the night. They just packed up their clothes and stuff from the house and left. He dropped off a note at Joe's, left it on the back door that the cows had to be taken care of and the horses and chickens. I guess they couldn't make their payment on the ranch and so they just packed up and left. There are some pullets there that could be had cheap or for nothing. The bank don't want them," Victor told her.

"I'd like them. Maybe we could put a band on the pullets so we'd know the difference when we butchered the old ones. I really don't want to milk, if I can help it. I'd rather buy milk from here," Sarah told them. "If I have to, then I would, but then there's manure to clean out and feed and hay to get. It's enough with Bonnie, and Lee was talking of getting a pony for Cora Lee and he should have a horse for himself. That's enough feed and manure to take care of with Lee gone so early and getting home so late. And there's hen houses to clean once in a while too. What about the geese and ducks? Why don't we just feed them and keep them there and then we eat them for holidays? Anyway there ain't that many of them. Call them everybody's geese and ducks."

"Sounds good to me," Tony told her.

"You shouldn't have to buy any milk for a while with all the clothes you gave everybody," Johanna said. "I know I don't do the milking or take care of the cows, but Sarah wouldn't have had to give anybody those clothes. We got a lot of dollars worth of nice clothes, better than what we could have made with no time invested in doing them."

"We still want to buy the milk," Lee answered. "There'll be plenty of times when we need help or something and you'll help us then. If we could get milk about every other day in the winter and every morning in the summer, then that would be the right way. Milk keeps for a day in the summer in the pump house by the river. The chickens, we'll keep for eggs and butchering. And we'll have to buy meat from here. We want to help with the butchering, but we want to pay for the meat we take home. I don't want to keep any pigs down there. There ain't any place decent to keep them and no fences to keep them in. And we'll pay for the hay and feed for the horses, 'cause I ain't home to help put it up. We'll have to come to some kind of an agreement on the price so there ain't any bad feeling afterwards."

"And you certainly will want to plant garden with me, won't you?" Johanna asked Sarah.

"I sure would like to," Sarah answered.

"It'd be foolish to have your own garden 'cause of the irrigating we do on this one. We don't want to set up an irrigating system at two places," Victor told her.

"And we'll just continue to work at hoeing like we have done in the past, whenever we can we hoe and weed and pick potato bugs," Johanna told Sarah. "We try keep it pretty clean and when the men help when they can, then it makes such a difference. And it helps me so much when Cora Lee sits with the little ones."

"That reminds me, I need sugar. Maybe you can pick up a hundred pounds for me in Ponta or Windsor someday very soon. And we'll need flour this winter too. If you can get ahold of a big tin can, then we'll get it in fifty-pound bags."

"You know what sugar costs?" Lee asked her.

"A little over six dollars, something like fifteen or nineteen cents over six dollars. Flour runs about a dollar forty cents, around there."

"You could get flour here when we get ours ground," Victor told them.

"What with the wheat crop you got, Pa, will you even have enough for yourself and for feed?" Lee asked.

"You're right about that. Maybe it would be just better if you bought your own flour and we took care of our own. Less to deal with that way," Tony answered. "I talked to Hugh Epperson the other day in Ponta and he said he got a hundred eight-five bushels of wheat from ninety acres. And I don't think ours ran any better. Just glad we can sell some animals every week to the butcher shop. Each week it gets less and less to feed. Without that irrigated land, we'd be in bad shape."

"Like a lot of them are. More and more every day. This year really thinned out the ranchers and made the government owners of lots and lots of gumbo. Sarah, what about the rental agreement, we keep it just like it is?" Victor asked. "It ain't up yet but when it does, what you want to do about it?"

"Would you still like to keep it as it is now?" Lee asked.

"We would."

"It gives us some income off the land to pay taxes and a little besides. For now, let's just leave it as it is. When is the five years up?" Lee asked.

"Next year," Sarah answered. "That much time has already passed. I never dreamed when you came over that day and helped me after Ma died, that so much could happen to me."

"Just think, you could have been married to Earl Conway for all those years," Lee teased.

"If I had married him, I wouldn't have had Cora Lee for a daughter and that would have been terrible." They all laughed while Lee took one hand and squeezed her neck until she squirmed and finally added, "And I like you lots better than him."

"Thank you," he answered, laughing and caressing her shoulder.

CHAPTER XII

Johanna verified what Sarah had suspected. She was going to have a baby. For a while already she had wondered and finally she asked Johanna about it. The women figured the baby would be born in late June or early July. Johanna's ma had told her it took as long for a baby to grow inside a woman as a calf to grow inside a cow. Using this knowledge, the two women figured out the date as best they could. Lee, Tony and Victor shook their heads when they heard how the determination was made. The men thought a doctor would probably come up with the correct date, when Sarah finally did go see him. They would never tell Cora Lee. When she knew, the whole school would know and then the neighborhood.

Mornings, Sarah hated to get out of bed, for she knew that before long she would be hunched over the slop pail. She was thankful when Cora Lee left for school. Knowing how Sarah was feeling, Victor took the little girl most days with his car. And when the first snowstorm came, he took her in either the buggy or they rode horseback. As they lived on the border of the district it was a full five miles to the school, too far for the little girl to walk.

"I don't know how long you're gonna be able to keep Cora Lee from knowing something is wrong," Victor told Sarah one morning after he had taken her to school. "She asked me why you had to keep throwing up. She said that when she had a tummy ache it went away in a couple of days, but yours ain't."

"I wondered about that. When I get sick I try to go into the bedroom, where she can't see me, but I know she wonders. She's so smart, hard to fool her. And I don't want to say anything to her 'cause she'll tell the whole school and anyway she don't need to know anything yet."

"I don't know how long you're gonna be able to keep it secret. She's starting to worry about you. She knows her real ma is dead and I wonder if she ain't beginning to wonder what's happening to you. Like you said, she's not dumb at all," Victor answered, going out the door toward the car and home.

With the early morning sickness constantly with her, Sarah found that a piece of buttered bread, forced down as soon as she got up, helped ease the queasy feeling. By mid-morning she usually felt somewhat better but never as good as before she got pregnant And by evening she was so tired that she could be found in bed sometimes as early as seven o'clock. The only food that really appealed to her was soft-boiled eggs, bread and butter, bread toasted in the oven and buttered, and ice cream. She forced herself to eat a little meat most days.

The butchering week had always been a full hard week, but this fall, it was somewhat of a nightmare. Johanna made her lie down for a nap after dinner every day. Without this added rest, Sarah didn't know if she would have been able to make it through the week. As usual, the following week was old hen butchering and canning time. Victor went through the flock of Sarah and Lee's culling out the non-layers. Knowing how Sarah felt, he knew it wouldn't be easy for her to get it done by herself, so they butchered the two flocks together. With everyone working at it, the hens were finally ready for the canners. No one was happier than Sarah when those two weeks were over.

"What are you planning to do about Christmas presents this year?" Lee asked Sarah the week following the last of the butchering.

"I've been thinking about that. We've got Tony's name and Dorothy's name and Will's name. I wonder if they won't try to come this year 'cause she wanted to exchange names again, like before. Gertrude and her family, that is. They don't come much now, I think Gertrude feels funny with her pa and it's farther and they live on a ranch and that always makes it harder. Got to get someone to take care of the place."

"They've been here only once since they got married and that was last summer. But Pa heard from Gertrude yesterday, had a letter when he went to Ponta and got the mail. She planned to come, said all four were coming. They're gonna come here and also visit the Eppersons. She also told Pa that she was going to have a baby in March. At least she told him before she got here. I don't think she knows you're going to have a baby. I don't know if Pa wrote her that or not. I think the letters they exchange are about two a year."

"Johanna said maybe one of us should ask her about writing, exchanging letters 'cause then we'd keep up with the news and keep in touch. I think Johanna was gonna ask her when she saw her next. As far as gifts, there's your pa to get for and Cora Lee too," Sarah said. " I thought I could get material for a flannel shirt for Will and one for Tony. And maybe get Dorothy a game or a book to read or colors or a puzzle or something like that. I don't even know what size dress she'd wear. Or maybe make her a nightie, trimmed with lace and fancy rickrack. Get a nice piece of flannel and make one. That sounds good. Your pa, maybe a new overall jacket or overalls."

"You gonna be able to sew all that?"

"If I can live through these last weeks, then I'll get the sewing done too. Johanna suggested we make candy together and cookies too and she's gonna take care of the shopping for your pa, what he gives everybody. I guess she wondered if

I'd get any of that done and I wonder too when I get up in the morning. I don't think I'll ever get over the wanting to throw up. It does help to eat the bread, but it's an awful feeling stuffing down bread when everything wants to come the other way."

"About Cora Lee," Lee said, "I wondered what you'd think about getting a set of play dishes for her. They have a really pretty set down in the dime store at Windsor. I walked through there the other day."

"That'd be fine. She has all the doll clothes I've ever made for her. I have to say that she really takes good care of what she's given. She may make a mess of things when she plays but she cleans and puts away everything so nice. And the dolls are in good shape too so I think doll dishes would be fine. That would save me having to sew something for her."

"Then next Saturday afternoon why don't you try to get into Ponta and get the stuff you need and you can meet the train when I come in? If you got everything you need on hand , then when you feel like it, you can sew on it. And for Christmas baking and candy, what gets done is done and what don't get done, we'll live without. Maybe pick up some hard candy, the ribbon candy. I like that and so does everyone else. Cora Lee ain't still hovering over you like she was doing when she realized you were having the tummy upset for so long?" Lee asked.

"She still watches me a lot. If she weren't so smart, it would help, but I think being around older people all the time makes her pick up ideas she wouldn't otherwise. At least that's what Victor thinks. Johanna asked me the other night how I was and Cora Lee right away came to stand right by my side, close to me so she wouldn't miss a word being said. I finally got her to go and play."

"Does her doing that bother you?" Lee asked.

"Sometimes it does but I try to remember that she ain't got no ma but me and I just try to get her to do something else, like play or set table or whatever. It's the worse when I get up and I feel sick and she smothers me. But when it's school days, then I get her out the door without her having time to worry about me. And you're here on Sunday and Saturdays she's been going with you to stay all day with Frieda and that helps so much."

"In her mind you've replaced her ma you know, even if she does call you Sarah. And I wonder when this baby starts to call you Ma, if Cora Lee won't too. Maybe not, but I would be surprised if she don't. She don't remember Annie much," Lee said. "You don't worry anymore about being mean to her, do you?"

"Sometimes. But that thinking gets less and less."

"Forget it," Lee told her. You couldn't be mean to her or hit her if you wanted to. It just ain't in you." Seeing the look on Sarah's face, Lee spoke again. "Forget it. You're like your Uncle John, not your ma."

Lee picked up the doll dishes in Windsor the next day. Sarah hid them in the boxes stored upstairs. Cora Lee had been given orders by Lee, when they moved there that she was not to touch anything upstairs. So Sarah knew that was a good place to hide her present. She had intended to drive into Ponta the following Saturday afternoon, do her shopping and then meet Lee when he came back on the train as he had planned, but that morning had been a bad one for Sarah. About eleven o'clock she sent Cora Lee down to see Victor with a note asking him to take her to town. At two o'clock, with the little girl playing at Johanna's, they drove out of the yard.

"You ain't gonna buy all kinds of material and try to make stuff, are you?" Victor asked as he drove.

"I thought so."

"You better go through your list again and get some store-bought stuff instead. You'll do good to just get through this holiday with doing what you got to do, without making yourself a whole lot more work. You think about that."

Walking around the fabric store, she made two complete rounds of the aisles and then headed to Penney's. Two good white shirts were bought and two neckties, one for Will and one for Tony, plus two pair of good socks for each man. A pair of bib overalls were gotten for Victor. Making a trip back to the fabric store, she picked out heavy flannel material to line the Victor's overalls. This was the only sewing she would have to do before Christmas, because she had decided to get something for Dorothy to play with in the dime store. A Chinese checker set and two large puzzles were picked out for the girl. She didn't have a thing to give Lee, she realized in a panic-stricken moment and then decided playing cards, three or four decks, a new checkers game and a bottle of good whiskey, that she would have Victor get, would take care of his present. On a whim, she also picked up a Chinese checkers game for an additional present for Lee. He enjoyed something like this on a Sunday evening. Most Sunday afternoons four people could be found available to play cards but the Sunday evenings were for each family in their own home with their own family and that was when Lee enjoyed playing card games or checkers with either his daughter or his wife or both. The treat of a bowl of popcorn, sprinkled with butter and salt, made the evening complete.

When Victor and Sarah picked up Lee when the train came in, he asked her how the shopping went.

"Your pa told me to redo my shopping list and so I did. Ain't got much sewing to have to worry about doing now. Bet it's the first time most everyone gets store-bought gifts for a long, long time. I know Mary sure never gave those kind of gifts." she answered.

"That's all right," Victor answered. "At least you ain't got to wonder how you're gonna get them done and lean over the slop pail at the same time."

She showed Lee what she had bought when they got

home and he told her he knew the men would appreciate a good shirt, a new tie and new socks. And he knew his pa would be very pleased with the lined overalls. He sure liked the pair she made for him and wore his many days to work. The extra layer of flannel on the inside made all the difference in the world for warmth at the depot and on his way getting there and back.

By the end of the week, Victor's present was done and all the gifts wrapped. The next week she spent working on the pile of mending she had let go when she felt so poorly. Most of all, she was thankful Cora Lee was in school everyday so she could rest in the afternoon. She knew unless she improved, there would be no extra sewing, rugs or curtains done during the months following Christmas.

When she put the final piece of mending away, she breathed a sigh of relief. A good job done because the following week was the candy-making and cookie-making. Johanna had already said Christmas dinner and supper would be down at her house and Sarah could have it next year. Sarah was very agreeable to the idea.

Sarah knew, regardless of how she felt, she would have to go to the Christmas program at school. She thought of how much she had wanted to go when she had been in school and her ma wouldn't let her. Now when she could go maybe she'd be too sick to. Cora Lee had been practicing her part in a little play about Santa Claus coming and she knew the songs she was to sing by heart. Sarah had looked through the box of clothing upstairs and had found a jumper and sweater for her to wear. It would probably have fit her better next year but with a little taking in here and there, Sarah knew it would be all right.

During the day of the program, Sarah thought back to the cleaning and preparations she could remember the teacher doing for the evening's festivities. Older children helped clean and straighten up the schoolroom and also scrub the blackboard clean. The smaller children cleaned out their desks and pounded the blackboard erasers until all the chalk dust was gone. Decorations made by the children were hung around the room. There were rings of colored paper glued together and strings of popcorn, colored Santas with reindeer and sleighs and wreaths colored with green leaves and red holly berries. Sweeping compound would be sprinkled on the floor and then swept up. Finally the teacher, with the help of the older boys and girls, would string a wire across the front of the room, about five feet out from the blackboard. On this wire would be strung white bed sheets. This was the stage curtain. It was always an important sought-after job to be one of those helping pull this curtain after each part of the program was completed. It was a night for the school children to remember and also a night for the adults of the community too. Sarah was thankful Cora Lee would have good memories.

By evening Sarah was so thankful to be feeling good enough that she was looking forward to the evening. With the program starting at eight o'clock, evening chores were started extra early. Cora Lee, already high with anticipation, greeted Lee when he came in from work with instructions to hurry and eat 'cause it was time to go.

"Let your pa eat his supper, Cora Lee. It ain't quite time to go yet."

"But I got to be there by seven thirty," she told Sarah.

"I know and we'll leave by seven. Your pa'll have his supper ate by then."

"You OK?" he asked Sarah.

"Yes," she answered, catching the interest Cora Lee had in her answer. "You can get your overshoes on and get your coat and mittens and cap," she told her.

"Everyone is going tonight, ain't they?" Lee asked.

"Everyone. First Labella in a Christmas program for a good many years and nobody's gonna miss that, besides Victor said, it's a chance to see all the old neighbors and visit. I sliced some beef real thin and made some sandwiches to take along for the lunch. Victor said those will go real fast 'cause some of the parents'll bring like they did for the picnic Labor Day. I told him that would be what Cora Lee and I would rather have. You done?"

"I could eat more but I think we had better go. Where did Cora Lee go? Oh, here you are. Ready? Then let's go."

The schoolhouse was as brightly lit as it could get with four kerosene lamps burning. Although Sarah and Lee were one of the first parents to arrive, it wasn't long before the room was full. The excitement of the children sifted through to the parents as each watched their offspring dart here and there until the teacher finally got them all seated, some behind the curtain and some in the first rows of desks. When Miss Schmitt stood in front of the pulled curtain, a hush came over the crowd. She thanked them for coming and asked the boys to pull the curtain so the program could begin.

The Labellas knew the littlest children were first. A lump came into each throat as they watched with pride as Cora Lee and two other little ones lined up and did their skit. It finished with "Up on the House Top" sung, not on key, but with enthusiasm. One by one the skits and songs continued as each grade did their part. The final part of the program was a song sung by the entire school. Leon Rumney finished the evening by thanking everyone for coming and he gave extra thanks to Miss Schmitt for the excellent program that was enjoyed by each and everyone. And as everyone knows, he told them, the evening wasn't ended as the visiting and lunch were there to enjoy yet. With this, Betty Rumney and Edith Snazzle set up the lunch and with Leon's help the coffee from the large coffee pot was poured.

About half an hour later, before anyone had left for home, the outside door opened and a gasp came over the children as in strode Santa Claus, complete with his bag of goodies. For once in her life, Cora Lee was speechless. She bounded over to her pa and climbed on to his lap. As Santa came through the crowd, each child was given an apple and an orange and wished a very Merry Christmas. Cora Lee's eyes got wide when he stopped before her. She whispered her thank you when handed her gift.

When they got home that night and Cora Lee was in bed, Lee and Sarah talked for a few minutes over another cup of coffee.

"You're feeling better, ain't you?" he asked.

"Tonight was the best I've felt for a long time. I enjoyed the evening and Cora Lee was great. What she lacked in her voice, she made up with her spirit," Sarah answered.

"It was a nice evening, I would have hated to have missed it. When I watched the kids there tonight and how nervous and anxious they all were with their parts and their singing, I thought about how hurt you must have been when you watched all the getting ready and the preparing and the learning of the parts and then couldn't come back and be a part of it. I can't figure out anyone being like your ma."

"She went the first couple of years when I was small. There was a women that lived close to school and she used to take me there and leave me with her. I remember she was fat and that's about all I remember about her. I didn't cry when she left me there 'cause I knew after Ma left that I'd get a couple of cookies to eat. That's about all I can remember about the woman. Later, when I was in school, then she quit going."

"I suppose she knew she would be asked where you were?"

"I suppose so. Anyway, Ma..." Sarah looked upward. "I got there tonight and I enjoyed the whole thing."

"Good girl," Lee told her. "Now let's got to bed. It's going to be a short night. I got to get to work in the morning."

The gifts Sarah had bought for Tony, Will and Dorothy were very much appreciated. Gertrude said her two girls would get a lot of pleasure out of the Chinese checkers game and the two puzzles as they didn't have anything like that. Will's new shirt and tie would be saved for his nephew's wedding in spring and Tony's would be used when one of his good friends got married this summer. Sarah felt good about the gifts when she found this out. Lee's new cards were tried out the very day he got them, while the whiskey Victor had picked up for Sarah to give to Lee was also tapped. From Cora Lee, Sarah got two pairs of new silk stockings that she needed and from Gertrude, who had her name, she got a very nice piece of material for a good dress. Gertrude said she probably would appreciate having something new later in the summer. But the gift she got from Lee was the most appreciated, a spanking brand-new wooden ice cream freezer. Many times these past months when it was cold enough to freeze ice outside, Sarah had borrowed the ice cream freezer from the big house and made ice cream. This was one food she couldn't get enough of as her pregnancy continued.

After Christmas and the New Year, Sarah felt good enough to make window coverings for the house. Using the curtains she had found in the boxes from the banker's family, she was able to fashion curtains for Cora Lee's bedroom. Granted, they were pieced here and there, but with the use of lace she also found in the boxes, she made them look very nice. Sarah bought new material for their bedroom curtains, making them like the one she had made for the little house.

The kitchen curtains were made out of white feed sacks, the ruffles trimmed with red rickrack and white gathered lace. She was able to use the curtain from her bedroom in the little house for the window in the dining room by piecing it with part of another pair of the banker's curtains. She was well satisfied with the frothy results.

The parlor had a large bay window facing the south

with two smaller windows on the west. These were a challenge. Sarah had found large curtains in the boxes upstairs sufficient for two of the windows, with enough for half of the third. The panels were a shimmery white material. She had also found six wide panels of heavier lace that also wasn't enough for the entire room. Johanna finally came up with the idea of using the shimmery material for the bottom three-fourths of each window, piecing white muslin on the top fourth that she also had in the banker's boxes and making a valance of the heavy lace over the top third of the window covering the muslin. After much figuring by both women, the curtains were finally cut, pieced and finished. The results were stunning.

Sarah spent the next days after she had finished the curtains, fashioning a wardrobe to fit over her new shape. Several everyday dresses were split down the front. She made three extra-large aprons to wear over the top of these split dresses. This would have to do for everyday. For good, she took a pattern of Johanna's and making it larger, made herself one good dress. Another apron was made for good. When the weather got terribly cold, she put on one of Lee's large flannel shirts over the top of the split dress and apron. Standing in front of the dresser mirror, she shook her head and threw her hands out in disgust at how sloppy she looked.

"Good thing nobody much sees me," she murmured as she patted her growing tummy. "And I've got all those months yet before I start to look like me again."

"Here's a fancy baptismal dress on the top," Johanna told Sarah as they started going through the boxes that had baby clothes in them that had come from the doctor's family.

"And here are diapers, lots of them, six, nine, twelve, fifteen, twenty here," Sarah counted. "And they look like they're in good shape. No holes even. And here's undershirts," she said, holding one up.

"Imagine, store-bought ones," Johanna said. "And under them are kimonos and lots of them, more than you'll need. And baby blankets. And all colors, pink and yellow and green and blue and white."

"Yeah, all kinds of them. And look here, a big blanket for a baby and here's another one and here's two more, just like brand-new out of a store. And more diapers. And baby booties, knit ones that'll be nice and warm. And bonnets and knit caps, green ones and yellow ones."

"You can put them on either a boy or girl," Johanna told her. "That way you don't have to put a pink one on a boy. I don't think you'll need anything else. She must have sent everything she had in baby clothes. Must not figure on having any more babies."

"Or else getting brand-new stuff if she did. These are such nice things, better than if I had to make them. Fancy edgings on some of these, must have used them for Sunday only, cause they ain't even faded."

"Look here Sarah, on the bottom of the box, a big piece of flannel, white and here's some more flannel, green, and some more here, yellow."

"I'll put that away. I don't need to cut into any of this for this baby. Can you imagine Johanna, just packing up all those boxes of stuff and selling it and having to replace it all when you get moved to California?"

"That's if she has another baby. And maybe she's got more money to do it with than we would have. I couldn't hardly believe it when I saw the upstairs here after Lee moved it all in and saw all those boxes of stuff. Have you gotten through all of those boxes yet?"

"I think so. I went through everything but these boxes after we moved in here. I knew these had baby clothes so I left them. The only thing that's left is some of those big-sized clothing up there and I figured to make Cora Lee coats and clothes out of those when she needed them. I could even make myself clothes out of some of them 'cause they are big, big in size. Fit some mighty huge people."

"She didn't just give it away when she didn't need it anymore, though. She packed it away and saved it and Lee did pay for it. And it sure came in handy for you, saved you lots of buying and lots and lots of sewing, when you ain't feeling as good as you could be."

Knowing she didn't have any sewing to do for the coming baby, Sarah asked Lee to set up the quilting frame in the parlor. She had sewed three quilt tops during the previous winters in the little house and thought she felt good enough now to get them done. Two only needed to be quilted using a darning needle and heavy yarn, lying them every six inches in squares. By working on them a few hours every afternoon, she slowly got one by one done. She had only one that required intricate hand-stitching and that was the last one she did. As she hand-stitched each afternoon, a design emerged. Many hours later she finished the quilt. Lee wondered if it was really worth the effort she put into it but when she used it on their bed for a bedspread even he had to admit it was a lovely quilt, every bit a masterpiece of art.

Before Sarah was truly done with the new quilts she took feed sacks and made quilt protectors. This was a piece of material the width of the quilt that covered the top of the quilt about a foot down on both front and back. It was loosely hand-stitched to the quilt so it could be taken off for washing. This kept the top of the quilt clean when it was pulled up to a person's chin. The grease from their face and hair stayed on the quilt protector thus saving the quilt from getting dirty. It was impossible to wash these quilts as the batting inside was either wool or a cotton batting that wasn't washable.

Toward the end of April, Lee took Sarah to see Doctor Larson. He thought she should go and see him before the baby came. She knew he was an older, nice and considerate man from when he had been to see Victor when he had quinsy. His manner made her feel very good. He told her the delivery shouldn't be more than twenty-five dollars and the hospital cost would be about thirty. He also told her that after the baby was born she would have to stay in the hospital for ten days or more. This she already knew from Johanna. When she asked him how she would know when she should come to the hospital, she was told she would know when the pains started, as they were different than other pains.

When Lee asked her on the way home if she had learned anything from the visit, she told him most of it she had already learned from Johanna.

"You've been through this before with Annie. So I am hoping you'll help me," she told him.

"I only took her to the hospital. I never saw her again until the day after the baby was born," he answered.

"But you knew when to take her, when she needed to go," she told him.

"That much she knew. It must be something that comes with being a woman. She just knew," he answered.

"I think I'll go back and talk to Johanna," she said. "I'll be glad when it's done and over with."

"I can't remember Annie being as large as you are though."

"Johanna wasn't either. I asked Dr. Larson about that and he said every woman carries a baby different," she answered.

"Did the doctor tell you when the baby should be born?" Lee asked.

"The middle of June or right about there, maybe a week later but somewhere about then."

"Then you and Johanna were right in when you thought," Lee told her.

"Yeah, we were. Not so dumb like you men thought, were we?"

"You're both real smart," Lee answered. "Both smart enough to marry Tony and me. Now how much more could you want?"

"The end of June to be here," she answered. Lee roared with laughter.

This year, 1935, the weather was different. Enough snow came during the winter that the dams were full and the rivers were too. The warm spring rains made the prairie come alive with grass and wild sweet peas and other wild flowers. Wild onion flourished making the cow's milk almost impossible to drink. As the spring turned into early summer, the rains continued to come, bringing with it the feeling of survival for the ranch people left on the prairie. This year the men didn't have to spend hours working on the irrigation. Gardens grew as if by magic, along with the weeds that took hours and hours of hoeing.

Poor Bud found a porcupine and wished he hadn't. He lay crying and whimpering on the porch when Lee came out on his way to work.

"Oh, oh, you poor soul. Sarah, I've got to run over to Pa's and have him come over as soon as he can and pull all of these out." Sarah patted the dog on his back as he lay in misery. His face and ears had a few quills sticking in them but his mouth was the big problem. He couldn't get it shut as it was full of the razor-sharp needlelike quills. As soon as he could, Victor came with his pliers and pulled them out, one by one. Sarah sat beside the dog, petting him and talking to him. Victor was afraid that the dog would try to bite him when he started on the quills but he didn't. After they were all pulled out, he took a big drink of water and then crawled under the porch where he lay for several days. He only came out for an occasional drink of water. Sarah finally coaxed him to eat some bread soaked with milk. His mouth finally healed and he never tangled with a porcupine again.

The twentieth day of June, Sarah knew something was different. She felt great. She had ambition, really felt like working. Chicken chores were first. Mixing up a batch of bread was second and then washing clothes. After emptying out the wash water, she saved enough rinse water to wipe up the kitchen floor, pantry floor and finally, the toilet floor. Since getting down on her hands and knees was something she couldn't do anymore, she took a mop to the floors in the house and a broom to the toilet.

Waiting for the floor to dry, Sarah sat on the porch steps watching Cora Lee, Johanna and her two children coming with a pan of strawberries. Cora Lee still had her job every morning watching Martha and Harvey while Johanna picked the berries or hoed in the garden. She didn't mind, as she liked to have someone to play with. They played close enough to Johanna so she could keep an eye on them yet they were far enough away so they weren't walking on everything that was growing .

"Oh, they're so nice and large this year," Sarah said as Johanna gave her the pan.

"I think they're the nicest berries we have ever had. Rain at just the right time and plenty of manure, Tony says makes the difference. It's so nice to have the rain we need this summer, better than irrigating and lots less work for the men. Makes everyone feel good. See, you've got a big washing out. Looks like you changed bedding too."

"I'll make them back up as soon as the sheets are dry and it won't take long, as breezy as it is. I'm not even going to press the sheets, just put them back on 'cause they smell so good and so I'm going to be lazy and not press them. I'm waiting for the floor to dry right now. Took a mop to it and the pantry. As soon as it's dry, I'll pick over a few berries for us to eat for dinner. Thanks so much for the berries. There's just no way that I could ever get them picked," she told Johanna.

"That I know. And with Cora Lee watching Martha and Harvey, it goes real good. It's so funny cause she's finally taught Martha how to jump rope. Cora Lee's pretty good at it while Martha has all she can do just to keep from falling down as she hops over the rope. And she's finally got her looking for the thimble when they try to play 'hide the thimble' this morning in the house. They'll have more fun together when Martha gets a little older. Now she just imitates her bigger cousin, but it sure is funny to watch. Wonder what else Cora Lee will learn at school, 'cause it sure didn't take her long to learn these games." Turning around, Johanna started toward home, adding, "Going back now so I get dinner for us. I want to have some fresh berries too. Made some baking powder biscuits this morning right away so we'll have shortcake. Sounds so good with fresh cream. Bye now."

"We got any biscuits?" Cora Lee asked.

"We got some from supper last night when I ran out of bread and I made some then. You know that sounds good. Maybe just biscuits and berries for dinner and cream too. We won't tell anyone we didn't eat any bread." Cora Lee snickered as she shared the secret.

"Ummm, that was so good," Cora Lee told Sarah as she scraped the last spoonful of crumbs out of the bowl.

"They did hit the spot," Sarah agreed. "I'll clean the rest of these and put them down in the springhouse to keep cool. Got to churn some butter today too. We're about out. That has to go down to the springhouse too, when I get it done."

"Can I start to churn it? I can turn it for a while," Cora Lee pleaded.

"Sure, I'll get it ready for you to start right after I fire the cook stove. My bread is about ready to bake. Before you can start the butter, I'll have to get the cream from the springhouse and then you can start." She took the bottom of the butter churn with her as she went out the door. Pulling the container full of cream from the water, she took off the cover and poured the churn full. Back in the house, she put the cover on and set it where Cora Lee could turn the handle.

While Cora Lee worked on churning the butter, Sarah slid the bread tins in the oven and then finished cleaning the berries. Seeing Cora Lee was starting to get tired of her job, Sarah took over finishing the butter. Lightly salting it, she took out enough for supper and then took the rest and the berries to the springhouse. She put the two into the cans they kept there for storing the food. As she lowered the cans into the cold water she thought of the women, the day of the school cleaning, who had said how hard it was to keep food because they didn't have a springhouse over any river. They had no way to keep food cold in the summer so their cream soured. They only fixed meat for one meal. The butter got rancid and those that had to haul water in ten-gallon cans never had cold water to drink. How lucky she was to have this nice building built over the river.

On the way back, she gathered the bedding off the line and made up the beds. Putting on the sad irons to heat, she went back to the wash line and brought in the rest of the clothes. Getting out the ironing board, she pressed some, folded some and sprinkled some.

"Ummm, the bread smells so good," Cora Lee told her when she took out the baked loaves and lightly smeared lard on the crusts.

"It does smell good. We'll have fresh bread and some canned liver sausage for supper. And strawberries and biscuits. And radishes and winter onions. It's hot in here with the stove going but I'll have to keep it going 'cause I can't heat the sausage any other way. But I'll do the ironing up while the stove is hot and then that'll be done."

"Can I go over and play with Martha and Harvey now? They should be done with their napping by now."

"Yes, providing you ask Johanna first if you can. I'm coming over to the garden to get some radishes and onions

before long. But you be back here by five thirty so you're back when your pa comes home so we can eat."

With a wave and the bang of the screen door, Cora Lee was gone. Sarah ironed the sprinkled clothes, piece by piece until she finally had the last one done. She moved her body this way and that way, trying to ease the backache she felt.

"It's no wonder it hurts with all the weight I'm carrying in the front of me," she murmured to herself. "Got to put these away and then get the onions and radishes. Feel tired now."

Halfway over to the garden, she was met by Cora Lee carrying some onions and radishes.

"Johanna pulled some radishes and onions for them so she just pulled some more so you'd have some too," Cora Lee told her, handing her the panful and tearing back down the road to play with her cousins.

"Tell her thank you. It saved me walking way over to the garden," she called as the little girl ran. The vegetables cleaned, she went to the basement and got the jar of liver sausage up. Before putting the sausage into the fry pan, she went again to the chickens to gather the eggs and make sure they had water. They were fed in the morning only. The rest of the day they had to pick up bugs, grasshoppers and whatever else they could find. Back in the house the fry pan of sausage was slid into the oven, the stove fired once more and the eggs that were dirty washed so they could be taken down to the springhouse the next time someone had to go after something. All done, Sarah went outside to sit on the steps of the porch.

"Not one more step can I make," she told Bud, as he crawled up beside her to get petted. "I'm completely tired out." She was still sitting there when Cora Lee came back.

"Go and wash your hands and you can set the table for me," she told her. "Then when you're done, you can come back and wait with me for your pa." They were both sitting there when Lee drove into the yard.

"You look tired," he told Sarah and, looking at Cora Lee, he added, "You even look tired."

"I watched Martha and Harvey while Johanna picked strawberries and then played with them this afternoon after they got done with their nap. I churned the butter, well, started to churn it anyway. Pa, we had strawberries for dinner and a biscuit and no bread. I wasn't supposed to tell anybody we didn't have any bread, was I?" she asked Sarah, giggling.

"I guess it's all right if you did," Sarah told her laughing as Lee joined in.

"Sounds like you had a busy day. And what did you do?" he asked Sarah.

"Can I tell Pa?" Cora Lee begged.

"Go ahead," Sarah told her.

"She washed clothes and made up the beds fresh and they smell good too. And cleaned the berries and ironed and we're having radishes and onions for supper and liver sausage. Did I miss anything? Oh gave the chickens water and picked the eggs and churned the butter and the wet floor," she ended with a long sigh.

"No wonder you both look tired. I'm hungry, so let's do it," Lee said, giving Sarah his hand to help her up. "You ain't getting any smaller, are you?" he teased as they went in the kitchen. "My ma used to say that the day you were going to have a baby was the day when you felt like tearing the world apart doing so much work," Lee told Sarah after supper, when the dishes were done and they went to sit on the porch steps where it was a little cooler. Cora Lee had run to catch one of the kittens that she saw scampering in the yard.

"In that case then you'd better make sure there's gas in the car 'cause I felt like working this morning for the first time for a long time. Now, I'm just plain tired and want to go to bed. I can't believe Cora Lee don't know something is different with me getting this big but she just don't say nothing. I don't think she knows there's a baby coming."

"Pa said she told him you were really getting fat and maybe that's why you don't have any get-up-and-go. He asked her if she thought you were eating too much food and if that was why you were getting so fat. And she shrugged her shoulders and said she didn't know. It's nice that she's so innocent and don't," Lee answered.

After sitting a little while on the porch, Sarah went back into the house and into the pantry, taking along a dipper of hot water and her nightie.

"Guess we know where Sarah's going, don't we?" he told Cora Lee as he heard the pantry door shut.

"She's going to clean up and go to bed," Cora Lee answered. "I'm want to stay outside and play with the cats. There's the mama cat down by the fence. I'm gonna pet her a while. She's got the other kitten with her too."

'You OK?" Lee asked Sarah when she came out of the pantry to stand by the porch door.

"Tired. And I've got a backache."

"Where?"

She rubbed the small of her back. "I'm going to lay down. And why the raised eyebrows?"

"Worked like a slave all day and now got a backache. Sounds like a trip to town to me."

"Dr. Larson said I'd know when the time came and I don't feel anything but tired. I'll let you know when I feel something else. I still don't know what I'm supposed to feel that's different."

Several hours later Sarah woke to a different kind of pain. Lying so quiet, she waited until another pain came and after that another one. She supposed this was the beginning of what was called labor. She thought of her ma and wondered if she had hated the pains when she had been born. There had to be some reason why she had hated Sarah so. Maybe it was the pain her ma had felt when she was born.

When Lee came to bed, Sarah told him that maybe he should take Cora Lee down to Johanna's to sleep. She felt some different pains but they didn't hurt much.

"She's sleeping already down there. Johanna wondered about you working so much today and your back hurting you and so she suggested that Cora Lee stay there tonight and if you're here in the morning she'll just send her back. You want to go to town now or what?"

"I don't think so. You might as well lay down and sleep."

"Wake me then when you need to."

Sarah dozed off and on the rest of the night, occasionally feeling pains that came and went with no set pattern. Lee debated what to do in the morning and finally Sarah told him to go to work. She couldn't see any reason why he had to stay home when she wasn't any sicker than this. She spent the morning wandering around the house and yard and finally ended up at the garden. Dinner was eaten with Victor, Johanna and the children, as Tony had to go to town for some supplies.

"I'm going home and lay down for a while," Sarah told Johanna after they finished the dishes. "I don't feel sick, I don't feel right, I don't feel like doing anything at all. Yesterday I felt so good and felt like tearing the world apart. Today I just feel miserable and uncomfortable and huge."

"I think you covered it all," Johanna told her, laughing. "You still got little pains coming and going?"

"Like I did last night, only not as hard. Just small ones."

"One of these times, they'll get going and then you'll get the job done," Johanna answered. "That's why Victor's staying around the buildings, just in case."

Tired from the night before's uneasiness, Sarah fell into a deep sleep, awakening with a jolt as a deep pain wrenched through her back. In a few minutes another pain came and then another after that. She knew that she needed to find Victor. She couldn't wait until Lee came home from work. Hearing steps on the porch, she got up to find Victor in her kitchen.

"Oh, did I wake you up? I'm sorry but I wanted to

look in on you before I went to look at the dam on the east pasture," he told her.

"You didn't wake me up. I'm glad you stopped before you left the buildings. I think you'd better take me to town. I don't think I can wait until Lee gets home. And," she held her breath as another pain came, "I think we should go now."

"I've got the car outside. I'll run back and tell Johanna and be right back," he said, scurrying out the door and down the steps. Half an hour later, Sarah was in the hospital. From there Victor went to the Ponta depot and had that depot agent send a message over the wire to Lee at Windsor.

"Oh, I wonder how Sarah's doing?" Johanna told the men at supper. "I think of her all the time and wish I knew."

"You should have seen Cora Lee when I told her I took Sarah to the hospital to have a baby. She was gonna have a baby brother or sister. I don't think I ever saw anyone's eyes get that big and for a minute or two she was speechless and from then on the questions flew." Victor was still laughing just thinking about it. "And I don't think she's shut up since either. I wonder how Sarah is too."

"You'll know when Lee gets home," Tony told her. "And who knows when that'll be. I hear a car coming down the lane." Getting up, he walked over to the door. "It's Lee. Cora Lee heard the car too. See her running."

"Pa, have I got a baby brother or sister?" Cora Lee shouted before the car even stopped. "You've got to tell me.".

"Maybe there ain't anything to tell," Victor told her.

"You got to tell us something," Johanna told Lee. "Before we all burst with wondering."

"It was all over by the time I got there. I got the message about three o'clock and got to the hospital about five thirty and they were already born."

"They?" Johanna shrieked.

"They. Twin boys. And they look so much alike you can't tell which is which. I saw them before I came home and saw Sarah too."

"Oh my. Twins," Johanna said. " I'm so glad for her it's over with and glad the babies are all right. Imagine! Twin boys. Oh, it's a good thing she's got all that extra flannel for diapers. She's gonna need them."

"So you see, Cora Lee, you've got two baby brothers," Lee told his daughter. Her eyes gleamed and her only comment was "Ohhh."

Twelve days later Sarah came home with the two babies. She and Lee had spent time different days trying to decide on names, finally coming up with Clyde John and Charles John. Because of the kindness her Uncle John had given her, Lee knew she wanted to use that name for a middle name. Sarah was afraid Victor would feel slighted but Lee told her Victor hated his name so she didn't need to feel bad about not using his name. Cora Lee was ecstatic. Her own little babies, not just cousins, but her own baby brothers.

"When can I hold them?" she asked Sarah.

"There'll be plenty of times you can hold them. I can feed only one baby at a time and if they're both crying, then I'll be glad for your help," she assured her. "And I'll probably be sorry to see school start this fall 'cause then you'll be gone all day long and I won't have any help."

"I can stay home, well, maybe not all the time 'cause I like to go to school."

"You go to school. I'll get along somehow until you come home."

"Johanna sent over fresh-baked bread and a custard pie this morning. And I got up a jar of canned chicken to go with it before I went to work this morning. Pa got the fire going so we can have some supper," Lee told Sarah as he added wood to the fire in the cook stove.

"I've got to have some boiling water to pour over these bottles and nipples you got at the store. They sent enough milk along for tonight but then we'll have to boil some cow's milk tomorrow and thin it down with water and then add some syrup. Have to have fresh milk everyday so it ain't sour 'cause that'd make 'em sick."

"Glad this here is Saturday, then I've got tomorrow off if there's anything you need me to do," Lee answered. "Oh, I hear one now."

"I'll get him before he wakes up the other one. Wait, Cora Lee, don't try to pick him up. See, I've got to change his diaper first." Cora Lee watched Sarah as she did this, taking notice of every little detail. "Now you sit down in the rocker and I'll give him to you." Her eyes huge, Cora Lee crawled into the rocker and held out her arms. Sarah gave her the baby. By that time, the other baby was crying, so she went to him.

"Here, let me hold him while you get the bottles ready," Lee told her, holding out his arms. When Sarah came with the bottles, Lee fed the one he was holding, while Cora Lee watched Sarah feed the other one.

"How are you ever going to tell them apart?" Lee asked. "They're so much alike. I can't see any difference in their faces at all."

"There's a small birthmark by Charlie's ear and an-other small one under his chin. That's all the difference the nurses could find between the two of them. Clyde don't have any marks on his face at all," she answered. "They suggested I pin a different colored ribbon on each one of their kimo-nos so I'd know who I had fed and whose diaper I had changed."

"You got to boil the milk from the barn?" Lee asked.

"Yeah. Then add corn syrup to each bottle. I'll have to get some milk out of the springhouse every night before I go to bed so it don't spoil before morning. The nurses told me I should get them off the bottle, onto a glass, before next spring, so I only have the rest of this summer and winter to worry about bottles. Johanna said it sure was easier for her when she nursed her babies than this bottle business, but I don't have any choice."

"Why not, Sarah?" asked Cora Lee.

"Just because. You go and set the table please for me," Sarah answered, with Lee's laughter softly floating across the room. "I don't talk enough when I'm away from home and too much here."

That night with Cora Lee sleeping in her bedroom down the hall and the twins finally asleep in their crib, Sarah came to the bedroom window to watch with Lee as the moonlight shone so brightly they could see one of the barn cats stalking some unsuspecting little animal for its supper. Lee put his arm around Sarah while she put her head against his shoulder.

"When Annie died, I thought my chance for a happy married life was over. I knew men that had married again, but mostly so there was a housekeeper in their home and someone to take care of their kids. I didn't have to worry about that with Annie's ma taking care of Cora Lee at first and then us moving in with Pa. Then you came along and before long I knew I wanted to marry again. I wonder if you ever realize how much you mean to me." Sarah drew away from him to look up at his face while he talked. "Annie was my first love, when I was younger and we'd have stayed married forever if she hadn't died, but you are my love for the rest of my older life. And Cora Lee loving you like she does only makes it better. Now, with these two babies it's the frosting on the cake, as my grandma that died long ago used to say. The frosting on the cake to only make it better. Tears, Sarah?"

He held her tight against him while she softy cried. "You are so dear to me. So very dear to me," he told her.

"Reach me a hankie. Thank you," she said as she wiped the tears and blew her nose. "Yeah Ma, I think I finally buried you. I never will figure out why she hated me so and why she treated me like she did. I worried so about how I'd feel about my little baby and when they laid them in my arms, I knew I could never treat them like I was treated. I could only love them. So in this house of hers, I've finally come out over the top, won the battle. I've finally decided it don't really matter why she did what she did, 'cause I'll never do it to my babies. I have won the war. I got you, who I love dearly and three children who I love dearly and I can let my ma be. 'Cause she'll never hurt me again, regardless of how many bad things we have happen, she can never hurt me again. So many times I wished, these past days, that Uncle John could have lived to have met you and seen my babies.

"He'd have been glad. But I have to believe someone like him is in heaven and he's looking down from up there in heaven and he sees. He sees."

Lee stood holding her against him, until finally they turned and went to bed.

One of the lucky ones... Sarah.

BOOKS BY SHIRLEY DUMMER

- *Therese, My Love,* ISBN 0-941187-00-4

- *We've Climbed the Mountains,* ISBN 0-9633479-0-X

- *Lost Love,* ISBN 0-9633479-2-6

- *Old Man,* ISBN 0-9633479-3-4

- *Sarah,* ISBN 0-9633479-4-2